CASKET GIRLS

A NOVEL

ELISABETH SEREDA

Copyright © 2024 Elisabeth Sereda.

All rights reserved. No part of this book may be used or reproduced by any means, graphic, electronic, or mechanical, including photocopying, recording, taping or by any information storage retrieval system without the written permission of the author except in the case of brief quotations embodied in critical articles and reviews.

This is a work of fiction. All of the characters, names, incidents, organizations, and dialogue in this novel are either the products of the author's imagination or are used fictitiously.

Archway Publishing books may be ordered through booksellers or by contacting:

Archway Publishing
1663 Liberty Drive
Bloomington, IN 47403
www.archwaypublishing.com
844-669-3957

Because of the dynamic nature of the Internet, any web addresses or links contained in this book may have changed since publication and may no longer be valid. The views expressed in this work are solely those of the author and do not necessarily reflect the views of the publisher, and the publisher hereby disclaims any responsibility for them.

Any people depicted in stock imagery provided by Getty Images are models, and such images are being used for illustrative purposes only. Certain stock imagery © Getty Images.

Interior Image Credit: The Historic New Orleans Collection / THNOC

ISBN: 978-1-6657-6055-3 (sc)
ISBN: 978-1-6657-6057-7 (hc)
ISBN: 978-1-6657-6056-0 (e)

Library of Congress Control Number: 2024910475

Print information available on the last page.

Archway Publishing rev. date: 10/15/2024

for Al Jarreau …

… who always knew

CONTENTS

Author's Note ix
Prologue xv

PART 1: THE GRAND VOYAGE

Chapter 1 1
Chapter 2 13
Chapter 3 29

PART 2: THE CRESCENT CITY

Chapter 4 41
Chapter 5 53
Chapter 6 66
Chapter 7 81
Chapter 8 93
Chapter 9 102
Chapter 10 126
Chapter 11 145
Chapter 12 162
Chapter 13 173
Chapter 14 182
Chapter 15 192
Chapter 16 208

Chapter 17 217
Chapter 18 226

PART 3: THE WINDS OF CHANGE

Chapter 19 237
Chapter 20 250
Chapter 21 266
Chapter 22 275
Chapter 23 289
Chapter 24 297
Chapter 25 310
Chapter 26 320
Chapter 27 333
Chapter 28 346

PART 4: OF SECRETS AND SCARS

Chapter 29 365
Chapter 30 386
Chapter 31 406

Epilogue 419

AUTHOR'S NOTE

When I was about eight years old, a family friend gave me a book about New Orleans ghost stories. I was an avid reader, even at that age. Or—as my parents put it: "She eats books for breakfast." I had my favorites, loved adventure and crime stories and anything mystical. The book drew me in, but it was not so much the scary ghosts and their mostly evil deeds as it was the vibrant description of the city they roamed, the places they haunted. Buildings full of history, misty bayous, cypress trees and the moss-covered branches of the old oaks came alive in my imagination and an eerie feeling of familiarity fell over me—as if I had lived there before…

When I got older, I read literature of the South, fell in love with the characters, watched films that told their stories and daydreamed about becoming a 'Southern writer'. I moved to the US at twenty-one and wanted to attend Bennington, widely considered the best writers' college. Sadly, as a foreigner, I was not eligible for a scholarship and lacking the financial means, I had to abandon the idea. My interest in the rich and often complicated and painful history of the South never waned, however. New Orleans, the city that had drawn me to her long before I ever visited, held and holds a special place in my heart.

I did not find the story of the Casket Girls, it found me. I was sitting on the floor of the Faulkner House bookstore on Pirate's Alley in the French Quarter, leafing through books as I have done often, delighted that New Orleans, unlike other cities, still has bookstores. There, in the foreword of a small non-fiction edition on a completely different subject was the mention of the Casket Girls. No other explanation, just those two words. They jumped out at me. I was intrigued. Back at my laptop I began a mad online search. And found nothing. At dinner that same night, I asked my friends, native New Orleanians about the Casket Girls and they, too, shook their heads. Only their then twelve-year-old daughter said that she had just written a paper about them. Hand it over, I said. It was short, like any six-grader's school assignment and it made me even more determined to find out more.

What followed was years-long research into eighteenth-century history. I learned that it is no coincidence that New Orleans is referred to as a 'she', for it is women who have built this city, who have tended to her culture, furthered her economy and created her mystique. All the way back to— well—the Casket Girls. Since there was not much to be found on the internet, I did my research old school: I immersed myself in census records, took up residency at The New Orleans Historic Society, studied the history of the Ursulines and contacted historians that specialize in the period. I read non-fiction books such as Shannon Lee Dawdy's "Building the Devil's Empire: French Colonial New Orleans", Emily Clark's "Masterless Mistresses" and Marie Madeleine Hachard's collection of letters, "Voices from an Early American Convent" that I quote from in the novel. Most of all I walked the same streets as my characters, cooked and ate the kind of foods that nourished them and tried to channel their traumas, joys, triumphs and struggles. Each of them became companions and confidantes while I tried to hear their voices in order to tell their story.

A few notes on my use of language and terminology: I decided to refer to the indigenous tribes that inhabited the land by their tribal names such as Choctaw and Natchez to preserve the authenticity of their culture and the era, while also being sensitive to our changing times. The term 'Native American', while now considered politically correct, would be incorrect if used in this context; Louisiana (La Louisiane) was a French and for almost forty years starting in the early 1760s a Spanish colony until Napoleon sold it to Thomas Jefferson in the Louisiana Purchase of 1803. For the same reason I do not use 'African American'—there was nothing American about them yet: black women and men of the period were either free or enslaved people of color. They called themselves negroes or colored people, in French *nègre* and *négresse* as well as *les personnes de couleur,* and used other French words to distinguish between mulattos, quadroons, octoroons, etc. Creoles are descendants of all settlers regardless of color of skin or social class, if they were born in Louisiana. This distinguishes them from the original French settlers and later arrivals from France, Spain and Africa. I also use the spelling 'vodou' or 'vodoun' instead of the more common contemporary 'voodoo' to separate what was a pagan religion and healing practice, from today's common view of it as 'black magic' and card-reading.

From the beginning, there was a lot of mixture, or to use the french word *metissage,* whether it pertained to status, business or marriages between Europeans, Indigenous people, Acadians (= Cajuns), free people of color and immigrants from the West Indies. The predominant religion for all people in La Nouvelle Orleàns was Catholicism. It co-existed with pagan culture. Even vodou priestesses were Catholic. This is due to the early arrival of Capuchins and Jesuits, but it is the Ursulines who deserve most of the credit. The Sisters arrived in 1727 and started a school for girls. They did not distinguish between race, color, nationality or social status but accepted all females to attend their classes, including enslaved women and girls. There was no equivalent for boys; if a family was not wealthy enough to send their sons back to Paris for schooling or hire private tutors, they had very little access to education. (It was the rivalry between Jesuits and Capuchins that hindered efforts to start a boys' school). This led to a stunning statistic: by the 1750s, 73% of women were educated and able to read and write compared to only 22% of men. Thus, females contributed tremendously to the economy, running their husbands' or fathers' businesses or starting their own.

Unlike the other thirteen colonies that were British, Louisiana's slavery laws were governed by the French *Code Noir* and later the equivalent Spanish *Código Negro*. These laws provided the right to education and marriage. Separation of married couples and mothers and their children as well as torture by the owner was prohibited. The law, when broken, was often challenged in court, in most cases to no avail. The enslaved were also not permitted to work more than twelve hours a day, six days a week, and many of them took advantage of being allowed to earn money on their day off, which led to more of them being able to buy their freedom in Louisiana than anywhere else in the South. The Code Noir forbade intermarriage between whites and indentured servants, but relationships—*plaçages*—between them were widely formed and accepted. Many children who resulted from these arrangements were freed by their white fathers. As early as 1730, there were more free people of color living in Louisiana than in states governed by Anglo-American laws. After the Louisiana Purchase, America tried to impose their binary slave laws, but this was, for a while at least, forcefully and successfully rejected by the Creoles.

CASKET GIRLS begins in 1727 with the voyage and arrival of the Ursulines. They bring with them the Casket Girls: a scandalous Parisian aristocrat, a criminal taken off the streets, a widow with two young children, a naive country girl from rural France, a scarred free woman of color from Cuba and an enslaved girl from St. Domingue (today's Haiti), skilled in the practice of vodou. They all have dark secrets which are revealed over a period of a generation. An Acadian girl with unusual skills, a prostitute, a traitorous Natchez tribal woman, pirates, smugglers, high ranking military men and a merchant with a big heart round out the novel's main characters.

While they are on the hunt for suitable husbands all these women regardless of skin color and social class are being educated by the Ursulines at the first girls' school in New Orleans. They are safe inside the convent's walls, but outside of them the city is a dangerous place.

Their fates are intertwined as they face—and commit—crimes, fend off attackers, endure court trials and survive a hurricane. One of them marries well yet carries on an affair with a pirate. Some find true love; others cannot escape the tragedy of their dark past.

I have tried to stay as accurate as possible as far as historical facts, culture and terminology as well as occurrences, the Natchez massacre and the hurricane of 1732 included. And although this is a work of fiction, some characters, like Marie Madeleine Hachard/Sister Stanislaus, are real and many, like Commander de Valdeterre and the Bèranger brothers are based on real people, and in some cases I have not changed their names.

CASKET GIRLS is part one of a story that I have planned as a trilogy: the descendants of my characters will live on through the Spanish period, and their descendants through the years after the Louisiana Purchase and Antebellum America.

PROLOGUE

One by one they stepped off the *pirogues*, the shallow rough-hewn boats, over the plank onto muddy soil. Twelve nuns were the first to disembark, each one of them carrying a small black leather bag. Impatiently hurrying behind them was a tall young woman of regal stature. Her blonde locks in an elaborate but messy updo, she looked tired from the long journey. Her brocade dress clung to her body, her eyes took in the scenery, moving quickly from side to side. She was not impressed.

This is supposed to be la grande porte, the grand harbor of this new colony?

She snorted in disgust as her shoes sank into the swampy ground. With her pale skin, chiseled face with high cheekbones and this gaze symbolizing millennia of eugenics she looked thoroughly out of place.

A few yards behind her, a lady with brown hair and green eyes was holding the hand of her older child, while carrying her toddler on her arm. As soon as she was on land, she turned around to those behind her: "Let me help you, *ma cher*," she said to the shy young girl who staggered unsteadily on the piece of wood. She extended her hand and pulled the girl onto the ground. As soon as she let go of her hand, the girl stumbled again and almost fell into the breakwater.

The first *pirogue* moved back, steered by a sailor as the next one floated in. A handsome, middle-aged gentleman barked orders to a group of black women as he jumped off the boat, the shallow water almost reaching the top of his boots. He fastened the plank and extended his hand to lead the women and one small girl across.

The last young woman stood out from the rest: holding her head high she ignored him, lifted the skirt of her thin cotton dress as if it were a ball gown and walked the narrow wood like it was a marble hallway. The gentleman watched her.

There is something about this one…

Behind them the Latin group disembarked. There was a sense of purpose about them as one by one they balanced on the plank with their colorful cotton bags slung over their shoulders while commenting on the surroundings in their Spanish dialect.

The eclectic group turned to look out over the water where more pirogues and flatboats arrived. Sailors delivered their belongings; two big trunks for the tall blonde, another large one for the lady with her children. There was nothing for the women of color, but two sailors carried *casquettes*, long narrow wooden boxes that resembled small coffins, and handed one each to the two noblewomen and the shy young girl. The blonde dismissed the casquette, paying attention only to her big trunks while the others clutched theirs. The gentleman oversaw the offloading of twenty-two crates, counting them and checking the markings on each: indigo, corn, sugar, candles and nails. A priest approached the weary travelers. He greeted his fellow brothers and the nuns before looking over the rest of the group.

Ah, la filles a la casquettes.

The priest's face showed worry, and he made the sign of the cross which was repeated by the Sisters and the Cuban women. After another weeklong journey on smaller boats through the meandering Mississippi Delta and on foot, the group arrived at their final destination, La Nouvelle Orleáns, on August 30, 1727.

∼

The loud noise woke up the neighborhood on this early summer morning as Marie Tranchepain, the Reverend Mother St. Augustin dropped her wooden travel box. Her hand flew to her mouth. Looking up at the building the usually eloquent Abbess was at a loss for words. Next to her, Sister Stanislaus began to move her lips in prayer:

Lord be merciful…

The sore sight before them was the convent, their new home. The broken windows, some panes on the upper floor balancing dangerously above them, hanging on by one nail and the front door, its sun-bleached wood contorted by the weather, was not what shocked them most. A gaping hole in the mansard roof was visible from the street. There was no doubt that this building had been magnificent once, a stately mansion located only a block from the quay on Rue de Bienville. Named after the current Governor, it was his former home, the nuns had been told.

He must have abandoned it a while ago, thought Sister Stanislaus whose secular name was Marie Madeleine Hachard. She had felt so much relief upon stepping on land at long last a week earlier when they had arrived at the Delta's Mouth, and had put her feelings into words in a letter to her father:

> "We arrived on July 23, five months to the day since our departure. Far from Rouen, about 2,400 leagues, it is a port located at the entrance of the Mississippi River on the western shore. It would be too long and even useless to express to you, my dear father, our joy at the sight of the land, for which we had longed for such a long time and how great our consolation when we set foot on land…"

That sense of relief was gone at the sight of the building. The Sister looked at the colorful group behind her. The nuns' expressions mirrored that of their Mother Superior. Florence Bourget, the young

Parisian seemed more concerned with Madame LaCour's big trunks than with what was before her. Geneviève LaCour herself was trying to calm Delphine, the crying baby daughter on her arm while holding the hand of her five-year-old son Pierre. Sister Stanislaus could not read the expression on the faces of the Cuban women,

"Are we home?" asked Louise Mariette, the shy country girl.

She slowly took a step towards the house. Before the group could follow there was another loud crash, this one deliberate. Josephine de Chavin, the *Vicomtesse*, had thrown her casket to the ground:

"This?!" she screamed. "We are supposed to live in this decrepit…I would not even know what to call it, a shack?!"

Frére Antoine, the priest who had welcomed them when their ship had arrived on the Louisiana shores and had accompanied them to the city, stepped in. He was a timid man and no match for the aristocrat:

"This is Governor Bienville's former mansion, Mademoiselle…that he kindly decided to offer you as a home until…"

Josephine sneered: "It is Vicomtesse, Frére. And if you call this a mansion, no wonder he moved!"

Sister Stanislaus interrupted: "Let us go inside. Maybe the inside of the house is not so bad."

She ushered them in. The interior of their new home was not much better than the outside. The rough wooden floors were uneven, the walls needed a fresh coat of paint, the splintered staircase posed a visible danger to anyone walking upstairs. The nuns carefully explored the downstairs area shaking their heads at the water damage in what must have been the Governor's salon. Margarita Cortez, the Cuban cook, headed straight to the kitchen.

O dios mio.

The stove, blackened from grease, needed proper cleaning, and all she could find was one pot with a hole in its bottom.

A loud shriek from upstairs interrupted the gloomy silence. "There are no beds! Where am I expected to sleep?" Josephine's voice had reached its highest pitch. Sister Stanislaus went upstairs, careful not to break the creaking staircase. The Vicomtesse pointed at the empty rooms, just as the rain began to fall outside. The Sister was less concerned with the lack of furniture and more with what was above them: the gaping hole in the roof she had noticed from the outside. Below them, there was a tense exchange of words between the Abbess and the Jesuit:

"I know this is not ideal…" the priest stammered, embarrassed at the miserable condition of the house. The Mother Superior, hands on her hips, lost her countenance:

"Not ideal, Frére? We were promised a convent. Not an unfinished construction site! This is stated in the contract between the Jesuits and the Ursulines. And it is stated very clearly. I shall speak to your superior, Father de Beaubois right away."

"We were not able to have the building finished in time for your arrival."

"We arrived one month and a half behind schedule."

"The summer rains made it impossible to get the roof done."

A crash followed by a splash and a shrill *"Merde!"* could be heard from upstairs, where a big shingle and rainwater fell on Josephine and Sister Stanislaus. The nuns and Casket Girls stared at them descending the stairs, both drenched, Josephine's hairdo ruined and the Sister trying to wring out her heavy woolen habit. A small wooden plank on the stairs broke underneath the Sister's feet. She barely avoided a fall. Josephine continued to curse. In the back of the hallway, Monsieur Henry de Roche, the Creole merchant and landowner walked through the open door with his nine enslaved women in tow. Sister Stanislaus, safely at the bottom of the staircase, took one look at him and breathed a sigh of relief. This man had been so helpful on the last part of their journey, she had no doubt, he would again lend a hand in their newest predicament.

∼

The Sister's instinct about Monsieur de Roche had proven right. A month had come and gone and even though not everything had been restored, the building was more livable now and began to look like a convent. If it had not been for the generosity of the man, they would not even have cots to sleep on. The merchant had shown a kindness towards the nuns and the girls that surprised her. Her first impression had not been favorable. She had thought him to be interested only in money and his plantation when they met in Port-au-Prince, but de Roche did not only oversee the repairs, he stepped in when Father de Beaubois, the cleric in charge whose signature was on the contract, tried to hold off the Mother Superior with one excuse after another. In a very stern voice de Roche told the Jesuit that the Sisters and their charges could not wait for the next ship to arrive with furniture—*when? Five, six months in the future?*—to get a good night's sleep. De Roche then sent for a carpenter and paid him twice his price to encourage the man to work faster and harder to build beds for the convent.

The Sister thought of all that had happened in these long seven months since she had left France on that big sailing vessel, the Gironde. A breeze made her skirts pillow as she walked towards the river. She was ever so grateful for the light winds that made the heat a bit more bearable. Sister Stanislaus had been adamant to regard everything as a blessing. She would not waver in her conviction that her life choices had been guided by the Lord, no matter how many times she was tested. Yet she shuddered at the memory of one such recent test on their sea voyage just after she had written what was only her second letter to her father…

PART ONE

THE GRAND VOYAGE

"Louisiana, the blessed country for which I long as if it were the Promised Land. I would like with all my heart, to be there in the monastery that has been built for us."

Marie Madeleine Hachard in a letter to her father

CHAPTER 1

Mon Papá, it is on this day, the fourteenth of May in the year of the Christ 1727 that I can finally find the solace and the opportunity to write to you again. The storms have been hard on everyone, we only advanced fifteen leagues a day, and I must admit my faith was tested. But the winds have calmed down now. Captain Vauberci says we are not making enough headway and will most likely have a longer journey than he is used to for this sea route. For now, though, I am breathing a sigh of relief. The bad weather made for some uncomfortable bickering among the passengers who, as you know, are mostly women. We are all the same in the eyes of the Lord, but they do not see it this way. We are hoping to reach the islands in a month's time to restock the supplies and pick up more passengers.

Food is getting scarce; of the five hundred lambs and chickens we brought with us forty-nine suffocated in the heat, and only the Sisters are used to fasting this much. We have been eating rice with water and salted beef. Some of the bacon was so bad we had to throw it overboard. Not having butter, we had to prepare our beans with lard. Some of us have had stomach distress.

I trust I can send all my letters that I have written to you so far from Caille St. Louis, the port of Saint Domingue. You may even receive them before I reach my final destination. May these letters serve as my journal.

My dear father,
Your very humble and obedient daughter and servant,
Marie Madeleine

She knew better than to sign as Sister Stanislaus or to invoke God's name too many times in her writings. Her father was not a man of great faith, and to him she would always be Marie Madeleine, the daughter that, in his mind, he had lost forever. She breathed in the ocean air, folded the letter and put her ink and pen back in their wooden box. Louise Mariette was watching her from a distance. Louise would never interrupt the Sister while she was writing or praying, but the girl was a constant presence. Sister Stanislaus was a patient woman, and she knew Louise adored her. She would teach her how to read and write. She would teach all of them. For now, she could not speak of that, though. She noticed the Vicomtesse in conversation with the First Mate. The young noblewoman was giggling. The Sister tried not to judge. Her attention wandered as she caught sight of the Jesuits huddled together in prayer behind the mast. She looked back at Louise, surprised that their eyes did not meet. The girl seemed distracted. She was standing up and bending over the railing, staring out at the horizon.

Suddenly, her hand went to her mouth. The Sister moved closer. There was terror on Louise's face. When the Sister approached, Louise tried to speak, but no words came out. She was waving her arms wildly and pointing towards the horizon. The waving and pointing attracted everyone else's attention on deck, and they all gathered around the girl. Then they saw it, too. A ship in the distance, hoisting the unmistakable black flag with a skull and crossbones.

"Pirates!" squealed Josephine de Chavin and grabbed the arm of the First Mate, but he ran off to alert the Captain and the crew.

Sister Stanislaus took Louise's hand and ushered everyone down to the galley. The rest of the passengers were already gathering there. They heard the First Mate bellowing orders to the sailors to get the canons ready. Captain Christophe Vauberci entered the dining room and was met with a flurry of anxious questions. He put up both hands:

"Yes, it is a Corsair, a pirate vessel. We are prepared for such an occurrence, but we do not have as much manpower as is usually the case for this kind of voyage," he said looking over the mostly female passengers. His gaze fell on the Jesuits.

"I need you to shed your habits and put on sailor uniforms. We have boxes of them in the cargo area."

The Jesuits exchanged frightened words in hushed voices.

We are not trained to fight! Nor does our faith allow us to attack others.

"You are permitted to defend yourselves and the lives of the ones entrusted to you," the Captain said as if he were reading their minds.

He did not pose it as a question. The priests slowly nodded. A sailor led them out to change. Immediately the noise increased as the women began to talk over each other. One voice was louder than everyone else's. Florence had been listening closely to Vauberci's words when he spoke to the priests:

"We can help, Captain."

Florence had an idea, and she would make sure she got the Captain's attention.

~

As Captain Vauberci left the room, he was twirling his beard, deep in thought. Only he and the nuns knew about the woman's past life under the bridges of Paris, and he had no reason to trust her, but her crazy idea might work. He was surprised that Sister Stanislaus agreed to it so quickly, against the protestations of her fellow Sisters, and less so that the Reverend Mother Superior outright forbade them to follow the plan. But once the *forçat* had convinced him, even the Abbess listened as he painted a dire picture of what would happen, if the pirates captured them and took the ship.

~

Jean Bèranger had spotted the ship from fifteen miles away. The weather was finally clear, and he was determined to make the most of the opportunity that had just presented itself. He was desperate to make bounty for his brother who was incarcerated in Port-au-Prince, and this ship was big. He saw the French colors on the flag and became even more excited. All his worries were over now. The wind was in their favor. They could take the ship within the hour. He stared through the telescope as they sailed closer. These French vessels were usually on their way to the colonies and carried large quantities of goods. As for their human cargo, he expected to see mostly females. He would make sure to capture them. He did not like killing women; they were worth more alive than dead.

The pirates readied their cannons and pulled their ladders up to the ropes. They would need them. Jean knew the element of surprise was going to be lost as they got closer.

"Fire!" he yelled.

The first cannon went off. And nowhere. Jean had anticipated this. It was only meant to open the attack and show their power. He put the telescope to his eye again. Then dropped it.

What the devil's foot?

He picked it up again and put it to his eye. He could not believe what he saw.

This is not supposed to be a military ship! There is nothing but uniformed sailors on board!

There were at least a hundred of them, from what he was able to make out. He could not continue his thought. A cannonball smashed into the deck beneath his feet, and he jumped away from the smoldering floorboards.

"Turn the ship!" he shouted, as he ran to the rudder to help his mates steer their damaged ship into the opposite winds.

∽

Louise, Florence, almost all the Sisters, and even Josephine, were rolling the ammunition to the cannons and handing them to the sailors. They kept firing, but most of the shots fell short. Only one hit the pirate ship, but that seemed enough.

"They are turning!" screamed one sailor.

The women, breathing heavily, fell on their backs, relieved. They were a wild sight. All of them wore uniforms, most of them so big they looked like costumes on travelling actors from the *comedie de l'arte*. As the pirates sailed off, Sister Stanislaus saw a big grin on Florence's face. She jumped up and, almost tripped over her pants.

"We did it! It worked!"

Vauberci grinned broadly: "It sure did."

"Let's go after them! Let's sink their ship!" she exclaimed.

Vauberci cautioned: "Not a good plan. The ruse worked, but we will never beat them in a real fight. Now, go get your warrior women and join me in the galley. We don't have much, but this calls for a celebration."

As the nun led the women downstairs, she felt unease. Florence would be a handful.

The night after turned stormy, and for the next two weeks, the weather was so bad that everyone was forced to stay in their cabins. The confinement led to arguments among the young women and tensions even among the nuns. Most suffered from terrible seasickness. Sister Stanislaus had a robust condition, the strongest of all the Sisters, but even she had trouble keeping control of her stomach in the tight quarters below. Disregarding the Captain's warnings about gusty winds she climbed the narrow stairs to the upper deck.

The heavy cloth of her habit got caught in one of the wooden planks as she stepped up to be closer to the railing, and the fabric tore a little. She paid it no mind. The air was cold, but she welcomed it for now. She had done her research and knew they would soon enter much warmer waters and with those waters, a sweltering heat none of them was accustomed to. She started to shiver and wrapped her arms around herself, but the thought of going back down to the stench in the cabins, the result of days and days of seasickness and barely emptied buckets, was unbearable. So, she held on to the railing with one hand, staring out over the dark ocean.

There was no moon under the heavy cloud cover. The Sister put her other hand into the pocket of her overcoat and gripped her rosary.

Lord, be merciful and keep us safe on this journey.

It was her daily prayer. It never varied much, and she never asked for better conditions, just safety for all on board. When she could barely feel her fingers on the wet ropes, she turned to go back inside. As she took a few steps towards the door, she heard sobbing from the other side of the ship. She followed the sound to discover the Mariette girl hunched over a barrel, crying uncontrollably. Louise did not hear the Sister coming and only stopped briefly when her downcast eyes fell on the worn black boots.

"Child, what troubles you?" Sister Stanislaus asked while putting her hand underneath the young one's chin to lift her face. The girl was unable to speak, her sobbing turning into small whimpers. The nun did not have to ask—Louise Mariette, barely fourteen, had never been off her father's farm before embarking on this month–long voyage to a new continent. She was an outsider among outsiders on this ship and did not know the ways of the world.

At twenty-three, Sister Stanislaus felt like a wise, old woman. She had chosen to enter the convent against her father's wishes, and she had chosen to travel to this colony. She was full of purpose and had never wavered in her conviction that this was her calling, not just becoming a nun, but dedicating her life to doing missionary work. This country girl was under her and her fellow sisters' care now, as were the others that suffered below. Even the rich aristocrat who pretended to know it all and rubbed everyone's noses in her wealth. The Sister felt responsible for all of them, but none more so than the girl. She had read the contract Monsieur Mariette had signed for his daughter. She was to be married in the new world. Like all the others, she had been given a casket by the government in Paris, filled with a dowry. The nun stroked the girl's wet hair.

"You are shivering, you must go back down before you catch a cold. Will you help me clean out the cabins for the others?"

The girl nodded and let the nun aid her in climbing the steep ladder they called stairs. As she stepped back down behind the kind Sister into the belly of the ship, Louise Mariette contemplated her fate. None of what had happened to her made any sense. Not even in that ‚God knows best what leads to heaven'-way that had been drilled into her by the parish priest, from an early age.

Why of all his children has Papá sent me away? What have I done wrong?

~

In one of the bigger cabins Josephine de Chavin punched her fist into the mattress while stifling tears. She wanted to scream. She had that feeling several times a day, sometimes every hour. She refrained. There was no use. She knew and resented that everyone called her 'mighty Princess' behind her back and that she was stuck on this ship, and worse, stuck in her cabin because of the bad weather. She had no one to talk to, at least no one on her level. Except for the Widow LaCour, a *baronesse*, none of the others were of aristocratic descent, and the woman was so preoccupied with making friends with the lower classes and endearing herself to the nuns that she neglected to spend time with her. The Baronesse even insisted on everyone calling her simply Madame LaCour. Josephine's anger belied her fear and loneliness.

No one knows how much I have lost…

The life as she knew it was gone, taken from her by cruel fate. It was all her family's fault. And that man's…

Her mind drifted, and there was a hint of pain flashing across her face that cut much deeper than her tears. She had been given no other choice than to leave everything she was accustomed to. She had tried to fight her father and uncle, but known it was futile. Being an outcast in Paris was worse than starting anew at the end of the world. This is how she regarded the place she was bound for. The end of the world. She had heard only rumors of the strange reptiles, the insects, the wetness of the land; and worse – of the wild native tribes that speared strange animals for food. But she had also read about the grandiose plans the government in Paris had for the place. The building of a modern city had already begun. It would not be Paris, though. Nothing could replace her fondness for her birthplace. She dragged herself off the bed. As much as she dreaded the company of the other women, she could no longer bear to stare at the wooden walls and the tiny cub hole.

∼

In the galley, Geneviève, the Widow LaCour comforted the frightened children. The ship made loud creaking noises every time she was hit by a wave. They had to hold on to the wooden bench or they would be thrown across the room as the Gironde swayed from one side to the other. Pierre, her five-year-old put on a brave face as he had done every day since his father passed. Her brother and sister-in-law had told the boy that he was now the man of the family, and he had taken this new role very seriously. She considered the notion foolish. He was only five, and she felt the heavy responsibility resting solely on her. She brushed away a tear from little Delphine's cheek. The angelic looking baby-girl was barely eighteen months on this earth and had endured more upheaval than most grown-ups, culminating in this voyage and a new beginning in the colony.

Geneviève liked most of her compatriots and felt very protective of them, especially the shy Louise who seemed so out of sorts with everything and everyone. The girl needed mothering most. Geneviève had decided early on to ignore Josephine de Chavin as best as she could.

She knew certain things about Josephine's past that she could easily hold over her, but they were based on rumors, and she did not want to repeat the typical behavior of Parisian society in such matters. She herself had been the victim of idle gossip and, like her or not, she was not willing to subject the Vicomtesse to the same treatment.

Geneviève had learned more about what was waiting for them in La Nouvelle Orleàns than any of her fellow travelers except for the Captain. Her brother was acquainted with a few people who had already settled there, but this too, she kept to herself; no need to let anyone know her business or the reasons why she fought so hard to get the last space on the ship for herself and her children. She had made friends with the nuns whom she admired for their sense of mission, especially Sister Stanislaus who was so much more educated than the rest. Geneviève felt a little pang of guilt that she had deceived everyone by telling them that her husband had died in poverty, and that this move to another continent was her and her children's only way to survive. Nothing could be further from the truth. For the devout Catholic woman she was, it caused her considerable regret, but survival trumped all; and keeping the utter and horrible truth a secret.

Florence Bourget, too, had lots of hidden secrets including her one talent. As the storm drowned out every other noise, she climbed the stairs to the main deck just as Josephine closed the door on her cabin. Florence waited until the aristocrat had disappeared. She was not meant to be on this deck; the Captain had told them to stay downstairs on the midlevel of the Gironde. The lower level was designated for the sailors, the midlevel was reserved for the nuns and priests, and all the other passengers, and the upper deck belonged to the Captain, his first mate and now the mighty Princess. It was also where the galley, the pantry and a common room were located. She was sleeping in a berth right next to Louise which was fine as far as she was concerned. The country girl did not talk much.

Florence minded much more that the nuns were watching her every move, especially that Sister Stanislaus. This nun was the smartest of them. Constantly writing in her journal when she wasn't praying. Writing letters to her father, too. By the time they would get to that colony, and the Sister could put those letters on another ship back to the homeland, her father could be dead. Florence had a very dour view on life. This journey hadn't been her decision but the government's. She was glad but not happy. *Oui*, she now had her freedom and the chance to leave her past behind, but who knew if they'd even survive this whole trip. In case they did, well, she'd be prepared. She glanced around the corner from her hiding place. The Princess had left the deck.

She must have gotten sick of the sick people. Her narrow little bourgeois nose couldn't stand the stench any longer.

To Florence the bad odors were nothing. She'd smelled much worse. She slowly tiptoed to the door, opened it, snuck in, and closed it behind her.

Now, where would a princess hide her finery?

Florence was not sure what she was looking for; anything shiny and valuable would do if she could sell it later. A big trunk was wedged between the bed and the wall. It was locked. She could have picked the delicate lock but not without breaking it, so she made a quick decision to look for something else. She knelt down and saw a slightly smaller trunk underneath the bed; it was unlocked. She pulled it out and flipped it open. Dresses and silken undergarments spilled out.

Nice but useless.

Florence couldn't sell those, or even trade them. She dug to the bottom. Nothing but clothes. She growled. But then an uneven part of the trunk's inside wall caught her eye. The fine leather had been carefully lifted from the wood and something had been stuck between it and the outside shell. Using her long fingernails, she pulled it back. A small, almost flat velvet pouch came into sight. She pulled it out and emptied its contents into her hand.

Ah oui! These will do!

She picked up the exquisite earrings of ornate gold, and what she recognized as diamonds and rubies set in a design of some sort of crest. She slipped them into the pocket of her heavy linen dress and was about to put the velvet back behind the leather but stopped herself; chances were slim the Princess would take out such fine jewelry while they were on the ship, but she could check if they were still there by running her hand over the leather. Florence looked around and saw the splintered armrest of a wooden chair. She broke off some splinters and put them into the pouch, smoothed back the leather, and tested her work.

There was only one place to hide the earrings. Like all the other girls she had had to turn in that casket she had been given. The first mate had stored it away with the rest of the cargo. The girls had been told that since everything in their casquettes was to be used only once they were betrothed, they wouldn't need them for a while. Clothes and personal items would be provided by the nuns once they reached the convent. So, she carefully opened the door just a crack and looked out. No one was around. She moved quickly down to the midlevel deck then stopped in front of another cabin. She hesitated.

Madame LaCour was such a nice woman, and she felt bad stealing from her. But she had heard the rumors: Madame was in fact a baroness, and therefore she must be wealthy. Florence put her ear against the door. It was so easy to determine if someone was in Madame's cabin. Those little brats always cried or made some other noise. There was only silence. She slipped inside. Madame's luggage was in plain sight; one big piece held together by thick leather straps. That made it easy. She unfastened the straps and carefully opened the trunk.

For an aristocrat Madame LaCour certainly travels light. Two dresses, a few pieces of clothing for the children, some toys, soaps, and an unopened bottle of perfume. How can this be all?

Florence felt deeper into the suitcase.

Merde! This is a false bottom!

She quickly took everything out of the trunk and noticed a tiny opening, not wider than a small finger. She put her pinkie inside and carefully lifted it. And gasped. She was staring at a treasure. Gold and silver coins wrapped in paper and cotton cloth, two golden candlesticks, a rolled-up tapestry and a bible.

Florence couldn't read, but the cross on the black leather cover was unmistakable. Some papers had been folded inside the holy book, but she was not interested in them. She still couldn't believe her luck. And her misfortune. There was no way she could take and hide all that money. This thievery of hers had to be carefully planned and spread out, so no one would catch on. She took a piece of cloth and grabbed a handful of the coins, put them in her other skirt pocket, then carefully replaced the false bottom, put everything else back inside and closed the trunk. Now she just had to find her casket. It had her initials on them, and she would recognize the F and the B.

Chapter 2

"Port of Call!" the First Mate shouted.

I know in my heart that my father and mother and all my siblings must have sent prayers, for our own cannot have been enough to fend off all the trouble that has followed us throughout our voyage. I am certain that their prayers were strongest during the attack. I am still filled with wonder that we did not perish, as so many others have done. Every one of the sailors on the Gironde told us that out of ten boats this has happened to, not one could escape. But it was not our fate, and for that I am grateful.

Sister Stanislaus put down her journal and let out a deep breath of relief. By the time Caille St. Louis, the port on the Island of Saint Domingue came into view, the passengers of the Gironde had been sailing the oceans for five months. They had been spared another pirate attack but had not gotten used to the heat yet. The humidity gave Josephine another reason to complain and was especially hard on the older nuns and the Jesuits. They only had their woolen habits and were constantly fanning themselves with their bibles. Louise still clung to Sister Stanislaus, Madame LaCour kept playing peacemaker whenever an argument broke out, and Florence mostly kept to herself. As the Gironde docked in the harbor around midday they were surprised by the amount and more so the mixture of people who were moving goods and selling and trading at the market stands. Women of all colors, wearing cotton dresses in vibrant shades of red, blue, green, yellow and purple, their hair up and bound in silk or cotton *tignons*. There were merchants and traders, workmen, and shady figures with no good intentions.

The Captain had extended an invitation for tonight, a *soirée* at the plantation of one of the richest Creole merchants on the island. Even the nuns were looking forward to spending an evening in different company. Vauberci had told Sister Stanislaus and the Mother Superior that said merchant would join them on the rest of their journey, and that he would bring at least ten more passengers with him. As they stepped off the ship onto the pier, some of them were overcome by dizziness.

"You are land-sick," the Captain smiled, "after such a long time at sea, you have gotten used to the ship's motion, and now the land feels strange to you."

The land feels strange in any case, Geneviève LaCour thought.

Between the mix of people, the palm trees lining the roads, and the small but charming houses, it was mostly the smells they were not used to; a mix of strong spices that were sold at the market, fish, sweat and a sweetness in the air, the Caribbean Isle felt like an exotic tale only described in books she had read a long time ago as a child. The Captain had encouraged them to explore this town called Port-au-Prince and had instructed the First Mate to accompany them. By dusk they would be met by carriages and brought to the plantation. Vauberci had warned the nuns, and first and foremost the outspoken Sister Stanislaus, not to question the sometime rough practice of slavery they may witness: "It is their custom," he had stated without further explanation.

∽

The day before, the pirate Jean Bèranger had walked into the port town's municipal building.

I am going to get my brother out of jail no matter what it takes. I am a businessman after all.

A businessman without funds but with a purpose. Armed with that he marched into the government office and demanded his brother's release. The official, not surprisingly, denied the request if one can call it such; because the pirate pulled his bayonet, grabbed the man and held the knife against his throat.

"If this is what it takes..." the pirate said and let the threat linger. The official's eyes showed fear, he barely nodded, and Jean let him go. The official fell back into his chair. Jean leaned against the desk, towering over the man.

"My brother has been rotting in that cell for months. The fact that you have not set a trial is proof that his incarceration is sheer malice on your part."

The official's voice got defensive: "I am just following orders..."

"Then follow this; you release him now, and I make it worth your while. Or not..."

"I have heard of the vampires on your ships..."

Jean smiled. He had done nothing to dispel that notion, even if the stories about him had taken on epic proportions involving sea monsters and bloodsucking otherworldly creatures. The truth was much more mundane. And more frightening. The official knew he would have to explain the release of a well-known pirate to his superiors. He had to keep partial control:

"I cannot return your brother's ship. Michél Beranger has violated the piracy laws. The ship has been seized and sold off."

"So they say."

"And you must pay bail and fee."

Jean's face darkened. He had counted on the loot from the French vessel to pay for Michél's freedom. Again, he took a step towards the man who shrank in his chair.

"I can provide you with my very last and best barrel of crude rum from Cuba as payment…"

The official's face lit up a bit. Cuban rum was far superior to the liquor available here, and the man was a connoisseur. Jean stared him down:

"… if you release my brother by morning. I trust you will have found a good excuse to free him by then."

He deliberately put the bayonet on the desk pointing towards the official and walked out.

∼

In the morning Jean reunited with his brother on the plaza. Jean loved his brother, impulsive as he was. He had taken care of Michél, who was four years younger, as long as he could remember. He had a cabin ready for him and a new set of clothes. His ship showed no sign of its true purpose now, the skull flags had been removed and stowed away. As he dropped his brother off, Jean could not believe what he was seeing. He immediately recognized the Gironde. There seemed to be no one on board except for some sailors maintaining the deck. Then he saw her: a woman emerged, fidgeting, her hands twitching before she climbed off the ship.

She is hiding something! Did she rob the ship? Is she from the island?

Nothing about what he had just witnessed made sense to him.

This is a military ship, dressed up as a civilian vessel, is it not? So where are the soldiers? And what is a woman doing here? She does not look like the harbor girls that the sailors pay for an hour of company. If she is a thief, what does she expect to find on a military ship?

The fact that she had white skin made even less sense to him. White women on the island were upper class, married to wealthy men, and would certainly not be wandering around the harbor by themselves.

This one did not look like a rich lady. His curiosity was peaked, and he decided to follow her.

~

Florence breathed a sigh of relief. Her plan had worked. She had feigned exhaustion, and the others had taken off without her. The remaining sailors were preoccupied with replacing ropes and fixing minor damage, and she was undisturbed. A few more of Madame LaCour's gold coins had made their way into Florence's casket.

Like any visitor to the island, the woman was drawn to the stands with their overflowing wares. Jean watched her enter the market. He stood a short distance away as she picked up a silver bracelet from a local craftsman. When the man told her the price she put it back down.

Ah oui, she is certainly not a wealthy woman.

Jean Bèranger saw the craftsman turn to help another customer. Within the glimpse of an eye the woman picked up the bracelet, slipped it into her corsage and strolled away with leisure. Jean had seen a lot in his life, but this here surprised even the worldly man he considered himself to be. There was not one moment's hesitation in the woman's deed. She was not new at this.

Florence smiled broadly as she disappeared into the crowds. She turned a corner into a narrow street and bumped into a man.

"*Excusé moi.*" She said and tried to pass, but the stranger would not let her. He had a dark beard and wore a black leather vest over a white shirt despite the heat.

"Monsieur, *s'il vous plaît...*"

The stranger towered over her, broad shouldered, his arms stretched out to the sides, his hands against the walls of the buildings. His dark, fiery eyes bore into her as he slowly put his hand over the fabric of her dress between her breasts. She jumped back:

"Monsieur, I'm not a prostitute!"

"*Non*, Mademoiselle, you are a thief."

It was time to run. She ducked under his arm, but he grabbed her. She struggled. He had his arm wrapped around her waist, holding her close.

"A very good thief…"

Florence stopped moving. Was this stranger paying her a compliment?

Jean Bèranger let go of her, knowing she would not try to run now, judging from the curious look on her face.

"Hand it over" he commanded.

She reached into her corsage, his eyes following her move. She pulled out the bracelet but did not give it to him:

"Don't touch it." He snagged it from her, held it up against the sun. Then he bit into it: "Not worth much." He slowly slipped it back into her corsage. His hand lingered. She slapped him. He laughed.

"Pleasure to make your acquaintance, Mademoiselle…"

"Florence." She was intrigued by him but determined not to show it.

"I could use someone as crafty as you, Mademoiselle Florence…"

This man is not going to hand me over to the police! He is a forçat, a criminal himself!

"I do not make my living here, Monsieur…"

"Jean."

"Monsieur Jean… I am on a journey to the colony of Louisiana; we are continuing in the morning."

Continuing?! So, she is a passenger…

There was only one ship leaving for Louisiana the next day the port master had told him, and only one in the harbor large enough for such a voyage. Anger flashed across his face as he suddenly connected all this information. They had been fooled. The Gironde was a passenger vessel after all. And this woman, Florence, was not the only female on board he guessed. He was determined to get to the bottom of this.

"We should meet this evening to discuss our further business dealings. That is unless you prefer that I fetch the shop keeper you stole from."

It was not an empty threat. He would not hand her to the police himself, given his occupation. He would let the shop keeper do it for him.

I must get out of this predicament.

Florence was a believer in truth when truth was the best option to escape a difficult situation.

"Monsieur, this evening I am to attend a soirée at a merchant's house. We are traveling under the care of ordained women of the Ursulines and getting out of joining them at this gathering is not possible."

Jean could barely conceal his growing anger.

Ursulines? They had been beaten into retreat by nuns?! How?!

"Well, then I will find a way to secure an invitation and see you there. What is the host's name?"

"I don't know, only that he is to join us on the ship tomorrow with all his servants."

Jean had no doubt that she really did not know the man's identity, but this was not hard to find out; not that many merchants would have booked the voyage to Louisiana. He bowed.

"I shall see you tonight."

On the outskirts of Port-au-Prince, Zulimé, a fifteen-year-old girl, looked down at her bound wrists. The woman in front of her stumbled and immediately felt the whip of one of the two slavecatchers. The women were all bound together, all nine of them. Zulimé had made out the number the night before, when she had been thrown into a cage and heard the voices of the others in the darkness. Most were older than her, but there was one little girl who could not be more than seven. She thought of the Larrác plantation, her home, and her *Mamán* and *Grandmère*…

They must be worried sick about me.

Zulimé's eyes darted left and right while she was trying to spot anyone who might recognize her and end this nightmare.

Would Monsieur send someone to look for me? Would they find me?

She thought they had walked past the mansion of a lady her mother worked for, but it was too early in the day for anyone to be outside, and these two men knew how to avoid any area of the city where they would be questioned about their prisoners. Every other block, the bigger one took out his whip and hit the group, not caring whom he reached. The little girl was crying out. She had been walking too slow and incurred his wrath. Zulimé had so far escaped the beating. She had been singled out for her slightly lighter skin color, the bigger catcher telling the other one not to tear her skin. She knew what that meant, and when she saw the auction block on the far side of the market a dreaded feeling of doom rose up, blocking her lungs and throat. A large group of males were sold one by one.

They must be from Africa.

They were naked, save for some rags that covered their man parts, with metal collars around their necks, and chains tied to their hands and feet. She shuddered in the heat. The usual price for an enslaved male was one thousand *livrés,* females went for half that. The auction went fast as most landowners purchased them in bulk; not only did they need lots of laborers for their sugar, coffee and spice plantations, but one could also negotiate a better price for ten or more. Zulimé had watched this before, the dealing and haggling and loud bidding that went on. She had never imagined she would end up here, so protected had she been by her family and by Monsieur Larrac. As reality sank in, she felt like someone had punched her in the stomach. And yet…

I can never give up; I can never give up.

She straightened her back, bracing for a fight, and in her head and heart, calling all the spirits for help.

Henry de Roche, the Creole merchant, watched the auction from the sidelines. He never delighted in the spectacle, but the plantation needed workers, and not just the one he owned on the island. He had bought land in Louisiana and had agreed to share in the transport of Africans with his neighbor, Louis Blanchard.

He took a long drag from his pipe. He was here for the females. The male auction was almost over. De Roche watched two rugged looking men push a line of girls up to the block.

Les petite gens, low class people.

He almost said it out loud and meant not the girls but the two men. He hated these slave traders. Dirty scoundrels with no good sense of making their wares look presentable. The women were soiled from whatever they had been sleeping on. The older ones, he knew, could not work in the fields.

And then, what is this? A little girl?

She had welts all over her arms from a whipping she must have received recently. From the way in which they were dressed—and that they wore clothes at all—Monsieur de Roche suspected that these women had not just come off a ship from Senegambia or the Congo region. He was aware of the practice of stealing enslaved people by abduction from plantations and selling them here. He watched the trader describe one by one in glowing words that could not be further from the truth.

Strong? This one can barely stand up.

Most of the bidders had left. There was no big interest in females today. De Roche needed to make a decision. His eyes squinted in the sun, and his gaze fell on a beautiful girl that looked different than the others.

"Now this here is a special one, a real diamond in the rough!" the trader shouted. He tried to force her mouth open, she bit his hand and spit at him. He yanked her chain.

"Lively, too!" He pulled her close, putting his mouth to her ear: "If you try this again, I will strip you naked and whip you right here for all to see."

She turned her head up. Before anyone knew what was happening, she lifted her free leg and pushed her knee into her captor's groin. He bent over and groaned.

She screamed: "*Je suis un negresse libre*! I am a free negress!"

Before she could repeat her claim, the trader raised his chain to hit her.

Monsieur de Roche parted the crowd: "Stop!"

The trader's arm was in midair. De Roche jumped on the block: "I take them all! Two thousand livrés for the whole lot!"

"Four thousand!" the trader hissed.

"Not after what I just witnessed! Twenty-five hundred is my final bid. No one here is even trying to get in on this auction!"

"You can have them; they are nothing but trouble!"

De Roche handed the man his money and had his coachman load them onto the horse cart. The beautiful girl kept saying the same thing over and over, her voice trailing off the more she repeated it:

"Je suis un negresse libre…" She kept repeating her claim even once they got to his plantation. It was as if she were in a trance.

Je suis un affranchitte, je suis un negresse libre…

De Roche tended to believe her, but he was in a bind. He needed a certain number of females to run the plantation efficiently. And he had run out of time. For weeks, he had been trying to buy more women, but the offerings had been scarce to non-existent. His deal with neighbor Blanchard was a trade: Blanchard had bought fourteen men on his last trip to the island and was willing to exchange four of them for six females if de Roche paid for their fare on a ship. De Roche wished the numbers would be more even, but women were not worth as much as men. The nine that he had bought this morning would not make for a good trade, either. If he gave up the most valuable one, he would lose more than he would gain. And there was something else… Underneath his calculating demeanor he was mystified by this girl. He promised himself to treat her well. For now, that meant that he had instructed the cook to wash her, give her a nicer dress, and a small room in the house to sleep in.

∽

That night on the foothills above the city's most affluent area, Josephine de Chavin had visions of her beloved Paris as she entered the grand hall of Henry de Roche's mansion. There must have been a thousand candles on the glittering crystal chandeliers, illuminating the whole house and casting a warm light over the guests. A long *banquette* with white porcelain plates, chiseled wine goblets and decanters invoked memories of a time long since passed. And yet it all had an exotic element that she had never seen before. The trays were overflowing with strange fruit and greens, the smell of spices, unfamiliar to her nose, emanated from the *brochettes* of meat and poultry. And then there was another smell that wafted in from the gardens and filled the air.

"What is this delicious scent?" she whispered to herself but loud enough for her host to hear.

"Plumeria, Vicomtesse," de Roche explained, "a flower specific to the islands."

For the first time in months Josephine was enchanted. She stepped out on the terrace in the back of the hall and took long, deep breaths.

∼

Sister Stanislaus stood in the entrance hall with a group of nuns. Unlike the other Sisters who had not looked forward to such a worldly event as a soirée, she was curious about this island and grateful they were able to break up the monotony of the last five months on the ship. Except for the two aristocrats, all the women stared at the splendor, some of them open-mouthed. Their reaction to the luxurious surroundings was quite different from the Sister's. The Marie Madeleine part of her marveled at the architecture, but her demeanor showed detachment; she observed the Casket Girls, her eyes following one after the other.

Louise Mariette was admiring the grandeur of what she considered a palace when she heard a noise. A girl with dark skin who seemed to be her age was rustling the heavy silken drapes behind her. Louise observed the girl watching her: *"Bon jour. Je m'apelle* Louise…"

"I am Zulimé."

There was something disconcerting about the girl, Louise thought. After taking in the customs of this place, she had decided that the class structure was very simple: there were the white people who owned the island, and there were the very, very dark people who worked for them. This girl, though, did not fit into this simplicity. She was not as dark as the others, but she was not white, either. She was not wearing one of those dresses with the little aprons like the other servants. And she was not walking with her head bowed. Before Louise's curiosity could prompt her to ask, an older black woman appeared and pulled the girl with her.

A commotion at the entrance to the salon turned all heads. A wild looking man with black, curly hair had entered, and Monsieur de Roche seemed unamused. Everyone followed the loud voices, trying to hear what was going on.

When Jean Bèranger had discovered the identity of the rich merchant who was hosting the soirée for the passengers of the Gironde, he had felt bile rising in his throat.

De Roche! The man who had conspired with his good friend, the Governor, to tighten the laws against piracy!

The one who had spent his own money to strengthen the military force to aid the battle against men like Jean and Michél. The same man who was ultimately responsible for his brother's capture and incarceration. Jean knew that Henry de Roche was not doing all this out of the goodness of his heart or respect for the law. With the pirates out of the way, men like him had no competition on the high seas. They could trade and drive prices up as they pleased. Jean had briefly considered to stay away. Jean Bèranger, the uninvited but not the unwanted. If they could prove anything, his face would be on banners all over town. In the end his pride and his recklessness had gotten the better of him. No sooner had he gotten off his horse and into the mansion, had the man who was his nemesis confronted him.

"I am not in the habit of permitting criminals to enter my home!" De Roche was as angry as he was shocked. Like most merchants on the island, he disliked pirates and despised Bèranger above all, but he also feared the man everyone called the king of the high seas; not that he believed the countless stories of wide-eyed creatures on the man's ship, and that pirates drank the blood of their victims. Those were fairy tales told by the fish mongers and market women. But he was aware of Bèranger's vengeful nature; cross him and one would regret it. De Roche was determined to keep him away from this house. The altercation drew a crowd, and from the midst of it stepped a young woman:

"Jean! What took you so long? I thought you would be here to walk me inside!"

Florence took Bèranger's arm and proceeded to walk him down the hallway. In passing she turned to de Roche and whispered coquettishly: "I do apologize, Monsieur, I should have announced my companion's arrival. I do hope, you will forgive me."

De Roche was stunned, and so was Jean, if for different reasons.

This cunning woman has outwitted my most powerful foe.

Jean glanced at Florence. She was worth forming an alliance with. She led him to the terrace. He picked up two goblets of wine, handed one to her and toasted:

"To a most resourceful young wench."

"Monsieur..."

"Jean, s'il vous plait. After all, we're old friends."

Florence had surprised herself. She was quick when it came to pickpocketing jewels, money and other valuable items, but she had not thought herself capable of thinking so fast and taking charge of a very delicate situation. She had kept an eye out for the mysterious man from the market as soon as they had arrived at this big house, and when he caused such commotion, she was certain Henry de Roche's footman would throw him down the front stairs. Her actions had been more of a reflex than the result of a plan. She was aware that everyone's eyes were on them. She would have some explaining to do with the nuns later.

Sister Stanislaus had watched the scene with growing concern. A crease formed between her eyes.

∽

Zulimé sat at the kitchen table, her head low, a bowl of rice and beans in front of her. She had put the little girl to bed and waited for her to fall asleep. Back in the kitchen, she had not touched the food Mama Maramé, the cook, had put out. The kind woman had let her know that the master did not want her outside with the guests after he had watched her interaction with the country girl Louise.

I wonder why. Could he be afraid I would tell everyone that I am not a slave?

A hopelessness engulfed her whole being. The master's house was too far from Monsieur Larrac's plantation. Even if she snuck out and ran, she would not make it back to Mamán and Grandmère. She had heard about runaway slaves. They were always caught and whipped or worse. The thought of being forced to leave this island in the morning on a big ship, cut off the air flowing to her lungs. She choked. The pit in her stomach that Mamán called *woulou*, was in knots. There were no circles of light emanating from it as Grandmère had said. She had taught her granddaughter that light had to flow through all the woulous of the body to be alive and connected to the heavens.

Am I dying? Is all this killing my light?

It was in this moment that Zulimé felt a force of power coming from deep inside her.

I am not going to die. I can and I will conquer whatever bad and dark happens to me.

She had seen this kind of power before when she had secretly watched her mother's ceremonies, hidden behind the thick trunk of a tree, but she had never felt it herself. She lifted her head and sat upright.

Familiar sounds were drifting through the window from somewhere on the property. She got up and climbed through the kitchen window into the garden. She followed the sounds until she got to the edge of the lawn where a low fence separated it from the sugar cane fields. She climbed over the fence and saw an opening in between the stalks. A group of Africans danced around a man. On the other side were a few men playing various instruments. She recognized a *lambi*, a conch shell in the form of a horn that made deep, full sounds. And an *ogan*, a flattened bell that her grandmother had told her came from Africa. There were other drum-like instruments, and the man in the middle held a *kulev*, a harmless snake, native to the island that represented the serpent-deities who are the sky-power and cosmic protector and bestow blessings. She knew all of these, and seeing the group made her feel safe and calm. These were her people, her ancestor's people. She joined the dance. When the playing and chanting stopped, she went up to the man in the middle and bowed:

"Can you help me?"

"We know all about you. But we cannot help you escape. The powers are against us."

"I know," she whispered. "But can you get a message to my family? Just to let them know I am alive, but forced to go on a ship?"

The man put the snake around her neck and made a blessing sign: "Oui, petit mademoiselle. We will."

She caressed the snake, then handed it back to him. When she returned to the big house, she was filled with a sense of peace she had not thought possible a few minutes earlier. That her family would know that she was alive, even if she never saw them again, was most important to her.

∼

Captain Vauberci had watched the confrontation between Henry de Roche and Jean Bèranger along with the Sisters and the Jesuits. He was the only one who knew of Bèranger's reputation, and he had every intention of keeping this knowledge to himself. There was no point in frightening them. The suspicion that it was Bèranger's ship that had attacked them entered his mind, but he dismissed it. There were too many pirate ships on this route and accusing one without proof would only lead to a fight. Vauberci had also watched with consternation how Florence Bourget had diffused the situation.

What is this woman up to? And how does she know the pirate?

Other than the Mother Superior, Vauberci was the only one who had seen Florence's papers and was aware of her history. An alliance between her and Bèranger was bad, very bad. De Roche, still seething, walked up: "Christophe, have a drink with me!"

The Captain excused himself and joined his host and friend. The two men huddled in a corner, engaged in heavy conversation.

"Do you know that he got his brother released?" De Roche said: "There must be a way to throw him in jail where he belongs!"

"We cannot prove anything, you know that. He's a clever bastard. But I swear, I shall keep an eye on the girl. It escapes me how she would know him after only a few hours on the island."

De Roche downed his drink with one gulp and slammed the glass on the mantle.

CHAPTER 3

Praise the Lord for the good weather.

On deck the next morning Sister Stanislaus practiced gratitude over exasperation. The Gironde had gotten crowded with Monsieur de Roche and his entourage and more than twenty crates of cargo onboard. The Sister thought of all the women under their care, their upbringings, so different from one another and now the addition of foreign cultures and skin-colors…

When the First Mate sounded the horn as the island of Cuba came into sight, she came out of her thoughts and into the present. The Captain came over to encourage the women to explore Havaña before dusk.

"There is to be no roaming around the streets after dark," he cautioned.

Florence was on her best behavior after Saint Domingue and because she was very much aware that both the Captain and Henry de Roche were watching her closely. Her new friendship with Jean was not doing her any favors with either man. She quietly followed Geneviève and Louise to the marketplace in front of the cathedral. Cigar smoke wafted through the narrow lanes between the stands, and she watched de Roche negotiating prices for crates of tobacco and crude rum. Louise and Geneviève were drawn to the strong herbal scents. The country girl carried little Delphine, and Pierre held onto his mother's hand, hopping along excitedly, and pointing to different products on the tables. When they passed a stand with wood crafts, the boy did not want to move on.

"*Alors*, I shall get you a toy," his mother consented. Geneviève let him pick out a carved donkey and paid for it with a silver coin. The craftsman had no change for the French currency and offered her half his wood figures in return. She declined, but when he yelled in Spanish to a woman with a coffee cart, she was too polite to say no to the cups of dark brew that the woman handed to her and her companions. Too polite and too tempted; even for the higher classes, coffee was still a luxury in France, and the watered-down mix that was served in Paris cafés could not compare to the strong smell filling her nose when she raised the cup. Louise did not even recognize the delicious, thick, hot concoction as coffee. In her world, the drink had been a rare treat, reserved for Sundays and holidays, and even then, she had never developed a taste for it. This here was invigorating. The nice coffee woman called over to a boy who pushed a strange looking iron cart. He pulled it over and grabbed a long piece of sugar cane from the cotton bag that was slung over his shoulder, fastened it between two metal tubes and, with one quick arm move, the wheel on the side of the tubes spun, thus squeezing the cane. Brown juice squirted into a metal cup that he handed to Pierre. Before her son could take a sip, Geneviéve snatched it out of his hand and inspected it.

"*Señora, este sola una copa con agua de azucar.*" the boy said.

Geneviève drank from it, smiled and handed the cup to Pierre. The drink tasted surprisingly refreshing and not sugary at all. The boy offered more to the women which they eagerly accepted.

The following morning when eleven local women made their way up the gang plank of the Gironde, Geneviève recognized the coffee lady among them. She introduced herself as Margarita Cortez and explained in broken French and a lot of hand gestures that she was one of three cooks that would make the journey to Louisiana. Margarita was to prepare meals at the convent. The other eight women were nurses and hired to work at the Ursuline hospital, once it was set up. Geneviève had a hard time guessing the cook's age. She was older than the others. The crease on her forehead spoke of a hard life, and her eyes told a story of a woman who had endured much and survived it.

Margarita was combing her long, wavy hair on deck. With her head bent forward, the long tresses fell to the floor as she rubbed scented oils into them. Unlike the French women who—even in the hot weather— would not expose their upper arms and had sleeves that reached to their elbows if not their wrists, Margarita and her companions wore cotton dresses with very short sleeves. Josephine called them indecent, but the Cuban women paid it no mind. Their customs were different, in many ways freer and certainly more accommodating to this climate. Zulimé, with the little girl clinging to her, watched as the Cuban cook was working the oils into her hair. When Margarita was done, she threw her head back and the shiny waves cascaded down her back, reaching to her waist. She noticed the fascinated look on Zulimé's face.

"*Viene acquí!*"

Zulimé shyly approached her. Margarita took her hands, palms up, and poured a little oil on them, rubbed the palms together and put them on the girl's head. Zulimé smoothed down her curls and inhaled the sweet scent.

"You may always ask me for more. I brought enough of these oils."

Zulimé thanked her, then used the excess oil for the little girl's hair. The child had not spoken a word since they had left Saint Domingue. No one seemed to know her name, so Zulimé had decided to call her Bebé. Margarita searched her skirt pockets and came up with sticky caramels that she offered the girls. They smiled and retreated to the other side of the ship. Margarita braided her hair and tied it in a bun at the nape of her neck before wrapping an orange and blue scarf around her head. She picked up a piece of broken glass and held it up to see her own reflection. Thank God, for her dark coloring. The bruises were barely visible, the swelling had gone down and the cut on her temple was covered by her hair. These wounds would heal soon enough. She worried more about the ones on the inside.

I must forget the past.

She reached into her pocket and clutched a tiny wooden doll.

Clodumare, protect me through the Orishas from the dark Ogun...

She kept chanting the words over and over, using the Santería words for God, the deities and aggressiveness.

∼

"Balise, Louisiana! Bienvenue, *Mesdames et Messieurs*!"

The First Mate was yelling the obvious as the Gironde entered the widest of the waterways that snaked their way through the Mississippi Delta. They had arrived in the colony. Not everyone understood what was going on when the sailors threw out the anchors and started bringing up luggage.

"This does not look like a big city. Where are we?" Louise asked.

"The ship is too big to sail up to La Nouvelle Orleàns, silly," Josephine chided the girl. "We have to take boats the rest of the way."

Geneviève looked the aristocrat over, then laughed: "Silly yourself! You are dressed for an afternoon in Paris in this heavy brocade. Not very practical for a weeklong journey through swampland."

Josephine ignored her. She was going to arrive in style no matter how much she suffered in the heat. One by one the passengers disembarked and climbed onto pirogues and flatboats steered by no more than one or two sailors. Their belongings were loaded onto separate barges. Zulimé was wedged between the enslaved women, but this was fine with her. She was afraid of the water, always had been. Her grandmother had taught her spells to chase away the fear, and Zulimé was repeating them in her head now. She was determined not to show how terrified she was on the boat with the river water lapping at her feet.

Monsieur de Roche will never take me seriously if I behave like all the others.

She could not act frightened in front of Bebé, either. So, she stood with her chin up, back straight and eyes fixed on the horizon. Bebé was clutching Zulimé's hand and burying her head in the older girl's frock.

Frère Antoine Dourot watched in amazement as, one by one, the pirogues anchored in the shallow water and deposited all these different groups of women. The priest had made the trip down here to welcome the Sisters. He had high hopes for the Ursulines. The convent, unfinished yet, was to become the center of clerical missions in the colony, and the establishing of a hospital essential to the survival of the soldiers. Frère Antoine was a man of the cloth, but he also possessed a practical mind. The Jesuits had not had much success as missionaries in this place. The people from the various tribes were difficult customers, and his Brothers not adept at selling and spreading the word of God. It was easier with the enslaved, but even that was up to their owners, and not all merchants, businessmen, politicians, and aristocrats running the plantations were God-fearing people. Their Lord and Master was mostly gold and riches and coming to church on Sunday was more an unavoidable social event than a holy ritual. The priests were not willing to do the hard work of going from house to house and convincing the locals to live by the laws of the Father, the Son and the Holy Spirit. It had always been women who spread the bible, and these Sisters might succeed where both, Jesuits and Capuchins had failed. What Frère Antoine was not expecting were the brown people. At least the Cuban women did not need converting.

But what about this group of slaves?

He pushed the thought out of his mind. He was not here to judge but to welcome.

∼

In the dead of night, the Vicomtesse awoke with a scream when Florence slapped her face.

What the hell was the forçat doing? How dare she?

Josephine grabbed the woman's hand.

"I saw something crawling on you!" Florence hissed.

"You enjoyed this!"

Only the night's darkness could hide Florence's smirk. The moon was full and illuminated the sleeping quarters—if the make-shift beds on wooden stilts, surrounded by burning ember could be called that. Sleep eluded most of the weary travelers. It was their third night, and none of them was used to this land yet. Frère Antoine had told them that August was one of the three hottest months and one of the most humid. The swamps smelled of strange plants and fish, and the insects attacked mostly after dusk. The nuns constantly swatted them away from their hands and faces, and the rich women used their fans. Only the darker-skinned people seemed immune to the stinging little creatures. Zulimé had told her that islanders had developed a tolerance. What Florence saw crawling across Josephine's face was far from a little insect, though. She had no idea what to make of this thing with four little legs and a pointed snout, long tail and huge eyes that seemed to be able to stare in all directions at once. For a moment, she had contemplated leaving it be.

Let the mighty Princess suffer in case this thing bit her.

The little animal scurried off into the swamp just as the Vicomtesse yelled. "I cannot take this anymore!" Josephine was waking up the whole camp. "How much longer until we reach the city?"

"We are at the halfway point, and if everything goes according to plan, we will get to La Nouvelle Orleàns on Friday." Frère Antoine said.

The nuns were suffering silently. Their woolen habits were inappropriate for this climate.

Only three more days... God willing...

Sister Stanislaus was still detailing every part of their journey in her letters to her father but was careful to leave out the particularly grueling events. Zulimé got up from her sleeping place and sat down next to Florence who tried to describe the animal:

"Big eyes. But it was not bigger than my hand," she said.

"What you are describing is a crocodile, and I doubt they exist in miniature form," Josephine argued.

Zulimé interrupted: "There are only two reptiles that look like this…"

"What would you know about it?" Josephine was not used to discussing any topic with a servant, especially not one she clearly knew less about.

"We have them on the island," Zulimé continued: "These big eyes belong either to an iguana…"

"*No es possible,*" Margarita spoke up: "Iguanas are bigger than your hand."

"…or to a gecko." Zulimé's voice carried so much authority that she had everyone's attention.

"Are geckos dangerous?" Florence asked out loud what everyone was thinking.

"No, they are harmless, we used to play with them," Zulimé answered.

When Josephine heard this, her fear and disgust turned into her usual annoyance: "Well, I do not want to play with them, and I do not want them to crawl over me."

"Since we are all up now, would you like some coffee?" Margarita, the ever practical, was already hunched over her little metal pot that hung over the fire. She fanned the embers to get the water to boil. The woman was a godsend as far as Geneviève LaCour was concerned. Her delicious brew had saved the day, every day. It was even good when it was cold. Margarita's coffee was not the only thing Geneviève was grateful for. Miraculously the little ones had been easy to handle. Pierre was fascinated by this strange land and went off exploring each evening with one of the sailors once they had found a place for their nightly camp. And tiny Delphine had not cried once. She too, seemed enthralled with her surroundings, and she loved sucking on the sugar canes Margarita carried in her cotton bag. The children also did not mind the heat. It was not indecent for them to wear thin cotton, so Geneviève dressed them only in what were otherwise considered undergarments.

Like the others, Florence was not able to resist the strong coffee smell but retreated to the edge of the camp once she got her cup, not wanting to attract further attention after the gecko incident. Jean Bèranger was constantly on her mind and in her heart. She was not willing to admit this part. She was interested in the man only for reasons of business, she told herself.

He must be a very rich criminal.

Florence was daydreaming of grand heists in which she would be his companion and night dreaming of a different kind of companionship. She woke up sweating, not entirely sure whether it should be attributed to the hot weather or her own excitement. She had no doubt he would come for her once they settled in the city. He would find her. Her hands shook as she held the steaming cup of coffee from Margarita.

PART TWO

THE CRESCENT CITY

"It is enough to tell you that here one publicly sings a song in which there is only this city which resembles the city of Paris. This tells you everything."

Marie Madeleine Hachard

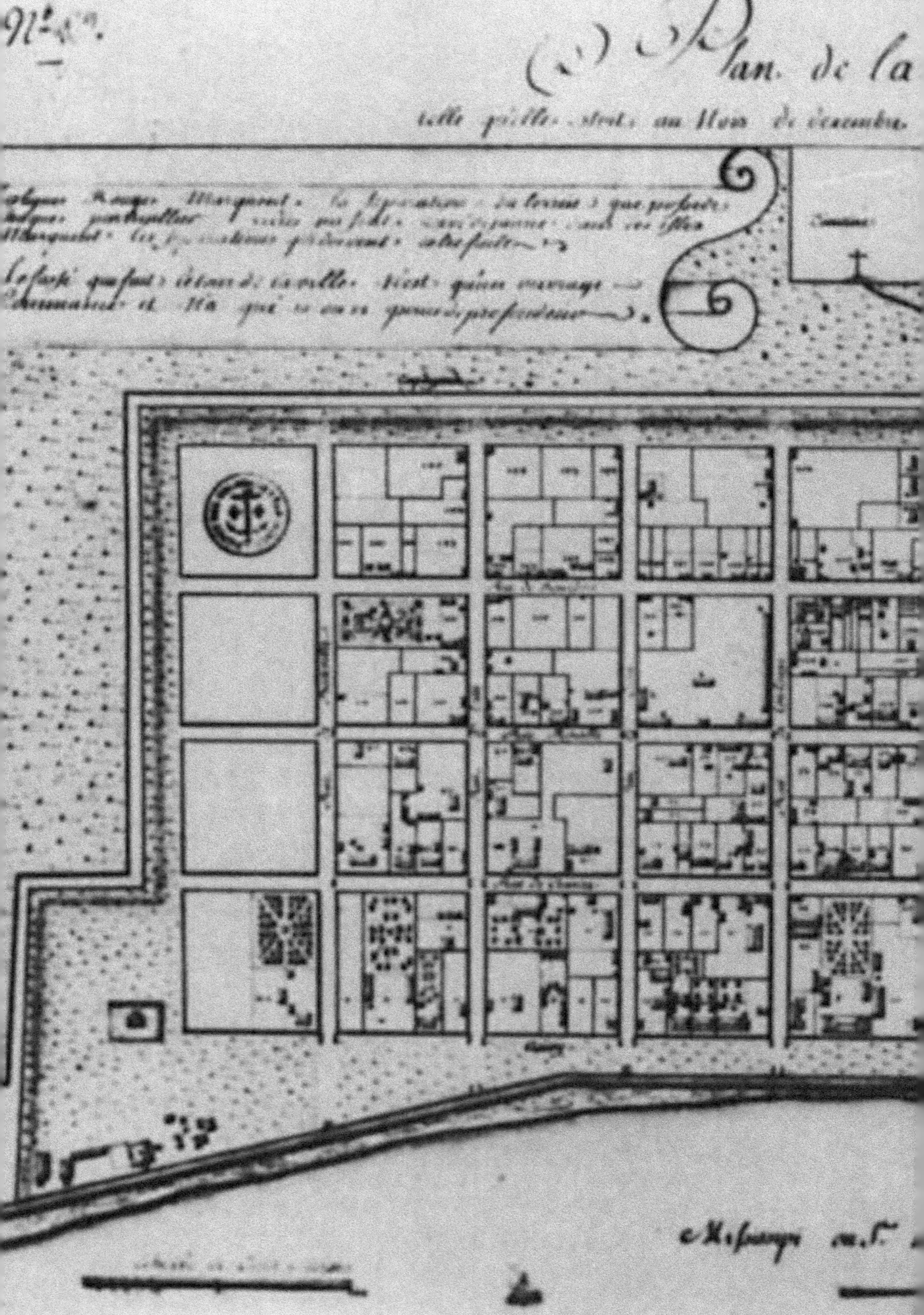
N.o 8
Plan de la

Map of New Orleans circa 1731

CHAPTER 4

We have a courtyard and a garden, which adjoin each other on one side, and at the end are wild trees of prodigious height and girth. This makes us among the first for an infinite number of visits from mosquitoes and the Frappes d'abord, and a type of flies and gnats whose species I still do not know... These bad insects sting without mercy. We are assaulted by them at night... Whatever precautions we take, we are unable to escape carrying their marks.
Marie Madeleine Hachard in a letter to her father

The moon had barely faded, the sun not yet risen when the Sister walked out of the convent, even at this early hour swatting away flies with a cotton handkerchief that had become her constant companion. She walked down Rue Saint Anne, past the whitewashed houses towards the market. Some of these buildings were two or three stories high with parterre gardens, others were smaller. All of them were made from timber. Cypress shingles lined their roofs. Despite the early hour the market was bustling with activity. The fishermen were unloading their catch on wooden tables, the artisans laid out their wares. She marveled at the variety of goods: there were the local products like sugar, rice, tobacco, and rum, as well as indigo, imports from Europe and indigenous crafts. Silk and other cloth, silver, wine, salt and household sundries could be found on the stands and the produce that farmers brought into the city: sweet potatoes, eggs, figs and greens. Lumber and tar, so needed for building and furnishings, were transported from the north shores of Lake Pontchartrain.

Sister Stanislaus was especially fascinated by the strange objects that came from the tribes of lower Louisiana. The Choctaw, Chitimacha, Chickasaw and others laid out deerskin, bear oil, bison tongues, game, corn, herbs and persimmon bread, the last one a delicacy she had savored many times since their arrival, after she had convinced the Mother Superior that it would save money to feed everyone at the convent with this specialty rather than hoping for wheat to arrive from French settlements all the way from Illinois. The shipment of goods from the far north could never be counted on with regularity. The frontier land was too far away and the water- and landways too treacherous.

Is it strange that I feel so much more of the world here than the last six years at the convent in France?

She longed to being called by her given name. She felt like Marie Madeleine in this vibrant place, where the lines between the clergy and the people were blurred, where the colorful life seeped into every corner of being, never to be avoided or shut out completely. But the last two living beings, her father and her cousin, who still referred to her as Marie Madeleine were an ocean away.

The Sister's musings were interrupted by the cheerful greeting from the big woman at the grocery stand who had prepared a cart filled with fruit, okra, potatoes, and rice.

While wheeling the heavy cart across the market, she caught a glimpse of a blue dress disappearing behind one of the stands. The Sister would recognize this dress anywhere. It was the only one Florence Bourget owned.

What mischief was this woman up to? Had she been out all night?

The Mother Superior had imposed a strict curfew after their arrival. Marie Madeleine sighed and concentrated on the cart. Every time the wheel hit a pothole, fruits tumbled off it, and she had to pick them up again. Her thoughts returned to the strange dichotomy of feeling like two persons in one body. Sister Stanislaus was the one with the convictions, the deep prayers, the commitment to God. Marie Madeleine was the practical woman who organized the girls, shopped for groceries and pushed the food cart. The Sister was best left at the convent while the practical woman was doing the chores and all that was necessary.

∽

What a night!
Florence did not quite know what to make of the endless conversation she had with the pirate. She had found him. Or had he found her? She could not be sure about anything concerning Jean Bèranger. She had been exploring the city almost every night since they had arrived. The Mother Superior's curfew did not stop her. The pirate had seen her first. She was outside a *cabarét* called Flamand's Tavern, on the sidewalk, fending off a drunkard. Not a very tough task for someone as street savvy as her. Besides, the man almost fell over as he was trying to touch her breast. A little shove, and he ended up flat on his face. As she turned away from the drunkard, there was Jean. Giving her his amused smile, one eye squinted in the light of the flickering candles from inside the bar.
"Always in trouble, aren't you?" He laughed.
She tried her best to hide the excitement of finally running into him: "I can handle myself."
He winked at her: "Ah, oui, we have seen that."
Bèranger led her into the bar where everyone seemed to know him and greeted him with loud hollers and back slapping. Florence was so giddy with excitement that she did not pay attention to how often he refilled her cup with crude rum. The rest of the night was a blur. She was not used to the drink, and he knew it. He emptied his own cup much faster than she, but the rum seemed to have no effect on him, he was in total control. Bèranger's face darkened when he thought of Saint Domingue, but a sense of ease returned to his features when he watched

the excited forçat. If it had been her looks that first made him notice her, it was her mind that kept him interested.

An exceptional mind for a woman.

She was unsure if his flirtatious ways were meant to lead her into his bed or if he used them to pry information out of her about her past, her business. Because this was all he talked about—business. And yet he was charming her. Florence had dealt with men all her life. From her nasty father who had drunk himself into the gutter to all the rogues she worked with but never for. She had learned to keep them at arm's length. Never had she answered to a man, never had she delivered the goods to one boss. She stole, but she stole for herself. She had explored the scene in Paris and made connections, so she would not depend on a middleman to sell her loot. It was dangerous for a woman, but it was better to get into a fight than to be regularly beaten up by some thief master for not bringing him enough valuables and having to depend on pocket money or worse, a few scraps of food and a dirty cot underneath the Pont Neuf among the drunks and *clochards*. She owed a lot of her feistiness to her brothers...

~

"*Allez, petite lapin!*" Aubin, her oldest brother yelled. His big hand tightened around hers and he dragged her along. She hated being called 'little bunny' by her three brothers. She was eight years old after all. And wasn't a bunny little already? Aubin did not care. He was tall and seemed like a grownup to her at thirteen years of age. Emile was ten and Bastien nine, barely a year older than her. Bastien called her 'Flo *lapin*'. She could not decide which nickname she disliked more. Yet she loved her brothers. They protected and defended her, first against their always angry father who had beaten up on them and did not spare his daughter in his drunken rages. And later against anyone who came too close to her, including the policemen of the *Guet Royal* who patrolled the river's edge where the homeless roamed and crime was rampant. As a child she never considered herself homeless. Her brothers knew how to construct a tent from a large piece of tarpaulin that they kept hidden in a hollow tree during the day, and in the winter when it was too cold to sleep under the bridges, they sought shelter at a nearby church. Aubin ran what he called 'the Bourget gang'. He gave her the first lesson in life—how to pick the pockets of unsuspecting strangers.

"You are so little, and you are a girl, they'll never suspect you," he told her. She stole her first coins when she was five. At six, she had perfected the art of snatching *reticules*, the small, often ornately embroidered handbags of the rich ladies, and she was so fast, they never noticed until she had long disappeared behind a corner. At seven, she knew how to sneak into a shop, hide behind a curtain or under a piece of furniture and let herself get locked in when the shopkeeper closed for the night. Then her brothers would wait in the back, Emile would find an opening, often a basement window, and they would remove what she had chosen. They let her decide, because after a night where they had hauled big items that had turned out to be worthless, they trusted her to pick glassware, ladies clothing like gloves and scarves, small bronze sculptures and on very good days, jewelry. If the store had only a tiny escape, it would be Bastien who helped her. She loved him most. He was closest to her age and always had a joke on his lips, unlike Aubin who had inherited their father's anger and Emile who did not speak much. When Bastien died of pneumonia two years later, she was heartbroken for the first time in her young life. She had never known her mother who had passed giving birth to her. And when their father was found dead on the street, they had all been relieved to be rid of him. After her youngest brother's death, she became sullen. That's when the two older boys taught her to fight:

"You have to learn to defend yourself when you can't outrun them," Aubin drilled into her. He made her practice the shin kick—a fast hit with the side of the shoe or a piece of wood, and the belly ram, where the smaller person rammed their head straight into the opponent's stomach, cutting off his air. When she got older and taller she became very good at the groin beat—kicking her knee into a man's tender parts, and the elbow slice, a quick raise and turn of the elbow to hit across her foe's face. She almost always carried a rock in her fist when she was out late, to harden her punches. During the following three years she liked getting into fights and did so intentionally at times. Kicking, punching and screaming brought some relief from the pain over losing Bastien. And later, after Emile had gotten himself killed when he provoked a police guard. A year after that, Aubin was arrested and thrown into Bicêtre prison. She was fourteen and on her own but bolstered by her street skills, and no man ever gained any power over her.

∽

Florence was not about to change her ways in the new world. Yet she was so drawn to the pirate that she longed to be with him. But…non, non, non! She would not work for him.

"So, what do you think?" His question interrupted her train of thought. She had gotten lost in her own head, she felt hazy from the strong alcohol.

"About what?"

He laughed again: "No more rum for you. How can we make a business deal if you fall asleep while sitting up?"

What did he say? Business deal?

She had to be alert for this, and she most definitely was not.

"Mademoiselle Bourget, I believe we will continue this conversation, when you are awake. Shall we say tonight?"

"It is tonight."

"No, it is morning. Look…" He took her arm and pulled her up. The sky outside was a honey-colored grey. She needed to get back to the convent before the nuns finished their morning prayers. And not in the state she was in. He was reading her mind: "I suggest you run to the market for a strong cup of coffee."

Good thought. She leaned in.

For what? A kiss?

He smiled, grabbed her shoulders and stretched his arms to create space between them. "Until tonight. Off you go."

She turned and walked away, embarrassed.

I will never drink rum again. They call this eau de vie? More like eau de mort.

At the market, she spotted the Sister and barely had time to run around the corner and disappear between the stands. She had grabbed coffee but was spilling it now while trying to avoid the nun.

Merde!

She ran back to the convent and snuck in through the hole in the wall before the Sister returned. She was so tired; she fell asleep as soon as her head rested on her pillow.

∾

Unlike the white women Zulimé was not allowed to leave the convent. To say that this rule upset her was an understatement, yet she knew that she had every reason to be grateful.

Monsieur de Roche had every right to move me upriver… all the way to his plantation. Or worse, sell me to another owner.

Instead, he had asked Mother St. Augustin to keep the girl in the convent. After all de Roche had done for them, the Mother Superior could hardly refuse but made it clear to him that she did not need a servant at this time and that Zulimé would be treated equally to all her other charges. What surprised her most was that he seemed relieved rather than opposed.

Monsieur mystifies me. I am his property, yet…

Zulimé could not finish the thought, could not articulate the strange power that she had over him and that he seemed to fully accept. She used that power by insisting that he leave little Bebé with her.

Zulimé did not mind the separation of sleeping quarters. Hers and Bebé's were upstairs in a vast space underneath the attic, designed for servants, while the French slept downstairs in community rooms near the main hall and the kitchen. The nuns' apartments were in the back, close to a newly erected chapel, and the Madame with her two children stayed in a room originally created as an office. The blonde noblewoman had insisted on her own quarters, so she and Louise had to drag her bed into the library which was the only other semi-private space in the convent. Margarita was assigned a cot in the community room but had opted to sleep upstairs with them. Zulimé liked and trusted the Cuban cook. Margarita had been nothing but kind to them and reminded her of her mother.

Still, that she was considered a slave and not allowed to leave, made her not just uncomfortable but filled her with anxiety. She had grown up roaming around freely wherever she wanted, and here there was not even a decent yard to speak of.

I need to convince the Mother Superior of a chore that only I can do. One that takes me into the city.

The chance presented itself two months after they had arrived. Madame LaCour's baby daughter Delphine fell ill, and the one local doctor could not seem to find a cure. Delphine's fever had not broken for two weeks, and her mother was beside herself. Then Louise started feeling sick. None of the white doctor's remedies helped, but Zulimé remembered the symptoms from when she was little, and all the children at the plantation had suffered from them in the early autumn. It was not until her *grandmère* had made a concoction of herbs that she brewed for a whole day over the open fire and then force-fed the children that their fever had gone away. Zulimé later identified the terrible taste as a mixture of wormwood, nettle and the bitter green herb they grew next to the flowers.

I must find these herbs.

There was no point in asking the Mother Superior directly. She would speak to Sister Stanislaus and to Madame. Delphine's mamán was desperate enough to try anything.

Geneviève LaCour rarely lost her composure, but watching her tiny daughter suffer day after day and night after night was too much for her to bear. Neither the syrupy liquid that the local *docteur* had prescribed for Delphine nor the vinegar wraps he recommended, did anything to relieve her symptoms. Louise had helped Geneviève care for the baby girl until she, too, had fallen ill. The nuns' answer to all this was to pray. Geneviève was a practical woman and could not think of anything that was a bigger waste of time than praying. She was not willing to watch the baby die that had entered this world against all odds and under particularly difficult circumstances. Sitting at her daughter's bed with her head in her hands, tired from nights without sleep trying to comfort Delphine, she did not hear Zulimé.

"Madame…"

Startled, Geneviève raised her head.

"Madame, I know what will help your little one…"

How could this young slave possibly know about illnesses and cures?

"What are you talking about?"

Zulimé was undeterred by Madame's doubtful tone: "The children on the plantation I grew up on suffered the same fever. And my grandmother made a remedy that cured them all."

"What was in it?" Geneviéve's interest was piqued.

"I am not sure, but I think I can make it if I can find the herbs."

The answer did not induce trust but after two weeks, Geneviéve was grasping at straws: "Where could you find the herbs? At the market?"

"No, Madame, they grow in the wild. If you can convince the Mother Superior to let me search for them, I will do my best to make a healing concoction for your child…"

Geneviève could not care less about the rules that the head of the convent had imposed on the girl. After a brief discussion with Sister Stanislaus, the two women marched into the Mother Superior's office and insisted that Zulimé would be allowed to venture outside the convent to search for the healing herbs.

"Mother St. Augustin," Geneviève said, "Monsieur le docteur has proven useless, and I need you to give the girl permission."

The head of the convent objected: "What if she runs off? Monsieur de Roche has entrusted her to us, and after all he has done for us, I cannot risk this."

"Forgive me, Mother," Sister Stanislaus interjected, "Zulimé has already proven herself worthy of your trust. Just remember how much she helped us with our habits."

Mother St. Augustin had to admit that they were right. Without the young St. Dominguan who knew how to mix indigo with coal to make a dark dye, they would all be wearing light colored natural cotton or suffer in their old woolen habits.

"And besides, where would she run to?" Geneviève added.

"*D'accord*, she is permitted outside, but only during daylight hours. And only accompanied by one of the Cubans," Mother St. Augustin relented.

When Zulimé was told that she could leave the confinement of the convent, she could hardly contain her excitement. Margarita was to join her on her searching mission. Zulimé would have preferred to go alone but was not about to argue and risk her newfound freedom.

I must deliver. I must find the cure.

~

The Dominguan girl and the Cuban cook set off that same afternoon. Margarita had been outside the convent a few times for market shopping, but she was not that familiar with the city. Zulimé knew that she had to follow her own instincts if she wanted to find her way to the outskirts with the meadows along the river she had heard of. They first crossed the Place d'Armes towards the river. At the market Zulimé turned east. She noticed Margarita's questioning look.

"If I want to find wild herbs, I first have to find the wild. We must get away from the houses, from the city."

After a few blocks, they reached a divide. Behind it were only fields and no sign of homes or other buildings. They walked deeper into nature, Zulimé's nose trying to detect a familiar smell. She silently called on Loco, the vodou God of wild vegetation with all its gifts, and the patron deity of doctors. After what seemed like an eternity to Margarita, Zulimé stopped and parted the grass. Underneath grew what looked like a robust little plant with tiny olive-colored leaves covering the swamp ground.

"Oui, oui, oui!" Zulimé exclaimed. "The first one found."

The second herb grew only in the shade. She scanned the horizon. Far off in the distance she saw what she thought could be a tree and when she got closer, she breathed a sigh of relief.

This looks like the brush around the plantation on the island–dense bushes and trees. There must be nettle.

She spotted it on the wet ground and began tearing it out in big bunches, not caring how much it stung her hands. She carried it back in the folds of her skirt. Zulimé was beaming, but her pride and relief at having found the two herbs soon gave way to doubt and worry: the third one would be so much harder to discover, she suspected.

After an hour, they gave up. The sun was beginning to set, and they had to make their way back if the Mother Superior were to ever allow her to go outside again. With a mixture of elatedness and disappointment, they walked towards the city with Zulimé stopping every so often to take in the scenery and stare at the beautiful rose-colored sunset that reminded her so much of her home. A tear rolled down her cheek. The Cuban woman noticed but did not mention it.

When they arrived at the convent an anxious Madame LaCour

was waiting. They dumped their finds on the kitchen table: "I am still missing the third ingredient…"

"Can you not do without?" Geneviève asked.

"It would not have the necessary strength. I must find wormwood."

Margarita held up a hand: "*Espere*. Wait. Why did you not say that it is wormwood you are looking for? I saw some at the market. The strange old man was selling it the other morning."

Margarita was referring to a scary man sitting behind his cart, whom she had seen a week ago, when she had helped Sister Stanislaus with the groceries. He was dark, but in a different color than Zulimé, and had strange markings all over his face and arms. He was barely clothed, wearing only leather rags and a painted feather in his waist long hair. Around his neck were strings with pouches. He kept the herbs in clay pots.

"He looked frightening," Margarita said.

Geneviève was not letting fear of a strange looking man overtake her determination to find help for her daughter: "I do not care. If he has wormwood, we will buy it from him!"

CHAPTER 5

Josephine de Chavin felt so restricted at the convent that she was spending her afternoons walking through the city and the nights looking for its darker side. During daylight she was memorizing street names and studying the grandest mansions, often standing in front of them for an hour, taking in every architectural detail and watching the comings and goings of their inhabitants. She discovered that the wealthiest and most powerful citizens lived closest to the waterfront, on Rue des Chartres. The second row was Rue Royale where the homes of artisans like carpenters, blacksmiths, coopers, candlemakers and tailors were located. Behind it was Rue de Bourbon. She rarely crossed that street, at least not during daytime. Beyond it was only the moat. On the riverside, the Quay was reserved for government buildings and divided by the Place d'Armes in the center. She was dying to visit Governor Jean-Baptiste Le Moyne de Bienville's palatial plantation about an hour's ride outside the city. It was described as a smaller version of the grand Versailles.

No wonder he had abandoned his measly residence in the city. How convenient for him to dump it on the nuns. I cannot wait to see his palace.

Yet to venture past the moat that separated the main *cité* from the outskirts to the west, she would need a male companion and a coach. Why the plantation of the highest-ranking official bordered on African territory she could not understand. Enslaved people and servants were housed in the swampland to the north and east of it. Josephine had no intention of accidentally crossing the wrong street and ending up there. As she walked down Rue de Chartres, she looked up at a particularly nice house and swallowed hard to avoid tears. The beautifully crafted slope of its roof reminded her of her childhood home in Paris. She quickly wiped away a tear and decided to cross over to the French market.

Maybe the pâtissier has the delicious biscuits that always make me feel sweeter.

∼

Josephine's nightly adventures were not as careful and harmless. She craved excitement and this night was no different; she put on the act of a perfectly bored aristocrat who retreated to her quarters after dinner only to emerge in secret and sneak out through the corner hole in the convent wall she had discovered soon after their arrival. Once she was on the street, she headed straight to the part of the city she avoided during her daily strolls: that last row of houses behind Rue de Bourbon. This was where the taverns and cabaréts were located, the area where no one ever seemed to sleep and *eau de vie,* crude rum, and brandy was served all night long. Several times a week, she went there, carefully dressed in simpler clothes than befit her social stature.

I do not want to be recognized or become a criminal's prey.

The same people she looked down on when it was light, drew her to them when it was dark. The Vicomtesse had always been strangely enthralled by the edges of society and the opposite of what she had been raised to be. It was as if two souls lived in her, one battling the other. So far, she had not summoned the courage to enter one of the bars. She was watching the patrons from across the street, more fascinated by their behavior than by the rich gents and ladies she was observing when the sun was up. At night she had noticed all sorts of women, seemingly on their own, entering these places and taking part in the drinking and laughing with the men. She took a deep breath and crossed the street.

It was still early, and the counter was not crowded. Josephine asked for a cup of rum. She had never tasted this drink and was surprised by its sweetness.

No wonder they call it eau de vie! Water of life.

A few more of these and she would be dancing. The bartender watched her through squinted eyes. Josephine could dress down all she wanted; she would still be out of place here. She was aware of this fact, but the rum seeping down her throat and warming her from the inside, filled her with courage.

"Be careful. You don't look like you're used to it."

The voice came from behind her, and when she turned around, she almost dropped her cup.

I know this man! He is the one that caused all the trouble in Saint Domingue!

If Jean Bèranger, in return recognized her, he did not show it. She looked past him and locked eyes with a man standing behind him. She saw the similarities in their features and gathered that the men were brothers. If Jean had made an impression as a troublemaker, his brother exuded danger—an unfortunate character trait that she had been drawn to all her life.

"May we join you, Mademoiselle?" The younger Bèranger said with a smile. He put his arm around her waist. In another world, during daylight hours, she would have slapped away his hands and called the police on any man who touched her this intimately in public. But here, in this candlelit tavern, she was frozen and mesmerized, terrified and charmed at the same time by this charismatic man. Her gilded manners, her societal education, her snobbery towards anyone she considered lower class vanished for the moment. She could not be sure if it was the rum, or the man that intoxicated her more.

Jean moved to her other side: "Mademoiselle, may I introduce my brother Michél? You and I already made the acquaintance, even if it was only across the hall of an island mansion."

Ah, he remembers me, too! He must be aware that I am a noblewoman. But he calls me Mademoiselle… Is he trying to fool his own brother?

"Monsieur, I do not know what you are referring to. I do not remember meeting you."

If he kept it up, so would she.

"Well, in that case: I am Jean."

He smiled but before she could reply, she felt a push on her back and heard a familiar voice: "Look who got off her throne and joined the *les petite gens*!"

Florence sneered at the aristocrat and pushed herself between them, almost shoving Jean to the side and away from Josephine. "Isn't this bar a bit too dirty, too smelly, too crude for you? You know, they don't serve champagne here."

Everything in Josephine's nature wanted to put the woman in her place, but Michél's grip on her waist tightened and shot shivers up and down her body: "I am enjoying the eau de vie." She raised her cup. "Would you like one?" She pulled a few coins from her skirt pocket and put them on the counter: "Another one for my… friend, si'l vous plait."

She handed the cup to Florence who reluctantly accepted. But when Josephine raised hers for a toast, Florence turned to Jean and toasted him instead. Michél laughed:

"*Laissez les bons temps rouler!* Let the good times roll!"

He downed his own cup, slammed it on the bar and with one swift move faced Josephine, pressed his body into hers and planted a kiss on her mouth. As fast as he had moved in, he let go and turned to Jean: "Brother, we have business to discuss. Excusé moi, mademoiselles."

Florence interjected: "Am I not part of this business?"

"In a little while, *mon trésor*. Give us a minute but stay close."

They walked to a corner table. Both women were in a state of trance.

He called me mon trésor, my treasure!

Florence's eyes were wide but not as wide as Josephine's. A small voice in her brain said, ,*you should have screamed and hit him*', but it was drowned out by a much stronger feeling, a burn that spread from the lips he had kissed all the way to her toes. She was dizzy, had to hold onto the countertop or she would have fainted.

The bartender's voice pulled them out of their reverie: "You both need cold water."

"What are you doing here?" Florence's tone was no longer as harsh as it had been a few minutes ago.

It isn't Jean who is interested in the Princess…

"I was not aware that this tavern is exclusive to the likes of you." Josephine's own voice was quiet, and its soft tone belied her words: "Besides… we are both in trouble for sneaking out."

'If we're caught. I am good at sneaking back in."

Florence finally raised her cup and toasted the woman she never thought would lower herself to spend time with her, much less find herself in a place like this. They stood next to each other in silence, sipping their rum.

∽

The morning after shone a harsh light on both women. They had not had what one would call a real conversation but had formed a silent bond over breaking the Mother Superior's rules and being the subject of the Bèranger brothers' interest, not to say affection. Florence had only a vague recollection on how or when they got back to the convent. Josephine, secretly admiring how easily and nonchalantly rule-breaking came to Florence, had none. Her memory had a bigger hole in it than the one in the wall they had crawled back through when they had returned from Flamand's.

And the brats kept screaming!

Or so it seemed. Loud voices from the kitchen pounded Josephine's brain like hammers. She dragged herself from her bed and staggered to where the shouting originated from. The smell from one of the pots on the stove made her gag:

"I am going to be sick. And why are you screaming? *Arrêt!*"

She needed to stop the three excited voices that were talking over each other.

"We found the wormwood at the market! We can make the cure now!" said Zulimé and Margarita in unison.

Worm what?

"Unless it is a cure for my headache, I am hardly interested." Josephine put her hands on her forehead.

Geneviève pulled them away from her face: "No, you wouldn't be interested in anything other than yourself. My baby is sick, and I do not care to listen to your complaints of us being too loud, too excited or too anything for your taste. Everyone here has had it with your high and mighty attitude and your disregard for anyone but yourself. Refrain from talking or leave the kitchen."

Josephine retreated, not capable to respond in her condition.

"I do know a cure for her headache…", Zulimé said shyly.

"Don't waste it on her, she can learn not to spend her nights somewhere she should not be," Geneviève dismissed the notion. She turned to the pot: "What do we do now?"

"We need to let the concoction simmer until most of the water evaporates. It will take the whole day."

"The whole day?! But Delphine needs this desperately, her fever keeps rising."

"If it isn't made the right way, it will not work," Zulimé instructed with authority. Geneviève took a long breath. More patience while the worry for her daughter consumed her. Other voices resonated through the walls and echoed through the big rooms. Louise could hear them from her sick bed.

So unusual for the nuns to yell…

∼

In Mother St. Augustin's office, a loud male voice interrupted the female ones. From the kitchen Zulimé and Margarita listened intently and tried to make out the words. Florence and Josephine were closer to the source of the argument. Josephine had her ear pressed against the door.

"We do not have the means nor the space nor the staff needed to open the hospital! And by that, I mean furniture, medical help and medicines, as well as real doctors."

The Mother Superior's voice was deep and strong. Father de Beaubois, the Jesuit cleric in charge, slammed his fist on the desk, an unusually emotional outburst from an otherwise calm and measured man. Frère Antoine had acted as the unwilling messenger between the head of the Ursulines and the Jesuits for weeks, and Beaubois could not ignore the complaints any longer, much as he would have preferred to. On his way over to the convent, he had contemplated the best strategy and decided that attack was the best defense:

"We brought you here specifically to run a hospital. For no other reason!"

"Really? You mean to say that our mission means nothing? That spreading the word of the Lord in this colony is of no consideration? Against the promises made to the Abbé in Rouen?"

"No one keeps you from spreading the gospel to the wounded soldiers."

Mother St. Augustin leaned across her desk. She was exasperated: "The soldiers are already Catholic!" She mumbled to herself: "Like preaching to the converted."

Sister Stanislaus had been following the argument from the sideline. She was standing behind the Mother Superior. Now she stepped in front: "Excusé moi, Father. May I just ask when we would be able to get beds, medicines and staff?"

Ignace de Beaubois took a step back and cleared his throat. Truth be told he had no answer.

This Sister is a smart one.

Again, the Mother Superior was impressed with her favorite nun.

"Once the next ship arrives…"

"And when will that be?" Sister Stanislaus asked innocently. The Jesuit cleared his throat again: "That depends…"

Now Mother St. Augustin smiled at him: "So, you really don't know… I shall make you a deal: you find us a property close to the monastery, and we shall start preparing as much as we can without supplies and what little staff we have with the handful of Cuban nurses. But…" she raised her finger, "in the meantime we begin with a school for women and girls to stay true to our mission and spread God's word. After all, we already have the supplies for all that, the books, the pens, the rooms and certainly enough bibles."

"You cannot open a girls' school before we open one for boys."

The Mother Superior had to stop herself from laughing out loud, but she could not hide the sarcasm in her voice: "We? Would that be the Jesuits or the Capuchins? Or both?"

Sister Stanislaus knew she had hit a nerve. It was well known in church circles that the two orders were vying for control in La Nouvelle Orleàns and could not agree on very much at all. They both independently had come up with plans for a boys' school more than a decade ago, but finances would only permit that they open one together. Of course, Ignace de Beaubois, the Jesuit superior and Raphael de Luxembourg, the Capuchin friar serving as the head ecclesial official had not been willing to compromise on anything. Therefore, the subject of the school was a sore one, and everyone in the room knew it.

The Mother Superior was ashamed of the feeling of power that came over her, but at the same time she reveled in it: "Let us be useful while we wait for the medical supplies. And besides—you know as well as I do that the Lord's message is not preached by the fathers but by the mothers. It is and always has been women who teach religion to their children and set an example for them as *dévotes* by living true to our beliefs."

Father de Beaubois could not argue with that. It was the basis for

Catholic missions all over the world, in all colonies. But he had to make one last point: "You want to teach girls how to read and write while the young men remain uneducated? The church officials in France will not like this…"

Sister Stanislaus interjected: "But Father, we fully support a boys' school. However, this is entirely up to you and the church officials. We do not keep you from opening your school. We are not in competition."

The Jesuit knew he had run out of excuses. He sighed: "I shall forward your request to France. When they approve it, you may open your school."

He bid goodbye. As soon as the door closed behind him, the Sisters looked at each other with triumphant smiles.

"Well done, Sister Stanislaus!" The Mother Superior said proudly.

The younger nun felt good, too. The Ursulines had again lived up to their reputation as the dealmakers among the Catholic orders. But she had to ask: "Did the Abbé in Rouen give us permission for the school before we started the journey?"

"Of course, he did. And Beaubois agreed to score points with the order. But we do not have anything in writing." She inhaled deeply. "Which shall not stop us. And we shall not wait for one such written permission to make it all the way across the oceans back to us. The school is to be opened! Let us get to work."

Sister Stanislaus felt a sense of true excitement for the first time since they had settled in La Nouvelle Orleàns. When she was still little Marie Madeleine Hachard of Rouen, France, she had received a well-rounded education and could best determine the privileges and opportunities that came with it. To now oversee imparting knowledge to a group of girls as varied as their boarders filled her with new energy.

Behind the door, Florence snorted dismissively: "A school? What a waste of time."

Josephine looked at her with disdain: "Do you already know how to read and write? Did they teach you on the streets of the Isle de la Cité, Les Halles or wherever dirty part of Paris you roamed?"

Florence got angry again at the superior attitude. "Who needs it? What good did it do you? You may think you know so much more than us, but where did it get you from your fancy *hotel particuliers*, your townhouse in the Marais? Right here in this place with the rest of us, that's where!"

The woman was right, but Josephine would never admit it: "You want to go into business with Jean, do you not?"

She knew she had Florence's attention when she saw the insecure look on her face.

"Oui, but what does that have to do with reading and writing?"

"Everything, you foolish woman! You would be the greatest asset to him if you brought some education to the table. I assume, he does not know the alphabet. You would be the one in control."

Florence's crinkled forehead said it all.

Control is what I want, what I've always wanted...

"Fine, I will learn how to read and write."

"You are not doing me a favor; I already know how to do both. And I can do it very well."

Josephine shook her head.

The mood in the kitchen was quite different. The girls had not been able to make out every single word, but they had gotten the idea.

A school!

Zulimé was excited. For the first time since she had met the nuns and the Casket Girls, she did not feel inferior. For her best kept secret was that she already knew how to read and write…

∼

The large clock in the salon of the Larrác house was little Zulimé's favorite hiding spot. Monsieur's three white children, Benoit and Luques, the two boys, and Anne-Marie, who was only a year older than her and whom she affectionately called her sister friend, were getting their daily instructions from the *tuteur,* an old French man from Lyon who instructed the children in every subject, from mathematics to literature. He focused his attention on the sons and gave seven-year-old Anne-Marie a pass on whatever mistake she made. Girls, after all, were born to run households and birth heirs, not excel in knowledge. Anne-Marie was therefore a lazy student, knowing that there would be no repercussions if she made a spelling error, or her additions were not correct. Very often she did not pay attention during their lessons, unlike Zulimé who mouthed along when the boys read from a history book or were tested about a particular subject. Almost always, Zulimé had the right answer before they did. When their classes ended, she often quizzed them about this or that and soaked up whatever they would share with her.

On this day they were learning about Louis le Grand, the 14th King of France who was called the Sun King and had died only three years earlier. She was very fascinated by his mother, Queen Anne, a Spanish Austrian from the Habsburg dynasty, who had taken over the regency of her then young son until he became old enough to sit on the throne. In the meantime, she had ruled the country herself.

What a strong woman she must have been…

Zulimé was lost in thought, comparing the Queen of France to the two strong queens she knew, her Mamán and Grandmère, when a shadow fell over her. She jumped up and almost knocked over the clock. Embarrassed, she put her hands before her face, but she need not have worried. Monsieur Larrác took her hand and lead her to the table with his other children.

"May we borrow the book?" he said: "Seems, Zulimé here would like to have the whole story read to her."

The tutor turned his nose up at the suggestion of the plantation owner reading to a servant child but could hardly refuse his employer.

Anne-Marie giggled, earning her a kick from her brother: "What are you laughing at? Soon, Zulimé will read better than you! At least she pays attention," Benoit said.

The teacher harrumphed as it became clear that this brown girl had been listening in and the children knew it.

Larrác quickly led her out of the salon and sat her down on the porch: "Have you been sneaking into the lessons and listening to the lectures?"

"And learning all of it by heart," she responded.

"But you cannot read or write."

"Non, but I would like to…"

Her head was bowed, and he lifted her chin: "You know that it is forbidden for servants to learn the alphabet, don't you?"

"Oui, but…"

"But from now on you may join the children during their French classes and borrow their books when they don't need them."

She was so excited, she jumped into his arms. From that day on, she became a pupil.

~

As enthused as Zulimé was about the convent school at first, she worried that she may not be included. She had never heard of a slave who was allowed to attend a real school, and even Mamán and Grandmère had not considered the alphabet as important as their healing recipes and rituals and never paid much attention to her when she excitedly told them about a story, she had read with the Larrác children.

Will I be allowed to learn here?

She put her worries away for the moment to check on the big pot on the stove where the herbs for Delphine and Louise were still brewing. It was almost time.

"Will you tell Madame and Louise that the medicine will be ready in a little while?"

Margarita was already out the door. Zulimé took a piece of cotton they used for drying dishes and spread it across a smaller pot. Slowly she began pouring the thick concoction over the rag with a big wooden serving spoon, squeezing the liquid through it and into the small pot. So concentrated was she on this task that she did not hear Geneviève enter with Delphine on her arm and Louise behind her. When the baby let out a scream, she jumped and dropped the spoon.

"I am so sorry…" She picked up the spoon and wiped the splatter from stove and floor. "We need to give it a few minutes to let it cool down and then you can slowly sip a cup," she said to Louise. "I don't know how to feed it to the baby… it's very bitter, she won't swallow it… I can try to add sugar. Grandmère always had little children suck it from a sugar cane."

"Whatever will work. As long as she gets better." Geneviève sighed.

CHAPTER 6

You see, my dear Father, I cannot express to you the pleasure that I find in instructing all these young people, their little souls, and teaching them to know and love God. It is enough for us to consider the needs that they have. I pray the Lord will give me His grace to succeed in this. I am always very happy in this country and in my vocation.
Marie Madeleine Hachard

Louise's and little Delphine's recovery within a week had earned Zulimé a lot of respect from the nuns and an enormous amount of gratitude from Geneviève. The only two that could not have cared less were Josephine and Florence, both too busy with their almost nightly excursions. Through their hazy days, while they were waiting for the effects of the many cups of eau de vie to subside, they barely tolerated the noises of the convent, now getting busier with the opening of the new school.

Mother St. Augustin had assigned all preparations to be coordinated by Sister Stanislaus, and the nun had thrown herself into the work without hesitation and began to create a curriculum. Only once everyone knew the alphabet and was able to read a chapter from the bible, would they introduce other subjects such as the study of mathematics and physics. Sister Stanislaus was an expert in these. She had been fascinated by them to the bewilderment—and delight—of her father. Those were considered interests for men, but while the other girls in her school had practiced singing and needlework, she had always had her head in the books, trying to solve difficult equations and studying the teachings of Galilei. As she worked on the lesson schedule her mind drifted off...

∽

In the Cathédrale Notre-Dame de Rouen, the front row of the pew was filled with young novices, their faces behind white veils, their heads bowed, and their hands folded in prayer. One by one they were called to take their vows:

"... and so, you have chosen a name and shall forthwith only be called Sister Stanislaus..."

After the service, Marie Madeleine had searched the crowd for her father, but only her mother reached out her hand to caress her daughter's cheek, her show of emotion hesitant as if she were unsure about the appropriate behavior towards the newly obtained nun.

"Mamán, where is Papá?"

"You know how he feels... it was hard for him to see you during your novitiate. And now..."

"He was secretly hoping I would not go through with it."

Her mother nodded: "It will be even harder on him when you tell him that you are leaving."

Marie Madeleine remembered that night in her family's modest home in Rouen, sitting at the kitchen table across from her father. Her question tinged with a trace of despair: "Papá, is it too much to ask for your blessing before I go on this long voyage?"

Her father staring at her, forehead crinkled. Her pleading voice: "I do not know when I shall see you again... if ever... you do understand why I have to leave, don't you?"

Her almost breaking when he wiped away a tear: "I understand your desire to explore a foreign land much more than I shall ever understand your wish to join the order. You have a higher mind! You excelled at school, in every subject, even mathematics and geometry. I always called you the son I never had, but you are so much more. I am blessed to call you my daughter and cursed that you are willing to waste your knowledge and talent on the church!"

She knew in that moment that she would never forget his words. He took her hands in his.

"Marie Madeleine, you could be a scientist's, a doctor's apprentice or the head mistress of any school!"

And her response which now sounded like a prophecy: "I can still run a school. In fact, that is the plan once we get to La Nouvelle Orlèans. Joining the Ursuline Sisters was a calling from God I could not ignore."

"Marie Madeleine…"

"It is Sister Stanislaus now, Papá."

"I will never call you that."

What had hurt her more and was still causing pain every time she thought of it was that his words were not angry but filled with sadness.

"To me you shall always remain Marie Madeleine, my most incredible daughter."

She had promised to write him letters, many of them and hoped he would read them, she had said. And then there were his other words that she remembered fondly and proudly:

"I shall do more than that. I shall publish them."

∞

A small smile appeared on her face as she stared off into the distance, a tear appearing on her cheek. In the coming weeks, she worked hard to meet her own expectations of opening the school before month's end.

She called for Zulimé: "Like all the others, you shall attend classes," she told the girl whose eyes widened almost as much as her lips broadened. Sister Stanislaus chuckled at her surprise: "Did you think the Ursulines exclude women of different social classes and backgrounds? Or colors? We do not, and all are welcome to learn."

Zulimé was walking around with a big smile on her face for days after. The only thing that dampened her joy was Margarita showing no interest in school, citing her cooking chores as the reason. She found out what was truly behind the cook's excuses, when she asked the kind woman to write down the recipe for the herbal remedy she had made for Louise' and Delphine's ailment, to keep it handy for the nuns in case someone else got sick, and she, Zulimé, was not around. Margarita had stared at her and then honored her request by slowly taking the coal stick out of her hand. But instead of writing words, she had drawn the plants Zulimé had used on a piece of thin wood left behind by the carpenters and added a pot where she drew a waterline to show the amount in relation to the herbs. The piece of wood ended up nailed to the backwall of the kitchen, the part of the convent that had entirely fallen under the control of the cook.

Zulimé decided to simply bring her books and homework to the kitchen after class and teach her privately, the same way Monsieur Larrác had done when she had asked to catch up with the curriculum of his other children. Margarita meanwhile excelled at her craft. She had turned out to be a true magician at the stove, not only when she brewed her wonderful coffee, but once she had appointed herself the convent's main cook, creating the most delicious dishes. No one knew how she accomplished this or what spices made her cooking so tasty, but everyone loved what she put on the daily menu. There were tomatoes and pecans and the filé made from sassafras, a dried leaf that she added to the bison stew to thicken the sauce. She also smoked meat over the stove and seasoned it with an array of spices, many of which were the same or similar in her native Cuba. There was white pepper, smokey paprika that was called *pimentòn* and a hot chile sold by the old Choctaw woman at the market. Margarita used a lot of them on the days when she prepared a dish of alligator tail, hiding what it was under the strong spice taste.

May they all think it is duck, just like Madame Geneviève when she first tasted it. The French ladies and the nuns will never touch the gator if I tell them what it is.

Only Zulimé recognized the dish. For her it was nothing unusual. She had grown up eating what was put before her, all creatures and plants that land and sea provided. Zulimé thought back to her life on the island, and that brought up a quandary; she was torn about sharing her herbal cure so openly. This had been a constant source of quarrel in her family; Grandmère insisted that healing inspirations came from God and were there for the good of all. Mamán made the point that the recipes generated income and should be kept secret. Zulimé agreed with both, but how to combine these opposing views? She had spent hours in prayer asking for answers. And then they came. She would share the medicinal recipes and not give away the *gris gris*, the spells and the rituals she had watched her mother and grandmother perform. This solution seemed fair to her. But there was so much for her to learn yet. She had wanted to begin with her induction to all the secrets of vodou the day after her fifteenth birthday, as was custom. She shuddered at the memory of that day…

During my waking hours, I can control the demons.

There were the nightmares still, when dirty men appeared in her dreams, and she awoke drenched in cold sweat. She had cried out in her sleep, many times finding Margarita by her side, soothing her, stroking her hair, when she was again haunted by all that had happened to her on that day.

I must learn all the secrets of the vodou. There must be a priestess here to teach me all the wisdoms… this place does not look or feel that different from the island.

∾

The Widow LaCour had much more important things on her mind than worrying about education. Delphine was too small, and Pierre would not be allowed to attend a girls' school, she was convinced. She would have to tutor him herself. But first she needed to get settled and find the man who could set her up with the property she owned according to her contract. She rummaged through her trunk to find the deed among the papers. Something seemed not quite right. The book folder was laying lower than she remembered. She removed it and felt the cloth beneath that covered her money. She lifted the cotton fabric. The coins! She had stacked them with painstaking precision, twenty gold coins each, wrapped in cloth. Now they were all jumbled and lose. Had the trunk gotten so shaken up during the last part of the journey on the boats? Pearls of sweat formed on her forehead as she began counting. 110 gold coins were missing! Her head was spinning, she had to sit down.

How could this happen? I have hidden them well, I thought… even had the bagmaker build a false bottom…

Geneviève counted them again, hoping she had made a mistake, but the recount just confirmed it; 110 pieces gone. After a few moments trying to regain her composure, she removed the deed from the book, closed the trunk, locked it as securely as possible and walked out of the room, slamming the door. Her shock was slowly replaced by anger as she marched to the Mother Superior's office. Without knocking Geneviève entered and planted herself in front of the desk. Mother St. Augustin looked up, surprised: "Madame LaCour? How can I…"

"I don't know, frankly, how you can help, but help you must. I was robbed. And I expect your cooperation in finding the thief!" After recounting the details, she finished: "What are you going to do about it?"

The Mother Superior took a long breath: "We can call Father de Beaubois…"

"What is the Jesuit supposed to do? He cannot start an investigation!"

"Madame, whom would you like me to involve? You know that there is not much law enforcement in this city."

"Call on the Commander of the military. Something must be done. It is outrageous that such thievery can happen in a supposed holy place."

Mother St. Augustin had trouble concealing her own anger upon hearing this accusation: "You are not suggesting that one of the Sisters robbed you, are you?"

Geneviève sighed, realizing she had gone too far: "No, Mother Superior, of course I am not. But not everyone living at the convent is trustworthy. And I am not even sure this robbery happened here. It could have been on the ship. I watched my belongings, but I was certainly not able to sit on my luggage the entire time."

Geneviève knew there was not much chance of recovering her money. *Not unless…*

She left the office without another word to Mother St. Augustin. She had an appointment this afternoon, and the military office just happened to be on her way there.

It was almost dinner time when she returned and walked into the dining room, her anger still palpable and drafting in with her like a wave of bad air. All eyes were on her before she even spoke a word, bewilderment on their faces. Madame LaCour was known as a woman of quiet strength who had only shown emotions once—when her baby daughter was suffering. Her anger filled entry was out of character.

"Mademoiselles, I wish to introduce you to a man of importance. You should all know him." She pointed to the door that she had not closed all the way. A tall man in military uniform entered. "This is Commander Valdeterre, the enforcer of the rules of law in this city."

The embarrassment on the Commander's face was obvious. He wanted to be anywhere but here. He cleared his throat while nervously clutching his *epaulette*: "Madame LaCour asked me here because of a robbery…" He paused, not sure how to continue.

She stepped in: "Gold coins were stolen from my trunk, and I have asked the Commander to investigate this dreadful thievery. He and his men will examine all your belongings."

Florence's knuckles turned white. She did not move. Everyone else seemed frozen, too, except for the Sisters.

The Mother Superior had a frown on her face: "Surely this investigation does not include the women of the cloth…"

Commander Valdeterre's face was turning red: "Of course not, Mother Superior. But we need to see the women's casquettes and other luggage they brought with them. If you could please point my two soldiers toward that. Madame, if you would follow us, s'il vous plait. Everyone else stay at the table."

As soon as Valdeterre and Geneviève had left the dining room, the girls started chattering in hushed voices. Since it would have been futile to tell them to be quiet upon this disconcertment, the Mother Superior simply looked at her Sisters and shook her head. She was more than displeased that Madame LaCour had taken such drastic measures as bringing law enforcement into their sanctum. The chatter had barely stopped when, after what seemed like an eternity to some of the women, steps could be heard descending down the staircase, followed by loud voices.

"They did not fly away, Commander! You must search the rest of the building!" Geneviève's anger was now mixed with anguish.

"Madame, we cannot possibly go through the Sisters' rooms, nor can we disturb the peace of the chapel." Valdeterre's tone was at once deferential, apologetic and weak.

"They must be somewhere…" Geneviève's voice trailed off. She held on to the staircase. "It may not seem much to you, but it is part of my children's future."

The Commander tried to be sympathetic: "I understand, Madame. But you cannot say with certainty when the coins were stolen or if they were stolen after you arrived in La Nouvelle Orléans or before. And in this city even the greatest crimes remain unpunished for lack of police…"

He sighed. She looked at him incredulously: "Commander, you are the police!"

He sighed again, shrugging his shoulders: "Regretfully the ways to enforce our laws cannot be compared to those of France. There are simply not enough personnel."

Geneviève was grateful for the refined upbringing that kept her from slapping the man.

What incompetence! The governing in this place leaves a lot to be desired.

She stared at him, and he averted his eyes, uncomfortably: "*Je suis désolé*, Madame."

He bowed to her, waved to his men and walked out the front door.

Zulimé slowly lifted her head after she heard the door falling shut and the soldiers' footsteps disappearing. She had nothing to hide, but how many times had she watched when the enslaved on the plantations were blamed for crimes another committed? And even though her life with the Sisters did not reflect it, it was a moment like this that hit her like the slavecatcher's whip. Would Madame LaCour whose baby she had saved defend her against wrongful accusations? She could never be sure again. This loss of safety and trust was squashing her heart and forcing burning tears into her eyes during the many nights when the memories kept her awake. When she was consoling little Bebé whose nightmares were so gut wrenching she screamed out in her sleep, this small being who had never known a life without the prison bars they called fences that people like her were not permitted to cross. And this made her cry for Bebé and for herself, too. It was only when Madame LaCour came back into the dining room, sat down on the only free chair next to her, absentmindedly took her hand and stroked Bebé's head, that she relaxed.

Florence felt like she had held her breath for the entire hour it took the soldiers to search all the caskets. She was not worried about the gold coins. Those were safely hidden in a place no military man would dare to look through. It was Josephine's earrings that had her in a state of frenzy. She was sure the men had seen them in her belongings but—not knowing the stories behind the names on the caskets—must not have suspected anything. If they had, all her well-laid plans that included

Josephine's participation would have disappeared faster than she could say Salpetriére prison.

~

Zulimé woke early the following morning because of a persistent knock. The Sisters were in the chapel for morning prayers and did not hear it. Zulimé went downstairs and saw Margarita and her fellow cooks who had been up preparing breakfast in the kitchen, open the heavy door. Two wild looking men kicked the door open with their boots and pushed a girl inside.

"You take her!"

They threw a rag-tied bundle after her, turned around and left. Margarita stared at the girl while Zulimé hid a few steps behind the cook. This young woman looked scary and frightened at the same time. Her white skin contrasted with her dark eyes and ink-black curls. Her face was dirty, as were her partly torn clothes, made from a rough material that looked like bearskin mixed with coarse cotton. The curls were tangled and muddy. The girl picked up the bundle and held it tightly to her body.

"Who are you?" Zulimé asked in a small voice.

"Abondance Gravois... je suis Abondance *dit* Gravois...," the girl stammered: "de L'Acadie..."

Geneviève came down the stairs and overheard the last words: "You are from Acadia, all the way to the North?"

"Oui."

Margarita led the girl into the kitchen, sat her down and put a cup of steaming hot water in front of her that she spiced with cinnamon. The Acadian ignored the cup and instead stared longingly at a pot on the stove. She could not remember the last time she had eaten, only what. They had run out of food, not usually a problem for her family of fishermen, but in the waterways they had steered down on, the catch had gotten scarcer the further south they had traveled. The last thing she remembered was a slimy little creature that they had fished out and eaten alive. Margarita put a bowl of cold stew in front of her. And a spoon that Abondance ignored. She grabbed the bowl, buried half her head in it and devoured the stew with slurping sounds.

Zulimé and the other women watched her with bewilderment. The girl put the bowl on the table and asked for more. When Sister Stanislaus returned from the chapel, Geneviève explained what had just happened.

"Who are the men who dropped you at our door?" the Sister asked.

"*Mon Frère et mon Papá*, Pascal et Pasquerette dit Gravois."

She would not say more or answer any questions. Still clutching the bundle, she put her head on the table. The snoring sounds began a few moments later. It was then that the bundle on her lap moved. Zulimé who was closest to the Acadian, jumped backwards. The bundle dropped to the floor, still moving, until Margarita grabbed two large wooden spoons and used them to pick it up and drop it in the sink. She carefully loosened the straps. Between rags that looked like old clothes there was a strange looking animal, not fish, not reptile, with big red claws. It was the claws that moved slowly.

"*El grande camarón!*" the cook exclaimed. A crab. A very big one. Margarita took the steaming pot of water and poured it over the crustacean. A high-pitched squealing sound came from the crab, then nothing. Margarita used the wooden spoons again to pick it up and drop it in the pot. The splash woke up Abondance.

"*Non! La langoustine!*" she screamed.

She jumped up and ran to the stove. Tears poured down her dirt-streaked face as she saw the animal cooking in the pot. Zulimé was mesmerized.

This thing must have magical powers.

It seemed to her that what Margarita had just done could only be compared to someone boiling a snake in front of her mother and grandmother. They would have screamed, too. The snake, or *legba* was considered a holy symbol, a deity, not to be killed by a mere human. But then this girl did something that no one would ever dare to do to a serpent in Saint Domingue: she grabbed the langoustine with her bare hands in the boiling water, lifted it out, broke off its claws and sucked the white meat out of them. When she glimpsed Zulimé out of the corner of her eye, she reluctantly offered her a piece. Zulimé shook her head.

Sister Stanislaus regained her composure: "We must find your father and brother. But first, we shall clean you."

The Acadian slowly let go of the claw and followed the women. Zulimé went after them, too curious was she about this girl who fought them when they undressed her but was too weak to fend them off. They scrubbed her with wet cloths and soap until the last trace of mud, grease and the smell of rotting fish had come off and her skin was pink. Then they gave her a simple cotton dress to wear. Her hair, although rinsed, still looked like a cluster of seagrasses that had been twirled by waves and swept into the sand. Margarita came into the washing room with a jar of her oil, and the women used it to painstakingly detangle the curls. Once Abondance was clean and clothed, she sunk to the floor, sobbing.

"You must be tired. I will make up a bed," Zulimé whispered. The girl's pain affected her deeply.

Abondance felt as if her day had just changed colors from red to a dark brown. She hated red days. And there were many on this journey down south. Her father and brother had decided to leave their home in Acadia after her mother had died a few months ago. There was talk of an impending attack and occupation by the British. Many considered it a rumor, but her father did not want to risk staying. They had heard about this French colony at the southern end of the continent, and that they could make a living as fishermen, a trade they knew well. They had caught many big *langoustines*, the lobsters that inhabited their waters, put them in cages and bound those to the pirogues. She loved the *langoustines*. They represented abundance and wealth that had otherwise escaped her parents despite the name they had given to their only daughter. She hated her name, Abondance. It had nothing to do with her. It had not magically made their struggles any easier or their lives less hard. Surviving the harsh winters meant drying as much meat as they could hunt in the summer and autumn months. Catching fish from November to April was equally difficult under the sheets of ice and many weeks were spent near starvation each year. She called those periods her blue days. Blue was the color of coldness, the color her skin turned when she had to go outside. She did not like blue any more than red. Red was pain and fighting and sometimes anger; not her own but her father's and brother's, directed toward her and everything and everyone in sight. For Abondance saw and felt the world in colors.

There had been a lot of red in the past weeks. They had endured a broken *pirogue* that needed repairing which took days and getting stuck in the muddy swamps once they got closer to La Nouvelle Orleàns. And then there had been the alligator attack in the middle of the night. They had anchored the boat under a cypress tree. The moon was a bright yellow that night, one of her better colors. Until she woke from a snapping noise. All she had seen at first were the teeth chowing down on the edge of the boat, wood splinters flying. When the swamp water had begun lapping at their feet, her father and brother finally woke up while she, frozen in fear, watched the animal destroy the boat. Pasquerette had taken a spear and fended it off, pushing it back into the water. And then he had hit her for not moving, for not doing anything.

A yellow night had turned into a red morning with both so full of rage that all she could do was try and stay out of their way, an impossible task on the small boat. They had mended the damage done by the alligator as best as they could, but one of the cages containing the *langoustines* had broken and the lobsters had escaped. She knew this was a threat to their survival. It had been her Papá's plan to breed them after he had heard that there were no *langoustines* in Louisiana, and the immigrants were very open minded when it came to new foods. On their next stop, they had anchored near a plantation. Her father had asked the owner if he had use for a maidservant. When she had heard him ask the question, her eyes had gone blank, and her world had become dark grey like the cloudy sky above them.

My own Papá wants to rid himself of me.

The owner had declined but told them that there was a convent in the city that took in women. And now here she was, abandoned by her own family because she was of no use to them and would only be another mouth to feed. Everything had turned dark brown. Dark brown was almost black, the one that represented the end for her.

"If you do not like your given name, we shall call you Acadia," Sister Stanislaus declared at dinner in front of everybody.

"I like this name," the girl said. "It is the land I come from…"

"You want to be called after a country?" Geneviève asked.

"Oui. It makes me proud. My birthname never has."

Acadia's world had just changed colors again. It was now the calming green of summer leaves. Zulimé felt the change in her and reached out to touch her hand. She had found a kindred spirit.

Yet in the following weeks, Sister Stanislaus saw enough reason to worry. Acadia's mood—or as she called it, her colors—changed constantly. She was sullen and withdrawn on most days. The only one who seemed to get through to her was Zulimé. The Sister had noticed the two huddling in a corner and talking for hours. Every attempt made by the Mother Superior to find Acadia's father and brother had been met with disappointment. First, they seemed to have disappeared and for weeks no one knew about their whereabouts. They had not registered with the magistrate, a requirement for new settlers. Then they surfaced near the lower part of the bayou, a fact reported to the Abbess by Florence.

For once her nightly excursions have led to something worthwhile.

The head of the convent immediately sent out workmen, but when Pascal and Pasquerette Gravois were found, they made it very clear that they could not support Acadia and that she should remain with the nuns.

An agreement was made that once the Gravois had their fishing business up and running, they would pay the Ursulines a monthly stipend for her room and board. It had been another dark brown day for Acadia when she heard about the rejection and the deal.

CHAPTER 7

In the convent's kitchen Geneviève was sitting at the large table, pouring over papers that were spread out in front of her. Occasionally, she looked up, observing the cook. Two moons had flown by, and Margarita worried about all the special ingredients for the Christmas meal she was to prepare. She made drawings of the meats, fruits and vegetables, and Zulimé added the words for each of them on the grocery list. While the cook was mixing butter and lard with the last jar of the pepper spices for a meat marinade, she glanced through the open door every time she heard a noise.

It takes them very long today to get back from the market...

She could not finish the marinades without the spices the Sister and Zulimé were supposed to bring back, and the meats would not taste right, if they were not soaking in the mix for the next day and a half. She felt Madame LaCour watching her.

Ever since the perceived burglary, Geneviève had felt even more urgency to get her affairs in order and plan a life for her children outside the convent. The key to this was finding the man who had the other half of the deed in his possession. She silently cursed her decision to agree to split the document in half.

I should have stood up to the advocate who forced me to accept this.

There had not been much of a choice, though. Francois Montferrat, the man she was looking for, had insisted on assurance that his part of the investment would not be lost in case she never made it across the seas.

But now I am at his mercy and cannot even find him.

Geneviève spent her days tracking down his whereabouts with nothing but conflicting information. The magistrate at the courthouse told her he had registered the address of his plantation upriver, but the nice soldier at the military headquarters insisted that Lieutenant Montferrat—he was an officer—had been sent to Fort Rosalie in the Natchez territory. This being in opposite directions, she had no way to look for him. So, she was waiting anxiously while trying to figure out which property was hers; the advocate had not included an address on her part of the deed, and there was so much building going on in La Nouvelle Orleàns, it was near impossible to identify the one that was hers. Yet she persisted and talked to the workmen, the neighbors, even the street vendors. And, like now, she studied the documents over and over, searching for some clue she had overlooked. A small number on the bottom of one sheet caught her eye: 930.

930 what? It cannot be a street number. There are not that many in the city. Could it be square meters?

This made more sense. If the land was 930 square meters, the plan for a two-story home that the advocate had talked about, would fit. She sighed. Margarita turned around; the two women locked eyes. They had never had a conversation, had not spoken more than a polite 'bon jour' or '*buenos dias*', '*merci*' and '*gracias*' since the day they had met by chance in Havaña. And yet, the French Baronesse had recognized the Cuban's pain then as much as she did still. Margarita, in turn had noticed how the widow LaCour had fixated on the scar on her temple one day on the journey when she had not carefully covered it with her headscarf. The cook's hand had gone up in a reflex to hide it, but Madame had touched her gently and without a word brushed the curls from her own neck to reveal a mark that went all the way from behind her ear to the back of her skull. Margarita recognized the pattern. Only a deep cut by a very big knife would leave such a scar. The two women had stared at each other, forming a silent bond.

"How can I help?" Geneviève asked in the kitchen.

"Gracias, Señora... Madame... *pero necesito los alimentos de mercado...*"

Geneviève's understanding of Spanish was good enough to get what Margarita was saying, and she hoped the cook had picked up enough French in return: "Let me know what I can do. I can use a distraction."

When Sister Stanislaus entered the kitchen with Zulimé, they all took the groceries off the cart under Margarita's watchful eye.

"No café?" she asked.

"The shipment has not come in, Monsieur José said to expect it tomorrow. But you must inspect it yourself, we are not experts as you always say," the Sister replied.

There was a rumor at the market that Señor José, whose full name was José Castro, a merchant from Havaña, liked Margarita and had asked about her after one of her rare visits. Margarita's face darkened; she could not bring herself to return the smile. José had been nice to her, but he was a man, and she resented men too much to encourage him.

She lifted the Muscovy ducks off the cart and plucked the feathers from their skin. They had to be brined and marinated in a spice mix to keep fresh until she would make a slow roasted *grillade* the evening before Christmas. Zulimé collected the feathers from the floor, but instead of throwing them out, she hid them in the folds of her dress. The cook worked silently, and the others did not engage in conversation, either.

The gloomy mood enforced Sister Stanislaus' determination to find ways to make everyone a little happier. She appealed to the Mother Superior to loosen the strict rules for the Christmas celebration.

"These young women need comfort on their first holiday in this place. Comfort would also ensure their cooperation with the new school we are opening after New Year," she said.

"What do you have in mind?" the Abbess asked.

"They grew up with different traditions, different music, different ways to worship, even different foods… maybe we could fold those into our own way to celebrate… and little presents might brighten their souls…"

"I see no reason to not broaden the menu and gift them something, but if you are talking about pagan rituals, I must refuse you. They have no place in a convent. I insist that we adhere to our Catholic rules particularly on what is our greatest holiday."

The Mother St. Augustin had spoken and there was no convincing her otherwise.

She never considers how foreign her rules must feel to a Saint Dominguan slave, a Cuban cook, an Acadian and even an aristocrat who had only attended church as part of her social schedule.

Marie Madeleine Hachard dared to think these thoughts, but Sister Stanislaus could never say them out loud.

~

On Christmas morning, the smell of duck *grillade*, fresh baked bread and spiced cake pervaded the convent halls. Margarita ruled over her kitchen like a queen. She was proud that she had managed to incorporate every single request, from the cured pig's feet of her fellow Cubans to one very delicate dessert that the Vicomtesse demanded, and the cook was only able to create after the widow LaCour had described it to her in detail. Somehow Margarita had even gotten ahold of some crabs for Acadia, albeit not the *langoustines* the girl longed for. The variety of spices Margarita used in all the dishes would make for an eclectic feast. She had also managed to restock the coffee thanks to her admirer José. Her reluctance to go see him had given way to gratefulness when she realized that he was completely out of beans when she got to the market, but had set a bag aside for her in the hopes she would show up.

In the afternoon holy mass was performed in the church and

attended by everyone in the city, with people spilling out into the street. To the nuns' surprise Monsieur de Roche was there and later showed up at the convent door with crates of necessities that they did not expect until after the holidays. Books, paper, ink and feather pens for the school, cotton, silks and linens for clothes and sheets, leather for shoes and a special selection of cast iron pots that Margarita had given up on finding. The Mother Superior could hardly send him away after he so generously gifted them and invited him to join the meal. Between this treasure trove of things and Sister Stanislaus's presents, the children were squealing, and the girls were chattering excitedly. Even Florence and Josephine behaved. Everyone was beyond delighted. Everyone but Zulimé. The sudden appearance of Henry de Roche filled her with fear and dread.

Is he going to take me? Will I have to work on his plantation? Will he force Bebé to work?

Zulimé wanted to disappear, but there was no hiding place. She barely touched her food. When Margarita served the spiced cake and the special dessert that Josephine had requested, Sister Stanislaus got up: "Zulimé shall now sing for us. A song from her childhood."

The girl froze. All eyes were on her. The Sister took her hand and made her stand up.

I forgot that I promised to sing!

Zulimé had so looked forward to it, but now all it caused was unwanted attention from the man who owned her. She walked the long way around the table to avoid him. She had only ever sung this song with the other children at Monsieur Larrác's house, accompanied by the Africans with their instruments made of tree trunks and other materials found in nature. With shaking hands, she picked up a wooden board and one of the cooking brushes that Margarita used to spread the spice mixes over the meats. Slowly she began to hit the board with the brush, sliding it across the wood and creating a rhythmic swooshing sound. She opened her mouth. At first, she sounded weak, but when she found her strength, the voice that came out of her chest filled the room and echoed into the hallways. The song was in an ancient language that her grandmother said came from Africa's western shores. Her grasp of the melody had always been a surprise to her family. She had sung since she was tiny, and her voice mesmerized anyone who got to hear it.

Singing transported her to another world, so she did not notice how captivating she was. It was only when she got to the end that she saw tears in the eyes of many at the table and Henry de Roche's face lighting up. He looked at her with a mixture of bewilderment and sheer adoration. Then he slowly started clapping. The others joined in. Zulimé bowed her head. Not in gratitude, but because she wanted to be swallowed by the ground beneath her.

He will take me. He will remove me from the only place that gives me a little peace.

De Roche got up and walked over to her. He placed his hand on her shoulder and gently lifted her head.

"You are…" he could not find words. "…such a voice…"

He looked at the Sisters: "I do not want to interfere with your curriculum, but I do hope you have a music class on your schedule. This one should sing every day."

He led Zulimé back to her chair.

It took her a while to understand the meaning of his words. When she did, her heart jumped out of her chest and into the heavens.

He says I shall go to school!

The elation over this realization was tempered by a regret, one she could not explain. She shook it off. Everyone was congratulating her on the song, and even the mighty Princess gave her a smile. In all this celebrating she barely noticed Monsieur de Roche leaving. Only that—once the others had settled down—he was no longer there.

Neither were Josephine and Florence, as Sister Stanislaus noticed with a frown.

∽

Florence had winked at Josephine when she had gotten up to leave the table, a sign for the Vicomtesse that it was time. They had snuck out and were now on their way to their own celebration. Jean and Michél had returned after three weeks from what they called another trading voyage.

That all the reports of piracy between the Louisiana coast and the islands have increased during the time must be coincidence.

Except Josephine did not believe in coincidence, and Florence wished for an open talk with Jean.

"How can I work with him if he does not trust me enough to tell me what everyone knows anyway?" She asked.

Josephine laughed: "No one knows. Some suspect. Among them a few important city officials. I would not shout his real profession from the rooftops if I were you."

"But it is me, not some city official! There must be trust in a work liaison."

"A work liaison. Is that really all the liaison you are hoping for?"

Josephine laughed again. If there was one thing Florence could not handle, it was being made fun of. She had beaten up her brothers and even grown men in Paris when they had ridiculed her. And she would do the same to Josephine. Regardless of her new friendship with the Vicomtesse.

"You are the pot calling the kettle black, aren't you? What about Jean's brother?" Florence responded harshly.

"I have never said I aspired to work with Michél."

"Oh, but it can be work. Even between the silk sheets you are used to. And don't pretend you are this noble virgin, and I am this dirty forçat, no one believes that fairy tale!"

Now it was Josephine's turn to get angry: "You are cruder than the rum you are slurping every night!"

Florence pushed her off the sidewalk. Josephine's boot got caught in the mud as she stumbled onto the street. Before she could fall into the dirt, Florence caught her. They both took a deep breath.

"*Je suis desolé*," they said almost at the same time.

"Let us not fight but help each other. Particularly when it involves the brothers Bèranger." Josephine said. Florence nodded. They entered Flamand's arm in arm. The tavern owner whose real name was Jan Lamesse but was called 'le Flamand' after the pink long-legged wading bird he resembled and his alcohol-induced skin coloration, could not even muster the slightest cordiality while Jean and Michél were at sea. He secretly despised the women and only tolerated them in the company of the brothers. Not that he was a great admirer of theirs, either. He felt overcharged for the rum they sold him.

How much of an imbécile do they think I am?

His hunched back curled downwards, and the small eyes turned into yellow slits.

"He looks even more like the snake he is when he squints," Florence whispered. She was aware of the man's predicament. There were other sources for him to acquire alcohol. The Bèrangers did not have a monopoly on rum, as much as they wished they had, but the short man feared the pirates' well-known wrath. And that meant being nice to the brothers' acquaintances now that they had returned. Tonight, instead of ignoring the women like he had the past weeks, he led them to their favorite corner table with an exaggerated bow of his head and a wave of his arm. Then he hovered close by.

Women always talk too much. Wonder what secrets about the Bèrangers they will spill...

Josephine was no fool. "Flamand, would you be so kind and fetch us some eau de vie? Merci beaucoup!"

The witch.

He had no choice but to retreat. As soon as he was out of earshot, she spoke fast but quietly and with urgency:

"Florence, you sit him down tonight. You ask him outright what goods he brought back and that you would like to help him sell them. For a fee, of course. At least forty percent. You also tell him you will be able to write up contracts with prospective buyers soon. Contracts that will hold up under the law. Make it clear that you and only you can give him legitimacy so he cannot be touched. Or…"

She thought for a moment: "Better yet, I will bring it up. I will be the one telling Jean what a great business mind you have."

Florence listened intently. Josephine leaned back: "Now what are you going to do for me?"

Florence grinned: "Princess, you are in control. Michél wants you. Maybe this will get him going…"

She pulled Josephine's dress off her shoulders, exposing more of her bosom. The Vicomtesse blushed uncomfortably: "Not that. I must start thinking about my future. I need to get into a soirée at the Governor's mansion."

Florence stared at her: "Pardon? How can I help you with that?! You are the noblewoman; you should know how to get into a rich man's house."

"I need the brothers to find a safe way for me to get there. I can gain entrance by myself. But the Governor's house is outside the city. Next to the slave quarters."

There was unmistakable disdain in her voice as she spoke the last sentence. Florence was about to respond when they were interrupted.

"*Ah, mademoiselles, joyeux Noël!*"

The brothers had arrived, and each grabbed a girl and swung her around in a pretended dance move.

"We came bearing gifts!"

They both smelled of rum and sweat and animalistic charm that drew the women to them instead of repelling them. Jean pulled a gold pendant from his pant pocket and put it around Florence's neck. Michél did the same with a necklace full of glittering gemstones. But instead of Josephine's neck he wrapped it around her wrist three times, touching her hand a little longer than necessary. Florence was beaming. And

Josephine decided to be gracious and not let on that she was used to better jewels.

"Merci, messieurs! Merci, indeed."

The men squeezed into the small space around the table, each with his arm around a woman's waist. After a toast and at least two cups of rum, Florence kicked Josephine under the table.

"Jean, how was your voyage? Did you bring back enough goods to last this city for a time?"

The older Bèranger raised his cup and laughed: "Enough to keep the patrons of this establishment in libations!" He took a large sip: It was a very successful voyage, wouldn't you say, mon petit frère?"

The edge of Michél's mouth turned up just enough to show the hint of a smile: "Considering that it was not only the barrels we brought back…"

This was enough of a cue for Josephine: "With all your success in… trading… should you not have someone in town to oversee your sales? Someone you can trust?"

The brothers exchanged glances. She continued: "See, Florence here knows how to make deals. She will also be able to write contracts soon. Contracts that turn any business legitimate…"

She let the suggestion hang in the air when she saw interest in Jean's eyes.

Legitimacy is protection against the law…this woman has a sharp mind.

Bèranger had taken his brother's incarceration in Port-au-Prince as a warning to be careful at sea. But he had not taken their trading on land into consideration.

"And speaking of legitimacy," Florence interjected, "whereas I can help with the buyers, Josephine can do a lot with her influence in certain circles."

"What kind of circles?" Michél looked at the Vicomtesse. His eyes were so intense that she had to avert hers.

"Let's just say, Josephine could make friends with the Governor."

Jean nodded. It made sense.

I saw this woman in Port-au-Prince. She does not come from the streets. She moves and acts like upper class even when she tries to hide it.

The rest of the night was spent discussing details of their plan. And drinking even more than usual. By the time the sun came up, Florence had gained Jean's interest in her as a partner and lost his interest in her as a woman. Bèranger sealed the deal with a handshake. Michél sealed his with a kiss. He insisted on accompanying Josephine back to the convent while his brother finished his conversation with his new trade partner. Josephine did not object but was taken by surprise when he pushed her roughly against the wall of a cottage:

"I will make sure of your safe passage to the Governor's estate." His mouth was on her neck just below her ear, and his hand was on her bottom, pressing her up against him. "But I will also collect a price for my troubles."

Before she could respond, his lips were on hers and his tongue forced her mouth open. She felt him through her thick brocade dress. All of him. She went limp. He held her up as he stopped kissing her. She wanted him to leave, and she wanted him not to let go. He took a step back, then took her arm and led her towards the convent. No more words were spoken. She disappeared through the wall, then caught her breath in the courtyard. This was how Florence found her a few minutes later. She did not have to ask any questions. The red mark on Josephine's neck and her bright, swollen lips told her enough.

Josephine very much kept to herself the following week and made-up excuses when Florence asked her to come out with her at night.

It isn't Michél who frightens me but myself...

Josephine had liked what he had done to her despite the shock over the forceful way he had touched and kissed her. She could not help reliving the short few moments and every time she did, she was gripped by an excitement she was barely willing to admit to herself, much less to Florence who could not stop telling her how Michél asked about her every night. The woman brought up the subject again on New Year's Eve:

"He and Jean are having a celebration tonight! You cannot miss it."

"I have decided to go to mass this evening."

Florence's mouth dropped open. Then she laughed:

"Why? To confess your sins? Or his?"

The thought of Josephine going to church without being forced to by the rules set forth by the Mother Superior put Florence's mind in a jumble. She had never found out exactly how far Michél had gone with the Vicomtesse, only that he had gone farther than she and Jean had ever done and judging from his new business minded behavior, would ever go. This made Florence uneasy about her own desires. In her daydreams, she imagined the perfect combination of shared money ventures and private passion.

"Alors, suit yourself," she finally said. "But do not forget that we have a plan. And we need Jean and Michél to get you to the Governor's mansion."

This very plan had been weighing on Josephine for the past days.

Florence is not wrong. I cannot avoid Michél forever.

Chapter 8

New Year's 1728 was greeted by a strong rainstorm that transformed the streets into muddy rivers. Sister Stanislaus delayed her trip to the market. She thought of the priest's sermon from this morning, words he repeated every New Year's, about gratitude for what had passed and faith in a new beginning. It was this faith that she struggled with when she watched the Casket Girls, each of them bringing with them their own set of troubles.

She bumped into Louise Mariette in the hallway. The girl flinched and began to breathlessly apologize, even though it was not her fault. Louise had begun acting more and more like an outsider among outsiders, as if looking in on secrets she was not supposed to see. It seemed to the Sister that Louise did not understand this new world she had been swept into, and she made no effort to do so. She retreated into herself, into an inner space which protected her like a soft, warm blanket. One that was torn away by loud voices, disagreements and intrusions. Acadia's arrival had been such an intrusion.

With misery written all over her face, Louise blurted out: "I tried to convince my father to let me join the holy order."

She could still see the look on his face in the light of the flickering candle…

~

In his humble Rouen farmhouse, Monsieur Mariette stared at his daughter, then averted his eyes. They sat at the rough wooden table in the small kitchen.

"You will not have to become a nun…"

"Papá, if you cannot pay for another dowry, I have resigned myself to devote my life to the Lord. So, my sister won't have to…"

He could not look at her when he reached into his overcoat and pulled out a paper: "This here is a contract I signed today. You are to travel to the town of Orleàns in the French colony of La Louisiane and work to the best of your ability until you get married."

His voice was stern, and her eyes widened in shock. He continued: "For that I have been given two hundred livrés to assemble your trousseau and fifteen sols per day until you set off from La Rochelle."

She was unable to speak, and she saw that it pained him, too. He shook his head: "I have no choice. Your mother's illness… I cannot even pay for her funeral…"

Her tears came suddenly. She sobbed and pleaded with him to not send her away, promised to work harder, but knew before the words were out of her mouth that it was of no use. There was no work. All the farmers had lost their crops after a two-year drought that had ruined the village. She would not be able to make two hundred livrés even if she worked herself to the bone for a year. This much money would save her family from certain famine and death.

"We have to make this sacrifice," he said.

Not we. I am the sacrifice…

∼

Louise told her story to the Sister. It all came out between heavy breaths. At the end she swallowed hard:

"I want to be like you. I want to join the holy order of St. Ursula."

The words tumbled out of her mouth. It was more than she had spoken in weeks. Sister Stanislaus was not surprised. But when she answered it was not in a nun's voice but Marie Madeleine Hachard's: "Joining the order is a decision reached only after long and careful consideration, a searching of the innermost longing and desire. You have not been with us very long."

Louise had expected the Sister to be overjoyed at the prospect of adding another nun to their group: "But I have considered it before my father sold me..." She frightened herself as the words came out. Never had she openly put it this way. In an instant she tried to distract from her judgement: "I have seen you and watched you for the past eight months... You are what I want to be."

"Child, aspiring to become a true daughter of God is not wanting to be like another earthly being but the continued struggle to become more like Him. No other human can or shall be your symbol of worship. We are all merely trying to live by his example."

Marie Madeleine put her hand on the girl's shoulder: "Are you certain of your true desires? Are you sure it is not a husband you wish for? Children of your own?" She continued when she saw the insecure look in Louise's eyes: "I see that you are in pain. But this is not a calling to be a nun. It is a sign of your loneliness. Joining the order would mean escape from that loneliness, an escape from yourself. Not a longing to serve the Lord."

She saw a tear rolling down Louise's cheek. In her most soothing voice, she said: "Let us make an agreement; tomorrow we open the school. You shall put all your attention towards learning until summertime. You shall participate in all that is going on, not merely mass and classes. If you then still feel the desire to become a nun, so it shall be."

Louise nodded slowly and apologized for the interruption. With her head hung low she walked back upstairs. The Sister retreated to the kitchen where Margarita uncovered a large bowl in which she had mixed milk with yeast the night before to let it thicken. Skillfully, the cook put equal parts of butter and sugar in a skillet and heated it over a small flame. After the mixture dissolved, she set it aside for cooling and began beating twenty-one eggs that she had collected from the chicken coup. She added caraway seeds and a few ground coffee beans and combined all the ingredients in a large baking pan. When the consistency was to her liking, she shoved the pan inside the oven and fanned the flames. She took pride in the creation of her dishes, and this New Year's cake was no exception. It would take but an hour to rise in the oven. Sister Stanislaus watched her with a smile.

At least one of them is living her purpose.

~

In the courtyard, the rain notwithstanding, Zulimé and Acadia were huddled under a banana tree. The big leaves kept them dry. The two had formed a bond that reminded the Dominguan girl of her childhood friendship with Anne-Marie, whom she had always thought of as her older sister. They had been inseparable, playing tricks on the older brothers, building treehouses and hiding from Monsieur and Zulimé's mother who did not like their mischief. There was only one thing she was never allowed to share with Anne-Marie: *you cannot let her in on the secrets of the vodou*, her grandmother had drilled into her.

This was not the case with Acadia. As soon as Zulimé had seen her obsession with the big crab, she had felt a kinship to the girl that only deepened once they had shared stories on each other's upbringing and traditions. Zulimé was fascinated by Acadia's closeness to nature and her understanding of wild animals and sea creatures. Acadia, in turn, was drawn to the dark girl's knowledge of spells and her tales of the snake dances on Saint Domingue. The two decided to have a combined New Year's ritual. All they needed was an alligator tail, some sugar cane and certain herbs. The sugar cane was easy; Margarita kept loads of them in the kitchen cabinet. For the other things, they had to go to the market.

And so, they did something they had never dared to before—they left the convent without permission.

Only when they got to the stands, they realized that neither of them had any coins. Zulimé knew she could just ask the spice lady to put the herbs on the list with the all the other items that the Sisters picked up for the convent. This bill was paid once a week. But the alligator tail? There was only one seller, and he was a scary man who would not accept credit. Acadia seemed to think that since he was a swamp man, she could charm him into giving them what they asked for by telling him her own story. But Scary Alligator Man just narrowed his black eyes and spit out some tobacco. And then, within the blink of Zulimé's eye, Acadia grabbed a tail and ran off. Zulimé darted after her with Alligator Man hollering from behind.

He will catch up with us halfway down the first block!

And suddenly Zulimé remembered. And stopped. And turned around facing his oncoming rage. With her feet firmly planted on the ground and her hands resting on her hips, she concentrated hard and fixated her eyes on him. Acadia, not hearing Zulimé's steps behind her, stopped, too. What she saw made her mouth drop open. Alligator Man's sprint was halted as if he had crashed against an invisible wall. He seemed fixed in this position, unable to move and incapable of averting his eyes under Zulimé's intense stare. Acadia slowly moved closer to her friend. Before she could reach her, Alligator Man let out a small scream, turned his body but not his head and with sheer horror on his face ran back to where he came from. Zulimé's whole body relaxed, her arms fell by her side, her shoulders sunk back and when she faced Acadia, she seemed almost normal. Except for her eyes. They were glowing darkly and were looking through Acadia, not at her. Only once the girl spoke, was Zulimé able to shake off whatever she had used to chase the man away.

"How did you do this?" Acadia whispered.

"I remembered how my mother stopped a landowner that came to the plantation for a visit with Monsieur Larrác, and after his visit, he came to our house and wanted to harm me. Mamán murmured secret words over and over and stood in his way like I just did. Her eyes were very scary when she focused them on him. I remember the words..."

"What were they?"

"A protection spell..."

That was all Zulimé could say to Acadia. Telling her the exact words would have violated an unwritten but sacred law of the vodou.

~

New Year's mass and dinner were uneventful with all of them praising Margarita's efforts and delighting in her cake. After they finished the meal, everyone retreated to their beds. Everyone except three. The rain had not let up, so Acadia and Zulimé waited under the stairs until the house was quiet. Then they went to the kitchen, grabbed sugar cane, duck feathers Zulimé had hidden the day before Christmas and a still glimmering piece of wood from the stove. Zulimé coated the sticky cane with herbs, and the two carefully opened the creaking front door to the narrowly covered front porch. They had meant to retreat much further into the yard, but the rain would extinguish the burning wood, so they had to stay close to the door. Zulimé set a small flame to the cane, then blew it out and swung the smoking stick back and forth and over their heads while chanting more of her secret words. Acadia put the alligator tail on the ground and stomped on it. She sang a melody while she pulverized the dead animal.

What the hell is that smell?

Florence neared the front door when it went up her nostrils. It did not come from the kitchen and knowing Margarita, she would never have left anything uncleaned before she went to sleep. Florence opened the door and screamed. The two girls in front of her looked like crazy witches with the Acadian's hair flying, feathers all up in the air and the smoke from the cane making them look like creatures the devil may have sent. Zulimé and Acadia both stopped their ritual, but it was too late. Florence's scream had woken up Sister Stanislaus and two other nuns. In their flowing white nightgowns with their heads uncovered, they came running down the hall. Their ghostly appearance made the scene even eerier. Sister Stanislaus took in what was happening. All three girls had no reason for being here, but it was the smoking cane stick that was the most worrisome. The Sister took it out of Zulimé's hand and threw it on the wet ground. The other Sisters ushered the girls back inside and ordered them to go to bed at once. Acadia and Zulimé went upstairs, embarrassed for having been caught, but Florence could barely contain her anger at them and only managed not to yell because of the Sisters' presence.

Now I have to wait again until they are all asleep! She seethed.

～

The new year began with discontent. The nuns were more taken aback by Acadia's and Zulimé's rituals than they had shown when they sent them to bed that night.

"I shall send for Monsieur de Roche to fetch Zulimé," the Mother Superior said upon hearing about it.

"Mother, I am begging you to reconsider," pleaded Sister Stanislaus, "the girl is too young to do work in the fields…"

"Isn't this the reason de Roche acquired her? She was always to join the rest of his slaves at some point."

Sister Stanislaus could not come up with a way to express her uneasiness about slavery, so she resolved to share another worry with the Abbess:

"I have observed the merchant's behavior with Zulimé. Mother, he is enamored with the girl. Is it not against our beliefs to let her become the man's concubine? Can we—knowing how he feels towards her—allow this if it is in our power to keep her away from this situation, at least as long as he is willing to leave her with us?"

The Mother Superior sighed: "We cannot. And we cannot throw Acadia out on the street, either…But both need to be reminded that stomping on alligator tails and smoking out bad spirits with coated sugar cane is not very Christian and shall not be tolerated from here on!"

Marie Madeleine had prevailed. She conveyed the Abbess' stern warning to Zulimé and Acadia, reminded herself and her fellow Sisters that no one had said their missionary work would be easy and threw herself into the school opening.

∼

There are already more than thirty boarders from here and Balise and the surrounding area who insisted on being received, Sister Stanislaus wrote to her father: *The parents are carried with joy to see us, saying that they no longer worry that they will return to France since they have here what they need to educate their daughters. All overwhelm us with all kinds of presents. The inhabitants, seeing that we do not want to take any money for instructing the day students, are filled with gratitude and help us in every way they can. The marks of protection that we receive from the leading inhabitants of the country make us respected by everyone. That will not continue if our actions do not confirm their high regard for us.*

The school was thriving. Within three months, attendance had doubled; many of the city's craftsmen had begun sending their girls to the convent. And it was not only the working people. Just this morning the Mother Superior had received another visit from the matron of a noble family, asking when their ten-year-old daughter could start taking lessons.

Geneviève LaCour had opposing views of the school's progress; for one she was glad the Ursulines contributed so strongly to the education of La Nouvelle Orleàns. She knew this would lure more immigrants from France to these shores and elevate a swampy colony to a booming place of business and trade. Property values would increase as a result. On the other hand, the lesson schedules inconvenienced her greatly, as she had been free to come and go as she pleased and deal with finding the man who shared her deed, while leaving Pierre and Delphine in the good care of the nuns and some of the girls she trusted. Now she had to structure her day around classes.

Chapter 9

Bad winter storms were the reason that Josephine had not gotten very far with her plan to visit the Governor's mansion for one of the many soirées. The weather was atrocious as far she was concerned. Paris had its fair share of rain but nothing like the walls of water that fell here. If the streets in the city turned into muddy creeks, the roads outside of it were like rivers that only the biggest carriages could maneuver. She had found a hairdresser who knew about every social event, but the past two Sundays the weather had interfered. The Bèrangers were still at sea, and she dared not make her way there on her own. Florence had offered to accompany her and asked to wear one of her ball gowns so she would not "stick out like a bean in a bowl of apples," as she put it. Josephine could not bring herself to tell the woman that even in a nice dress she would still look like a bean. That Florence's language was so inappropriate and her dialect so clearly from the street that she would be unable to fool the city's upper class and that she, Josephine, could not risk having her reputation ruined because of it when she had not even begun to build one.

Ball season was almost over. The hairdresser had told her on her visit two days ago that some society ladies had booked her for Mardi Gras, the last big celebration before lent started and turned everyone into devout Catholics—or as she preferred to put it: praying bores—for the next forty days.

I must get to this one. It is this coming Tuesday!

The brothers would be back by week's end if not sooner. She had trodden carefully with Michél, permitting his advances at Flamand's, but finding excuses not to be alone with him. She told herself that he was a means to an end. What the end was she was not certain, only that it would restore her place in the upper echelons of society. And in those there was no room for a pirate.

Mardi Gras, in one great coincidence, was always a masked affair. *Which makes it so much easier to blend into the crowd!*

Josephine booked an appointment with the hairdresser and asked her to refer her to an artist that would create a mask to go with her grandest gown. She had to trade it for a bracelet but hoped it would be worth it. All preparations were made, and she prayed every day the brothers would return on time. The Vicomtesse could be very devout when it suited her. Her prayers were answered: the rains ended the day the Bèrangers walked into the tavern in a boisterous mood. It must have been a very profitable voyage, she thought, which Florence confirmed the next morning after doing the inventory.

Florence had made herself indispensable to Jean. She was quick in assessing the value of goods and even quicker in finding buyers. She had not mastered the art of drawing up contracts, but this was only a matter of time. When the nuns graded papers, it was always she who came out on top.

Josephine decided to take advantage of the brother's good mood: "Would you get a carriage to take me to Bienville's estate for the big Mardi Gras ball next week?"

Michél and Jean exchanged looks: "What kind of carriage?"

"One grand enough to make me look like I belong there."

Michél knew of one such carriage. It belonged to the Commander of the military, a man without a wife who would most likely not attend the ball unless he was summoned by the Governor himself. He might be persuaded to take Josephine with him. Just not by any man with the last name Bèranger.

Which makes me expendable...

A notion he disliked immensely. But short of stealing the carriage—the idea of an imbecile, given that everyone would recognize it—he would be of no use. *Unless...*

"I do know a man who owns a carriage. You would have to convince him to either lend it to you or invite you to join him. And insist that I am the only coachman you trust."

Josephine laughed: "You? A coachman?"

Michél's face went dark: "If I can steer a ship, I can handle some horses."

Josephine knew she had gone too far: "I apologize, I did not mean to question your abilities. I am just unsure of how to broach this to a man I do not know."

"Everyone here knows him. Or of him. He is the Commander of the military."

Josephine was stunned.

Valdeterre? The quiet man, intimidated by Baronesse LaCour?

She laughed again, but this time it was not at Michél, and she put her hand on his arm: "This is good news, Michél! I have met him. *Alors*, maybe not met him. We were never formerly introduced, but he came to the convent, and this is enough for me to approach him. And yes, I will suggest hiring you as a coachman for the night."

It was not what the younger Bèranger wanted to hear. Suggesting was not enough, she had to insist. He thought of pressing the subject, but then let it go.

She knows better how to treat rich people than I do.

∽

The next morning Josephine de Chavin marched into Commander Valdeterre's office just off the Place d'Armes. She demanded to see the Commander as she had a crime to report, she said. Valdeterre asked her to sit. Just as she remembered, he was a shy man and the silence between them was awkward until she spoke, reminding him where they had met. The Commander, familiar with the convent was nonetheless surprised to see that a Parisian aristocrat was among the women. What crime did she have to report, he asked, hoping it was not another burglary at St. Ursula's convent. Non, she said, smiling, not at all: "It happened on the Rue St. Louis. Near Flamand's tavern after sunset. A friend was touched in a very unsavory way by a small man with yellowish eyes."

She described Jan Lamesse, the tavern's owner in detail. Who is the friend and what was she doing on such a street after dark, he asked.

"I cannot say. She got lost. It was dusk, and she had just left an artisan on Rue de Bourbon that she had ordered her Mardi Gras mask from. She turned the wrong corner."

Josephine spun a story of this unfortunate noblewoman who found herself mistreated by a creepy bar owner.

"Your friend must come in herself and file a report." Valdeterre said.

Josephine looked at the floor: "*Monsieur le Commandeur*, this is not possible. My friend is a woman of stature and cannot risk ill repute just because she went the wrong way. You know how people talk."

And did he ever. The gossiping in this city where everyone knew one another was a great source of trouble to him and his soldiers who, in lieu of a real police force, had to discern between real threats and idle talk whenever a case was reported.

"Vicomtesse, all I can do is have my men patrol that block on Rue St. Louis and keep an eye out for the man you have described."

She faked blushing and looked at him with hooded eyes and a shy smile: "This would be greatly appreciated, Commander."

She got up and shook his hand, then held it: "Come to think of it: will you be attending the Governor's ball next week?"

He sighed: "Yes, Jean Baptiste personally asked me to. These functions are not my favorite pastime."

She smiled at him: "Maybe I could make this one more pleasurable for you? See, I am in a predicament. I have no carriage of my own yet and no way to get to the mansion…"

It took him a moment to understand her suggestion. When he did, his cheeks turned red, and he stammered: "It would be my pleasure to provide transportation, Vicomtesse."

She almost curtsied. He offered to pick her up from the convent, but she suggested to meet a block away. "The Sisters are not too fond of me going out at night, and besides, I do not want to create jealousy among the other women who are not as fortunate as I am."

He nodded. No mention was made of a special choice for coachman. Josephine left the Commander's office with a sense of joy she had not felt in over a year.

~

Wherever Geneviève turned in her search for Francois Montferrat, the man who held the other half of her deed, she met with a shut door. She kept hounding the military command to get word on when he would go on leave and return from Fort Rosalie. As it was, the old soldier had been correct, the Lieutenant was in fact stationed there for now. She had found out that he was unmarried and without children. But no one was able to tell her the exact location of his plantation or anything else that would have helped her.

Yet I must find him.

And so, like every week she was on her way to ask the same question.

I know that I am annoying the military command, but I do not have another choice. They will have to endure my continued badgering until they provide me with answers.

She was crossing the Place d'Armes when she saw Josephine coming out of the building.

The woman is practically skipping down the street. What trouble is she up to?

It was a rhetorical question. Geneviève had no interest in the Vicomtesse de Chavin if she stayed out of her way. A short while later Geneviève emerged from the same building as she had done so many times before: disappointed. She had not crossed the square yet when she heard hurried footsteps behind her. The Commander's aide, a Major Dumont, came running after her.

"Baronesse!" The corpulent man was wheezing. "Madame, the Lieutenant Colonel…"

He gasped for air, bending over and putting his fat hands on his knees. When he recovered, Geneviève was standing in front of him, arms folded, waiting.

"An invitation just arrived for the Lieutenant that will be delivered to him right away via courier…"

He was still panting. She was getting impatient: "And?"

The major finally caught his breath: "He is required to attend."

She was bewildered: "Attend what? Be clear, Major!"

He apologized: "Excusé moi, Madame, I thought I had said it… The Governor's Ball. On Tuesday."

She was taken aback: "And how will this help me?"

He was embarrassed: "Ah, Madame, I guessed you were going…"

"You guessed wrong. I have not been in La Nouvelle Orleàns long enough to receive such invitations."

The Major cleared his throat: "Madame LaCour, then it would be my honor to ask you to accompany me."

She hesitated for a moment, then thanked the Major for his kindness. And accepted. A door had just opened, and she was not about to refuse to walk through it just because the Major did not fit her idea of a perfect *rendezvous*.

I shall celebrate Fat Tuesday with the fat Major.

∼

The Vicomtesse and the Baronesse were occupied with their preparations for the ball, and both kept them secret from each other despite having made appointments with the one and only hairdresser on the day of, ordering masks from the same artisan and spending most of their time mending their best gowns. Josephine had the added heavy task of handling Michél Bèranger. Over the weekend, she avoided excursions to the tavern, but by Sunday night she knew she had to face him. Florence had gotten suspicious, so two nights before the Mardi Gras *fête* Josephine arrived at Flamand's with trepidation. She asked Michél to join her at the bar while Florence was busy doing what she had been doing for weeks: counting the earnings from their various sales with Jean before the rum prevented them both from adding correctly.

"Michél," Josephine said in her most soothing voice, "I have tried my utmost, even used my charm on the Commander, but he would not hear of using a coachman of my choosing for the night. It seems he is very attached to his own…"

When she saw Michél's eyes clouded in the now familiar darkness, she laid her hand on his arm, but he shook it off.

"Michél, je suis desolé… I am sorry…"

She saw that he did not believe her. But before he could respond, a commotion at the entrance distracted everyone. A disheveled Jan Lamesse stormed through the door, yelling bloody murder. It was hard to make out his words, but after a few minutes some sort of story emerged. Apparently, he had been interrogated by the soldiers for most of the day and had not been given food or water. They had accused him of attacking a woman of high standing, of touching her in unseemly ways, he said. Him, Le Flamand! A man of honor! Jean was not the only patron at the bar who chuckled at his last words. The distraction provided Josephine with a chance to slip away.

∽

At breakfast in the convent on Monday Florence treated Josephine frostily, which was unusual, but the Vicomtesse was so preoccupied she hardly noticed. Her every thought revolved around the ball. Geneviève had informed the Sisters about her invitation. The nuns treated Madame LaCour differently than the younger women wo were largely confined to the convent until the Mother Superior thought them ready to get married. That was after all the goal and the whole reason for their journey. The way they saw it, Madame LaCour would be perfectly capable of handling her own affairs should she choose to remarry.

It was shortly after sunset on Tuesday when Major Dumont's carriage arrived. Josephine was desperately searching for her most precious earrings to go with her best gown. The contents of her large suitcase were spread out all over the bed and floor. She was kneeling in front of it, remembering that she had hidden the jewels in one of the side walls of the case. In a panic, she felt around every inch of the inside.

There it is!

Her fingers touched the uneven part where the leather had been peeled away. A sigh of relief escaped her when she removed the velvet pouch, followed by a barely contained scream when the wood pieces that Florence had put there fell into her hand. Josephine gasped.

So, there is a thief! The Baronesse was not imagining it!

Josephine clenched her fist and knocked it into the suitcase so hard, blood appeared where the skin had met the edge. She hastily wrapped a silk handkerchief around the scratch and looked for her gloves. Her anger was greater than her shock or her pain, but she also knew it was time to go. She put on the gloves, grabbed her mask and opened the door to the hallway when she heard a knock. She retreated but caught a glimpse of the entrance. To her astonishment the Baronesse in full costume with her hair almost as fancy as her own opened the door, holding a mask. A fat, nervous soldier, sweating profusely, clumsily complimented her and led her to his carriage.

Josephine waited until the hoof steps and the rattle of the carriage could no longer be heard. The Commander was waiting for her a few blocks away. They rode to the Governor's mansion in silence. The Commander was too shy to start a conversation, and Josephine was seething from the loss of her jewels. She only came out of her reverie when the carriage took a turn and Valdeterre pointed out the large orange trees lining the lane leading up to the main house. The closer they got to the incredible mansion the more lights flickered around them. She thought at first the candles in the big glass vases were hung from the trees and only became aware of the *livréed* servants who held them up, when the lights illuminated more and more of the surroundings.

"The Governor must own a lot of slaves," she mused.

"He is running a very grand household, he could not do without," Valdeterre responded, happy that she had finally broken her silence. "That and the fields around the plantation require a lot of workers."

She looked at him curiously: "Do you own slaves?"

He shook his head: "Non, Vicomtesse, that would be a waste in a one-man household. Besides, I am living at military headquarters. Once I get lucky enough to find a wife, then maybe…"

The last sentence hung in the air. She had no response and was relieved when they arrived in the long line of carriages letting off passengers. As they ascended the big staircase leading up to the front porch and into the grand hall, they were greeted by the Governor and his wife, the only two who were not wearing any masks. A butler asked them for their names before announcing them to their hosts:

"Commander Drouot de Valdeterre and Vicomtesse Josephine de Chavin!"

Pleasantries were exchanged, and Josephine commented to her escort after they had passed into the main salon that if one did not pay attention to the announcement, the guests really were anonymous, so elaborate were the costumes and the masks that covered most parts of their faces. Josephine felt right at home in this incredible estate. For a moment she thought she was back in Paris, at one of the great balls of the carnival season she used to attend since she had made her debut at fourteen years old. Valdeterre was a very attentive companion who put a goblet of champagne in her hand before she had asked for one and led her around the house pointing out important guests that he recognized despite their masks.

She expected a formal dinner, but the Commander explained that customs had been loosened in recent years and veered away from the strict French setting of such soireés. There were tables with food, and trays of wine and champagne were passed around by the servants. Only one tradition was upheld: that of the *contredanse*, the popular dance where a line of the ladies faced a line of the gents, then one couple at a time came together, touched hands and moved down the middle by a series of easy steps in the first round. Josephine was familiar with the *contredanse*, having mastered the more complicated variations where both dancers crossed the floor and changed partners. She was very much looking forward to showing off her skills.

Between sips from her goblet and trying to have a light talk with the Commander, a difficult task for such a diffident man, she watched the Governor and his wife moving from one guest to the next, making short but polite conversation with each.

I hope they will engage us, too. It is never a mistake to make oneself known to the most important man in the city.

She steered Valdeterre into the Governor's path. Jean-Baptiste Le Moyne, Sieur de Bienville was the founder of Louisiana and was serving his third term as governor. Josephine prided herself on knowing as much about the important figures in the state as she could. He had built this beautiful grand estate as an homage to Versailles. Having been to the French court, Josephine could attest as to this wonderful accomplishment. The Bienville plantation truly reminded her of the grand palace.

"Bon soir, Monsieur le Commandeur!"

Bienville greeted Valdeterre with a strong handshake.

"May I present the Vicomtesse one more time, Governor?"

Bienville took time to eye her from the elaborate hairdo on her head to the tips of her intricately woven leather boots that stuck out from beneath her gold and green brocade gown. Then he took her hand and kissed it: "It's about time you showed up with a beautiful woman by your side!"

Bienville's wife giggled and took Josephine's hand: "Do not mind my husband. Although we would be very happy if he found himself a lady."

Despite her disinterest in the Commander as a suitor, Josephine blushed.

Across the room Geneviève LaCour closely watched them.

So, the mighty Princess found a prince.

Geneviéve felt a small sting of jealousy. While the Vicomtesse was here with the military commander, she had to content herself with his major, a man who tried her patience. Every chance he got he touched her hand or arm and would not leave her side. Unlike Josephine, Geneviéve had been very open about her reasons to attend the féte:

"Major, would you point out Lieutenant Montferrat?"

"Happy to oblige if I can make out his face beneath the mask. Although… the Lieutenant does have a very prominent chin." His eyes darted across the room. "This man over there near the fireplace might be him."

Geneviève took his arm and dragged him in the direction he was pointing to. When they reached the man, she gave Dumont a little shove.

"Lieutenant, is that you?" He stammered.

"Dumont, you are not allowed to unveil the masked guests yet," Montferrat chuckled.

"Excusé moi, but I would like to introduce the Baronesse…"

She interrupted him and put her hand out: "Geneviève LaCour, Lieutenant. I am sure you are familiar with my name from certain documents."

Montferrat ignored her outstretched hand. Even with his mask it was easy to tell that he was not pleased.

Did he harbor some hope that I would perish on the journey so he could keep the property for himself?

She decided to be as forceful as she could: "Lieutenant, you are a hard man to find. And I believe we have a lot of business to discuss. The Major tells me you will be in town for a few days, so I suggest we meet at your office first thing tomorrow morning."

Montferrat's lips tightened: "The Major here has a big mouth. But just as well. I assume you already know where my office is. Do not forget to bring the papers. You do have the papers, don't you?"

She smiled sweetly: "Certainly. I shall see you in the morning. *Enchanté*, Lieutenant."

She tilted her head slightly.

∼

"*Mesdames et Messieurs, la contredanse!*"

Josephine did not need much encouragement. As soon as she heard the announcement for the dance, she put down her champagne goblet and put her hand out for Valdeterre to lead her to the center of the salon. The Commander was reluctant but could not very well decline the Vicomtesse' invitation. The couple got in line, and as soon as the musicians started playing, moved down the line in the first simple formation. It was when the more intricate part of the famous dance began which required them to switch partners that Josephine noticed something familiar about a man only two couples away from them.

C'est impossible!

The man wore a black mask that covered most of his face but left the bearded chin visible. His black curls were spilling out from the high-collared white shirt under a black jacket. Her surprise turned to shock when he grabbed her hands moments later and pulled her closer than was custom. His musky scent left no doubt. Michél Bèranger had somehow gained entry to the ball. Before she was able to decide how to react to this disturbing realization, he let her go and allowed her to move on to the next partner.

How did he get here and get in? And does this mean his brother is here, too?

Josephine tried to survey the room without missing a step, but the next formation was so difficult that she had to pay attention. The ladies were now facing one another and so were the gentleman before once again zigzagging down the line, but this time locking into a position where the man had his arm around a woman's waist, swinging her in a circle before leading her to the next partner. Except that once she had met up with Michél again, he would not hand her over after she completed the twirl, but instead caught her and thrust his pelvis into hers, locking her into a position that did not allow her to move away. He broke the formation. The musicians could not see them and kept playing. Michél moved Josephine to the salon's backdoor, away from the crowd. It was then that she saw the woman. She noticed the earrings first. Her earrings. On this stranger who wore a purple and silver dress that had seen better days. Josephine opened her mouth, but when Michél swung her around in another circle the woman was gone. Josephine's shock wore off and gave way to anger. She hissed:

"Let me go!"

He only pushed her further away from the dancers into a dark corner where there were no flickering chandeliers:

"Did you think you could cut me out this easily?" His tone was threatening, his lower body was still pushing into hers, and she could feel his breath. She freed one hand and began pounding into his chest.

"We had a deal," he said under his breath.

He loosened his grip and gently brushed his fingers across her lips. She was too stunned to respond in any way, neither with words nor with actions. She stopped hitting him. His eyes bore into her and then, suddenly, he was gone.

Later Josephine would not be able to tell if Michél had slipped back into the crowd or into the gardens. She felt the wall behind her moving until she realized it was not the house, but she sliding to one side and unable to stop herself. An arm reached out, gripping her shoulder, pulling her up. The familiar voice of Madame LaCour parted the haze that had fallen like thick curtains around her brain:

"Can you stand up?" Geneviève asked.

Josephine nodded and the Baronesse let go of her: "Were you assaulted by that man?"

Oh no, she saw everything!

Josephine was not sure what disturbed her most—what had just happened or the fact that there was a witness.

"Non, he was only… he was trying… he is not a good dancer, he made a mistake and was too embarrassed to break the formation…"

Why am I defending this coquin?

Geneviève's face said it all; she did not believe a word out of the Vicomtesse' mouth. She handed her a glass of wine that Josephine accepted with a trembling hand.

"You may consider choosing your companions more wisely."

It was obvious that the Baronesse was not talking about the approaching Commander Valdeterre. Geneviève retreated when she saw the worry and care in his eyes.

"Vicomtesse, I lost you in the crowd after that dancer took you away. My deepest apologies. Are you alright?"

She mustered a small smile: "Oui, oui, he was just… twirling me too fast and I got dizzy. In fact, I still am. Would you mind taking me back to the city?"

"Certainly. Whatever you need me to do." He offered her his arm. When they crossed the salon, she thought she caught a glimpse of the woman in the purple and silver dress.

She stopped Valdeterre: "On second thought… it would be a shame to miss the unveiling of the masks. Maybe a refreshment will invigorate me."

Let's see who the thief is behind the ugly red mask!

Valdeterre bowed his head and lead her to the buffet. He accepted a plate from a waiter and carried it to the next room for her where several tables had been set. They sat down, and she ate a few bites.

The Commander is a gentleman. I must be friendlier and more inviting with him.

"Commander, why don't you fetch yourself something to eat and a glass of wine? We should enjoy this together."

With a pleased look on his face he went back to the buffet. Josephine, slowly regaining her composure, searched the room for a sign of Michél, Jean or the woman.

Who was she and how did she get my earrings?

It did not occur to Josephine to suspect anyone who was on the ship or living at the convent. Rather she thought, it must be a lady who had acquired the jewels from the original thief. For a price much lower than their actual worth, no doubt. One would have to know that the shape and pattern resembled her family crest to appreciate their true value. She did not spot the woman. And she was not about to get up and walk around. Whatever attention she got when the pirate disrupted the dance, it was better to wait before causing another commotion. She still could not admit to herself that yet again Michél's violent passion excited her as much as it frightened her. And so, she concentrated her thoughts on the Commander.

He is someone who seems to truly care about me… And he is in a good position to protect me…

Her musings were interrupted by Valdeterre's return. After he sat down, he touched her hand: "Are you feeling better? The Governor has a surprise when the clock strikes midnight and knowing him it might be a display of fireworks."

She smiled and did not withdraw her hand: "Before or after the unveiling?"

He shook his head: "That I would not know. Should we make our way to the balcony?"

Her smile deepened: "It would be my pleasure, Commander."

The balcony was built in a design that wrapped around the back and half the sides of the mansion, overlooking a garden constructed like the labyrinth at Versailles. The hedges here were not hornbeams, arborvitae and *privét* trees but local Louisiana plants like swamp cypress, palmettos and southern ferns. The grassy circles were planted with rosinweed and Woodland phlox, and the pots were overflowing with scarlet buckeye and indigo flowers. The edge of the plantation was lined with magnolia trees that flowered but once a year. The original idea of planting roses and tulips had failed miserably. The Louisiana weather did not permit much success with those. Nevertheless, the gardens looked as magnificent as the house. The center part of the balcony protruded out, about fifteen by twenty-five meters, and in its middle, there was a cannon. Below, the servants had spread out on a perfect square and as soon as the Governor gave the order, they began lighting the fireworks. They went off into the night sky and exploded in patterns of blue, white and red, the French colors.

Neither of the guests heard the shot on the right side of the mansion. Nor the gallop of the horses disappearing into the fields. It was too dark for the footman's body to be found until morning light.

On the balcony, the display ended with the cannon being fired and the butler yelling: "Unveil yourselves! Drop the masks!"

Far from dropping, the ladies fussed with the untying and disentangling of theirs and the gentlemen ripped theirs off their heads. Josephine pretended having difficulty with removing her mask while frantically looking in all directions to make out the faces of the other guests. Not a trace of the Bèranger brothers. And if the woman with her earrings were still here, Josephine did not see her. The Baronesse must have left as well. Neither she nor her fat companion were on the balcony.

"Would you join me on the dancefloor?"

The Commander held out his hand. She wanted to keep looking for the brothers and the woman, but how could she refuse? Josephine took his arm, and they went inside. Valdeterre had already proved to be a skilled dancer during the *contredanse*, albeit a very formal one. There was none of the heat she had felt in Michél's arms. The Commander brought back memories of her debutante ball in Paris when the son of her father's best friend had shyly led her down the grand hall of the palais, uncertain of his touch and afraid he might offend her if he pulled her too close.

After the dance guests proceeded to leave in their carriages. She was gracious and engaged the Commander in conversation on their ride back. When his carriage pulled around the corner at Rue de Bienville and the Quai, he jumped out, held the door, bowed and kissed her hand, holding it to his mouth while staring into her eyes. He then let go, but she held onto his hand. His surprise showed, but it was perhaps this tiny encouragement that gave him the chance to say out loud what he had been thinking about the entire evening:

"Vicomtesse, may I call on you? It would be my pleasure to take you to dinner soon."

Josephine smiled, nodded, then bid him good night. For a moment after he was gone, she considered to go to the tavern.

I wonder if they are there. I would love to see Michél's face when I walk in.

She decided against it. It may not be the smartest way of conduct to confront the man tonight when passions ran high. Besides, she could not very well walk into the seedy tavern dressed like she was with her mask in her hand. And she was too tired from the night's excitement to sneak into the convent, change and sneak out again.

∽

At Flamand's Florence sank into the back booth. Her hair was sticking out, her dress was splattered with mud and her ribcage and backside hurt from the long ride back. She had lost the mask somewhere along the way. Jean had thrown her on the horse and only stopped to let her adjust in front of him after screams of protest. His brother had scared her tonight. She did not pity Josephine, but Michél's vengeful behavior during the dance could have endangered their whole plan. Florence had warned them that it was madness to intrude on such a high-class affair as the Governor's ball, but the brothers would hear none of it, and if she were honest, she would have to concede that she herself was too riled up to stay behind. She still felt like she had to prove herself to Jean, and tonight she certainly had done that. But it had ended badly and no amount of eau de vie could erase the picture of the bloody hole in the footman's forehead when he fell to the ground right in front of her or the burnt smell emanating from the pistol. Rage overtook her when Michél walked up with a cup. She smashed it out of his hand:

"How dare you put us all in danger with the police by murdering the footman!" she hissed under her breath, but loud enough for him to hear her. Her hand went for his throat, but a stronger arm stopped her:

"Cool down. This is not my brother's fault."

If she had expected Jean to take her side, she had miscalculated; blood clearly ran deeper than business partners. Her anger prevented her from giving in:

"We planned everything for days! Arrive late after the Governor had greeted all his guests. I was to find the bedroom, unlock the balcony door from the inside, then go back downstairs and blend into the crowd. You were to wait outside for my sign to enter through the back and meet me upstairs. But no, you –," she jabbed her finger into Michél's chest, "you had to let your obsession take over and create a scene during the dance!"

When neither Michél nor Jean had an answer, she continued her ranting: "Why was it necessary to kill a man when he could not even see our faces behind the masks? Why was it necessary to show the mighty Princess that you can scare her? Why was it necessary to risk everything out of vengeance?!"

Her voice got louder, and Michél's face took on a darker color than she had ever seen before. He raised his hand against her and if Jean had not interfered, he would have hit her.

"No man gets to hit me!" she screamed before running out of the tavern.

∼

In the morning, the news spread like wildfire through La Nouvelle Orleàns. At the market, where the cooks went shopping, everyone was talking about it. A robbery and a murder had occurred at the Governor's mansion! The more the story got repeated the more it became embellished. By the time the cooks reached the convent, the murderer had shot seven bullets into the body of a servant, ripping his head and chest to threads, and the jewels stolen from the plantation might as well have been owned by Marie Antoinette. The truth as it emerged later was much more mundane, and much more upsetting. Josephine who woke late as usual heard the tale in its most outlandish version. According to rumor a band of pirates had entered the mansion by swinging from ropes fastened to a large oak tree, catapulting themselves onto the second-floor balcony. They had overpowered the governor's wife's maid, shot the lock on the metal box that contained the jewels—ten necklaces, six rings including the wedding bands, bracelets and a tiara— threw them into a flour sack and swung themselves back to the oak tree. This is where they were encountered by a servant who began screaming and was shot multiple times.

Josephine easily deducted truth from lore.

Pirates? Yes. But a band of them? Hardly.

She was not even certain that it was two, and she sincerely doubted the rope swinging. As for the jewels, oui, the Governor was rich, but ten necklaces and a tiara seemed a bit much. And the wedding band? The Governor's wife was wearing it during the evening. Josephine did not believe the extensive number of bullets supposedly shot into the servant's body, either. In the kitchen she asked where they had heard all this.

"Oh, everyone at the market was talking about it," one of the Cubans said.

The market, the place of fish mongering and tale telling.

Josephine hurriedly finished dressing and was on her way to get to the bottom of it all. If anyone would know the truth it was her new friend, the Commander. When she arrived at military command, she was told Valdeterre was very busy and on his way to the Governor's plantation in a few minutes. She waited by the door. When he came rushing out with the fat Major following a few steps behind, he was surprised to see her.

"Vicomtesse… I am so sorry, but I have a criminal investigation to take care of. Would you mind if we talked later?"

She was not going to let him leave: "Commander, a few minutes of your time, s'il vous plait. What I have to say pertains to your investigation."

He looked even more surprised.

What could this beautiful woman possibly know about such a gruesome crime?

He led her back to his office and offered her a seat across from his desk. Instead of taking it she walked to the window behind his chair and looked out. When she turned a ray of sun made her hair shine like spun gold. Valdeterre almost missed her first words, so captivated was he.

"Commander? Did you hear what I said?"

He composed himself: "Pardon, Vicomtesse, will you please repeat it?"

"I said, my earrings, a very valuable family heirloom were stolen.

This is why I was so quiet on our way to the ball. I was very upset by the loss."

Josephine proceeded to tell him about the masked woman who had worn her jewels at the ball and had then disappeared suddenly before the unveiling and the fireworks. This was the first time Valdeterre heard about the presence of a woman who might have been involved in the burglary. Or was it a coincidence and the two cases were not connected? He had to find out:

"May I ask what you know about the crime, Commander?" Josephine asked.

Valdeterre shared the meager facts: the number of criminals they were looking for was two, three at the most. They had stolen a necklace and two bracelets from the upstairs bedroom. They must have been discovered by a servant. He was shot in the head with one bullet. They did not know how the perpetrators had entered the bedroom and to find out, they were about to ride to the mansion to look at evidence. Valdeterre suspected that the only way the shot was not heard was during the fireworks when everyone was distracted by the noise. The presence of a mysterious woman wearing stolen earrings complicated the whole story. He asked Josephine to file a report about her jewels with the clerk and promised to keep her informed of their findings. He then took her hand and again held it a little longer than necessary.

Florence crawled out of bed around noon. Sleep had alluded her after her fight with the Bèrangers. She had to admit that she, too, had been careless and cursed herself for putting on Josephine's earrings. It was pure vanity that had prompted her to wear them. And maybe a tinge of vengefulness to flaunt them at a ball where the Vicomtesse was certain to spot them.

Florence tried to avoid Josephine, and the easiest way to do that was to attend class; no chance of running into her there and a very good one to find out if news of the murder had reached the convent. Her anxious questions were answered in the kitchen. It was lunch break, and the cooks were chattering about nothing else. Florence listened to the ridiculous stories that had little if anything to do with the truth.

A tiara? I only wish. Not that one could ever sell such a rarity.

She took a sip of steaming coffee and retreated into a classroom. Mathematics and geometry were on the schedule, and although she had no interest in the latter, the former was one of her favorite subjects.

Acting like nothing has happened is key now. That and hiding last night's loot in the attic with the other valuables in my casket.

Geneviève LaCour was a woman with a purpose when she marched into Lieutenant Montferrat's office.

This time he will not escape me.

She came armed with a small paper—her part of the deed—and a big determination. The Lieutenant was in a meeting, the soldier at the door told her. She did not care. She walked past the poor man and opened the door. Francois Montferrat was sitting in a big armchair in front of a fireplace smoking a pipe. There was no one else.

"Good morning, Lieutenant! I did assume the meeting your aide mentioned was with me. So glad you are taking the time!" She said cheerily and took the chair opposite him before the speechless Lieutenant could say a word and pulled the deed out of her bag.

"Madame…"

"Baronesse, Lieutenant. I am certain you are aware of my stature." She turned the paper over, so it faced him: "Let us not waste any more of my time. My children and I are eager to move into our home."

He coughed nervously: "I thought you were staying at the Ursuline convent."

"And we shall remain there until construction on our house is completed. Now I need you to sign and show me your part of the deed so I can do the same. And please give me the exact address of the property to hire builders and have them start the work."

Montferrat narrowed his eyes: "Madame… Baronesse… it is not this simple. There is a reason that you cannot own the property outright. It is called a law. A law that prohibits women from owning colonial land without a man as a *consignée*."

Geneviève slowly took her gloves off and locked eyes with him: "I am very aware of the law. I am also aware of my however limited rights. And I have a letter from the advocate in Paris stating clearly that it is within these —my— rights to have you sign the deed upon my arrival in La Nouvelle Orléans and hand over my part of the property which I understand is much smaller than yours. My arrival, Lieutenant, happened months ago."

The man keeps trying to evade me. What is he hiding?

"The address, Lieutenant!"

Montferrat stood up: "64 Rue St. Anne. But I do not have the deed with me. So, it will have to wait until my post at Fort Rosalie has been completed."

She knew he was lying, but there was nothing she could do. For now. At least she had the address. She got up and put her gloves back on: "You cannot evade me forever. Remember that. And know that I am not going away. You shall have to deal with me."

He let out a nasty laugh: "Is that a threat, Madame?"

She walked up to him and looked him straight into the eyes: "Take it however you want. I am not some poor little wife you can put in her place. I shall make use of my rights to the full extent the law provides me. And I shall also make use of my considerable influence with certain people."

Her quiet tone belied the rage underneath. Without another word she marched out of his office. As soon as she was on the street and around the corner she wanted to cry, yet her anger and purpose were stronger than her feelings of defeat.

I will not let yet another man take advantage of me.

She shook it off and walked straight to 64 Rue St. Anne which was only two blocks away. The property was desolate and had nothing but wild swamp grass on it. It was smaller than the 900 square meters she had expected after seeing the number on her deed. She walked around it.

Non, it is not as big as I had hoped, but there would be room to build a nice house with two stories, a balcony in front and a courtyard in the back.

To the left of it was a much bigger lot.

This must be Montferrat's…

CHAPTER 10

In the Mother Superior's office stood Ignace de Beaubois who had no choice but to confront the head of the Ursulines in person after Frère Antoine's delivery of orders to Mother St. Augustin had been ignored and the meek priest had been shown the door. It was another chapter in the ongoing hold-up to open the military hospital. Sister Stanislaus was with the Abbess.

"You have been here for eighteen months!" He raged. "It is about time you fulfilled your contract!"

"Père, I would urge you to calm yourself. This kind of anger is not only unbecoming of a man of God but may also harm your health."

The Jesuit lost his carefully prepared train of thought and with it the speech he had practiced in his head on the way to the convent. He began to stutter: "We need this hospital for the soldiers… this has been … this has been talked about for years… we only brought you over for… for this very purpose…"

Mother St. Augustin walked around her desk and put her hand on his arm. Almost sweetly she continued: "You see, Père, we Ursulines have many purposes."

He wanted to respond, but she cut him off: "And besides, where should we even house wounded soldiers? We have no room in this building that took us many months to repair after you so kindly settled us with it. All the while promising us a new convent."

"Didn't the engineer show you the new plans?" Beaubois asked.

"He did indeed, and we truly desire to move into our new house. Once it is built. And then care not only for the soldiers but for all the other sick in this city that die without said care. But alas, the first stone has yet to be set in the ground. After two years of mere talk. What are we supposed to do?"

Her ironic words were not lost on him: "You have a big property, a plantation, with grounds big enough to build the hospital and worry about the convent later."

"We have fields, Père. Fields that we cannot plow, seed or harvest for lack of laborers. Would the Jesuits provide us with half your workforce?"

He harrumphed: "You know very well that we cannot do that."

"Then, I'm afraid, we will not be in any position to proceed further. You know better than me that the women's orders are never given the same monetary help from the church as the male ones."

He knew. And he also knew that he had run out of arguments. To bring up the contract again would not change anything since that same piece of paper also stated that the Jesuits would lend financial support for a hospital. And they did not have any money to spare. He grudgingly excused himself.

Mother St. Augustin looked at Sister Stanislaus. "That was no lie. We really do lack laborers to work our plantation."

Sister Stanislaus nodded. She had been to the property, no more than wild fields where someone had planted tobacco and indigo years earlier, but without anyone tending to those crops, they had rotted away.

"We have to buy more negroes."

The Mother Superior's words tore her out of her thoughts "But we already have…"

"We have only the four that that the Jesuits originally sent over to work for the convent. They seed, grow and harvest vegetables and rice for our own needs, but they are not enough to plant all the other crops that we need to sell for us to become self-reliant. I cannot beg for money from France or the Jesuits and Capuchins."

Sister Stanislaus was upset: "I cannot condone this," she said, "we are all children of God, as you point out so often. Humans cannot own other humans and buy and sell them like goods."

"Without slave labor the convent cannot function. There is no money coming from Rouen, these fields are part of our property for the construction of a new building, so that we can leave this one that we are already outgrowing. It will never be done without laborers. And this includes sending some of the female boarders that are enslaved to work the fields."

In the corridor, Zulimé overheard the conversation. She held her breath at the Abbess' last words as fear gripped her. The door opened and slammed shut. Sister Stanislaus stared at Zulimé who stared back, frozen.

"I cannot work the fields, I will die." Zulimé's voice was filled with anguish.

Sister Stanislaus' softened: "You will not have to. You are Monsieur de Roche's property not ours, and he put you here to go to school. And besides, we need you for all your healing recipes. Now go on and do your homework. And do not listen in on conversations that are not meant for your ears."

Zulimé was so relieved that she did not even mind being chided for her nosiness by the Sister. After she had gone, the nun straightened her back and returned to the Mother Superior's office.

"Are you done with slamming doors?" The Abbess asked.

The Sister knew that she had to find a compromise to avoid having her relationship to her superior harden to the point where she would have no influence in the decision making at all.

"Mother St. Augustin, I apologize for my anger. But not for my conviction that it is not God's will to send young girls to do backbreaking work when we might find grown men to do that."

"We do not have much of either. Nothing in this country can be done without the slaves. The church certainly will not spend money on free people that we would have to pay for their skills. This is how it is done here and who are we to impose our old-world views?"

"We are supposed to live up to a higher standard, we are supposed to be that higher standard, by example." Sister Stanislaus was not about to give in easily.

"We cannot afford it! It is as simple as that!"

The Mother Superior explained that it was a business decision. And a political one, too. The Ursulines had to hold their own against Jesuits and Capuchins. Not relying on the two orders for income was instrumental if they were to stay independent in their decision making. And so, the Abbess engaged Monsieur de Roche in the procuring of the slaves. The more Sister Stanislaus protested, the more she was rebuffed. Her focus should be the school, the Mother Superior had told her in a stern voice.

Zulimé had her own difficulties that she could not speak of. She was attending classes and had become a good student; she liked school even better than the private tutoring lessons on the Larrác plantation. There were more classes, more pupils, and she was never treated less than any other student. Not like le tuteur who had never called on her and had concentrated all his efforts on the three Creole children, even though she was better at most subjects. Here, she felt equal to all other girls in class, but she could not reconcile that the practice of Christian rule was the only accepted one. She secretly and silently rebelled and had found a like-minded friend in Acadia. They burnt incense, chanted in languages and dialects that were foreign to everyone else and showed apathy when the others recited blessings before meals.

Acadia missed her former life, as did Zulimé. The girl from up north even let her new friend in on the secret of the colors. Zulimé was now able to tell if Acadia had a dark brown day or a green one. The dark days happened when Acadia escaped the convent in search of her father and brother and was returned by a *patrolé*. And when the nuns told her that her family wanted nothing to do with her. Not even Zulimé could get through to her then, much less lift her spirits. Acadia was a wingless bird in those moments, a fish on land.

~

I know how dark it is for her, I have my grey days, too…

    Zulimé battled her demon spirits whenever she thought of her mother and grandmother. When the skeleton hand gripped her insides hard, and the pain kept her awake. When the only way to silence the demon was to walk up and down the stairs and along the hallways. One night she had a good dream; she saw her family dancing and singing with a group of negroes. One of the men had the face of the servant everyone else had danced around, the man in the middle, whom she had talked to at Monsieur de Roche's soirée the night before she was forced onto the ship. In her dream, he still held the snake, the *kulev*, then handed it to her mother. When she awoke, she knew with certainty that he had told them that she was alive. And for a short while she felt contentment and joy. But the demons returned. She knew in her heart that the only way to conquer them, to drive them out of her body, was to learn proper spells. Her grandma had told her that the secrets of vodou originated in Africa and were spread throughout the islands by their ancestors.

    She went to the kitchen to do her homework. It was her favorite place in the building. The cooks provided such warmth. Margarita spoke better French now and had taught her a little Spanish, too. She helped Zulimé with the herbs whenever someone was suffering from an illness. Today it was little Pierre and Bebé who were coughing and sniffling, and she had put a brew on the stove before class that she needed to check on. Margarita was watching her stir the thickening concoction.

"You should heal yourself," the cook said.

Zulimé was not surprised to hear these words. She had seen Margarita's knowing look, when she stood chanting over the pots whenever only the cook was around.

"You know that it is hardest if not impossible to put a healing spell on oneself?" Zulimé asked.

"*Sí. Mi abuela* was a Santoría in Havaña. She died from the same ailment that she cured in all others. She could chase away the demons who held everyone else captive but not her own."

The girl sat down and looked intently at the cook: "Margarita, can you help me find a priestess... or a Santoría who will teach me?"

The Cuban shook her head: "There isn't one. I had a talk with the old man at the market. He says he only knows Natchez and Chitimaca women who know tribal spells. And they are passing it on to their own, not outsiders. You are on your own. You must listen to the Gods and hear their words. I have complete trust in you. You knew nothing about healing teas and yet you have helped so many of us here simply by trusting yourself. You can do this."

Yes, I can do this.

Florence used the convent as a means to an end. She had a bed and got fed, she learned what she was interested in during the classes she bothered to attend. But mostly she used the attic as her personal storage space for all the stolen goods she had assembled. Including the jewels from the Bienville heist.

Jean Bèranger had become dependent on his business partner. Florence knew with certainty who to talk to, sell to and negotiate with. It was like a sixth sense, for she also knew whom to trust and whom to avoid. He admired that greatly. And her contracts? She put everyone they sold rum to in a vise, so tightly written were the agreements. Most of the uneducated tavern owners were not capable of reading and made their x without knowing what they were signing. Florence took full advantage of that. She inserted clauses that would drive the price up every three months and some that would guarantee them payment even if they could not deliver enough barrels due to unforeseen circumstances such as bad weather at sea or a lack of ships to take over. If you owned and ran a tavern or cabarét and you wanted to sell eau de vie, you had to be prepared to make regular payments to the Bèrangers. No one resented this more than Jan Lamesse, the yellow-eyed Flamand. He ranted and raged when Florence presented him with the piece of paper and refused to sign his x under it. He insisted to have it read to him by an unbiased outsider and once he did, ranted and raged some more. He even threatened her with bodily harm. She pushed the little man back and calmly told him to take it up with the brothers.

"This woman has ice in her veins!" He shouted for all his patrons to hear. "She is the devil!"

In the end, he had no option but to agree to the contract, knowing full well that he was charged more than the other tavern owners.

"They want me out," he kept telling everyone in earshot. And he could not be more correct.

Florence and Jean had searched the city for a place to open their own bar but most of the buildings between Rue de Bourbon and the city limits were either occupied or not yet finished. They could not buy a property since all the land had been allocated and short of dumping a barrel of gold coins on the table of a prospective seller, they were not trustworthy enough to be given a loan.

They had barely seen Josephine over the course of the year. She was avoiding Michél, and her contact with Florence was limited to the convent. When she went out at night, it was only with Valdeterre.

We are not good enough for the mighty princess.

Florence resented this but understood Josephine's reluctance to consort with the reckless Michél. Ever since that night of the Mardi

Gras ball she, too, had avoided being alone with him. The military police had questioned both brothers about the murder and robbery as they had done with every shady character in the city but had to let them go for lack of evidence. Jean had disposed of the pistol on one of their crossings to the islands. The victim was a slave, which simply meant that no one at military command really cared, and the Governor could afford to replace his wife's necklace and bracelets. It was just another one of the many unsolved crimes in La Nouvelle Orleàns. And so, the three of them thrived. Their trades had tripled over the last twelve months.

～

The intention of the Commandant and the principal inhabitants of this city is that we would also take the girls and the women of bad conduct. They let us hear that it would be a great good for the colony…
Marie Madeleine Hachard in her journal

On a cold and wet morning in late February Sister Stanislaus heard knocking just as she was getting the cart ready for her market run. She opened the heavy door and did not see anyone at first. Then a hand weakly grabbed her leg. She jumped back. In front of her was a woman in ragged clothes, hovering on the steps. Her hair was wet and messy from the rain, and there was not one part of her that was not dirty. Even her face was caked in mud. She was bleeding from a wound on her neck. She looked young, not more than twenty years of age, but the weary gaze in her eyes made her seem much older. The Sister pulled the shivering woman up and dragged her inside.

"Margarita! I need help!"

The cook appeared from the kitchen. Without a word, she took the woman into the tiny space that served as a washing room next to the kitchen. After Margarita fed her, Sister Stanislaus listened to her story:

"I am Jeanette. Five years ago, they…the magistrates in Paris sent me on a voyage over here…"

"You are a Casket Girl?" The nun was incredulous. "You've been living in La Nouvelle Orleàns for all these years?"

"Non, the ship never made it to La Louisiane, it was shot to pieces off the Mississippi coastline by pirates, and only a handful of us survived. I held on to a trunk, and with it I floated to the shore from where I made my way to Biloxi."

"How did you survive there? And why are you here now?"

Before Jeanette could think of an answer Florence walked in. One glance at the woman was enough. Jeanette noticed the look of recognition in Florence's eyes and tried to cover her arms, but Florence left the kitchen without a word.

Sister Stanislaus turned her attention back to the woman: "How have you made a living all this time?"

"I worked at the market in Biloxi…And in a tavern, serving food. Work ran out after a storm hit Biloxi and so I… I decided to make my way to the city here…"

Sister Stanislaus—or rather the secular part of her—was no fool. None of these stories sounded believable. She took Jeanette into the Mother Superior's office and made her repeat her tale.

The Abbess, too, was as doubtful: "I must admit I have a hard time understanding how a young woman is able to make such a long journey along the coast and through the swamps on her own. By foot, no less… And if you are a Casket Girl, why are you not married by now? Ships getting stranded in Mississippi and early arrivals of Casket Girls getting lost at sea, I have certainly heard about. We all have…" She shook her head. "But any woman who stayed alive has married a soldier, as was intended…"

Jeanette fidgeted with her hair and never looked Mother St. Augustin in the eye. The head of the convent took on a practical tone: "I need your full name…go on, what is it? You need to be registered as a boarder if you want to stay here. And do not lie to me. Your name?"

"Crozat… Jeanette Crozat…"

Mother St. Augustin wrote the name in her book and closed its cover. "You shall start attending school immediately if you desire to stay. Sister, please find Mademoiselle Crozat some more appropriate clothes and assign her a bed."

Do not judge her, Sister Stanislaus told herself.

Yet she could not shake a nervousness about the new arrival. And she was not alone. Jeanette made everyone feel uneasy. Madame LaCour took one look at her and asked for a lock to her room. Josephine did the same. Zulimé and Acadia moved their beds to the other end of the sleeping quarters, found fabric they used as a curtain and hung that from a beam, separating Jeanette from the others. Louise avoided her, too. Margarita was the only one who felt compassion and invited her to sit with her during Sunday mass, which Jeanette accepted since no one else wanted to be close to her. No one except Florence who took every opportunity to make her feel watched.

I know you. I know what you are. You will not get into my business or interfere with me in any way.

Sister Stanislaus urged the Mother Superior to make inquiries about Jeanette, not an easy task given that there was no Catholic order in Biloxi. If this was indeed where she had come from.

It all came to blows soon after when Florence, in one of her generous moments, brought much needed fabrics for new spring dresses and laid out various patterns on the community table. The nuns had given up on asking where she got the money to buy such fineries, instead accepting her willingness to share. Apart from the Vicomtesse and the Baronesse, the girls crowded around the table. Some of the fabrics were magnificent. Next to cotton there were rolls of silk voilé with delicate stitching. Everyone felt the softness and admired the colors. It was when Jeanette snatched a smaller piece and tried to hide it in her corsage that Florence exploded. She grabbed the woman's arm, ripped the fabric away from her and the two ended up on the floor, pulling each other's hair and slapping each other's faces. Finally, Florence gained the upper hand. She pinned Jeanette under her and pulled her dress off her shoulder. On Jeanette's upper back a branding of the *fleur de lis* was exposed.

"There!" Florence shouted. "Now we all know what you are!"

"It takes one to know one!" Jeanette hissed.

Louise and the others had blank looks on their faces.

A branding? What does it mean?

Sister Stanislaus raised her voice: "Enough! You shall all calm down and behave in a proper manner! We shall neither discuss brandings nor shall any of you engage in any gossip."

It was unusual to see the Sister this angry that everyone went quiet. "Let us all thank Mademoiselle Bourget for her generosity, and I shall take the fabrics for safekeeping until the tailor can sew new dresses."

The Sister gathered the rolls and went to the office.

As soon as she was gone, Florence leaned across the table: "Only inmates of the Salpetriére prison are branded with the fleur de lis. You are a forçat."

Jeanette's tone was defiant when she responded: "And so are you, otherwise how would you know about it?"

Florence would not back off: "Oui," she said to the group, "I was branded. I was thrown into jail for stealing fruit from a vendor because I was hungry. But unlike you," she fixed her eyes on Jeanette, "mine does not have a heart attached to it!"

She pulled back her right sleeve to show her tattoo. "A heart means that you are a lying, thieving, filthy *putain*!"

Prostitute!

Louise's hand went to her mouth in shock. She had never seen or met prostitutes. Jeanette raised a fist in response.

"She is living in fire red," Acadia said to Zulimé.

Acadia's code for Jeanette's recklessness described it perfectly.

Jeanette refused to attend church or class and came and went as she pleased. Her bed was usually unslept in. The Abbess considered to throw her out, but her faith prevented her from doing so. Secretly all the nuns were as relieved as the girls when Jeanette was out, and the convent was peaceful. No one warmed up to the prostitute from Biloxi. No one could figure out how she spent her time and with whom, except for Florence who had run into her outside a seedy tavern on Rue St. Louis. Jeanette was accepting a handful of coins from a drunk man. It was not hard to guess what kind of services she was providing. When Jeanette saw Florence, she provocatively put the coins into her corsage and shot her a defiant look. Florence shook her head and moved on.

As long as that woman stays out of my way I am not getting into her business.

Florence had the utmost disdain for women who sold themselves.

As if street life is not dangerous enough. As if a woman does not have to fight three times as hard as a man when poverty is the way of life and the only means for us to survive are strength and perseverance while we live on the edge of the law.

She had seen too many women die, whether it was of illness or by the hand of some suitor who used and then discarded them. She had fought off men like these her whole life. She had no compassion or even tolerance for the women who sold their bodies for she believed that their souls were lost, too.

Geneviève made Sister Stanislaus promise that there would be no contact between her children and Jeanette, when she was out to oversee the work on her house. She had never gotten Montferrat to sign the deed, but this not-so-little detail had not kept her from hiring builders, carpenters and blacksmiths to begin work on her home. Montferrat, stationed again at Fort Rosalie, was unavailable to her. With the house almost finished, she was waiting for the next ship to arrive from France, hoping that their cargo would include furniture, chandeliers and glass ware. She did not want to move in before everything was to her satisfaction. She also needed a housekeeper. Her first thought had been to ask Louise, but the girl had changed in the last few months. She had begun to venture outside the convent more often, encouraged by the Sisters who had been worried about her living like a hermit and hiding herself away from the world in general and from men in particular.

Although there was no suitor yet, Louise smiled more often and had blossomed into a young woman with opinions. One of these opinions was that she wanted to run her own household and that she was ready to get married as soon as a husband presented himself.

This is, after all, what my father had in mind for me when he sent me on this journey. I will not take a position working for another. I will advance my status in society, not remain a farmer's daughter for the rest of my life.

Louise had become very clear about her goals and not afraid to voice them. She was tired of being the shy, withdrawn country girl that always felt like she was not good enough. Neither important nor rich compared to Madame and the Vicomtesse, not skilled and practical compared to Margarita, not mysterious like the Dominguan girl and the Acadian, she studied hard at school, the only distraction from the constant upheavals at the convent. Her Catholic beliefs made her condemn women like Florence and Jeanette, but that same condemnation was the reason that she had abandoned the idea of becoming a nun. Sister Stanislaus was still the object of her unwavering admiration and the one who was preaching forgiveness for all sinners, a forgiveness that Louise could not find in her heart. She was aware of this shortcoming, but she could not bring herself to engage in any way with Jeanette or even say a kind bonjour to her.

Louise had begun accompanying the Sister on her market runs again and taking long walks to get to know the city. It was on one of these walks that she forgot the time, and when dusk settled over the city she was lost. She had never been this far down the river, at the end of the docks where soldiers and sailors spent their free time at the only bar near the shore. When she realized that she was walking in the wrong direction, away from the convent instead of toward it, it was too late.

"*Bon nuit, ma belle mademoiselle!*"

The soldiers came out of nowhere. One of them put his arm around her and drew her towards the entrance of the bar. She tried to escape, but other soldiers surrounded her, pushing her inside with them.

"Non!" She said anxiously, "I have to go home!"

They laughed: "You will not refuse a drink with us, ma belle, will you? That would be so impolite," another soldier said. They shoved a cup filled with a dark liquid in front of her: "*Á votre santé!*"

The soldier next to her guided her hand with the cup to her mouth and forced her to drink. Not ever having tasted crude rum before, she spit out the liquid, and it spilled all over the top of her dress. The man laughed and put his hand on her chest to wipe it off. She screamed and jumped back, but there was no room to move. The soldier had her up against the bar with her arms pinned behind her. He lifted her dress and pushed his hand between her legs, ripping the thin cotton of her undergarment. She tried to fight him, but the shock left her frozen. He violated her with his fingers while he continued to laugh. The others fired him up: "Make her feel like a woman!"

He used his other hand to undo the buttons on the front of his trousers. She closed her eyes, imagined herself on her father's land, the green fields full of spring flowers that she used to run through when she was a little child.

Anywhere but here…

She felt the pain, but she was in the fields, the burning banished to a place far away. And suddenly it ended. There was wide open space around her. It was the yelling that made her open her eyes. A tall soldier was beating the man who had been hurting her. The soldier sat on top of the man on the floor, hitting his face again and again. The other men moved in to stop him. He pulled a gun and waved it in a circle: "Back! All of you! Or I will take you all to prison!"

He pulled up the soldier whose face was beaten to a bloody pulp, his nose split and his right eye swollen so he could not see. His trousers were still open. Louise tried to hold on to the bar to keep from fainting. Her savior saw her sliding down. He turned the man on his back, almost breaking his arm and tied a rope around his wrists.

"I am ordering you to watch this animal. Do not go against my order. I am your superior officer. You!" He pointed to one of them: "Go get the garrison guard."

He pulled Louise up from the floor, and she immediately used her fists against him, fighting him now like she had wanted to fight her attacker.

"Shhhh, Mademoiselle, I am here to help."

His soothing words made her weak again. A crying sound escaped her mouth. He put his arm under her shoulder and around her waist to hold her up, led her outside and put her in a carriage.

"Where is your home?" he asked.

"Convent…" was all she could say.

He was surprised at first, but when he looked her over—the modest but well-made dress, the barely worn boots and the unpainted face—he regretted the first thought that had entered his mind when he had walked into the bar; that she was a prostitute who had not been paid in advance and was fighting the man who tried to get her services for free.

This young woman is not a prostitute. That she lives at the convent makes sense.

He felt for her, but no words seemed good enough, so their ride was silent. He helped her out of the carriage in front of the convent. She did not want him to walk her in but was too weak without his support. She made him promise not to tell anyone the gory details, only that she was attacked.

She need not have worried about anything he would say. Sister Stanislaus took one look at her and knew. So did Zulimé. The

Dominguan had seen too many young, enslaved girls with empty eyes after the overseer had taken them to the shack in the back of the barn. Some of these women got used to it. Others never re-entered the world of the living, doing their chores without ever speaking again. Zulimé had never quite grasped what had been done to them, just that a bad man could take the essence of a woman and never give it back. She was filled with sorrow for the country girl, but when she rushed up to her, Louise almost pushed her back.

I do not want some black magic coming at me! I need to be alone.

Louise rejected the Sister's touch, too, and went upstairs. It was up to the ever practical Margarita to go after her. Carrying a bowl of soup, the Cuban sat down on the edge of the young woman's bed. Louise was curled up, her head halfway under her pillow. The cook gently removed the pillow and caressed her cheek. "You must eat, *querida.*"

Margarita got her to sit up and fed her like a little child. As the warm liquid ran down Louise's throat, hot tears streamed down her cheeks, soundless crying in the darkness. When the bowl was empty, Margarita put it to the side and her hand up to the girl's face, wiping the tears away with her thumb. "What happened to you today happens to us all the time…"

Louise finally looked at her: "It happened to you?"

Margarita nodded. "More than once."

The girl's eyes widened: "Are you saying that this is normal? To be… touched like this by a man?"

The cook raised her head to avoid showing her own wet eyes. "No, it is not normal, it can never be normal, but it happens. My husband did it to me all the time."

"Your husband? But he is allowed to if he is your husband."

Margarita shook her head violently. Her voice turned hard when she forced out her next words: *"No! Nunca!* Never. *Ninguno hombre, esposo o no!* No man is ever allowed to do this, not even a husband! I left Cuba because of it."

She took Louise's face in both her hands: "*Escuche me*, listen: a man must respect a woman. He can touch her only when she wants him to. If he does not obey this rule, you run. You run as far as you can. You run from him if he is your husband or *un extraño*, a stranger. You also run if he hits you."

The sobs started rising from deep inside the girl: "I will never find a husband now…"

Margarita hugged her and rocked her back and forth: "*Si, ya verás!* Yes, you will. There are good men in the world."

In the darkness, leaning against the door frame, Geneviève was shaken to the core.

Too many bad memories…

Zulimé knew something had to be done. The French country girl could reject her help, but she remembered her Mamán's words: ,you do not always have to get permission to chase away the bad spirits…' An idea formed in her head. She went looking for Acadia.

Margarita held Louise until she fell asleep. It did not take long. The cook had seasoned the soup with a soothing herb, undetectable to taste, but strong enough to make Louise fall into a deep, dreamless slumber. Margarita knew the girl would not wake until many hours later. She knew because without that herb she herself would not have escaped her pain. When she left the room, she saw Geneviéve's shadow at the door. The Baronesse and the cook put their arms around each other in quiet understanding.

"How did you escape?" Geneviève asked.

"I fought back one day."

"So did I. And then, like you I found a ship."

There was no point in confiding to Margarita that she had done much more than fought back.

Better to keep the painful details to myself…

∽

"The shadows fall so deep, the spirits roam under the oaks' extended arms. Make them show themselves, Papa Legba! Make them come out of the trees' roots, Papa Legba, and send them to fiery heaven!"

It was past midnight under a new moon, and Zulimé danced in a circle in the courtyard's corner around the thick trunk of the old oak. Her arms swirling, her face turned to the soil, chanting the words over and over. Words she had made up, words that came to her after a long and quiet sitting during her excursion to the fields this morning with Acadia, who was now perched on a branch above her. When a cloud passed across the foggy moon, Zulimé reached up, and Acadia put a snake in her outstretched arms. Zulimé kept chanting the words, adding a ‚Papa Legba'—the name for the holy deity of the kulev—to each sentence, as Acadia slid down and began drumming on a hollow wood stick. Zulimé's chants got faster as the drumming increased. When they reached a crescendo, Acadia stopped and Zulimé held the serpent up with one last whisper of "Papa Legba!". Then she sank to the ground, spent from the ritual. Acadia took the snake from her and put it in its cage, hidden away from the nuns' prying eyes in the shack behind the convent's walls that only the workmen used to store their tools.

"I pray, this will work."

Acadia had learned how to use wood as an instrument for drumming at her friend's instruction. She was the one who had found a snake when Zulimé told her that only the vodou's highest symbol would get rid of the spirits that haunted so many of the women and had taken over the soul of Louise. Acadia did not question her friend's ability to perform this ritual. She had seen many ways to keep demons at bay while growing up. This was just another one.

"It will work," Zulimé said, "I may not have experienced all the teachings of my mother and grandmother, but Margarita is right; all I have to do is listen to my spirit angels to guide me."

∽

News came that the soldier who had raped the country girl had been stripped of his position and properly arrested. He was to be held indefinitely, but had escaped the next night, most likely with the help of some of his fellow officers. He had disappeared. The Sisters kept this information from Louise, but the others got wind of it. Margarita and Zulimé were most upset, and Acadia's eyes clouded over in the darkest color she had ever felt. While the others lamented that a bad man had gotten off, she did not utter a word. A few days later the soldier's body washed up on the banks of the river. A gator head was firmly implanted in his chest. Curiously, it looked dried and old and neatly severed from the rest of its body. Death by alligator attack was listed as the official cause of the man's demise, and no one questioned it.

CHAPTER 11

Father Antoine, in his sermons so emphasizes our duty to teach those entrusted to us, to guide them on their journey to become good Catholic people, and I cannot share with him my doubts on this matter. He does not sit with us at the table, does not hear the questions of the many women so different in faith, color and upbringing, does not see their struggle to abandon their pagan beliefs and rituals to heal their pain. I ask myself, if we are to be teachers are we not to listen and learn from them, too? The custom here is to marry the girls early. We have not been successful in doing so. It is the women who accompanied us on our journey that are of the most concern. Dare we marry them off as if they were our property?

In a quiet corner of the chapel, Sister Stanislaus dared to write in her journal the doubts that she could not share openly.

The matter of marriage was heavily on her superior's mind when Mother St. Augustin called all the Sisters into her office. The head of the convent wanted to know about the progress in finding husbands for the filles a la casquettes, the Casket Girls.

Louise had become a shadow of herself, barely making it to church. Florence was a lost cause that even the Mother Superior had given up on. That the Abbess allowed the forçat to stay was a testament to her Catholic faith. To everyone's surprise it was the aristocrat Josephine de Chavin who seemed the closest to marriage. For the past year, she had been escorted around town by Commander Valdeterre. It was only a matter of time until they were betrothed.

"The poor man. I hope he knows what he is signing up for," the Mother Superior sighed. As glad as she was to see one of her charges go off into a secure future, she was also realistic enough to see that Valdeterre was hardly equipped to handle the Vicomtesse with all her past burdens that only the nuns knew about and were certain the aristocrat had not shared with him.

"A world of trouble," Sister Stanislaus agreed. "We have to believe that she will make him a good wife."

The Mother Superior made the sign of the cross. "It has not been easy, dear Sisters…" The nuns looked at each other in agreement. "We have taken on a monumental task and trusted in the Lord to guide us. We must keep that trust no matter what we encounter, no matter what we must overcome. Another ship will soon deliver more Casket Girls to the city and to us. And yes, I know, progress on the construction of a new building is slow. But let us focus on how much we are achieving; our school is a success. We have tripled our students. We serve a community with no boundaries. Women of all social classes will be educated citizens in a few years' time, from the blacksmith's daughter to the wife of a workman. And the plantation owners are now permitting their enslaved women and girls to attend our Sunday curriculum. Affranchittes, free women of color and women from the tribes attend early or late classes. They will be well versed in spreading the word of God, and with his blessing we shall not fail."

She cleared her throat. "I will now hear your concerns and grievances. If there are any…" She hoped not but knew better.

Sister St. Therese, a soft-spoken nun raised her hand: "Not to diminish our advancements with the school… but we are dealing with terrible situations like the attack on Louise Mariette…"

"And prostitution," Sister St. Marthé chimed in.

"Not to mention not one but two forçats among our charges!"

"And all the pagan rituals of the girl from Saint Domingue and her friend, the Acadian!"

A chorus of voices talked over each other until the Mother Superior rose and raised her hands: "Sisters, please remember your faith. We are not here to judge."

Some of them quieted down and listened, others did not. Sister St. Anne said to Sister Stanislaus: "And just this morning the workmen discovered a snake in the woodshed." Her words, though spoken in a hushed voice were heard by all.

"A snake?"

"Oui! In a cage!"

The Mother Superior raised her voice. "Return to your chores, s'il vous plait. Sister Stanislaus, would you please stay?" The others left.

"A snake by itself is not unusual in the swamps, but a snake in a cage is a different story. One that poses the question…"

Sister Stanislaus finished the sentence for her: "I believe we have to talk to Zulimé."

The nun found the girl in her favorite class, reading. She asked her to step out and follow her to the shed. Awakened by the workmen and agitated, the snake was thrashing in its cage. Zulimé rushed over and put her hands on top of the bars, murmuring words that were foreign to Sister Stanislaus whose eyes widened in fear. She tried to pull the girl back, but Zulimé would have none of it until the snake was calmed. Only when the reptile recoiled and settled into the far corner, did the girl slowly turn around. There was as much fear in her eyes as there was in the nun's. Yet it was not her snake that scared her: "Please do not send me away," she said.

Marie Madeleine—for the Sister knew only the worldly part of her would be able to handle this situation—took her by the shoulders: "Child, it is not up to me what will happen now. You have defied every order to abstain from these pagan rituals, conducted in secret and behind our backs. And now you are involving dangerous animals that could threaten all of us. You can plead your case with the Mother Superior."

Zulimé's tears began to flow. With her head hung low, she followed the Sister back inside. Her day had gone from a rosy morning color to stormy indigo, as Acadia would say. Marie Madeleine did not want Zulimé to be sent away but believed that only the fear of this scenario would change her ways.

The Mother Superior leaned forward, her glasses low on her nose. "What do you have to say for yourself, child?"

Zulimé slowly looked up: "I did not want to endanger anyone here… that is why we… I… put it in a cage far away from the main house. It is not a poisonous snake, Mother. It is for healing only…"

The Mother Superior crinkled her forehead: "Healing? Healing what?"

Zulimé's voice grew more confident: "Louise. And everyone who is possessed by the demons that make their nights sleepless and their days dark."

The old nun lost her patience: "Only the Lord can do that. That is why he is called our savior! Not a reptile, poisonous or not, not a girl like you, who defies God's teachings, only the Lord himself!"

Zulimé knew that her future depended on her next words: "Mother, I never meant to offend you… or the Lord. My Mamán raised me in the Catholic faith. I am a good pupil. I read the bible every day. I go to church with the others. I pray. Our ancient rituals only serve in the healing. They do not keep me from my belief in God. All I ever use them for is to help others."

It was the longest speech she had ever given.

"But what do you need a snake for?" Sister Stanislaus asked.

"A serpent is not the symbol of danger and death… it represents the rainbow, the connection between the earth and heaven. It helps to send all the bad on the earth up to the heavens to be made into something good and beautiful…"

When she was not interrupted by the Mother Superior, she grew bolder.

"Isn't this better than the serpent in the bible? The one in the garden of Eden that stands only for temptation? In our tradition, it is the opposite, it is there but for the good of the humans who are in pain on this earth." Zulimé held her breath.

With her hands folded the older nun paused. When she spoke, it was in a measured tone that betrayed her mixed emotions: "The snake must be disposed of. As for you, I shall consider your explanation and your conduct and let you know my decision. You can go now."

Zulimé left the Abbess' office.

In the end it was not up to the Ursulines. Gossip was not only a favorite pastime among the city's residents, but it had also permeated the Catholic orders. Father de Beaubois got wind that a young, enslaved girl was living at the Ursuline convent, one that attended classes every day instead of only on weekends as it was the rule for indentured servants. Worse, said girl was known for her healing skills and treated illnesses like she was a docteur. This did not sit well with the Jesuit, and he called on Mother St. Augustin. He did not waste time with pleasantries:

"You refuse to open a hospital but employ a slave to cure the sick, who should work in your fields or at least in the house? With pagan rituals? This goes against every law put in place by the Governor of this colony, by the city command and the rules that we adhere to!" He raged.

When he finally took a breath, the Mother Superior responded:

"Father, we still have not received supplies, money or even a reply to our question about doctors for that hospital you keep holding over us. Furthermore, the slave girl is not our property. She was entrusted to us by a Creole merchant—who unlike the Jesuits—has helped us consistently ever since we got here. Without him we would not even have windowpanes much less beds. We owe him a great deal of gratitude. The least we can do is treat the girl the way he asked us to."

"If she is his property send her back to him! We don't need her witches' brews to heal the sick or make them sicker! She is not to continue practicing medicine or attending your school unless her owner brings her for Sunday classes! Is that understood?"

As much as the Mother Superior wanted to throw the Jesuit out, she knew that he had the upper hand. If word about Zulimé's healing concoctions had reached him, how long would it take until he found out about the snake?

After de Beaubois left, Mother St. Augustin sat in prayer for an hour asking the Lord to guide her in coming up with a solution. There was only one. She called Sister Stanislaus back in and relayed her argument with the Jesuit.

"We cannot tell Zulimé that she is being expelled over all the good she has done for everyone here… and I know you do not agree with expulsion," she said to Sister Stanislaus.

"I fear that sending her away will only throw her deeper into her misguided beliefs. The girl has no ill will. She has helped a lot of the women through illness and pain. Her explanation of the meaning of the serpent shows a quick mind."

The Mother Superior had to agree. "She is a smart one. But we do not know if her reasoning is true. And where did she get a snake in the first place?"

"She could have caught it in the swampland just outside the city. I am certain, Acadia would know where to find such an animal. She lived in rough nature up north."

The older nun shook her head: "Sister, I have no other choice than to take a strong stand here that will not get us into more trouble with the Jesuits. Morale is low. And all this threatens the school. Imagine if Father de Beaubois finds out about the snake next? All he needs is an excuse to shut us down. What if he writes to the Cardinal? You think anyone in France will have an open mind as to what a positive symbol a serpent is according to a colored girl from the islands?"

Sister Stanislaus sighed: "If we are concerned about threats to the school, we must look no further than to the woman who sells her body on the street. A woman that we give room and board to. And who, unlike Zulimé, is not coming to classes or attending daily prayer."

Mother St. Augustin rose from her chair and began pacing her office. Sister Stanislaus had a point, she had to admit. Yet she also knew that it would be easier to argue housing a prostitute than to explain a reptile ritual to the Jesuit clergymen. All she had to bring up in defense of the former was the bible. Mary Magdalene to be precise. And the mercy the Lord Jesus afforded her.

Right or wrong, French streetwalkers count higher in the eyes of the church than African slaves.

"I have no choice but to send you to the plantation," the Mother Superior informed Zulimé:

"You may attend Sunday school if Monsieur de Roche finds a way for you to travel down the river. Now go back to class until we can get word to him."

Zulimé slumped to the floor. Her worst nightmares were coming true. "What about Bebé?"

"Bebé can stay. She has done nothing wrong."

Sister Stanislaus guided Zulimé outside, then returned to the office, closing the door behind her. The Mother Superior looked up:

"I shall send a message to Monsieur de Roche," she said after a long pause.

Sister Stanislaus knew there was no way to change her mind now. Zulimé would have to be the sacrifice made to ensure the continuation of their mission.

The news of her friend's expulsion from the convent hit Acadia like a dark storm. She had not felt the black clouds closing in on her like this since her mother had died. And she had not cried since then, either. Not like this. Her sobbing woke everyone in the upstairs sleeping quarters. Zulimé, despite being crushed by her own despair, tried to soothe her.

"I will go to the Mother Superior and tell her that it was me who got you the snake," Acadia said under tears.

Zulimé caressed her unruly hair: "And what good would that do? She will throw you out on the street. I, at least, have a place to go to. However awful it is to live the life of a slave..."

They cried together and Zulimé made Acadia promise not to say anything about her involvement.

Margarita, too, was more distraught than she showed when she heard about Zulimé. She had grown fond of the girl that had so much dignity in her impossible situation. Even more than Sister Stanislaus, she doubted the official story that she had been told. She had taken one look at Zulimé on the ship and the way she behaved and was convinced that she had never been enslaved. The young woman's pride, the way she carried herself, that she could read and write; all of it spoke of a privileged upbringing for someone as dark as her.

Zulimé's departure happened faster than expected. Henry de Roche, having just returned from Saint Domingue, always made it a point to look in on the convent after a journey, to see what would be needed and how he could help. When he was told about the snake, it took him a minute to respond. And when he spoke it was in an apologetic tone, as if he was trying to excuse the bad behavior of an unruly child. She had to get used to the strict rules of the convent, he said. She had had more than a year to do that, Mother St. Augustin replied. She could not allow the girl to disrupt the already difficult life of her charges. De Roche knew there was no use arguing with the Mother Superior. Margarita stood in the hallway, one arm around the sobbing, inconsolable Acadia. She herself had tears in her eyes, and when Zulimé came down the stairs with her meager belongings wrapped in a cotton cloth, a sob escaped her, too. Zulimé was shaking with every step that got her closer to her owner.

I must not cry. I must not cry.

But when little Bebé came flying down the hall and threw herself into her arms screaming, she could not hold back the tears. With the child clinging to her, she slid to the floor. Bebé would not let go. She wanted to go with her, she cried. Zulimé tried to calm her, whispered in her ear that she would have it so much better here. Finally, Sister St. Marthé stepped in and pried the child from her arms. Zulimé got up and without another look back, she followed de Roche to his carriage. She was about to climb up to sit on top with the coachman or behind him as she had seen servants do. But de Roche ordered her inside the carriage. She slid into a corner on the bench across from him. He saw how much she tried to hide her fear:

"This was not my doing. I would have left you at the convent, snake or not."

Is he apologizing to me?

She looked at him, curiously.

"To be honest, I do not know what to do with you…" he continued. "I cannot send you to work in the fields, and you would not be of much use out there anyway. We have just begun to get them ready, and it is hard work that only men can do. Once it is harvesting time, it will be another story. But right now… I have a cook and one servant to clean the house, so all I can do is have you work with them…" De Roche was thinking out loud. All she heard was that she would not have to suffer. For now. She had seen what the cane could do to a body at the Larrác plantation. Had heard the cries of the exhausted field slaves, had felt the torn, raised skin on the arms of children far too young to do such hard labor. And even though there were no sugar plantations here, she knew of the damage indigo could do, too. The coughing of the slaves that had to cook it had kept her awake at night. Never mind the deep blue dye on them, so strong no skin was dark enough to hide it. And she had quietly blamed Monsieur Larrác, never quite able to reconcile his loving gentleness towards her and her mother with his orders for the indentured servants. She felt that same chasm of character in de Roche yet could not help but feel grateful that she was on the good side of his decisions.

"Monsieur, I will do my best, I promise! And if you are happy with me, will you let me attend Sunday school? The Mother Superior said I could…"

"We shall see. While I am here you can come with me since I go to the city for Sunday mass. But when I travel, you will have to stay on the plantation. There is no one who can take you."

It was not what she had wanted to hear but it was better than not being able to get away at all. They did not speak the rest of the way. De Roche had not been shocked when the Mother Superior had told him about the snake. On the island, people of color often kept snakes for their rituals. This had never bothered him much if they kept them outside. He considered himself a good Catholic and was all for baptizing his servants, but what harm would it do if they practiced their traditions on their own time? He remembered his own grandmother, who was darker than anyone in his family and her chanting behind the kitchen when she thought no one was around. As a little boy he had hid behind a tree, trying but never succeeding to make out the words. When he had asked her about the chants, she denied them, but he had known for a long time that mixed blood ran through his veins, however diluted. His father had been one of the first merchants to ship supplies from the island. The father's success as a planter and farmer and his own even bigger one could not erase his ancestry.

De Roche was born here, in La Louisiane, when it had been settled by the French at the turn of the century. This made him a true Creole unlike his father who hailed from Saint Domingue, the son of a French settler and his mother who was born in the island's rural area, her lineage not quite clear. Henry learned early that this was not something that was talked about in his family but having watched his mother often spending time with the servants and their rituals, caused him to question the ancient practices even less. Of course, he did not say any of this to the French nuns. They would never understand or condone such thinking. But he had not planned on taking Zulimé back so soon. The truth was that he needed every hand on the fields, male and female. He had acquired more enslaved men and women on his recent travels. Except for the oldest female they all did hard work outside. Only Cecile was working in the house. She did the cooking and cleaning. His reluctance to send Zulimé into the indigo and tobacco fields had to do less with hard labor and more with another matter; she was the most beautiful of all his servants, and the men would want her. He could not bear the thought of her being used as a breeder. And it was this thought that made him so uneasy.

Slaves breeding more slaves and increasing the workforce is the only way to turn a new, struggling plantation into a prosperous one.

As a businessman he knew that. It was the reason that he tried to keep the numbers even between the men and the women.

But not this girl... I must keep her from all that...

At the convent life went on as usual, if usual meant a barrel of secrets and troubles, hidden deep inside the attic and buried in the hearts and souls of some of its inhabitants. Sister Stanislaus had taken to watching over the original group of Casket Girls as if she were their mother. She missed Zulimé more than she wanted to admit. She was grateful that Acadia had found a safe place with Margarita who spent most of her time in the kitchen and on market runs, teaching Acadia about the unusual spices she had grown up with and adding them to many of the dishes. The blackened meats and poultry were liked by most. Only the Mother Superior and the older nuns complained about indigestion, so Margarita began to make their portions unsalted and unseasoned. Sister Stanislaus who had preferred vegetable dishes in the beginning, warmed up to the talented cook's delicious wild duck and bison creations.

∼

Geneviève looked up at her house where the roofers were adding shingles. When she bent down to inspect one of the *piliers*, the stilts that lifted the structure above ground, thus preventing the mud from seeping through the floorboards during the winter and summer rains, she felt a hand on her shoulder.

"Bon jour, Madame. I like what you have done here." Montferrat's smirk was as nasty as it was unwelcome. She was not looking forward to having him as a neighbor. She faced him: "Have you come to finally bring me the signed deed, Lieutenant?"

He laughed: "Indeed, I have." He pulled out a piece of paper, unfolded it and handed it to her: "You see, you are mistaken about the address. This property here is all mine. As you can read here,"—he pointed to the deed— "you own a part of land on the corner of Rue de Bourbon and Rue de Toulouse." He laughed again. "But I thank you for building such a nice house for me. I will, of course, reimburse you for the materials, should you insist."

Geneviève felt the ground under her turning to sludge and swallowing her.

I shall be damned if I let him see how upset I am!

She supported herself by holding on to the rough wall. Her knuckle was white as much from the effort of not falling over as from keeping herself from hitting him. She knew exactly where the supposed property was that he said belonged to her; a much smaller parcel of land on an unsavory corner of the city, surrounded by houses of ill repute: cabaréts, taverns and a brothel. She did not for an instance believe that this was the deal her brother had negotiated for her. Montferrat was a liar and a thief.

"Lieutenant, it is clearly you who is mistaken. My deed states that you and I are neighbors. Unless you own property on Rue de Bourbon, I am in the right place. The land next door is yours, is it not?"

His eyes narrowed. He realized a crucial oversight in his clever plan. "No, Madame, I am not your neighbor since this deed—" he flipped his fingers at the paper in her hands "—lists your address, and it is not this one here. I am the owner of both these properties." He pointed at the one next door. "And as grateful as I am to you for building a house for me, I must ask you to get off my land before I am forced to have you escorted off by my men."

She could not fight him in this moment but fight him she would. She crumpled up the deed and threw it at his feet, then thought better of it, picked it up and stomped away. She could hear his laughter following her halfway down the block and lingering in her ears like an echo of evil even after she was far away.

∼

Geneviève was still breathing heavily when she walked into Mother St. Augustin's office. The Mother Superior looked up from her desk.

Madame LaCour looks like she could use some water. I wonder what new drama has befallen us.

The Abbess poured water in a glass and handed it to Geneviève who drank it in one long gulp. She then told the nun the whole sordid story.

"My dear brother wanted to make sure my children and I would be taken care of after the loss of my husband. He negotiated this deal through his military connections. Since I am a woman, we needed a consignée to the deed."

The Mother Superior nodded. It did not surprise her that a man of influence had taken advantage of a woman in need.

"I shall fight him. In court if I must."

Mother St. Augustin could hear the despair in the widow's voice after her anger over this injustice had subsided.

"Madame, my advice to you is to speak with Commander Valdeterre before you decide. He is Lieutenant Montferrat's superior. I would also urge you to contact your brother in Paris. And lastly, I can only recommend deep prayer. Your children should not see you so upset. You have a home here for as long as you need it." She made the sign of the cross. "May the Lord be with you, Widow LaCour."

Geneviève knew she was dismissed.

Oui, I have a home here. As long as my money pays for it. I am the last woman the Ursulines would throw out...

Margarita had not been as kind and open towards the Baronesse as she used to be after Zulimé was gone. In her mind the defenseless girl had needed someone more powerful than a woman of color to stand up for her. When Geneviève walked into her kitchen, the cook did not turn from her stove to acknowledge her. It was only minutes later, when she still had not spoken that Margarita looked over her shoulder and saw Geneviève's head on the table between her folded arms. It was very unlike her to be in such a state, Margarita thought.

"*Que pasa*? What is with you? Are you ill?"

Geneviève lifted her head. She looked defeated. More sighing than speaking she conveyed what had happened. "Is my entire life ruled by fighting powerful men?" she finally asked.

Now it was Margarita's turn to sigh: "You at least, have the power to do something about it..." She ladled some rabbit stew from the big pot into a bowl and put it in front of her. For above all Margarita believed that good food was the best first remedy in all desperate situations.

～

At the chapel, quiet and empty during the early afternoons, Louise contemplated the upcoming Easter holiday and that it meant she would have to leave her seclusion and attend mass in the front row. There was a hierarchy to the way the congregation was seated on high holidays.

The Ursulines were in a separate section to the left of the altar, while the high-ranking soldiers and city officials sat in the first few rows on the right with their wives. On the other side it was the Casket Girls according to the time of their arrival in La Nouvelle Orleàns. It filled Louise with dread that made her stomach turn. On all other Sundays she could hide in the back closest to the entrance and easiest to get out after the last prayer and song.

The Holy Week also brought with it another Catholic burden: the confession. Louise would have to line up on Good Friday after the *via crucis*, the stations of the cross, with all the others to go into the dark booth and tell the parish priest about her sins.

What to say? That I have dirtied myself with something that will never wash off? That I have committed a deathly sin and broken the sixth commandment? That my punishment, my penance will be to never have a husband?

Despite Margarita's words, Louise regarded that day in the bar as her fault. At night, she lay awake eaten up by the thought of failure. Her failure.

Why did I not fight back harder to preserve my honor, my dignity as a woman? Why did I walk alone only to get lost and lose my way as a result?

These thoughts of guilt made a jumble of her mind. But to share them with a priest? She was so anguished that any attempt to hide it failed, and so absentminded in school that Sister Stanislaus asked her to stay after class.

"Louise, how can I help?"

And at that moment it broke out of her. All of it. Like an unstoppable rockslide rolling off the mountain of her guilt.

"Sister, you said my motives for joining the order were not guided by God. That it was my loneliness that was the reason for my wish. But now I have no other choice. I have failed God, I have let these terrible things happen to me, I sinned against his commandment, and I want to do penance, but how better to do that than by becoming one of you and dedicating the rest of my life to making up for what I did?"

Marie Madeleine Hachard was stunned. She had seen women like this country girl before, women who suffered at the hands of men. She strongly believed that there was happiness and light after the abyss. Once she had become Sister Stanislaus many of the abused had come to seek shelter at the convent in Rouen. Some souls healed like their bodies, and they went on to live normal lives. A few never got over it, and in some rare cases, they took their own lives. She would not let Louise join their ranks. Nor would she let her join the order. Sister Stanislaus took a deep breath and placed both her hands on the girl's shoulders:

"You had nothing to do with what this soldier did to you. You hear me? Nothing. God does not blame the victim. And a victim you are. God does not ask for penance for what another has done to you. Do you understand?"

Louise's blank look left no doubt that she did not. The Sister sighed: "God does not have to forgive you for a sin since you have not done anything that would be cause for redemption." She gently shook the girl: "I have seen women in your predicament. They healed. Inside and out, body and soul. They went on to lead fulfilled lives with a family of their own. You can, too. It is but a matter of time and will. God's will and yours. God does not want you to spend your life in agony. If he does not want this, why do you?"

Sister Stanislaus knew that what she was saying was not entirely in line with her Catholic teachings. The assumption of God's will was in itself a sin, but her heart told her to follow her instincts on this as it always had, even when the chasm between the bible and her own beliefs was as wide as the sea that separated her from her father. She saw that she had gotten through to the girl. There was a glimmer of hope in Louise's eyes.

"Does this mean I do not have to confess this?"

The Sister almost laughed: "Non, you do not have to confess another's sin, not at all.

The only sin you must confess on this Good Friday is the one of doubt. Doubt in the Lord that he can heal you."

When Louise left the classroom, a lot of weight had been lifted off her. Sister Stanislaus saw it in the way the girl walked out, with her head held just a little higher than before and her shoulders just a bit looser.

If only I could reconcile my own instincts about God's will, and the way the holy book tells me to interpret his rules. If defying the bible is the only way to help people, so help me Lord, I shall continue to do so.

And that was something Sister Stanislaus would tell the priest in her own confession.

CHAPTER 12

Josephine was blissfully unaware of everyone's travails, so occupied was she with much more pleasant possibilities concerning her own future. Valdeterre was a gentle and patient suitor, but he would propose marriage soon. She felt it in the way his eyes lingered when he thought she was not watching. How his thigh touched hers in the narrow carriage, and how he would not move it like he used to on their first rendezvous. He had kissed her good night the last few times when he had dropped her off, always a block away from the convent door to not cause her having to explain herself to the nuns or become the victim of the other women's gossip. His kisses were soft, almost like those of a shy young boy. Nothing like the ones she had experienced before.

Nothing like Michél's... or that man's in Paris...

That Drouot de Valdeterre was not the man who would take without asking, endeared him to her, and it made her long for more.

What kind of lover will he be? Will he become more passionate once we are married?

Thoughts of Michél rose to the surface, and she tried to suppress them, lock them in a far corner of her mind, but her body betrayed her every time she remembered his rough hands on her and his lips on her mouth. She had avoided him ever since that night at the Governor's ball, never venturing past Rue Royale, much less Rue de Bourbon.

The Vicomtesse was strolling along the river her arm intertwined with the Commander's. The weather had turned much more pleasant in the week before Easter. They were to attend an afternoon reception at the Governor's on Sunday after church. These visits to the mansion had become a regular occurrence, and Drouot seemed to have changed his mind about them being just a dreaded work obligation. With her by his side he truly began to enjoy them. Josephine was well versed in making conversation, charming their hosts, and delighting him while he watched her. He looked forward to Easter Sunday. If the ship from France made it on time, his plans for the day would unfold with perfect precision. While he was lost in his thoughts, she had some of her own. Josephine did not doubt his feelings for her. Did he need a little more encouragement? She stopped and faced him with her other arm now resting against his chest. She turned her face up to him, her lips slightly parted. He looked surprised at first, then met her when he felt her getting on her toes to be closer to him. It was the longest he had ever kissed her. And it was the first kiss in the light of day for all passerby to see. She would almost call it passionate if she did not have comparisons. It is progress, she thought.

Easter Sunday might just turn out to be the day...

She was not disappointed. He asked her to walk with him in the beautifully tended gardens of the Governor's mansion. In the hidden cove between the rose bushes, he knelt before her.

"My dear Vicomtesse, *ma chèrie* Josephine..." His shyness overwhelmed him as he cleared his throat for what seemed like an eternity. "I should be so honored if you would grant me your hand in marriage...Will you consider becoming my wife?"

Consider? She tugged her forelock, and giggling, bent to kiss him as he rose and met her halfway. "Oui, Monsieur," she sighed before melting into his embrace. Three years of burdens drained out of her as he put a magnificent emerald on her finger. Set in gold and flanked by tiny rubies on each side that reached to the creases between her fingers, it sparkled in the sun. She stole a look while he kissed her, holding her hand out to the side where the ring hit the light. She would be Madame de Valdeterre neé Vicomtesse de Chavin, wife of the second most powerful man in the colony of La Louisiane and lady of La Nouvelle Orleàns. She would run his household after the most talked about wedding this city had ever seen. She must find a dressmaker who is better than the tailor that everyone else went to. Madame de Bienville would surely know someone. And Margarita had to cook the wedding feast. And she would need to hire a maidservant. But first find a house. Or build a mansion almost as grand as this place they were standing in the middle of.

These were the thoughts in her head while her betrothed was kissing her deeply or trying to. He stopped and stared at her incredulously.

"*Ma chèrie*, what are you thinking of?"

She smiled at him.

I must not let him feel that I am not in this kiss but outside of my body.

"I am so overwhelmed, so excited that I shall become your wife!"

She saw in his relieved smile that he believed her.

"Let us go back to the house and tell everyone!"

She took his hand and not so much led but dragged him off behind her, still holding out her other arm admiring the precious stone as she skipped along the lawn. On the porch surrounded by their guests, the Governor and his wife held court. Madame de Bienville had a wide and knowing smile on her round face as she took one look at Josephine and the man behind her. "Ah, Jean-Baptiste," she said, tugging on her husband's sleeve: "I believe we have to celebrate a happy couple here!"

The Governor barked a "it was about time, Drouot," as he slapped Valdeterre's shoulder, then shook his hand. All the attention was on them for the rest of the afternoon with congratulations pouring over them from all sides, and the ladies oohing over her ring. Josephine basked in the attention.

Finally! I am a personage again, not to be trifled with.

Her world, her stature would be restored, leaving her past but a gilded painting of a forgotten time, more a bad dream than a living memory. Her biggest hope on this bright Easter Sunday was to have the wedding ceremony in this place, this house that so reminded her of the castles of her youth.

Madame de Bienville did not disappoint. She took Josephine aside after what seemed like an endless stream of well-wishers:

"My dearest Vicomtesse, it would be our honor—and yes, I am speaking for my husband without having asked him, mind you, but I know he will not refuse my wish—if we could offer to host your wedding right here in our home."

With a courteous smile Josephine accepted and asked about a dressmaker:

"Oh dear," the Governor's wife replied: "You must order the silks and lace from Paris, of course. I do have a dressmaker right here on the plantation. She is our most treasured slave. I do not share her services with anyone, but under the circumstances and as the Commander is my husband's most trusted man in the entire colony, I shall be happy to make an exception for you."

Josephine voiced her worry that the fabrics for her gown would not arrive in a timely manner. Madame de Bienville waved this off: "You have time. You do not want to get married during the wet and humid summer months. We would not want you to be a sweating bride now, would we? Give the engagement and the wedding preparations six months, until October, when the weather turns cooler and there is no chance of rain," she cautioned.

Josephine had not planned on such a long wait, and the thought of having to remain in her tiny, makeshift room at the convent for another six months filled her with dread, but she had to admit that it might be more sensible. And it would give her time to find a house for them first while she got ready for the ceremony. She told all this to her betrothed on their way back to the city. He listened as all the ideas tumbled out of her. He took her hands in his and described the house he had in mind for them. It would be close to the Place d'Armes, a stone's throw from his office and overlooking the river on one of the best blocks in all La

Nouvelle Orleàns. He did not tell her that he had already acquired the property and had the building plans drawn up. He would surprise her with a drawing once they got back. She could then still make changes before the work on it commenced.

Josephine was giddy when they arrived at the convent. The Commander had insisted on telling the Mother Superior first, considering her the substitute for his fiancé's absent parents. Mother St. Augustin hid her relief at the news.

The first one married off.
She wished them well and quietly sent a prayer to heaven.
Lord, give him the strength to handle her. Bless her with the patience and modesty that are the true virtues of a good wife. And forgive me for not believing that she will hear you.

Out loud she spoke of the sanctity of their union and that she would ask Father de Beaubois himself to conduct a modest ceremony in the church.

Modest? That nun has no idea!
Josephine kept herself from laughing by clutching Valdeterre's arm until the poor man flinched in pain.

"Mother Superior, this is too kind of you, but the Governor and his wife have generously offered the Bienville plantation for our wedding. I was hoping you could ask Father Beaubois to marry us on their beautiful porch where afterwards we shall have the celebration."

The Mother Superior swallowed words of caution of turning a holy union into such a lavish affair. It would be of no use to try to convince this aristocrat to do anything in a small and humble way. "As you wish. We will bring your casquette from the attic for you to inspect your belongings."

As soon as the word casquette was out of her mouth, Josephine hurriedly interrupted her: "I shall not be needing my additional luggage as I am ordering fabric from Paris for my wedding gown. Please let the less fortunate among the girls divide its contents among them. I am all too happy I can do something for them." She ushered her fiancé towards the front door: "And now Mother, you may forgive us. We shall say our goodbyes in private. It was such a long and exciting day for the Commander and me. And we plan on starting the preparations as early as tomorrow, isn't that so, *mon cher*?"

Valdeterre could only nod. As soon as they were outside, she threw her arms around his neck.

God, I hope he did not hear the word casquette!

She kissed him with more passion than ever before. He was surprised but all too happy to reciprocate as much as he was capable of. They agreed to meet at his office in the late morning.

Hovering in a dark corner just above the stairs Florence had heard every word that was said between them and the Abbess.

So, he does not know she is one of us. The poor fool has no idea his mighty Princess future wife is nothing but a Casket Girl...

The news of the betrothal spread through the convent the next day. Most were elated. Not because they wished the Vicomtesse the best but for the fact that there would be an end to her constant demands and complaints. Florence told everyone that Josephine would not be needing her dowry and that it should go to poor Acadia who did not own anything besides the clothes on her back.

I can hardly claim it for myself, better to be charitable.

There were no objections. Florence could not wait for Michél's reaction to the news.

Serves him right. Now he cannot touch his prey. She is out of reach for someone like him.

∽

At Flamand's, Michél Bèranger slammed his fist on the bar so hard that the cups were jumping. He got up to fetch more rum. His brother had a look on his face that was all too easy to read for Florence; Jean was plotting in his head how to best use the connection to the Commander and that it could only be accomplished by finding something to hold over Josephine. That the aristocrat had spent all those nights drinking with them in a seedy bar was hardly enough.

Florence turned to Jean with a wide grin on her face: "You are searching for a way to get to the future Madame de Valdeterre." It was not a question and once again Jean was impressed by her mind. "You need something to blackmail her with and I just might have it." She knew she had his full attention now. "The high and mighty Vicomtesse," she paused for a moment to give her next words even more weight, "is a Casket Girl!"

Now it was Jean's turn to laugh: "I hope you are not saying this merely for our amusement."

"Oh no, it is true. She came over under the same contract as the rest of us. Which means…"

"Which means there is something truly unsavory in her past…" he finished her sentence.

"Why else would an aristocrat be sent to the end of the world?"

They both laughed. Michél's reaction to what he had just overheard was quite different. He retreated to the bar deep in thought. Sadness spread across his face, a rare emotion he seldom shared in public.

She must have seen more darkness than I ever imagined…

For the truth, he admitted to himself, was that he cared about Josephine. It was not just her body he desired. He had felt a strange kinship with her that belied their different stations in life. He remembered the flickers of pain on her face when she thought no one was looking. It all made sense now. And he deeply regretted shooting the footman at the Governor's mansion. Not because he valued the man's life, but because his recklessness was the reason Josephine had avoided him for months. When he returned to the table, his brother and Florence were still laughing and discussing how they could use this juicy secret to their advantage.

This is not right. They should not hold her misfortune against her.

Their laughter reminded him of his childhood on the islands when Jean had made fun of him for standing up for all the weak children, the downtrodden and outcasts that Michél preferred to play with. Whenever someone came after them, they had to deal with him. Michél would stand up for Josephine, too, even against his brother. And even if she married the Commander.

Geneviève LaCour did not give the engagement a moment's thought. She was not surprised because she had seen the couple out on the town a few times and had bigger things on her mind. Montferrat had instructed the workmen and his soldiers not to permit her to come within a block of her house. The Lieutenant had left the city to return to Fort Rosalie and would not respond to her letters, her hopes for some sort of agreement dashed.

Josephine's nuptials come in handy. This will give me an excuse to talk to Montferrat's superior, the Commander himself when I pay him a visit.

Under the pretense of congratulating Valdeterre she gained entry to his office. After pleasantries were exchanged, she asked him for his help in filing a lawsuit. "Could you advise me as to how to put a case together?" she asked.

Valdeterre was astounded: "Madame, what kind of claim?"

"It is a delicate matter, I am afraid, since it unfortunately involves wrongdoing by one of your officers."

He sighed.

Not another one.

He prayed it was not a violent act committed against one of the women again, like the one that had so badly hurt Louise Mariette. He was almost relieved when Geneviève laid out her case. Almost, because the officer in question was high ranking enough to turn this into a difficult fight if the Baronesse insisted on starting proceedings. He did not like the Lieutenant and as his superior could force him to offer her a solution, but that again would lead to a confrontation that Valdeterre tried to avoid: "Madame, what if I were to speak with him?"

Geneviève was intrigued. Like everyone in the city she considered the Commander a weak law enforcement official who let his court handle criminal proceedings and did not involve himself personally in any other disagreements.

"If you believe you can make him honor my deed, please do so by all means. But know this: I shall not give up my house and watch Montferrat move in. He forged the address, and he shall not get away with it."

Valdeterre stopped pacing. "How do you know he forged the address? Do you have proof?"

"Aside from the ridiculous assumption that my brother would have bought property for me that is situated on one of the worst corners of La Nouvelle Orleàns, land surrounded by houses of ill repute that have been there since the beginning? I can assure you, Commander, my brother did his diligence and is well versed with the social lines of this place and the geographical setup of the homes. Aside from all of this, look at the deed." She unrolled the paper on his desk and tapped her finger at the address: "Do you have a magnifying glass, Commander?"

He shook his head.

"Well, I borrowed the Mother Superior's because something did not seem right when I moved my finger over it. And then I saw it; the parchment here is scratched like someone erased this line. And the ink the address is written in is slightly darker than the rest of the document. Not immediately visible to the naked eye but glaringly obvious under the magnifying glass."

Valdeterre studied the deed. Madame LaCour could be right. It did not surprise him. He considered Montferrat a man of shady reputation whose fortunes seemed to have no explainable origin. He sighed: "I shall do my best, Madame."

When Geneviève left the Place d'Armes she was only slightly more hopeful. If the Commander were a strong man, he would order his Lieutenant to return her property and be done with it. But Valdeterre was not that man.

God help him with Josephine! She will run him like a carriage horse.

She marveled at how little she had in common with the Vicomtesse. And how much of a deep connection she felt with a Cuban cook. Back in Paris she had never spent time with anyone outside her class, not because of arrogance like Josephine de Chavin but because of lack of opportunity. She had not experienced the kind of warmth that came with friendship. In France all she had was acquaintances, not friends. Yet Margarita was a friend, and Geneviève had noticed a nice change in her recently.

I hope she finds love with the coffee seller...

~

It was unlike Margarita to steal herself away from the convent. The wounds she was hiding were invisible as were the secrets bound to them. The Widow LaCour had been granted a glimpse, and only because of the unspoken understanding of their shared pains. Margarita was known to others as a simple woman, praised for her skills in the kitchen and relied upon as a calming presence around everyone else's storm. No one suspected the complexity of her heart, the buried hopes, and the hidden wishes. The secret she kept on this day was a sweet one, though. She had finally given in to José Castro's repeated request for a *cita romántica*, a rendezvous. The man was quiet but insistent. He did not seem to care that she was not a young woman. He had gifted her with a flower, a wood carving, a silken handkerchief or some other little token of affection every time she saw him at the market. He exuded a gentleness she had never known in a man. She told herself that she owed him a few hours in a cabarét and a drink or two.

José took Margarita not to one of the taverns that people of color frequented but to his aunt Juana's home, who had a Cuban meal prepared for them before she disappeared in the back. The two of them spent the rest of the evening in deep conversation.

"A terrible drought a decade ago that destroyed the coffee farms was the reason we left Cuba..." He saw her eyes widen at the word 'we'. "There was a storm on our passage... my wife and infant son were swept into the sea..."

She could hear traces of pain in his words but felt his distance to the loss that only time could provide. While her own past was too recent, his wounds had long since transformed into scars, reminders of a tragedy that were in a stage of healing she could not yet imagine for herself. What had brought her across the ocean, he asked.

"Great suffering at the hands of a bad man." The words were out before she realized she had spoken out loud. His eyes took on the sorrowful look of a man who knew pain and hardship. He reached for her hand, but she withdrew and lowered her head. He was wise enough not to push.

"*Lo siento...* I am sorry," he said.

He refilled her glass. They spoke of other things, unimportant ones. The new Choctaw traders that had moved downriver, the nosy woman who sold the rotten fish and the dependency on good weather for José's steady supply of coffee. Harmless pieces of conversation, desperately designed to avoid touching on painful personal matters. He was the perfect *gentilhombre*, a gentleman when he took her back to the convent later, never letting go of her arm until she was safely behind the gates where she leaned against the wall and took a deep breath.

I have never told anyone before...

She trusted José, a man from the same background, but most of all a man who understood a painful past. He made her feel safe. And this was new to her, an unfamiliar place to be, one she had only ever recognized in others, but never attained for herself. When she drifted off to sleep it was a peaceful one.

CHAPTER 13

Spring had turned into summer, and the humidity that came with it lay on the city like a hot, wet blanket. Its steamy weight plunged the brain into haziness and prevented quick movement.

The Governor's wife was so right—one cannot put on a wedding in such torturous heat!

Preparing for one was not much better, Josephine thought, as she walked to the market where, finally, the fabric for her gown had arrived. The breeze from the river provided temporary relief, but it also whipped up the smell from the horse droppings. She crinkled her nose in revulsion at the sour stench permeating from the ground. Soon she would have her own carriage and not be subjected to such disgusting encumbrances. She was about to dab a few of the last drops of her lavender oil under her nose which she had brought with her from Paris, when she felt an arm around her waist.

"Well, hello Josephine!" Florence was skipping down the street, dragging her along. "We must spend more time together again!" Florence babbled in a sing-song tone.

So unlike her, she must need something… This false alacrity is very displeasing.

Josephine disentangled herself: "We have barely spoken for a year, what is it you want?"

Florence laughed. "Oh, I simply miss our fun filled nights at the tavern. And since you will soon move out of the convent, we should really make the best of our remaining time together."

"Given that my days are occupied with preparations, and I need my nights to recover from the pressures and tensions that go into all this, I am sure you understand that I do not have a minute left for frivolous pastimes," Josephine replied coldly.

Florence narrowed her eyes. "I seem to remember how much you enjoyed our frivolous pastimes. And I am sure you would not want your betrothed to find out about just how frivolous they were."

Josephine stood her ground: "Let me assure you, I have confessed all my little sins to my future husband."

Florence laughed: "All of them, really? What about the not so little ones?"

Josephine's cheeks turned a dark color. She pulled Florence behind a market stand: "If I told my fiancé of Michél's upsetting behavior, how well do you think he and his brother would fare? Do you really want the attention of the Commander of the military on the Bèranger brothers and by extension, on you?"

If Florence understood the danger, she was not about to show it. She had one more ace up her not quite clean sleeve: "Ah non, I am not speaking of Michél's dreadful ways. He is a hot-headed brute, a constant threat to Jean's business and mine. I am simply thinking of the similar circumstances that brought both of us here. You and me…"

For a moment, Josephine was not quite certain what the woman was referring to.

What similar circumstances?

"That we were both on the same ship? The Commander knows that I came over on the Gironde."

Florence's smile turned at once cat-like. "Oui, and that we both came carrying the same kind of casquettes…"

This word alone carried within it a threat that was neither veiled nor idle. After almost two decades of Casket Girls arriving in the colony it was no longer believed by anyone that such a girl had the pedigree of a well-to-do and decent family, a noble title and the cushy security of a wealthy father. Too many had turned out to be forçats and women of ill repute. The best a soldier could hope for was a simple country girl like Louise. Josephine was an aristocrat, no one could take that from her. But the casquette would expose her, would be proof that she had been exiled, that her journey was by no means voluntary. Josephine had gone to great lengths to keep this from Valdeterre. She had told him of a family feud and her decision to explore the world before returning to Paris one day. She would not let Florence ruin her carefully constructed future. She hid the trembling in her voice:

"My husband-to-be knows of the colorful company I have kept these past two years in La Nouvelle Orleàns. Of course, I did have to hide from him the backgrounds of certain acquaintances…" She grabbed Florence's dress and pulled it off her shoulder. "Like the fleur de lis that marks you as a forçat from the Salpetriére prison!"

If Florence was surprised that Josephine knew about her branding—after all the mighty Princess had not been present during the altercation with Jeanette—she hid it well. Angrily she pulled her dress back up as the Vicomtesse went on:

"You see, I would not want to cause you or your business any trouble from the head of this city's law enforcement."

Florence saw the tables turned but would be damned if she let her have the last word: "You should make sure our businesses are not interfered with, and that Jean and I can go about it undisturbed, or it will be us creating trouble!" she growled.

When Florence left, Josephine took a long, deep breath. Even a hint of impropriety could threaten her impending nuptials. By now she knew Valdeterre well. He was not just quiet but possessed a hidden strength without which he would have never attained the position he occupied. He was honorable and expected the same from those closest to him. His family's good reputation reached back centuries, and no scandal had ever tainted it. Unlike hers…

The bitterness that crossed Josephine's features over Florence's threats belied a deeper sense of loss. Despite their class difference she had become used to the forçat, enjoyed her wicked sense of humor and their times spent together before the ball. She had missed her this last year. Florence came as close to a friend as Josephine ever had.

∽

At the chapel, Sister Stanislaus suddenly had a revelation while praying for guidance. She hurried to tell the Mother Superior:

"Mother, even though I believe that we are not schooled in being matchmakers, I do understand that the arrangement of marriages for the filles a la casquette is expected of us. I have prayed for an idea that I believe could help." Sister Stanislaus had gotten the Abbess's full attention: "Could we persuade Josephine de Chavin soon to be Madame de Valdeterre to host a gathering at her home after her wedding? A dinner for the Casked Girls perhaps, where she would invite eligible soldiers from the regiment?"

"She may very well resist this idea," the Mother Superior cautioned and was not wrong. When they broached the subject to Josephine, the Vicomtesse deliberately dropped her delicate fan and put her gloved hands on her hips: "I am not even married yet, and you want me to tell my future husband whose house I have not moved into to host an introduction to his men for these…these les petite gens, this lowest class of women?" The idea was not worth another thought as far as Josephine was concerned, but Sister Stanislaus lost her patience for the first time in the two years she had put up with the mighty Princess. When she spoke, it was in the sharp voice of Marie Madeleine Hachard:

"May I remind you that you, too, are a Casket Girl. And while you go to great length to keep this secret from your betrothed, it would behoove you to show a common decency towards those not as fortunate, or shall I say lucky as you to have found a man who will take care of them!"

If the Mother Superior was surprised, the Vicomtesse was downright shocked at the Sister's cutting tone.

Now these nuns are blackmailing me, too?

Josephine stormed out the convent, away from its literal and metaphorical confines to cool off despite the heat outside. She regretted that she had left her fan and decided to ignore the whole conversation. A visit to the dressmaker to look at the progress for her bridal gown made her forget what she considered a preposterous proposition. For the next few weeks, she put all her thoughts into the wedding.

On a glorious day in October the Vicomtesse Josephine de Chavin gave her hand in marriage to Drouot de Valdeterre, Commander of the military. The wedding was officiated by Father de Beaubois, presided over by the Governor, hosted by his wife, Madame Le Moyne de Bienville and attended by all of La Nouvelle Orlèans, so it seemed. It was the social event of the season, and even the uninvited lined the roads leading up to the Governor's plantation. If it had been up to Josephine, none of the les petite gens would have been allowed anywhere near the estate, but alas, it was not for her to decide. Madame de Bienville viewed this wedding as much a political occasion as a social one. Her husband's detractors in Paris had voiced their resistance to an extension of his term, and the ones criticizing his failed measures, such as gaining control over the many pirates inflating the price for goods, the slow development of the city, the ever-present crime and the growing unrest between the surrounding tribes, were becoming louder. Madame de Bienville had no intention to going back to Quebec, after having gotten used to the warm weather. Nor was she prepared to leave the grandiose home they had built. The more people attended this wedding, the better she could show the world the great sense of community and inclusion of all classes of residents.

And so, against the bride's wishes, she had not only invited the aristocracy, high military officers and clergy, but also the merchants, workers' families, craftsmen and all sorts of colorful folk. There was not much Josephine could object to. She was not the one paying for this lavish affair. She had hoped that, at least from the convent, only the Mother Superior, Sister Stanislaus and the Baronesse LaCour would show up, but no. All the nuns came with every single girl and woman in tow who boarded there. Josephine had asked Geneviève if little Pierre could serve as the ring bearer and had to swallow her anger when Geneviève dared to suggest that the young slave Bebé should be among the flower girls, because the Governor's wife had erupted in squeals of delight at this idea. It felt like none of the decisions made for her wedding were Josephine's.

Except for the gown. She relished how it looked on her, perfectly emphasizing her slender yet well-proportioned frame, the feel of the fine silk against her skin and the texture of the delicate lace she had waited so many months and ship arrivals for. The countless fittings with the tailor in the heat of the summer were well worth it, she thought, as she twirled in front of the gilded mirror in the biggest guest bedroom on the estate where she had stayed the week before the wedding day, and where the couple would also spend their first night together. It took four chambermaids to put the elaborate headdress on and two hairdressers to weave the ribbons through her locks and drape the veil. The carpenter's twin daughters had to lift her train as she descended the mansion's grand staircase to the adoring *ooh-la-lahs* of the assembled guests.

As Josephine was led out to the terrace where a canopy had been erected to shield her from the sun, she felt for once like a princess. And as Father de Beaubois performed the ceremony her mind drifted off.

My life just changed. I shall, at long last, get back the respect that is my birthright.

She looked at her groom who was completely entranced in whatever religious encouragements and warnings came out of the priest's mouth, words that were the same at every wedding, preached to every new couple. She paid no attention, thinking instead of the life that awaited her. A life of luxury and adoration. She had no doubt of her new husband's feelings.

This here is a stable, loyal man who admires me so deeply he will never deny me anything.

She was torn from her reverie when the priest got to the part of bearing children. It took all her countenance to refrain from flinching.

I will not put my life in danger. Again…

It was not until Valdeterre nudged her that she realized that they had come to the part where she had to say 'oui'. Josephine forced a smile when she looked into his eyes and was slightly disappointed when he put a chaste kiss on her forehead instead of her lips.

What a proper man I am marrying.

Père de Beaubois blessed the couple, and the crowd erupted in loud cheers. The next hour was a blur of people lining up according to their social status to congratulate them. After the Ursulines had wished them well, the bride feigned weakness to avoid the unimportant, the les petite gens and retreated into the house to ask for a glass of water. She walked to the other side of the mansion toward the front porch to be alone for a moment.

That is when she saw him. He rode straight up to the entrance as if he were an invited guest. Her breath caught somewhere between her stomach and her throat, she clasped onto the railing until her knuckles where white.

Michél Bèranger, the greatest threat to my future, has the audacity to show up on the most important day of my life!

Her shock turning to anger, she spotted two footmen nearby and called out: "Remove this man at once! He is not welcome here!" She pointed to the pirate. "You will be shot if you don't leave!"

Michél heaved himself up right in front of her, not bothering to take the stairs, his face inches from hers before she staggered back. "Afraid someone will kill me?" he mocked her. Then his demeanor softened: "Josephine, I only came to warn you. My brother will..."

He was interrupted and the look on his face changed again, having glimpsed someone behind her. So did his tone: "Madame, my sincerest congratulations. Unfortunately, I must be off." He jumped down, tipped his hat, mounted his horse and rode off. Josephine felt an arm around her waist.

"Who was that, ma chèrie?" Her new husband stood behind her.

"I do not know. A well-wisher, I presume," she whispered with a look of confusion.

He came to warn me. He did so despite of his brother…

Valdeterre stared at the back of the pirate on his horse until he had galloped out of sight. Josephine turned and put her arms around his neck: "I am very hungry. Will you take me to the banquet?"

"Mais oui." He smiled. Inside she regained her composure after drinking two glasses of champagne and eating a few bites of the delicious meats which twenty cooks under Margarita's watchful eye had prepared for the occasion. Josephine chatted with their hosts and exchanged pleasantries with her new husband's officers and their wives. She drank two more glasses, was more than tipsy when her husband asked her to dance and had only a vague recollection of how she got upstairs. When she awoke hours later the moon shone through the window and the shadow of the sycamores cast an eerie web on the white sheets. Although in her undergarments, she was certain Valdeterre had not touched her. She turned to the side to look at him. His eyes were open, and he smiled:

"Feeling better? You had too many toasts with our guests. And not enough food."

She nodded, and he leaned over. His kisses were slow, and when he got on top of her, she was prepared. His clumsiness while removing her garments and his, was endearing. But during his gentle lovemaking her mind wandered. She imagined the passion of another, the pirate's strong arms and the danger in his dark eyes.

Who am I? What kind of woman dreams of another man on her wedding night?

Tears of shame ran down her cheeks as the man on top of her reached his *le petit mort*. Tears that he mistook for the pain of her virginity he thought he had just taken. Caressing her cheek, he pulled her closer and fell asleep soon after while she lay awake for hours.

CHAPTER 14

The good Lord keeps testing our faith, our resolve. Whenever we are assured that everything is going well, there is another trial for our belief, our trust in God's ways.
Marie Madeleine Hachard

In the early hours of Wednesday, the first day of the month of December a lone rider arrived at the military command. His uniform torn, his face and hands blackened and his horse so weak it died on the spot as soon as he dismounted, he bled from a leg wound as he dragged himself upstairs. Barely able to stand before Valdeterre, his wheezing breath interrupting his speech, he stammered: "It is bad, Commander. Most are dead, only a few escaped to the woods… the *sauvages* put the heads of high-ranking officers on stakes."

Valdeterre's worst fears were realized. For days there had been rumors of a Natchez uprising near Fort Rosalie, and he had sent two officers from the garrison up there the night before. He himself had slept at his office, eager for news much to the dismay of his new bride who had to go to a dinner at Madame de Bienville's mansion all by herself. Now he feared for the two soldiers who were riding into a war zone. Relations with the Natchez had been testy for almost a year. The tribal chiefs had complained about getting shortchanged on their goods and that their territory had been encroached on by settlers. Valdeterre had left the negotiations to Lieutenant Montferrat and others. Fort Rosalie was a hundred miles away, too far for him to travel back and forth on a regular basis. It was beyond comprehension how this man standing before him had been able to ride all the way from up there overnight through the treacherous woods and bayous. He helped the man to a chair and called for water and food and the medic to clean his wound.

Over the next day news trickled in slowly but was kept from the citizens of La Nouvelle Orleàns out of fear of a mass panic gripping the city. The nuns were taken by surprise when by week's end, a sauvage, a woman from the Natchez tribe threw herself at the convent's door. Her hair half burnt, her eyes wild with terror, her mouth wide open but not a sound coming out, she fell to the floor grabbing on to the hem of Sister Stanislaus' habit. She was picked up and carried to a bed upstairs. Her feet were bare and raw, the dried blood caked her soles, her torn dress barely covering her body with etched markings all over her back and arms and thorns and twigs sticking to the thin fabric. When Margarita began cleaning her wounds, she thrashed about and knocked the bowl of water from the cook's hands. Acadia, standing a few feet away watched the scene.

Where is Zulimé when we need her? She would know what to do, she would make a salve for healing and brew a concoction to drink for calming.

It did take but a minute until the woman passed out, and Margarita was able to gently wipe the dirt off her, bandage her feet and hands and cover her with a blanket. The Mother Superior sent for the Commander but was told he was managing a crisis and would be unable to come to the convent.

A crisis? So are we!

It was out of character for Mother St. Augustin to lose her even tempered calmness, but no prayer could help in this moment. She sent Sister Stanislaus to the Place d'Armes to speak to Valdeterre. In full Marie Madeleine mode, the nun brushed past the soldier stationed in front of the closed door of the Commander's office. The man was not about to stop a woman of the cloth. Sister Stanislaus opened the door and saw five officers in an emergency meeting with Valdeterre. Without a greeting, she relayed the story of the Natchez woman's arrival and ended with a question: "Commander, what is going on? The young woman looks like she ran all the way from her territory."

Valdeterre scratched his head and shot a look at one of the officers. "Sister, what I am about to say shall be for your ears only and the Mother Superior's." He took a deep breath. No civilian, not even his wife who kept pestering him for information was told this news: "There was an uprising at Fort Rosalie on Monday. The Natchez attacked my men. Between the soldiers and the surrounding settlers more than four hundred were killed. Among them women and children. We only have patches of information as to the tribe's plans. You see why I want to keep this information from spreading before we know more. A panic is to be avoided."

The Sister stared at the men in disbelief. And confusion.

How does the woman fit into all this?

"From the looks of her, her torn clothes and bloodied feet she must have run one hundred miles to the city. She fell asleep before we could ask her what happened."

Another officer, an older man, crinkled his forehead: "Can you describe her? Does she have any tribal signs on her?"

"I would be hard pressed to describe them under all the soot and dirt, but there are markings on her. A few on her arms and back and one on her forehead. Like drawings made from little points made of raised skin that are lined up..."

Sister Stanislaus remembered having seen similar markings on some of the traders at the market.

"On her forehead?" The officer's voice raised alarm. "Is it pointed? Like an arrow?"

The nun narrowed her eyes, trying to conjure the woman's face from her memory: "It looks like a tooth… or rather a fang…"

The officer pursed his lips and blew out the air. The others stared at him, waiting for an explanation. When he spoke, he was looking at the Commander. "Only a female related to a chief would have a marking on her forehead. This one belongs to Inola. The fang of a fox. Because Inola means ‚black fox' in her native language."

Apparently, the other officers all understood the implications of what the officer was telling them, but Sister Stanislaus shook her head in confusion: "Who is Inola?" she asked, looking from one to the other. What they then told her raised more questions than it answered.

On her way back to the convent, the Sister tried to make sense of the information she had just received. Valdeterre had insisted on having the Natchez woman interrogated. Sister Stanislaus had persuaded him and his men to wait until the woman had recovered. When the Sister told the Mother Superior, the older nun agreed with her: "Whoever she is, whatever she has done, our convent is and shall remain a place of refuge. We shall not turn her over to the authorities in her condition."

During the next few weeks more survivors made their way to the city, and a gruesome picture of the attack emerged. The tribal men had entered the fort at dawn but apparently not by climbing the walls. This mystified the military. Fort Rosalie was deemed impenetrable. It had been built to withstand an attack with only one way in—through the main entrance, a heavy wooden door with metal enforcements that when opened caused a noise that would have woken the most drunken soldier. There was a small hidden door on the same side, but only the fort's inhabitants knew about it. So how did the Natchez get in? They killed the guards stationed on top of the wall in all four corners and surprised the soldiers who put up a mighty resistance. In the end, the military men had no chance. Their canons were useless against an enemy already inside their walls. Most of those who fled were captured and killed in the small town next to Fort Rosalie along with all the settlers who could not outrun their perpetrators. The survivors told of burnt homes and scalpings and a frantic determination by the Natchez who did not spare anyone or anything in their path, neither woman nor child.

The fallout of the attack weighed heavy on the Crescent City. The nuns took in thirty-two widows and orphans, turning the dining room into sleeping quarters. There were no beds, no cots, not even enough blankets and the refugees had to sleep on the floor. Classes were disrupted, and the cooks had to come up with the simplest of dishes to feed everyone, a version of stew or red beans and rice.

In her narrow bed upstairs, Inola woke up in so much pain, she opened her mouth with a whimpering cry interrupted by short bursts of breath. Her chest tight, her arms and legs rigid, she could not move. She had lost control of her limbs yet felt the burning wounds, the stinging scrapes as if ants had been poured onto them. She saw that her hands and feet had been wrapped in bleached cotton cloth, and she tried to tear it off with her teeth, but no attempt to lift even as much as a finger yielded any success. When she noticed a shadowy figure in the doorframe under the flickering light of a candle, her moaning turned into a bloodcurdling scream that stopped midair. In her mind she kept screaming but no sound came out.

Acadia slowly walked to the bed and sat down with the candle in her hand. Inola flinched, tried to move to the far end of the cot, her eyes showing a mixture of terror and incomprehension that had taken hold of her features the day it all happened. Acadia raised her other hand and caressed her head. Inola finally let go of the air stuck in her lungs. Her body relaxed a little under the gentle strokes. Acadia sat with her until she fell back into an uneasy slumber and stayed until the candle had burnt down and wax dripped on her hand.

It was almost a week later that the Natchez woman got up for the first time, her feet still bandaged but her hands freed of the cotton wraps. She walked slowly into the dining room. The simple dress Margarita had given her made her itch all over.

I am used to better cloth...

She returned the greeting by the Sisters.

Why are they staring at me? Who told them what I have done?

Margarita put a bowl of beans down and handed her a spoon. She ate, ravenous from days without food. She had refused the plates the Acadian girl had brought up to her bed, had only accepted some milk, unable to swallow, so raw was her throat from screaming at the horror her eyes had seen but her mind could not comprehend.

"Merci..." she said. No one even looked up.

And this is how it continued; she would try to be polite, saying 'bon jour' and 'bon nuit', 'merci' and 's'il vous plait' and get no response as if everyone around her were deaf. But this could not be the reason for their indifference.

They all know, and they hate me for it...

A loud bolt on the front door made everyone jump. Heavy steps on the floorboards echoed closer. Valdeterre walked in with three officers in tow. Two of them roughly pulled Inola from her chair. Beans from her spoon splattered all over her and the floor. Sister Stanislaus stepped in front of Valdeterre: "Commander, please, she is barely healed."

Valdeterre motioned his men to loosen their grip. Inola sank back into the chair, head bowed, hands on her knees.

"We need to take her to command to question her."

The nun put a soothing hand on his arm and led him off to a corner: "Can you not do this here? We shall go to the Mother Superior's office. The woman is more likely to talk here at the convent than at the command, do you not agree?" She whispered.

Valdeterre had to admit that the nun's sensible suggestion was worth considering. Yet after an hour, the officers' frustration turned to anger. Inola had not uttered a word.

Why do they keep asking me the same question over and over? I speak French. Why are they not hearing me?

When the officers again tried to arrest Inola, Sister Stanislaus interfered: "Commander, this convent is a sanctuary for women like her. And she is still wounded."

One officer snorted dismissively: "A sanctuary for criminals?"

"You have no proof for what you are accusing her of."

Another soldier spoke up: "The proof is the heads of our military men on stakes, the burnt bodies of the settlers! What more do we need?"

Valdeterre raised his hand: "Stand down. Give me and the Sister the room and take the Natchez back to the kitchen. Watch her!"

The three soldiers left with Inola. Sister Stanislaus did not wait for Valdeterre to make his case for an arrest: "Commander, what you have told me about the attack on Fort Rosalie, the Mother Superior and I have kept in strict confidence. We are watching the woman for any signs of what you believe to be true, but nothing so far has warranted your suspicions. She has been recuperating from whatever ordeal she has been through. She has not spoken. Not to me, my fellow Sisters or any of the other girls or women. In fact, she does not interact with anyone. Today is the first time she has eaten real food. I cannot let you in good conscience take her to prison without evidence of her supposed crime."

The Commander was not capable of standing his ground with the resolute nun. He did not have evidence, even if nothing but his theory made sense. "I shall give you one fortnight to get her to talk," he finally said. "After that I shall have to take her in. The city demands resolution and satisfaction for the crimes."

Sister Stanislaus breathed a quiet sigh of relief. She had just gained time to get to the bottom of what had bothered her the entire time Inola had been at the convent.

The silent cries of the woman, the wide-open eyes trying to engage whoever was talking to her...

She sensed a secret hidden behind the pain and despair.

I must get her to confide in me...

Back in the kitchen Acadia tried to do the same to no avail. When Sister Stanislaus came back, Acadia asked for a word: "Please bring Zulimé back! She is the only one who can help Inola. I have tried. I have searched my brain for a way to get her to answer me, but I cannot cut through the thickness of the blood underneath the grey fog around her."

The Sister had gotten used to Acadia's colorful way of painting moods and conditions. Hers was a near perfect description. The nun herself had thought of asking the Dominguan girl for help.

It should not be too hard once I mention that she may get the Natchez woman to talk. I shall ask the Commander to make sure the girl is brought here.

～

In the fields of the de Roche plantation, Jacques, the overseer spit globs of chewed tobacco out of his mouth and at the enslaved to amuse himself. His brutality of character showed in his features, the uneven mouth that was fixed in a perpetual frown, and the stinging eyes. He was never without his whip, aiming it at any man, woman or child whom he deemed lazy or not fast enough.

Only when Monsieur was not around, of course.

The overseer resented Zulimé most but could not go against the Master's instructions. The heat and humidity never bothered Zulimé, the fields were green and luscious, and they reminded her of her home, but she did not like roaming through them as she had done so frequently on the island. There was none of the carefree abandon left in her that had made those excursions so joyful at Monsieur Larrác's plantation. Now, when she walked through the fields, the other slaves looked at her with disdain. She was the only one, save for the old cook, not having to participate in plowing, seeding or harvesting. And so, she lived hated by all, not part of any group or class. She was neither field hand nor housemaid, neither slave nor free. She was suspended in a no man's land of not belonging. Her only joy were the Sundays when Monsieur took her with him to the city to attend church, and she could go to some classes while he went about his business or social visits in the afternoon. There was always enough time to spend an hour with Margarita and Acadia and play with Bebé who came flying into her arms when she arrived and hid crying under the stairs when she left. These excursions took all day, and she always dreaded the long week ahead on their carriage ride back to the plantation.

Zulimé was filled with a loneliness she had never experienced before. There was no friendly soul to talk to, no other girls her age, no neighbors. She sang to herself on her walks to the far ends of the property, but her voice was not as full as it had been at the convent and in church, her songs now fragmented pieces of her ancestors, tinged with anguish and isolation.

> *"Under the black trees*
> *Down by the river*
> *The kalfu is waiting,*
> *The kalfu is hungry for my soul,*
> *Ke'-m Pa Sote – but I'm not afraid*
> *Ke'-m Pa Sote – yet I', sad"*

Zulimé treasured the rare occasion when Monsieur was not occupied by his business or too tired to sit down on the porch after she served him dinner. When he invited her to join him, encouraged her to borrow a book from his library and discuss its contents after she finished reading it. It was then and only then that she felt the warmth of another human.

It was on one of the Sunday carriage rides back from the city on a hot July evening that Monsieur de Roche told her of his impending departure: "The first sugar harvest on Saint Domingue is bigger than I expected, the trade with the North is successful, and I am about to leave for the island to buy more slaves."

She flinched at the notion of this.

More people with dead eyes…

CHAPTER 15

Come along, come along, sweet child of the Gods,
Mamán will dry your tears, sweet child of the Gods,
Papá will bring you fruit, sweet child,
Don't cry, little child, don't cry.

Zulimé was singing one of her childhood songs, a sad ballad her Mamán had taught her under her protection tree after de Roche had left. The big oak on the far edge of the plantation had been planted along with twenty-three more many years ago by the first settler who owned this land. He had brought the trees over from a continent called Europe. Many plants had not survived the journey, and he had paid much attention to the ones that had. They had grown large in the past thirty years, their roots extending above ground, offering a comfortable place to sit and enough shade from the sun. Zulimé looked up into the dense canopy that only allowed for a few rays to shine through. Here was her peaceful place, the one she escaped to after she finished the housework. No one ever came here as it was far away from the fields, on the opposite end of the hustle and buzzle of the slave quarters.

Her quiet was interrupted by the sound of a horse's hooves. A rider galloped towards the main house. She got up and ran over. Any disruption from the daily monotony was welcomed. The rider jumped off, tied his horse to a post and walked in. His footsteps roused Cecile who seemed to spend more and more time sleeping on the old chaiselongue in the hallway.

"Urgent order from Commander Valdeterre!" the soldier bellowed.

"Master is not here…"

"No matter, I am to take the slave Zulimé to the Ursuline convent at once."

Zulimé, hiding behind the entrance, straightened her spine, raised her head and stepped into the hallway: "*Je suis* Zulimé,"

"Get on my horse and hold on," the man ordered.

Cecile put up a hand: "But she cannot leave the plantation without the overseer's permission."

The soldier waved her off: "She is to do as the Commander says. These are my orders."

He helped Zulimé into the saddle behind him. She had never been on a horse, and frankly, these animals frightened her, but her elation at being taken back to the convent and the people whom she loved, overcame her fear. She held on to the soldier as they galloped down the road.

Time flew by as did the cypresses while they passed over creeks and across the bayous towards La Nouvelle Orleàns. It took her a while to get used to the shaking and the uncomfortable way of sitting, but soon she became one with the horse's movement. When they entered the city, the soldier slowed to a trot. Zulimé let go of him and held onto the back of the saddle instead. She noticed the strange looks from the people on the street. She even thought she caught a glimpse of mighty Princess Josephine, now married to the Commander.

I wonder if it was her who sent for me…

She dismissed the thought. She did not care. As long as she could get away from the plantation. She was sure that Monsieur would not mind her being summoned to the convent.

I just pray he is back before I am…

She feared the overseer's wrath once he got wind of her leaving.

"Get off."

Zulimé had been so lost in thought she had not realized they had arrived. The soldier walked her to the open door where classes had just ended, and the girls who were not boarders spilled out. She slowly made her way in adjusting her eyes to the darkness. She had missed the smell of the wooden floor mixed with Margarita's fragrant cooking from the kitchen down the hallway. She breathed in the delicious scents. There was delighted squealing from her friends, curious looks from all the new boarders, a big hug from Margarita. And one excited yelp from Bebé who pushed the chair she had sat on aside and ran to her. She found herself immersed in the biggest embrace by all who had missed her. Sister Stanislaus' entrance caused them to slowly let go of her.

"Thank you for coming" the Sister said.

Zulimé had forgotten the politeness, the class-less manner in which life was conducted at the Ursulines'. Here she was equal to all and beneath no other. A human to be respected and heard, not property, pushed aside, mistreated or, at best, ignored. Margarita served her a bowl of rice and beans, and she ate the simple yet delicious dish while her curiosity got the better of her: "Why did the Commander send for me?" she asked.

"It was not the Commander, it was the Mother Superior and me," the Sister explained. "Finish your food, then come to Mother St. Augustin's office, s'il vous plait."

By the time Zulimé was done eating, she already knew the reason she had been summoned. Acadia had whispered the whole story in her ear. Still, she listened intently to the nuns and wondered what to make of this information. She had been unaware of the Natchez attack, so far removed from life outside the plantation now that Monsieur was traveling. The nuns had only conveyed the utmost necessary, leaving out the most important part, the one only they knew, but Zulimé sensed that there was more to their story.

"We only have one week until the Commander arrests her, unless we get her to speak for herself," the Mother Superior said.

When Zulimé left the Abbess' office with Sister Stanislaus, she saw other refugees, victims of the attack, all the grief-stricken figures wandering the halls with their dead eyes who were in dire need of ailment for body and soul.

Sister Stanislaus watched her and cautioned: "Your banishment is not over, but for a month or so, until they move out of the convent, we also need you to brew healing concoctions and do whatever it is you do to make these poor people better."

If Zulimé would have known what irony was, she could have put a word to her feelings.

Now they want me to do what they punished me for. Now my spells are needed.

Mostly, she was overjoyed and filled with gratitude towards the nuns.

The irony of having to call on the Dominguan girl to mend the sick while the Mother Superior kept refusing to open a proper hospital did not escape Sister Stanislaus.

Better make sure the good Père de Beaubois never finds out who is healing the poor victims of Natchez...

~

Inola retreated as soon as she saw Zulimé go near her bed. Acadia took her hand and pulled her closer. "This is my friend," she said in a soothing voice. "She can help you; she has magical powers."

I need no help, I only need you all to listen to me, not dismiss me as soon as I open my mouth!

Inola felt like yelling. She formed the words; she said them out loud but recognized no understanding in the two girls' eyes.

Je parle français!

Zulimé put her fingers on Inola's lips. The Natchez woman bit her, drawing a droplet of blood. Yet instead of retreating, Zulimé wiped it off and took Inola's head between her hands, staring into her wild eyes, trying to read what was behind them.

"She cannot cut through the thick grey fog and there is blood under it," Acadia stated. Zulimé let go of Inola and turned to her friend:

"You are right. She is possessed by a spirit that we must drive out of her. But first we need to make her breathe without fear." She got up and went downstairs and began brewing a tea. It took three days until Acadia proclaimed what Zulimé felt: "The fog is lifting! But the redness is still strong."

The woman did not retreat any longer, instead her pain was raw. She still refused to speak. Or did she? Zulimé had spent hours watching her. There was an urgency in Inola, she moved fast from one end of the room to the other, waving her arms, making signs with her hands, opening her mouth.

I must help this poor soul. I must solve this mystery. And maybe if I do, the Sisters will let me stay…

Zulimé dismissed the selfish part of her thought. Her grandmother had taught her to never use her power based on a condition. But she could hope. And then it came to her as she again watched Inola's face.

She wants to speak! She is trying to tell us!

Zulimé bolted downstairs. Without knocking she burst into the Mother Superior's office: "Inola is mute! She has lost her speech because of a terrible demon… thing… situation… that happened to her…"

Mother St. Augustin looked at Sister Stanislaus.

This all makes sense. She turned mute because of the atrocities she witnessed. Given what we know, yes, it made sense.

"She thinks she can speak. She does not understand why we won't hear her. Her mouth forms the words without a sound." Zulimé anticipated the question before it was asked: "And I think I can help find her voice."

"What do you need from us?" The Mother Superior was matter of fact.

"Time," said Zulimé.

Sister Stanislaus shook her head in frustration. "The only thing we do not have."

"The trees would help, the grass, the river… she must watch peaceful things that God created. Water that moves, windswept flowers… all that may make her find the words much faster."

The Mother Superior was not convinced: "If the Commander finds out we let out his prisoner…"

Sister Stanislaus opened the door for her to leave the room, and Zulimé knew the reason. Her favorite nun would now have to convince Mother St. Augustin. And make it possible for her to stay and do the work she loved most, her magic.

Valdeterre was not happy when Sister Stanislaus begged him for more time with the Natchez woman. Pressure was mounting to find the culprit for a massacre that had cost more than two hundred of his men and countless civilians their lives. He needed a show trial to put the proverbial head on the stake to calm the citizens and his own military. The sooner this happened the better. The fair judge in him would have preferred to investigate thoroughly, but it was too dangerous to send more men to Fort Rosalie. He agreed to give the Ursulines one more week. Zulimé was disappointed, she had hoped to spend Christmas at the convent after which Monsieur would certainly be back.

Mother St. Augustin permitted Acadia and Zulimé to venture to the meadows upriver, but she instructed Sister Stanislaus and one of the workmen to accompany them. What the nun knew about Valdeterre's suspicion made her cautious of underestimating the Natchez woman.

On the fourth day after Zulimé had been chanting the vodou words for peace, calm and unblocking the sun point of the throat, the breakthrough happened. It started with a whisper. No one understood the words for Inola spoke in her native tongue, but she spoke. When the sounds grew louder, and she held on to Acadia's hand and they locked eyes, a deep moaning rose from her insides. Inola let go of Acadia's hand and put hers before her face, then stretched them towards the sky and raised her face to the sun. Tears were streaming down, and her words changed to French: "Forgive me, my love, forgive me, my love…"

The others stood, mesmerized, as she continued: "I did not mean to take your spirit…" She turned to the group: "I did not mean to take anyone's spirit."

Zulimé touched her arm, and Sister Stanislaus said: "You will have to tell this—all of it—to the Mother Superior."

The Sister led them back to the convent marveling at what Zulimé had accomplished. In her heart, she regarded the Dominguan's chanting as just another form of prayer while her mind told her that this kind of paganism was to be condemned by a Catholic nun. What mattered now was that it yielded results.

I want the Mother Superior to hear the woman's story before she is turned over to the Commander.

Inola refused to divulge more than she had, only repeating her cries for forgiveness. Questions from the Mother Superior, Sister Stanislaus or any of the girls remained unanswered. Once Valdeterre was informed that she had regained her speech, he had her picked up and taken to prison. She did not go quietly. The officers had to restrain her after she scratched their faces and lashed out at them. And then she stopped speaking completely, this time out of her own accord. The Commander set a trial date for the first month after the holiday, January of 1730.

∼

The convent had gotten so crammed with refugees from the uprising that Geneviève could not wait for the day when she was able to move herself and her children to their new house. Unlike everyone else she was not gloomy, quite the contrary. The one good thing that had come out of the attack? That devil Montferrat was one of the high-ranking officers whose heads had ended up on a stake, his smirk forever frozen, his mean-spirited tongue forever silenced. He had no heirs, no family to speak of, and the Baronesse was certain that this was her gain. She had already spoken to Valdeterre, since she feared that the *greffier*, the royal notary, would put Montferrat's property up for public auction. The *crieur*, the town crier, would shout out the announcement at every intersection of the city and post it on three consecutive Sundays on the front door of the church at the end of high mass: a very efficient way of attracting prospective bidders.

This needs to be avoided at all costs.

Geneviève need not have worried. The Commander was dealing with much bigger problems than to argue over her sly suggestion to dismiss the court case, and with one stroke of his pen he signed the *la dite sentence arbitralle*, the said judgment of possession, and the property reverted to her. It was now just a matter of time until the work on her house was finished.

My house. It is really mine now. And not just this one.

She had every intention of taking possession of Montferrat's, too, since the original deed had been halved. The foreman working on the building had found the Lieutenant's part of the deed and—for a sizeable sum of her gold coins—had willingly handed it over.

Zulimé begged Sister Stanislaus to allow for an extension over the Christmas holiday, but it was not to be. She was sent back to the de Roche plantation in anticipation of her owner's return. The closer she got to the house the more she was gripped by fear.

Acadia would say a thick, dark rock is laying on top of my heart.

When she walked in, the look on Cecile's face confirmed her worst thoughts: "You better have a real good explanation for your absence, girl," Cecile told her: "You lucky the bastard is already asleep with all the rum he drank."

Zulimé did not have to ask whom Cecile meant by 'the bastard'. It was Jacques, the overseer's unofficial title. She went to bed quietly but was forcefully torn from her sleep when Jacques stomped into her room, yanked her from the bed by her hair and dragged her outside. It was not dawn yet.

"You think, you can disappear for weeks and we'll all just be smiling? I'll show you what happens to dirty slaves when they try to run away!"

He took a long chain and tied her to a post in the middle of the slave quarters. No protestations, no mention of the nuns, the officers or anything else would calm the man down. The slaves woke up from his loud yelling. He took the whip conveniently hanging from the wooden rafter as a constant reminder for the slaves and ripped Zulimé's dress from the back, top to bottom that her body was completely exposed. He raised his arm, then stopped for a second admiring her backside with a leering desire clouding his eyes.

When the lashes began, Zulimé retreated into a place deep within her, yet so far from this land it might have been a thousand stars away. She would not scream. She would not close her eyes. What she saw was men and women who stood in the doorframes of their huts, half hidden in the shadows. None stepped forward. None spoke up. None dared to defy her torturer out of fear they would be next. And she saw something else. A satisfaction that it was her, their owner's favorite, the one who did not have to work in the fields. The one who did not belong. Only Touton, the biggest and kindest of them made a move toward her as if he wanted to help but was held back by the others.

Zulimé did not count the lashes and could not remember when she lost consciousness. When she came to, she was on her stomach on a bench. The sun was burning down on her, and she smelled the overseer before she could hear him: "Tonight, I'll bend you in other ways. You better be at my house at dusk. And don't worry about your back. I'll have you on your knees."

His tongue licked her ear, and it took her last strength to raise her head and spit into his face. He slammed his fist down on her. She passed out again. It was afternoon when the pain woke her. She found herself on the chaiselongue in the big house. Touton must have carried her there, she thought. Cecile was too weak for that, and she doubted any of the other slaves would have helped. She knew what would stop her body's pain, had the remedy in her head, but who would collect the herbs, who would make an ointment?

"Cecile…" she moaned.

The woman shuffled over from the kitchen: "I warned you what would happen. I did." The cook sounded as if she were looking for redemption.

"It is not your fault…"

She needed to convince Cecile to find some chamomile. She knew there was a basket in the kitchen for when Monsieur wanted tea.

"I cleaned your wounds," the old woman said.

"Merci… please brew me some tea and let it cool. Then soak a cotton cloth and put it on my back…"

Cecile went to the kitchen. Zulimé slowly got up. Every movement hurt, but she needed to find a hideaway.

I will not have the bastard touch me.

After revisiting every spot on the plantation in her mind, she realized that there was only one safe place, right here in this house. Everywhere else she was in danger of being found. When Zulimé heard Cecile snoring just as the sun set, she walked upstairs careful to avoid the creaking boards on the stairs and opened the door to the Master's sleeping suite. From the Master's dressing room, she heard Jacques enter the house a short while later, angrily yelling for her, waking Cecile, threatening her with a beating. Cecile was afraid but stood her ground.

That bastard would not hurt an old woman!

Zulimé hid between de Roche's overcoats. The yelling stopped, but she stayed hidden breathing in the faint tobacco smell emanating from the clothes. Monsieur's scent was strangely comforting. She got lost in thought for a moment until heavy footsteps on the stairs made her heart clench.

He could not! He would not dare come upstairs… would he? Defy Monsieur and enter his private rooms?

She stopped breathing when the door opened, and the footsteps came closer, then sank to the floor with a whimper. She felt herself lifted and carried to the settee. De Roche cradled her in his arms until he heard her crying out in pain. He let go and saw her bloodied dress, held together by the pin Cecile had put there, covering the chamomile-drenched cloth. She flinched when he took out the pin and removed the wet rag.

"Merde!" He exclaimed. "Who did this to you?"

"The overseer…" she whispered.

De Roche wanted to jump up and go after the man he had entrusted his household, his fields, his plantation and his workers to. But the girl clutched the lapels of his coat, her head buried in the fabric. He could not leave her like this, nor did he want to. He caressed her hair and her arms, the only parts of her that were not raw from the wounds. She breathed in his smell, so comforting, so strong it felt like a safe place. His mind was racing while he held her, a thousand angry thoughts on how to avenge her, wrestling with a few coherent plans on taking the overseer to prison and seeing him convicted of violations against the *code noir*.

He never stopped soothing her while he juggled the options in his head until he felt her letting go. She had drifted into sleep. He carefully placed her head on the settee, lifted her legs up and made sure she lay on her side, the torn skin not touching anything that would cause her more pain. He left the room quietly and went downstairs where he instructed Cecile to watch her and clean and bandage her back. The barely contained anger made his voice shake. He bolted out the door, ripping the riding crop off his saddle as he passed his horse. His determined stride made Jacques jump up from the bench in front of his house. The man dropped his rum cup: "That woman ran away for three weeks, I had to make sure the others were not getting any ideas in their heads about doing the same."

The overseer could not finish as the crop came down and tore his cheek. He cursed as de Roche lifted his arm for a second strike, then halted in midair: "Is this how she screamed? Is this how she bled?"

De Roche's words echoed through the night and could be heard all the way to the slave quarters. He felt a rage he had not known in himself.

I must get ahold of myself.

He lowered the crop and called for his two strongest men: "Antoine! Touton! Take this man to the barn, tie his hands and feet and chain him to the beam. And watch him until morning. He is not to get away."

Let the authorities deal with him.

All the way down to La Nouvelle Orleàns, Jacques tried to barter with his employer; he was only doing what he was hired to do, he was only trying to keep the plantation running. The slave girl thought she was better than the others. It was when he brought up Zulimé that de Roche lost his last ounce of hard-fought patience: "You whipped this young woman until her body gave out! You shall be prosecuted under the full extent of the law! I shall make sure of that!"

The man sneered: "No one has ever been thrown in jail for keeping some dirty slave under control."

It was exactly what the Commander told de Roche in legal language a short while later, when the merchant dropped the overseer at military headquarters: "I do understand your anger, Monsieur de Roche. Like you I abhor this kind of violence and do not believe that slaves and servants become better and more loyal workers by being beaten. But although the *code noir* is law, no one has ever brought a court case against a violator. I shall be hard pressed to find a judge or an advocate to take it on. Are you certain this is what you want?"

De Roche did not hesitate: "Oui, Commander. And if my case serves as a warning, a precedent if you will, so be it."

Valdeterre was cautious. "Was the slave otherwise... violated... by your overseer?"

De Roche swallowed hard. It was the one question that had plagued him since last night. The one question he had not been able to ask Zulimé. "I cannot be sure..."

"What is the overseer's reasoning for the beating?" Valdeterre asked.

"He says she disappeared for three weeks."

"And returned to your plantation of her own free will? Runaways don't come back." Valdeterre stopped suddenly: "Monsieur, what is the slave's name?" De Roche's answer confirmed the Commander's suspicion: "Zulimé was ordered by me to help with a situation at the Ursuline convent. In your absence, your overseer was supposed to be informed of this when I sent an officer to your plantation to pick her up. The man could not talk to him for he was passed out drunk."

De Roche's anger only increased when he heard this: "I want him prosecuted. I want him rotting in a cell for the rest of his miserable life. Hanged, if that is what the judge decides."

Valdeterre knew he would not be able to deter the merchant from seeking prosecution, no more than he had known the Baronesse could not be dissuaded from suing Montferrat. When that case went away in the wake of the Natchez massacre and the death of his Lieutenant, whom he had not shed a tear over, he was relieved. And now there was another court drama that had landed at his door. He liked de Roche. The Creole was a noble man who stood up for what was right. And this was why he felt compelled to warn him: "The *code noir* lays responsibility of its enforcement on the slave owner, not the employee hired by such. Given that you were on an overseas journey, a judge may absolve you of this responsibility. Do you have proof that you left the overseer in charge?"

De Roche shrugged his shoulders: "Who else would I have entrusted with running my plantation?"

"It will take more than your word to win this. Is the slave prepared to testify?"

"Non!" De Roche's answer came fast and loud. He took a deep breath: "I shall testify on her behalf."

Valdeterre shook his head: "You cannot testify, you are not a witness to the crime." He could relate to the man's frustration: "This girl, Zulimé is important to you. I can see why. She is quite something. A bright mind and more sense than one could expect from an islander. But still... why hedge your bets? If you are held responsible for what transpired on your property, it is you who might go to jail."

"Commander, I am prepared to take this risk."

Before the merchant left the city, he went to the market to buy silk cloth. And he had one more stop to make. What he proposed to the Mother Superior took some convincing on his part, but after an hour they had made an agreement. Just before he left, the Cuban cook asked him for a word. Margarita had unwittingly heard what he had told Mother St. Augustin about Zulimé. She handed de Roche four bundles of herbs wrapped in cotton and gave him instructions on how to use them: "Zulimé has healed a lot of poor souls here at the convent and taught some of us how to brew these. May her own cures now heal her." She made the sign of the cross.

Henry de Roche left the convent relieved and much calmer than he had been in the last twenty-four hours. On his way back to his plantation, he could think of nothing but how to ease Zulimé's pain. And finally admitted to himself the depth of his feelings.

Zulimé drifted in and out of sleep, no position was comfortable. Cecile had helped her to a narrow daybed in the backroom behind the kitchen. The young woman's wounds were still burning. It was dark outside when she felt a presence in the tiny room. She flinched, then relaxed. It was

Monsieur. He lit a small candle, and she could see the concern in his eyes. "You are burning up. The Ursuline's cook, Margarita is her name, I believe, she gave me some herbs for you. If you tell me how to prepare them, I can put them on your wounds."

The thought of Monsieur brewing something in the kitchen made her smile despite the pain. "Are some of them leaves?" she asked.

"I believe so."

"Soak them in water for a while, then put them on me. And take equal parts of the others and cook them on the fire until morning. I must drink the liquid as soon as possible, but it must stew until the sun comes up."

She wanted to teach him the secret vodou words to say while he put them in the pot but thought better of it. She had to say them to herself in her mind while he did as she had instructed.

～

A week went by. Days of solitude and healing. Zulimé slept through most of it. In her waking hours, she had come to enjoy Monsieur's visits. He would not let Cecile take over the changing of the bandages and application of the leaves. He held her hand when the stinging made her moan until she told him that this was how she knew the herbs were working. She had no appetite but forced herself to eat the soups that Cecile brought her. She missed Christmas, having lost track of the days. One evening at the turn of the year, she got up for the first time since the whipping. She followed the smoke from Monsieur's pipe and found him on the front porch. He was looking out at the rose-colored sunset coming through streaks between the clouds. The crickets made loud sounds down below, and the fireflies were dancing in the darkness of the bushes behind them. She had not found her voice yet to sing again but in this moment, there was song back in her heart. He must have felt her presence for he turned around. He put down his pipe. What she saw in his eyes was unfamiliar yet spellbinding, and she took a step towards him. He put his hands on both sides of her head, gently.

The crickets grew quiet, and the fireflies stopped dancing, suspended in the night sky like tiny stars. She felt his lips on her forehead, then on her lids as she closed her eyes. His mouth slowly moved to the tender place behind her ear. She could not remember her arms moving upwards, but there they were, around his neck, pulling him close as his own drew her in, on her waist, careful to avoid her still healing flesh. She opened her eyes when his lips were on hers, in a kiss that would not end. When he did let go, one hand was on her cheek, the other rested lightly on the small of her back. None of them wanted to break the touch.

"I have made arrangements with the Mother Superior," he said, "you will go back to the convent until I have sorted out what to do with you. Until I have hired a better man to run this place during my travels."

I should be delighted to go back to the Ursulines, but after this kiss...

He saw her mixed emotions. I want you to be safe. I need you to be safe, *mon amour*."

It was these words that echoed in her heart for the days, weeks and months to come when she was happily back with her friends, and her dreams were free from demons for the first time since she had set foot on this land.

CHAPTER 16

Josephine Valdeterre neé de Chavin thoroughly enjoyed her new status as the well-respected wife of the Commander of the military. When she walked through the city with her head held high, she never tired of the gentlemen tipping their hats and the ladies' shy greeting when she rushed past. So regal was her walk that some almost curtsied before her. The way people treated her brought back memories of her youth in Paris. She had barely noticed the reverence of the people around her then but taken for granted that she was the princess of the ball, any ball. She was aware of it now and found herself going on walks without aim simply to revel in everyone's adoration. One afternoon she ventured over to Rue Bourbon, carefully lifting her skirts to avoid getting the hems muddy and dirty. While city officials had planks put on the streets in the well-to-do parts, there were still no more than dirt roads north of Rue Royale. Yet it seemed to her that the amount of respect grew with the amount of the mud. Artisans and workers, indentured servants and even the les petite gens went out of their way to make room for her. If she would have looked closely at their faces, she might have discovered the hint of disdain and resentment for the high and mighty lady beneath the forced kowtowing. But she never did.

One day as she turned the corner on Rue Toulouse, she noticed a woman bellowing orders to two workmen pushing barrels through the door of a tavern. She could not make out the woman's face, but she would have recognized her voice anywhere. Josephine stopped and watched as Florence commanded the men, being completely in charge. And for the first time since her wedding day an unsettling feeling took hold. Seeing Florence full of purpose was in stark contrast to her own life of leisure. She tripped over a piece of wood left on the street and would have fallen down face first, had there not been a man to catch her. She barely thanked him while shaking herself off and hurrying back towards the better side of the city. Safely home and sitting down on the slanted chaiselongue in her boudoir, she finally admitted to herself the boredom and restlessness that had overtaken her.

Josephine did not dare to admit it, but she longed for Florence's company because she had no friends to speak of and no exciting acquaintances save for Madame de Bienville. She attended a few soirées at some of the officers' homes but found no common ground with their wives. Most were much older than her and some were of questionable lineage in her opinion. Her husband had chided her when she had treated them with condescension. They had their first fight over his long work hours, her insisting that he take her to dinner at least three times a week and him growing impatient when she refused to understand the demands of his position.

"What do you expect of me? Sit around and do needlepoint all day?" she yelled.

Josephine pressed him on government matters and became angry when he explained to her why he could not divulge anything that related to his work. Their lovemaking was too infrequent to provide relief for either of them and too unskilled on his part to give her satisfaction. She was aware of his wish for children, but the thought of spending her days by herself with a screaming *bebé* made her uneasy.

It was in one of these moods that she wandered the streets one afternoon, conjuring old images from her beloved Paris that grew more magical in her mind the longer she was gone. She walked without a destination and suddenly found herself in front of Flamand's. The tavern looked different. The sign was tattered, and the place looked dirtier than she remembered. As she contemplated on whether to go inside, she heard screaming and recognized familiar voices:

"You will not get my hard-earned money, you wretched wench!"

Josephine saw Florence pinned against the wall by two of Flamand's employees. The sleazy bar owner was yelling at her. Florence struggled to breathe with one of the men's arms against her throat. Josephine, never one to interfere in physical altercations, nevertheless stepped forward and planted herself in front of Flamand. Taller than him, she looked down: "You will have to answer to Jean and Michél Bèranger for this. Why not just pay her and avoid their fury?"

Flamand was loath to give in to a woman, but this aristocrat had always made him uncomfortable. He waved to the men who let go of Florence who shook herself off and stepped right up to the bar owner who pulled a handful of coins from his pocket. She counted them.

"You owe 180.-, this is not even half."

"I don't make enough to pay your exorbitant fees!"

Florence looked around: "Clean up this stink-hole, maybe that will entice more customers to drink here. It's our good rum that keeps you in business not your hospitality. I give you one more week to come up with the full amount."

Flamand mumbled a curse but walked away. Florence turned to Josephine: "Well, well, look what the cat dragged over. You must be lost. The Commander's wife on the wrong side of the tracks."

Florence's words belied her shakiness after the encounter. Josephine wanted to reply sharply but thought otherwise.

"A simple 'merci' for helping you would have been nice… And I am not lost. I wanted to see you."

The words were out before she could stop them. It was the most honest Josephine had been in a long time. She had missed her crazy outings with the forçat, missed the excitement of sneaking in and out of the convent. And despite the woman's scheming, the unpleasantness surrounding her dealings with the Bèrangers, Josephine would welcome any of their adventures to disrupt the predictability of her current life. She registered surprise on Florence's face who asked:

"What do you want from me?"

Josephine managed a smile: "A cup of eau de vie. An hour of pleasant conversation?"

Florence laughed: "You are a bit overdressed for this hole, don't you think? Not even I would be caught drinking in this place. Not anymore. I only come here to collect Flamand's protection money. Every time Jean is out of town, I am forced to deal with the same refusal from that weasel. And because he is such a little rat, he sets his bloodhounds on me, because he knows I'd win any fight with him. He only feels like a man when Jean is not here. I am so sick of needing the protection of a man!"

She would have gone on, but Josephine steered her toward the door: "Let us find another tavern."

Florence nodded: "There are much better *etablissements* around the corner from here. Not that you would know."

"Show me."

Josephine linked her arm under Florence's.

"You are serious about this." Florence shrugged her shoulders and led Josephine down the street to Paramour, a cabarét that was brightened up not by its grandeur but by the ladies that justified its name.

"Yes, they are for hire," she answered Josephine's unspoken question, "but at least here the glasses are clean, and the tables are wiped. Two cups of eau de vie, s'il vous plait!" she shouted at the bartender. "So, how is high society life?"

"Oh, it is *magnifique*. As you know my husband is very connected, and we spend all our free time with soirées and balls."

Florence narrowed her eyes: "You are bored out of your prettily coiffed head."

Josephine wanted to object but changed the conversation instead:

"Judging from that little incident back there, you are still in business with Jean."

Florence laughed. "And you should see the money under my mattress. So to speak. Of course, I don't keep it under my mattress."

"Ah, and is that mattress still at the convent?"

Florence's grin froze. This was a sore subject. "Not for very much longer. I made enough to afford a *garconniere* on Rue St. Louis." She stopped talking for a moment, sizing up her vis-à-vis. "Two cups of rum, and you have not asked about Michél…"

Josephine blushed. "Why would I care about him? I am a married woman."

Florence laughed. "Sure. Well, let me tell you, Michél certainly cares about you. He has not stopped talking about you."

As much as this was an exaggeration, it had the desired effect. For a blink of an eye Josephine showed pleasant surprise before her eyes clouded over, and she waved it off: "And I am certain he is busy committing crimes and consorting with harlots."

Florence waited before she answered: "I don't know about his business outside of what he does with his brother, but he does have a girl."

The flash of jealousy disappeared as fast as Josephine could get control of herself. But it was there, and Florence noted it with a satisfaction she was almost ashamed of.

I did miss the mighty Princess.

～

Two more cups of rum later Josephine staggered home, filled with a mixture of excitement over having spent the first memorable evening in months and at the same time an unease about the man who could still arouse such strong feelings in her. Her husband awaited, having come home hours earlier. She was forced to explain the smell of alcohol on her breath: "I spent time with an old friend from the convent. We had too much champagne, I am afraid. I shall retire early."

He looked at her with suspicion: "Early? Early was when I got home with plans to take my wife to one of the new cabaréts on the river."

"Ah, pardon, mon cher. Why did you not tell me this morning? We could have made plans. Now I am too tired, having spent hours talking to my friend."

"What friend?"

"Louise Mariette," she said hastily.

"Really? Is she doing better now?"

"Oui, oui, she is fine."

She could tell that he did not believe her.

Why could I not have said that I went out with the Baronesse? It would have made much more sense.

Valdeterre decided not to press the matter. He did not want another argument.

Josephine began seeing Florence regularly, dressing down when she went to Rue Bourbon for their meetings and careful not to be seen by any of the society ladies. She heard gossip from the convent and pieces of information about the Bèrangers and their trades. Florence did not mention Michél again, only saying that the brothers were at sea which put Josephine at ease about going to the taverns the two men controlled and would frequent if they were back in the city. The forçat had her own reasons for furthering contact between them.

"Rumor has it that the Governor has new ideas about an additional tax… Is this true?" she asked.

"What are you talking about?"

"A new tax on everything to be imposed on all goods that do not come from France. Which would cost other merchants considerably."

"Other merchants? You mean pirates and smugglers. You mean Jean," Josephine said with a smirk.

Florence raised her voice: "Don't you see that this tax would ruin my business, too?"

"I can see that it would deter pirates from finding customers once they are forced to raise their prices. A pretty clever measure, I must say."

"Clever? Sinister is what it is! Everyone affected would struggle to make deals, all the while being kept out of the prison cells that are now needed for the perpetrators of the Natchez uprising!"

Josephine's brow furrowed. "In other words, the city would profit from piracy without having to spend one *livré* on housing the criminals. But why are you telling me about your concerns?"

Florence looked at her incredulously: "Because you are the wife of the second most powerful man in the city and must know what's going on."

"My husband does not share governmental issues with me. And I have no interest in politics."

Florence was visibly disappointed. She went to the convent's attic to count the ever-growing amount of gold coins, a favorite pastime of hers. The sound of her foot on a creaking floorboard woke Acadia, and she had to make up a story of strange noises to explain why she was up there. She was waiting for Acadia's curiosity to get the better of her: "Is someone trapped in the attic?"

"Oui," Florence replied, "but it is not a being of flesh and blood..."

Acadia's hand flew to her mouth, her eyes widened: "A ghost?"

"Or more than one..."

Florence let the words hang in the air. She had complete faith in Acadia's inability to keep the ghost story to herself.

This will prevent them all from searching the attic and my treasures.

Sure enough, Acadia spread the story all over the convent the next morning. With every mention the number of ghosts increased, and discussion on whether they were male or female, dominated every conversation. Madame LaCour was the only one who laughed at it and warned them about frightening little Pierre and Delphine with their silly tales. Margarita, who believed in the dead, the undead and spirits of all kinds but doubted their existence under the convent's roof had forbidden any mention in her kitchen and the dining room. "Or I will tell Mother St. Augustin about it," she threatened.

Florence could not have been more pleased with herself.

My money is safe until it is time for me to move out of this house. Soon...

A few days later Florence decided to surprise Josephine. They were trading gossip at Paramour when the Bèrangers walked in. Josephine turned pale at the site of them. Her first instinct was to flee. Her second was the result of locking eyes with Michél, and she was incapable of moving. He bowed: "Madame, what a pleasure to see you!" He took one look at her cup and exclaimed: "This is no drink for a lady. *Garçon, s'il vous plaît*, we need champagne!"

There was champagne in this etablissement? And what about his manners? He has never been this cordial before. Or talked this much.

Once a bottle of fine champagne appeared at their table, Michél Bèranger entertained them with stories from the brothers' journeys, and—made up or not—they were simply delightful and entertaining. Josephine began to relax and laugh with the others. Michél put her at ease with his charm. The past, his resentment of her, his behavior at the masked ball and his appearance at the wedding seemed all but forgotten. He smiled a lot, touched her arm ever so often, yet never did so in the threatening manner he had exhibited before. He pulled her in with compliments and gestures, playing the lighthearted conversationalist. Nothing in his tone suggested otherwise.

Valdeterre had no time for suspecting his wife of anything untoward. The rare nights when he came home late and Josephine was not there, she always had a good story and an even better reason. She was helping the Ursulines with the refugees, she was meeting the Baronesse LaCour, she had gotten caught up at the hairdresser's or the dress maker's house. He had so much on his mind, he never questioned her explanations.

The trial against Inola, whom the citizens had taken to calling the savage maiden was about to begin. The Natchez woman had not spoken or responded to any of the officers interrogating her since she had been arrested. Sister Stanislaus and the Acadian girl had visited regularly. Rumor had it that she was speaking with them, but neither the nun nor the girl were willing to disclose the nature of their conversations.

Inola herself was feeling sick to her stomach. Her damp cell, the lack of light and the bad food contributed to her discomfort, but these were not the only reasons. She had been throwing up every day. Inola wanted to tell the truth about what had happened at the fort, wanted to appeal to the Sister's good heart. She suspected that the nun knew the whole sordid story—from the military's point, not hers. Inola's guilt kept her from talking about it. For she knew she was guilty. Just not to the extent they were going to accuse her of.

CHAPTER 17

The tribunal started on the 25th day of January, a dreary morning with wind and rain. The charges against Inola were treason and murder. It was to be one of the biggest trials ever held in the colony of New France, and the Governor himself would be sitting in on crucial days and in the end deliver the verdict. Governor Bienville was joined by the King's lieutenant, a specially appointed official from Paris and crown representative, as well as a procurer general and an appointed attorney called the Senior Councilor, who was the head of the superior council whose three members also made up the quorum and sat *en banc*. The Councilor would be asking questions of the witnesses. Valdeterre opened the trial for the public, and the citizens, clamoring for excitement were pushing and shoving to get into the courtroom. Those who were kept outside in long queues were shouting for the clerk to leave the courtroom door open so they could hear the proceedings. The city was rife with wild rumors and tales about the massacre, painting Inola as a fiery devil slaughtering soldiers with a tomahawk, like a savage version of Jeanne d'Arc.

The first witness was a soldier. He hobbled to the stand with a cane having lost his leg after a Natchez had shot an arrow into him. While he had fled down south, gangrene had set in, and his leg needed to be amputated once he reached the city: "It was barely dawn when out of the shadows they were everywhere. These red devils were quiet. Not like the hollering we were used to from their tribal dances. They speared the watch guards first."

"Did you see that with your own eyes?" the Councilor asked.

"No, sir, I was the one who found the dead guards. By then the Natchez had gone into the barracks in search of the Commander, killing everyone in their way. Most of the soldiers were unarmed and murdered in their sleep."

"Commander Chepart?"

"Yes, sir. The Commander's quarters were above the others."

"Was the accused with him?"

"No, sir, she must have left her husband during the night knowing what was coming."

Loud gasps were heard from the gallery. Acadia looked at Sister Stanislaus: "Her husband? So Inola is… was… Sieur de Chepart's wife?"

The Sister nodded, to her this was not news. Acadia's view turned blurry and a fiery color as this piece of information sank in. Shouts of "Hang her!", "String her up!" and "Burn the witch!" could be heard. The Governor slammed down the gavel: "Silence!" he thundered.

The crowd quieted down only because they were eager to hear more detailed accounts.

In the days following, witness after witness took the stand. Credible accounts of the massacre mixed with conjecture and wild theories made it difficult to discern truth from lore. The picture that emerged from the soldiers' and settlers' testimonies could neither sufficiently prove a motive on Inola's part, nor did it explain how the Natchez had entered Fort Rosalie undetected. To the public, she was guilty nonetheless, based at this point only on the color of her skin. One of the surviving Majors recounted how Chepart, shortly after Inola and he were married, had insisted on taking the savage maiden to Paris:

"Many felt it was sheer audacity on his part when he presented her to the French court. What with her gaudy costume, trying to pass as a white lady? Commander Chepart was blind to it, so enamored was he with that sauvage. She made our whole delegation a laughingstock."

The Major was asked to describe in detail the gaudy costume he had referred to. Was she wearing tribal clothes? No, quite the opposite, he said. But he was no expert in dresses, so his wife should be the one describing that savage, he continued. The Councilor, weary of allowing this case to become a circus, reluctantly called the Major's wife after the crowd loudly demanded it. A beaming, plump woman, she walked to the front, basking in her sudden importance: "Your honor, she was just disgraceful. Wearing a damask gown in a flame color with gold flowers. She looked like a bird. Everything had gold in it, even the petticoats were gold!"

The Councilor interrupted: "Madame, the undergarments of the accused are of no interest to this court."

The woman could not be deterred: "She wore two pairs of bodices underneath it, too! And six lace shifts with ribbons in gold and silver and silk stockings. The lace-up booties were bronze-colored, who has ever heard of such audaciousness!" she exclaimed, talking not to the court but to a very responsive audience.

The Councilor had difficulty getting her off the stand, she kept babbling on even after he had her escorted out. The Major was recalled, to finish his testimony.

Throughout it all Inola sat in the enclosed box with a stoic expression on her face. She had her eyes fixed on the Major until he complained to the council that she was trying to put a devil's curse on him. She lowered her head before the Councilor could instruct her to do so. With every testimony, it became clearer how much the military under Chepart's command had resented his red bride, although many of them were either also married to tribal women or kept them as concubines. After a week, the whole town was on pins and needles when the King's Lieutenant announced on Friday that the next person to take the stand would be the accused.

On Monday morning at first light Sister Stanislaus headed for the prison. She had not asked permission and suspected that Mother St. Augustin would disapprove of her visiting the Natchez woman on the most crucial day of the proceedings. Yet Marie Madeleine Hachard felt in the pit of her stomach that Inola needed to hear what she had to say. The nun was a familiar visitor at the jail, so she did not arouse suspicion despite the early hour. Inside Inola's cold cell she had only one advice for the woman: "Be truthful. Whatever you have done, do not lie on the stand. Tell your truth with sincerity. And most of all: speak. God will help you find your voice and the ability to tell your side of the story with dignity."

Inola looked at her without indication that the nun's words had reached her. Marie Madeleine knew that the court would not acquit, even if Inola had not committed the crime of which she stood accused. She prayed that Inola would break her silence for she knew she had regained her voice if not her willingness to speak. The nun feared that she would come across as cold and unfeeling. But Inola surprised everyone.

"State your name and relations!" the Councilor instructed when she took the stand a few hours later.

"I am Inola, daughter of the Natchez, known as Madame de Chepart."

"What is your relation to the tribal chiefs of the Natchez?"

"The Great Sun was my father who passed over to the spirits fifty moons ago. His brother, my uncle, the Tattooed Serpent, named my brother as his successor." With every word her voice grew stronger. "My marriage was an arrangement to strengthen the ties between my tribe and the colonists, but it was not a sacrifice. I came to regard my husband with deep affection, and he loved me in return."

Dismissive sounds from the audience interrupted her at these last words, until again, the Governor slammed down the gavel. She continued: "As for him taking me on his journey to his motherland that the Major talked about… my husband insisted that I accompany him. I was so worried about embarrassing him and the delegation, I had the seamstress copy the painting of a dress I found in a book. It was of a noblewoman in Paris. All I wanted is to belong."

Again, snickering could be heard from the gallery. Below Sister Stanislaus and Acadia sat, mesmerized.

She has not uttered so many words in the two months since her appearance. Inola is giving a speech! And she does so in near perfect French.

"What happened on the morning of the 29th day of November?"

"To truly understand it, you must consider the events that came before."

"What events are you referring to?"

Again, Inola inhaled deeply before continuing: "The wars that came before, the injustice at the White Apple settlement. When a villager from my tribe was murdered by a French trader and my husband's predecessor let him go free."

The Councilor lost his patience: "Woman, what are you talking about? This was years ago. The trader was reprimanded and lost his license."

She looked him in the eye, incredulously: "He murdered one of my own and all he lost was a trading license. But this was not the only injustice. My people were being driven out of their homes, and the military demanded that White Apple chief was turned over to them after the warriors rose up."

"The warriors as you call them, attacked the nearby settlements. It was your own uncle, Tattooed Serpent who turned the chief over to us."

There were cheers from the citizens.

"Only under pressure. Only to restore the peace. A peace that could not outlast my own husband's ill-fated decision to drive out the Natchez once and for all to vacate the village, so he could use the land for a new tobacco plantation. I warned him not to do this to my people. I warned him they would fight before they would let their children starve. I arranged a meeting between him and the chiefs. They did not come to an agreement. Whatever my husband offered was not enough to make up for the lack of food, the lack of supplies. His plan broke all contracts and trade deals. I had to do something! I could not let my people die!"

The Councilor's tone was icy when he asked the question everyone in the room wanted answered: "What did you do?"

Inola's breathing could be heard all the way to the last row. At last, she raised her head: "I told the Great Sun, my brother, of the secret door to the fort. When he sent me a signal the night before I unlocked the latch…"

Angry voices rose up and went like a wave around the courtroom. "Murderess!", "Kill her!", "Put her head on a stake like these savages did to our own!"

Inola held on to the wooden panel. When the Councilor demanded silence, she spoke in a quiet tone: "The Commander was never meant to be killed in the rebellion. For this is what it was. A rebellion. Against starvation, against injustice…" Her voice trailed off as she lost control over her limbs and slid to the floor. The shouting never stopped until she was carried back to her cell by two officers. Acadia hung on to Sister Stanislaus when the nun pushed her way through the angry crowds to the Governor's bench: "Monsieur le Governeur, s'il vous plait, I must see the defendant. She is not well."

He was about to deny her request when Valdeterre stepped up: "What harm could it do? Can we not let the Sister bring the woman some food and water?"

The Governor relented.

When Sister Stanislaus got to the cell Inola was heaving. She refused the bread they handed her, only taking a few sips of water. Then she forced herself to get up from her cot while protectively holding her stomach. The Sister looked from Inola's hands to her eyes. Inola nodded faintly, almost invisibly. The Sister made the sign of the cross.

"Yes, I am with child. That is why I asked my brother to spare the Commander. My husband was supposed to live to see his son born. And now if they hang me none of us will survive…"

Sister Stanislaus put her hand on Inola's: "God will not let this happen." Secretly she knew that the chance of the court sparing the woman's life were slim.

God allows a lot of death to happen and saves his explanation for it for the afterlife.

The Sister could not bring herself to feel guilty for her cynicism. It was Marie Madeleine talking after all.

On Tuesday morning, the members of the court retreated to Valdeterre's office for deliberations. Though the Commander was the head of law enforcement, not justice, he weighed in and pleaded for imprisonment instead of the death penalty. In the end, it all came down to politics and fear of angry citizens. The verdict was to be delivered on Wednesday. The Mother Superior herself accompanied Sister Stanislaus to the courthouse. While Acadia and other inhabitants of the convent were confined to the standing-room-only gallery, the ordained women sat prominently right behind the accused. The Governor called for Inola to step into the wooden box.

"In the matter of the territories of the New France versus Inola, Madame de Chepart, the court has come to a decision…"

Sister Stanislaus felt a flare of hope.

He called her Madame de Chepart, a connection the Councilor has avoided throughout the trial, to not raise sympathy.

The Governor continued: "In the charges of murder and treason the court finds the accused guilty."

As the gavel came down, the crowd erupted in loud cheering. The Sisters looked at each in shock. Inola stood frozen.

"The sentence is death by decapitation and shall be carried out this Saturday, the 4th day of February at dawn on the Place d'Armes."

When she told of the events later, Sister Stanislaus could not recall how she ended up standing in front of the Governor's bench moments after the verdict. She must have jumped over the barrier. There she stood with both arms raised as if embracing a higher justice that had eluded everyone else: "Sieur, I demand to be heard!"

The courtroom had quieted at the sight of the nun. Before Bienville could respond she spoke: "Inola... Madame de Chepart is carrying her husband's, the Commander's child. In the Lord's name, I am appealing this verdict for it would end the life of an unborn. A child of God. And God does not want to punish the innocent. In his name, I beg you to reconsider."

When the crowd reacted to her statement, it was not favorable. Shouts of "Kill the bastard child!" rang out. The King's Lieutenant had to step in and order the soldiers to move the citizens outside. He ordered the doors closed. After a few minutes of whispered deliberations, the Councilor addressed Inola who had not moved: "Is what the Sister says the truth? Are you with child?"

She raised her head: "My... the Commander's son will be born in four moons."

The Governor shook his head. In view of this new information, I am ordering a halt to the carrying out of the judgement until such time as the child is born. This is my final verdict!"

If Sister Stanislaus had hoped for a conversion of the death penalty to life imprisonment, she did not show it. Any attempts on her part to have Inola moved to the convent to keep her healthy for the remainder of her pregnancy were denied by the Governor. Too many boarders were victims of the attack and if the citizens found out that the murderess of Fort Rosalie had been allowed to spend her last months in comfort, they would riot, he feared. And so, accompanied by Acadia and Zulimé, daily visits to the prison became a routine. They brought Inola food and blankets to keep her warm during the winter months. One day, with her belly growing, she asked Zulimé for special herbs. After they left the cell, Zulimé was unusually quiet on their way back to the convent.

"Is something wrong?" the Sister asked.

"The herbs Inola asked for...they will kill the bebé inside her... I believe, she knows this. She wants to end her life and the child's by her own hand. She does not want to give that last power over to her jailers. And she does not want the child to be born in captivity. I can understand, but…"

Sister Stanislaus' shock over what she had just heard, turned into determination: "But non! We cannot let this happen. I have spoken to the Mother Superior, and it has been decided that the child will be raised at the convent. By us."

On their next visit, Zulimé told Inola that she had not been able to get the specific mixture, but that she had come up with a similar recipe. Zulimé's herbs would strengthen the baby and its mother, not end their lives.

Chapter 18

In their bedroom one morning as Valdeterre woke his wife, he turned her face to the window and saw the dark circles under her eyes: "What worries you so that you are getting no sleep?"

That my friend, the forçat will get assaulted by some drunk in a seedy bar in a part of town you would never find yourself in? That I revel in the company of a man you would put behind bars?

Josephine clenched her teeth and tried to turn away from him. He took her in his arms:

"My dear wife, please take better care of yourself. I regret that my work keeps me up deep

into the night. You must rest. I hope to have more time to spend with you soon. And then we shall try again for a child."

Josephine shuddered inside. It was the last thing she wanted to think about.

How much longer can I keep the truth from him? That I may not be able to conceive… that I do not want to take care of a child…

She forced a smile. Patted his hand. Reassuring gestures to end the conversation. Josephine was intent on drowning her woes and misgivings about her marriage. The rum made her reckless. When Florence told her about one of the taverns on the river, one known to serve a better clientele, Josephine threw caution to the wind. Instead of declining to accompany Florence to a place where she could be recognized, to sell champagne that she knew must have been acquired by questionable if not criminal means, the aristocrat agreed to join the forçat.

The Bèrangers met the women at the bar, Michél dressed in nicer attire than his usual ragged shirt. Florence asked them to sit with Josephine while she talked to the owner. Clean clothes notwithstanding, Florence knew that the brothers would hinder not help negotiations with such an establishment. Josephine, sitting with her back to the room was suddenly uneasy when Michél's hand touched hers on the table.

Someone is watching me... us....

She turned and saw Major Dumont staring at her: "Madame de Valdeterre..."

As soon as her name was out of his mouth Josephine jumped up and left. She knew the moment she was around the corner that running away was a mistake. She did not see if he followed her, could not know if he had spotted the Bèrangers or watched them come in together.

He will tell my husband... how will I possibly explain?

Back at her house, Josephine had another sleepless night, this time not from adventure but apprehension. Major Dumont must not have seen my husband yet, she thought at breakfast the following morning when Valdeterre acted his usual self, preoccupied with work and papers strewn out on the dining table before he hurried back to headquarters. The Commander was curious about his first appointment. The Ursuline nun had sent a message that she needed to talk to him. When Sister Stanislaus walked in an hour later, he had no idea what her concern would be and was surprised by her request:

"Commander, the Mother Superior and all our Sisters were not only tasked to put a roof over the heads of the Casket Girls that came with us from France, but also entrusted us to find them suitable husbands. This part has proven difficult. Except for your wife..." She stopped herself.

Remember, he does not know that Josephine is a Casket Girl and who am I to ruin a marriage?

"...who was born a Vicomtesse, of course, with the advantage to meet a good man like yourself under natural circumstances, we have not had any luck with the Casket Girls who all come from quite different paths of life and upbringing." The Sister hoped Valdeterre had not noticed her mentioning his wife in the same breath as the other girls.

He furrowed his brow: "Over the years some of my men have married Casket Girls."

"Oui, and those were the lucky ones. Before we opened the convent many of them were lost. Commander, I do not know how your men met their wives. If there were gatherings where they could become acquainted...We Ursulines do not know how to make an introduction. And this is where we need your help."

"You would like me to introduce my soldiers to the women?"

"Oui, at some sort of gathering that you and Madame Valdeterre would host."

"Have you spoken to my wife about it?"

Sister Stanislaus refused to lie: "The Mother Superior has. A while ago. Your wife seemed...reluctant."

"I shall bring this up with her. We could host a soirée at our home, I suppose."

"Very much appreciated, Commander. The Mother Superior will be filled with gratitude."

∼

Back home that evening Valdeterre had two difficult subject matters to bring up to his wife. Josephine sensed the trouble when he marched into the salon. No warm greeting, no usual kiss on the cheek. His measured tone belied his dismay:

"Major Dumont said he saw you at one of the taverns on the river last night. You ran out when you recognized him, apparently. Is this what causes your exhaustion? Gallivanting in bars?"

Josephine had prepared herself all day for this confrontation. She forced a laugh:

"Your Major must be losing his eyesight. Or his mind. Why would I go to some river tavern? And even if I did why would I run from the Major, a man I know from numerous soirées and receptions?"

So convincing was her lie that he was unsure of his accusations. The Major was not a man of gossip, but these taverns were dark, and he could have made a mistake. Valdeterre decided to broach the other subject: "Speaking of soirées, we are to host one. Or a ball if you prefer to call it that. For the Casket Girls."

Josephine's first instinct, as always was to protest, but in view of having just narrowly escaped what could cause a big rift in her marriage she thought better of it: "Do you mind telling me the occasion? These girls do not even own the proper dress for a ball. And who would they be dancing with?"

Valdeterre sighed: "My men or some of them. The unmarried kind. The good Sister came to me with a request from the Mother Superior."

So, these nuns would not let this pass!

"The Ursulines want us to arrange a ball for the sole purpose of helping them get rid of boarders?"

"To find them husbands."

"That is what I said." Her voice grew hard before she caught herself. "Fine. Let us find husbands for the poor and downtrodden."

Valdeterre had prepared himself for a much bigger argument and was relieved she consented. As for the other subject matter, he could not bring himself to admit to a nagging suspicion that his wife was dishonest.

Josephine loathed having to throw a ball for the Casket Girls. With gritted teeth she half-heartedly began with the preparations leaving most of the work to the housekeeper and servants.

"Get whatever flower arrangements you want. And decide on a three-course supper, not a five-course one. I do not care what we serve, and our guests will not know the difference," she instructed them.

The result were plants that did not match the tablecloth and food that was half decent but far from Margarita's delicious dishes. The only two matters she paid the utmost attention to, were her own dress and Florence. Josephine was determined to outshine them all and put them in their place.

I must find Florence.

The need to get ahold of the rum mistress was of greater importance than her gown. Florence's was on the list of attendees' names Sister Stanislaus had given to Valdeterre. Josephine had to make sure the forçat would not show up. One slip of Florence's tongue and all the denials about Josephine's nightly outings would expose her as a liar. The two women had a silent agreement to not socialize or even greet each other at and after church with Josephine sitting with her husband and among their peers and Florence with the Casket Girls.

"I shall talk to Sister Stanislaus and inspect the gowns for the women. We cannot introduce a badly dressed bunch to your men," she informed the Commander and headed into the convent. The excitement over the invitation was palpable when Josephine entered the dining room and endured a few minutes of getting stared at by everyone. She had no intention of inspecting dresses or talking to Sister Stanislaus and pulled Florence into the hallway: "I need you to not attend my ball."

Florence was not surprised by the request, having mulled it over for days and looking for an excuse to bow out, but now Josephine's tone annoyed her: "I cannot promise you that. I still live here and must honor the Sisters' orders."

Josephine laughed wryly: "When have you ever honored what the nuns asked of you?"

"As I said, I cannot promise anything. If I do come, I will behave if that is what you are concerned about."

Florence walked back into the dining room. Josephine was left none the wiser.

Most of the Casket Girls were looking forward to the ball, even the ones who resisted the real reason for the event.

"I am curious to see the house. I've always wanted to know how the mighty Princess and the Commander live!" said Acadia to Madame LaCour. Geneviève sighed. For her, attending this affair was a futile exercise. She would only go to not seem ungrateful to the Ursulines.

Who would want to marry a widow with two children? Not that I have any interest in a new husband.

Acadia's curiosity for Josephine's mansion outweighed her interest in marriage. Margarita, given her feelings towards José only agreed to go out of respect for the Sisters. Jeanette was the most delighted. When Mother St. Augustin tried to force Louise Mariette to attend—"she is a Casket Girl after all"—the Sister objected and prevailed: "How can we force this poor soul to sit in a ballroom full of soldiers waiting to be asked to dance by them after what happened to her?"

On the night of the ball, it was raining and Valdeterre sent carriages for the Casket Girls. He had invited more than twenty of his unmarried officers including—to Josephine's dread—Major Dumont. As the hour approached when the Valdeterres had to welcome their guests, Josephine's anxiety grew. The Major was not her only concern for she still had no inkling of whether Florence would show.

Sister Stanislaus was the first one to step off the carriage and walk into the mansion. Josephine greeted her with a minimum of respect but merely nodded her head to the girls as one by one they entered with wide open eyes, their awe showing on their faces. The Commander welcomed everyone warmly, extending his hand and calling them by their names. They were led into the salon where Valdeterre's officers had gathered.

Josephine breathed a sigh of relief. Florence was not among her guests. The girls huddled in one corner not daring to cross an invisible line to the other side of the room. It was left to Valdeterre to make the introductions. Sister Stanislaus felt everyone's awkwardness. Madame LaCour was the only one who looked and acted as if she belonged. Margarita Cortez, disinterested in the soldiers, was merely admiring the polished wood floors, the brocade curtains and the gold leaf wallpaper that Acadia Gravois was touching which earned her a scolding from one of the servants. When a quartet of musicians appeared and began playing, the tension eased a little.

"Are we supposed to dance now?" Acadia asked.

"Not until after supper," Geneviève explained.

Josephine's relief was short lived when the door opened, and Florence walked in wearing a garish gown of bright blue silk with gold ribbons that was at least one size too small to fully cover her bosom.

Lord Jesus, Sister Stanislaus thought. *After all the time we spent making sure Jeanette and the rest would be clothed appropriately...*

Florence floated through the room, took Valdeterre's hand and breathed: "My apologies, Commander. I had urgent business to attend to. I hope I did not miss anything."

Valdeterre was too stupefied by her boldness to do anything but stare as Florence retreated with a smile to join the others. Josephine's lips turned into a thin line and as soon as an opportunity presented itself, she pulled Florence into the hallway: "You couldn't stay away, could you?"

"No, my curiosity got the better of me. I really wanted to see how you live."

Josephine chose calm over anger: "Do not make this difficult for me, s'il vous plait. I will not be able to spend time with you if you expose me."

"Don't worry, your secret is safe."

And one can only hope the Major will not call me out, either.

Josephine need not have worried about Major Dumont. He had meddled with the place cards at the table to sit next to Geneviève LaCour. The Baronesse was less than delighted of having to spend the evening in the company of the boorish military man. The unease among the other women only increased during supper as they were all placed between the soldiers. The conversations seemed forced, Acadia did not know what fork to use for the main course, and Margarita's disdain of the lackluster dishes was written all over her face. Sister Stanislaus observed the room from her chair at the head of the table next to the Commander. The only one who seemed engaged with the man seated next to her was Jeanette Crozat. A little too engaged, the Sister thought. Florence downed one goblet of champagne after another, loudly asking for more when the server was not refilling her glass fast enough and cheering on the Lieutenant next to her who tried to keep up.

Things did not improve after the meal. Once again, the women retreated to one side of the salon, the soldiers to the other. Some of them leered at the Casket Girls. This evening was a welcome distraction for the soldiers, the girls their prey. When the musicians played again, the Valdeterres took to the dance floor first as was custom. The women were expected to dance solo before being joined by the men on the floor. Jeanette twirled across the room provocatively. Margarita's lack of enthusiasm for the whole affair showed not only on her features but also in her moves. She thought of José, then looked at her dance partner who lost in comparison. And whatever Acadia was doing was as far from dancing as her provenance was from Paris. With her arms in the air, she looked uncomfortable in a gown that was wearing her, not the other way around. Sister Stanislaus took in the scene and her discomfort grew.

There isn't much difference between an auction block and this. A meat market disguised as a ball. Women being forced to show themselves off to men.

In this moment, the nun did not fault Florence for preferring champagne over selling herself on the dancefloor. The forçat was the only one refusing to take part in the demeaning exercise.

At the other end of the salon Josephine felt similar displeasure, if for entirely different reasons. When the soldiers joined the women in their dances, she excused herself.

I need a break from this farce.

She went into her husband's study and lit a candle. The smoke from his pipe lingered in the air, a scent that always calmed her down, reminding her of the carefree days of their courtship when she first smelled the distinctive aroma of this specially blended cherry tobacco on him. She sat on the chaiselongue and put her feet up. She must have drifted off to sleep. The candle had burned halfway down when she awoke, startled by Jeanette Crozat's yelling.

"Non!" Sister Stanislaus held Jeanette's wrist in a firm grip. The nun's voice was quiet but forceful: "Put. It. Back."

Josephine rushed up to them and took hold of Jeanette's hand. Her fingers clasped the small, golden statue of a horse, a Valdeterre family heirloom that they kept on a mantle: "You thieving putain!" Josephine ripped the horse from the woman's hand: "Leave our house! In fact," she stormed into the salon, waving the statue, "All of you, get out! I shall not tolerate you thieving les petite gens a moment longer!" Josephine walked up to her husband and held up the golden horse: "They tried to burglarize our home!"

Sister Stanislaus stepped forward, looked at the Commander while ignoring his wife and said with a tinge of embarrassment: "Not we. One girl. One girl made a mistake, regretfully. I apologize and humbly ask for your forgiveness on her behalf. We shall all leave your home forthwith."

Valdeterre was too stunned to speak. The Casket Girls knew it was their cue and made their way to the door. Florence had disappeared in the commotion. On the carriage ride home no one spoke. Sister Stanislaus was torn between her discomfort and a feeling of relief that the humiliating evening was over. And disconcerted that she had to tell Mother St. Augustin about the utter failure of the ball.

PART THREE

THE WINDS OF CHANGE

"In the end, the devil has a great empire here, but this does not take away from us the hope of destroying him, with God's love."

Marie Madeleine Hachard

CHAPTER 19

The year of 1730 brought forth another courtroom drama, this one involving Jacques, the overseer at Henry de Roche's plantation. From the commencement of the trial the defendant was defiant, blaming his employer's long absences on his actions. It was unusual to start proceedings by calling the accused to the stand, but nothing about this trial was considered normal. The Councilor had objected to Zulimé's testimony, citing no precedent for an enslaved person serving as a witness, but had been overruled by the Governor at Valdeterre's urging. Zulimé would take the stand. By then even the most hardened court officers had been surprised by the overseer's utter lack of remorse. The man was cursing and spitting during de Roche's testimony, in which he described Zulimé's wounds in detail. De Roche spoke of her long recovery, of the pain she endured and hinted at another abuse, the one he dared not imagine, the one he could not be sure about, the one she had never spoken of, neither confirming nor denying it.

"Monsieur de Roche, you are aware that the laws apply to the property owner, property being slaves, are you not? And that your travels do not absolve you of the responsibility over said property?"

These were the questions that de Roche and Valdeterre feared could alter the outcome of the trial. The Governor had asked the Councilor to add one crucial question: "Monsieur, did you then, before the commencement of your journey or at any time before, order your overseer to punish the slaves as he sees fit?"

"No. I instructed him only to run my plantation in my absence and prevent slaves from escaping. Not by beating them but by enforcing the fence around my property. I do not believe in whipping. I do know that it is common practice on other plantations, but I have never seen a better harvest, stronger field hands or a better work ethic because of beatings. In fact, quite the opposite is true. Abused slaves are more likely to run away than those who are treated with dignity. My success as a Creole and as a merchant with plantations here and on the islands, my crops and my income are proof of this. Furthermore, I am strongly opposed to beating women, and my overseer was very aware of that."

The snickering of a handful of landowners who attended the proceedings showed that not everyone agreed with the merchant's view. But de Roche had made his case.

Zulimé had opted not to attend the trial until the day she had to speak about her ordeal. She could not close her eyes the night before, calling on her spirits to protect her and grant her the words to convince the court of not only her story, but of her Master's innocence. She had studied the code noir and knew the law. De Roche had sent an advocate to the convent to prepare her for the trial and go over the Councilor's possible questions. This, too, had never been done before. On the day of Zulimé's testimony the gallery filled up with most of the city's indentured servants. If this trial would go Zulimé's way, they too, might have more power in the future.

Zulimé entered accompanied by Sister Stanislaus. The joint appearance was a statement in itself and gave credence to her testimony. If the Councilor was surprised by a slave who held her head high and answered with clarity and precision, he tried not to show it. He had expected a timid girl with limited language skills. Instead, what he saw was a young woman with an almost regal air about her who spoke eloquently and in perfect French. She showed no emotion at first.

"Is it not custom for runaway slaves to get punished by anywhere between twenty and a hundred lashes of the whip?" the Councilor asked.

"Monsieur Councilor, I am not a runaway. Or have you ever heard of a runaway coming back of their own volition?"

Zulimé recounted the events that lead to her leaving, facts that were confirmed by the Mother Superior and the soldier who had picked her up and returned her back to the plantation. It was not until the Councilor asked her to describe the whipping that she faltered and stumbled over her words: "He dragged me out to the middle of the slave quarters... he tied me to the post... and ripped my clothes and then my skin..."

Zulimé's voice trailed off. The Councilor continued: "How many lashes did he punish you with?"

From his box the overseer commented with a nasty laugh: "Not enough."

Zulimé who had avoided looking at him, lowered her head and put her arms protectively around herself. The Councilor reprimanded the man and continued his query: "Can you remember how many times the whip came down on you?"

She looked up. "No, sir. I cannot recall. After a while I lost all sense of time."

"We have heard your Master's testimony in which he stated that he found you in his dressing room. What happened between the beating and Monsieur de Roche discovering you?"

"Sir, I am not sure what you mean."

The Councilor took a breath. The next question was not easy for him, either. "Did the overseer take... advantage of you?"

It took Zulimé a while to understand what he was asking. When it sank in, she straightened her spine and stood tall and proud: "Non, sir! I hid from him. And if he had found me, I would have fought to my death. For I will never let a man touch me or take advantage of me like that. Ever!"

De Roche was afraid that everyone in the courtroom heard the sigh of relief that escaped his lips. He caught Zulimé's eye as she was excused and stepped down. His was a look of the purest compassion that made her want to run up and throw her arms around him. It took all her composure to walk out of the courtroom. In the end, it was Valdeterre's testimony that cinched the outcome of the trial once he told the court that it was on his orders that Zulimé was fetched from the plantation.

The overseer was pronounced guilty, but in the eyes of many his punishment did not fit the crime: he was sentenced to a public whipping of thirty lashes and ordered to leave the state of New France.

Zulimé only wished for all of it to be put behind her and did not attend the public lashing. Yet even though she wanted no reminders of her ordeal, Zulimé's case became a cause célèbre, and she became famous because of it. Her carefree days filled with study, market runs and excursions to the river's edge in search of herbs were tempered by her notoriety. In the days after the verdict, she was hounded by indentured servants who asked for advice on how to sue their owners. When she had none, they turned on her, disappointed. White people crossed the street when they saw her. Some made nasty remarks or spit at her. To the masters, the landowners, the rich and the entitled Zulimé posed a threat. Her precedent-setting trial had empowered their servants and slaves, had given rise to complaints and thinly veiled warnings. The plantation owners depended on their overseers, and unlike Henry de Roche did not believe in the proper treatment of slaves. Most of them violated the code noir on a regular basis. So far without repercussions, but this had changed when the verdict came down. They knew that from that day forth they, too could end up in court and worse, end up losing.

The Mother Superior, meanwhile, went to great length to make sure Père de Beaubois did not find out that the now notorious Dominguan was the same girl he had forced the nuns to banish for making witch's brew. Luckily, the priest never made the connection.

Zulimé stopped going to the market but could not bring herself to give up her other pastime. To avoid confrontations, she now snuck out at dawn or just before dusk and never alone. She convinced Acadia to accompany her.

Sometimes Margarita joined them on their walks through the meadows and along the river. As Zulimé picked nettles and other plants, the rest of them carried them back in big cotton pouches. She never explained exactly what they were for, and only Margarita knew, for Zulimé trusted her. The cook knew enough Santoría secrets to understand and support the girl's need to practice her vodou spells. Margarita even slipped her colored string to make *gris-gris* pouches and let her do them in the kitchen when no one else was around.

At night Zulimé lay dreaming with eyes wide open.

That look on Monsieur's face in the courtroom!

A warm cloud had engulfed her, and she was still feeling its comfort. She longed to see him, but he had gone off on another one of his journeys, this time north. De Roche had left the plantation under the care of his strongest and smartest man, Touton, who he considered loyal. To ensure that Touton would not take advantage of his position and run away, de Roche had paid him twenty livrés with the prospect of another twenty once he returned and saw that Touton had taken his responsibility seriously. Zulimé liked Touton. He was the only one among the Master's enslaved peoples who always had a kind word for her.

Florence had not watched Zulimé take the stand in the trial against the overseer but cared a great deal about its outcome and made sure to see the punishment being carried out.

That slave girl stood up against a man who abused his power. Just like I always stood up for myself in Paris when I was her age. These low-lives on the plantations treat servants the same way the police treated the poor population in Paris—with disdain and violence.

In Florence's opinion it was men like the overseer, the pimps and the crime lords of Montmartre who deserved to be whipped.

∼

At La Cocotte, by now the most desirable of all the cabaréts, Josephine restlessly moved in her seat. She kept trying to pry information out of Florence about the brothers' return.

"All I know is, this voyage is a short one. They are only traveling to the port of Balise and collecting goods on the waterways," was all Josephine got out of Florence. The nights out with the forçat were fine, but the Vicomtesse missed the excitement she felt when Michél was around. He continued to intrigue her. He was considerate and charming yet kept his hands to himself. Whenever he walked her a few blocks in the direction of her home—never all the way as she was worried, they might be seen—he kissed her hand and acted like the gentleman he was most definitely not.

The longer his absence the more Josephine wished for Michél's return, taking extra care while getting ready for the night out despite wearing the simplest dress in her closet to not attract unwanted attention. Her locks were always shiny, her skin glowing, and she used cochineal, a carmine-colored extract derived from insects to stain her lips red. Never too much, as she did not want to be mistaken for a prostitute or one of the painted women she had seen in the theater and circus back in Paris. There was no difference between an actress and a prostitute in her mind, and she had no intention to be confused with either. She knew of some society women who used the liquid squeezed out of the belladonna plant to give their eyes a more luminous appearance, but it was poisonous, and she had no need for it; the excitement gave her eyes a natural shine.

And yet Josephine was unprepared for Michél when she ran into him. Their reunion did not happen late at night at La Cocotte or one of the other cabaréts, but near the shipyard where Josephine had gone to collect a package from France. It was not midday yet. As Josephine was paying the merchant, she felt a hand lightly touching her back. She smelled the familiar scent before she turned around. Michél offered her his arm which she took after a moment's hesitation.

"Mademoiselle," he said, continuing to call her that, in complete disregard of not only her title but her marital status, "it has been too long. Would you mind if I accompanied you on a walk and maybe we could share a refreshment?"

He had a market vendor fill a bottle with sugarcane juice. It was a warm day, so they circled up the river and around the city's eastern edge. They barely talked. She felt his arm through the fabric of her sleeve, a little hotter than made sense in this temperature.

"Would you like to take our refreshment over there?" he asked pointing towards the fields.

"Oui," she said, only briefly thinking of what might happen to her dress if she sat down in the high grass. He spread out his jacket after removing a flask and poured the rum into the bottle with the juice.

She laughed. "Monsieur! Drinking before sunset? How naughty of us."

Michél took a swig before handing it to her. Josephine did not wipe the rim before doing the same. His callused finger lightly brushed her lips before he put it on his own and licked it while never breaking eye contact. He leaned over her and pushed her slowly down on the ground, pinning her arms above her head with his left arm. His right hand unlaced the front of her corsage until she was exposed down to her waist. She dared not move except for the trembling she could not stop and barely breathed as he ran his hand from her breasts to her navel. He let go of her arms, but when she flung them around his neck, he pushed them back down.

"Non!", was all he said.

Her arms stayed where he had pinned them, when he released his grip to pull up her dress. She was ready for him, and as careful as he had been to not ruin her corsage, her undergarments he ripped apart with one hand while unfastening his trousers with the other. She thought she heard moans until she realized it was her making these sounds when he was inside her. He was rough yet deliberate. She could not tell if it was the rum or his passion that made her feel like floating in warm water. Until a hot wave raised her up, her whole body contracted and erupted in spasms. She barely felt him do the same, and it took her what seemed like hours to regain regular breathing.

So, this is what they call le petit mort.

She had closed her eyes, and when she openend them she saw his face above hers. She was surprised to see gentleness in his eyes.

"Ah oui, Mademoiselle. Let me help you."

He laced up her corsage while she stared at him, surprised by all of it. He kissed her for the first time on this day and got up.

"We should not walk back together, I presume…"

Josephine nodded. Michél kissed her again, then waved *adieu*. She pulled herself together and hurried back toward the city in the opposite direction. Her undergarments were beyond repair, and she felt her nakedness underneath her dress. The feeling excited as much as it mortified her. She thought that everyone could see what had happened and was relieved when she entered the cool quietude of her house. She fell into her bed, after removing her dress and shoes and burning her ripped garment in the kitchen. Her short time of peace ended when she heard her husband coming home much earlier than anticipated. He called for her from downstairs, and when she did not respond he soon stood in the bedroom. She feigned sleep until he sat down on the bed and carressed her hair. She could not bear his touch and opened her eyes while she moved from his reach.

"Are you ill?" he asked, concerned.

"I felt faint when I went to the dock," she answered, her voice cracking. A deep crease formed between his brows.

Does he know? Can he smell Michél on me?

She misinterpreted the look on his face. He reached for her hand which she reluctantly gave him.

"I came home early to take you to supper at Bienville's."

Her eyes widened in surprise.

"I have not forgotten that you wanted us to attend… Josephine, I know I have been absent and working longer hours than I should. I truly regret not paying my wife the attention she deserves."

Josephine dreaded being alone with her husband after Michél, but an evening in the lively company of the Bienvilles and their friends may take her mind off the pirate. She managed a small smile:

"I am happy you came to your senses. I shall get dressed and be ready in two hours." She saw that he wanted to respond: "I cannot be appropriately adorned for a supper at the Governor's home unless you give me time. I thought we would not make it because of your work and did not plan accordingly. Better be late than in disarray."

Hours later—after she had made it through the supper party, distracted from her thoughts and emotions by the chatty wives and their gossip—she knew she had to fend off her husband who had been amorous all through the evening, touching her arm and waist. On the way home, she pretended to faint and let him put her to bed but insisted that he sleep in the other bedroom:

"I am still feeling ill, and the wine and excitement tonight did not help."

As much as Valdeterre tried to please his wife in the coming weeks, another matter occupied his time. Inola, the savage maiden, still incarcerated, but visited by the Sister and the Dominguan girl regularly, was soon to give birth to the child of her slain husband. Sister Stanislaus had been to the Commander's office nearly every day trying to persuade him to let Inola spend her last weeks on earth at the convent. Valdeterre knew he could never justify a release from prison to any of his military men, much less to the Governor. Whether or not the Natchez woman had meant for her husband and another four hundred people to be killed, her treason had led to their demise. Even half innocent, she had to be the sacrificial lamb. Valdeterre had already heard of complaints when he had postponed her execution. Some even wanted her to be tortured to death, in what was called *a petit feu*, where the accused is suspended above a fire that burns the body parts one by one in a form of slow cooking, with blood and fat dripping on the ground, carried out with help from the Tunica tribe whose men originally invented it. The Commander considered it bastardly and pagan and swept the suggestion off the table immediately. This method of execution turned Valdeterre's stomach. He had witnessed it in the past. Still, his men would have been all too happy to hang her with her unborn child. But then even Père de Beaubois was pleading for the woman to be sent to the convent. The Commander was pulled in all directions over this matter, the world on one side, the clergy on the other. In the end, it was all settled when Inola's labor started two weeks early. The guards who heard her screams ignored them. She gave birth to a baby girl in her damp and dirty cell, severing the umbilical cord with her teeth. Zulimé found Inola and the child in their own blood and excrement, hanging on to the bars, exhausted from the ordeal. Zulimé screamed for help, but considered a slave she, too, was ignored by the guards. All she could do was reach for the baby. With it in her arms she ran back to the convent, where Sister Stanislaus sent for a nursemaid.

One day later, Inola was executed in a public hanging attended by most citizens of La Nouvelle Orleàns. They screamed "murderess!", "dirty savage!" and other insults when she was dragged up the steps to the gallows. She was asked if she had any last words as was custom but looked stoically above the crowd. She made no sound as the executioner kicked away the ladder. The cheering crowd quieted down; many a mouth dropped in shock when instead of turning downwards Inola's face rose to the heavens as she fell to her death.

∽

In the Mother Superior's office, Sister Stanislaus cautioned:

"We must make sure Inola's child does not suffer revenge. The sins of the mother shall not be visited upon the daughter."

They agreed it was a blessing that the baby was a female. Had it been a boy, the Ursulines would have had a hard time explaining why they would raise him at a convent reserved for women. Not to mention that a half-red male would be seen as a threat to be dealt with by the soldiers loyal to their fallen comrades. The Sisters had named the tiny creature Marianne, and she was baptized within a few days of her arrival. Zulimé and Acadia had decided that the tiny baby should also have a Natchez name, Ayita, that meant 'First to Dance'.

Marianne/Ayita was not welcomed by all. Jeanette complained about the crying and was scolded by Sister Stanislaus: "You, of all people, have no right to make a complaint, any kind of complaint! You are not abiding by the rules of this house, you refuse to go to school and are out in the streets all night. You should thank the Lord that you have not been expelled yet."

A short time after, the Sister overheard Louise voicing her discontent over the child: "She is a *métis*, half white, half red. The product of a plaçage. She should not be raised by holy nuns."

The Sister stepped in: "We do not care what color our charges are any more than we care what social background they come from, aristocrat or farmer's daughter." The rebuke stung, and the nun continued: "Marianne Chepart is not the product of a plaçage but the child of a married couple, her father having been a high-ranking official in the military. She is as you know, also an orphan. It would behoove every Christian in this house to welcome her."

The Sister hoped that her words had not fallen on deaf ears, but a few days later she watched as Louise chided Bebé for leaving her schoolbooks on the dining table. Bebé quickly picked them up and ran out in tears. This did not sit well with the Sister: "It is not right to make a little girl cry."

"She is a slave. She should be cleaning or doing her chores, not attending school and dropping her books everywhere."

"Bebé is permitted to go to school and learn just like Casket Girls from the countryside, orphanages or the street. I have told you this before; we do not make a difference, and no one is above or below another."

The Sister's tone was cutting; she would not let this stand. Louise had become bitter in the year after she had been assaulted. Gone was the wide-eyed country girl full of curiosity and wonder. Her shyness had given way to a tight-lipped judgement of others, her fears turned into inflexible rules for herself and expectation of those around her to follow them as well. She was in Sister Stanislaus' prayers and the hopes of the Mother Superior which the head of the convent voiced in a meeting with the nuns one morning while discussing prospective suitors for the Casket Girls:

"We have looked at possible husbands for Louise Mariette but given what happened to her, we must rule out all soldiers and military officials. Most of the artisans are already married. The landowners are aristocrats from noble families who will not give her a second look, much less consider her a suitable match to bear children who can carry on their lineage. This leaves us with merchants and traders. May her hardened heart be opened by a good man."

The Sisters could not foresee that the solution to the Louise problem would present itself in the most unlikely way before the year was over.

"What about Mademoiselle Bourget?" the Mother Superior asked, moving on to the next one.

"We should not concern ourselves with Florence Bourget who seems to be perfectly capable of taking care of herself. Or Jeanette Crozat. They are the reason the Lord welcomed the sinners, so we must do the same." Said Sister Marthé.

Mother St. Augustin took a deep breath: "Well then, we best concentrate our efforts on Mademoiselle Mariette and Abondance Gravois."

The rest of the nuns looked confused.

"Acadia, as she now calls herself."

Hardly anyone but Sister Stanislaus and the Mother Superior remembered Acadia's real name.

CHAPTER 20

Summer came and brought with it a life changing moment for Zulimé. Henry de Roche had returned from a voyage to Saint Domingue a month ago and ridden down from the plantation to faithfully attend mass every Sunday. It was less his yearning for prayer and the Lord and more his longing to see Zulimé that compelled him to make the trip. They had been stealing glances from different sides of the nave, her sitting on pews toward the back of the female section, de Roche always seated on the aisle to make sure that turning to see her would not attract too much attention. Whenever invited, the merchant joined the Sisters for an after-church lunch at the convent and when not, he found other ways to gain entrance, usually bearing gifts or offering services or necessary goods to the Ursulines. The ever-observant Margarita often found reasons to have him visit the kitchen—a broken piece of the stove that needed mending or inspecting the pots so he could order more sizes. She made sure to ask him only when Zulimé was nearby. Margarita would then excuse herself for a few minutes, so they could steal a kiss, a shy embrace, a few words.

Not a day or night had gone by that de Roche had not been on Zulimé's mind since their magical moment on his porch at New Years. She pushed aside her mixed feelings about him, the man who adored her yet the same man who owned her still. On one of his visits in the kitchen with Margarita keeping watch outside he touched her face, and his eyes took on a strange and intense stare. She could see his thoughts spinning in his head, but they were tumbling so fast she was not able to guess them clearly. Only that whatever he was about to say was of great importance.

"Ma petit chèrie, I would like you to live with me."

There they were, the words she had been longing to hear. Not for a moment did she mistake their meaning. He did not just want her back on the plantation to work, although this was what he would tell the nuns right after.

Non, he wants to be with me as a man is with a woman.

Her heart woulou did not jump out of her chest, it expanded beyond her body, encompassing them both, standing near the boiling pots on the stove.

"Oui, Monsieur," she whispered, her voice breaking from emotion.

"You shall call me Henry when we are alone, mon amour." He touched a ringlet of her hair that had escaped and caressed her cheek.

After he spoke to the Mother Superior, Zulimé packed her meager belongings and said a teary goodbye to Acadia and Bebé. De Roche pulled her up on his horse in front of him, and as soon as they reached the outskirts of the city, she nestled up against him, feeling his warmth through her thin dress, a mixture of safety and a tingling sensation of what was to come as they galloped toward the plantation.

This is what Mamán must have felt when she was called to the big house…

Zulimé remembered that, when she was still a little girl, her mother had been getting ready to go to Monsieur Larrác's rooms, the dancing lights in her eyes while she washed herself with a cloth dipped in hibiscus flowers and something secret that she would not talk about. Then she would put on her only silk dress. It was loose, and the fabric was thin and shiny. Zulimé now felt like her mother had looked – like her insides were made of thousands of fireflies.

I wish I had a dress like Mamán's…

When they arrived, he took her hand and led her into the house. Cecile greeted them with a crooked smile for her Master and a condescending stare for Zulimé. It was obvious, the Master had not brought the girl back for the housework. De Roche took Zulimé's hand and led her upstairs. She asked to be allowed to wash up after the long ride, and he pointed her to his bathroom. She kept him waiting while she cleaned up, regretting that she had no other dress and grateful when she found one of Margarita's oils in her pocket.

It is nothing like Mamán's intoxicating scent, but it does smell nice.

She dabbed it on the back of her neck, between her breasts and just above her most private spot. She was nervous, because her grandmother had always shielded her from the young men who had shown interest in her, as far back as before she had any curves.

The spot between your legs is its own woulou, she had said. *You do not open it for just any man. It is your power, your sacred part.*

Her grandmother's words rang in her ear. The old woman would approve of Henry de Roche, Zulimé was certain of it. And she even dared to think that her mother would, too. She remembered watching her with Monsieur Larrác. How he had gently swept the locks off her face when he had come to visit. His hands lingering on Mamán's shoulders when he stood behind her, her smile so different than the one she gave the rest of them. And their retreat to her bedroom late at night, Mamán's forlorn look in the morning when he was long gone…

Of course, Zulimé knew about the physical part of what was about to happen for she had seen the animals do it on the island. Yet she could not imagine it being like that.

Or at least, I hope it will be different…

The thoughts were racing through her brain, her hands were shaking. Finally, she could not make him wait any longer. Zulimé stared at herself in the small, gilded mirror above the bowl and took a deep breath. When she walked into the bedroom, Henry de Roche was standing near the bedpost. He had taken off his jacket and loosened his shirt. What she saw in his eyes would have made her knees buckle, had he not drawn her into his arms. There was a gentle hesitation in him before he kissed her. He, too, was strangely nervous. He felt his chest expanding. He slowly undressed her. Every part of her that he freed from the dress, he showered with more kisses until she sank onto the bed. His hands were everywhere.

She felt like the finest silk to him. His gentleness never wavered, not when she felt his strength inside her, not when she moved with him, not afterwards when their bodies were pressed against each other, and she found her place in the nook under his arm. He kissed the top of her head, caressed her arms and intertwined his fingers with hers. Neither spoke for fear of breaking this magical spell that engulfed them. They could not remember falling asleep, and in the middle of the night woke up still entangled, with the light of the full moon shining through the folds of the curtains. He saw the tiny sparkles in her dark eyes. They made love once more, then drifted off again until it was day.

When she woke, she could not feel him next to her. She sat up, covering her nakedness. As she pulled the sheet over her breasts, she saw it, a dress, just like her mothers. He had laid it out on top of the bedspread and put a wildflower at the neckline. She got up and held the fine material against her in front of the long, narrow mirror, smelling the flower. She saw his reflection in the glass as he entered the room and stood, mesmerized at the sight of her. He cleared his throat: "You are not making it easy to leave you, but I have work to do. Wear this dress tonight, s'il vous plait. We shall have supper on the porch."

His eyes took her in one more time before he left. He bolted downstairs, fast.

It is too hard to not turn around if I slow down.

∽

Zulimé spent her nights in Henry's loving embrace and her days worrying about her practice of vodou for she felt a limit to her abilities that she could not seem to overcome. One night she had a dream; she saw herself sitting under the big oak, her arms folded at first as she was chanting and as her voice grew louder, reaching up to the night sky through the tree's canopy. She saw tears on her face from despair, her features distorted from trying to reach the spirit Gods, her eyes blind to the moonlight that broke through the thick foliage and illuminated the Spanish moss. Her head sunk before she could notice the fireflies dancing and forming a circle around her, the wind parting the branches and engulfing her whole being in a white and purple fog. She saw herself not seeing any of it.

She woke up with a jolt, sat upright in the bed, the tears she had seen in her dream now flowing down her cheeks. She took a deep breath.

This is what keeps me from reaching the spirits! From achieving what I set out to do. I am so desperately concentrating on the wanting that the wanting becomes the goal, instead of the goal itself. I have been doing this wrong all along. I need to be open to the signs, the fireflies, the parted tree branches and the light behind the fog.

Zulimé climbed out of bed, careful not to wake Henry. On bare feet she tiptoed down the stairs, soundlessly opened the heavy front door and ran towards the sacred place on the creek's edge. Once there, she sat down on the soft mossy ground and raised her head up to the sky.

Thank you for this dream, great Damballah and your wife, the rainbow Goddess Ayida.

She saw a snake crawling up to her, lifted it up with both hands and bowed her head to it. Zulimé was certain that it was Damballah, the serpent deity, the earth creator and life-force whose manifestation she held in her hands. She bowed once more before she let him go. He circled up the trunk of the oak, his sacred tree until she could no longer see him, but his presence was all around her. And she began to sing. A song full of elation and hope. Her voice was full and loud:

Ala lwa mache nan dlo,	*Look, how the lwa walks on water,*
Se Danbala o!	*Oh, it is Damballah!*
Ala lwa mache nan dlo,	*Look, how the lwa walks on water,*

Se Danbala o!   *Oh, it is Damballah!*
Papa Danbala se tèt dlo!   *Papa Damballah is the water's spring!*
Papa Danbala se tèt dlo! Abobo!   *Papa Damballah is the water's spring! Abobo!*

Zulimé felt a major shift after that night. She had always been good at the medicinal part of vodou, relying mostly on her memory of her grandmother's recipes to heal others. But now, as she began experimenting, she followed her instincts, or signs as she called them, combining herbs that before her revelation would have seemed too strange a mix. She had a newfound trust in herself that transformed her former insecurities to certainties. The struggle to call on the Gods made way for an ease she had never known. There was no ailment of body or soul she could not cure, and everyone on the plantation relied on her including the enslaved people who were slowly warming up to *the special one* as they called her.

~

When October came and the days were getting colder, the thick summer air gave way to clear skies and endless sunshine. Zulimé and Henry spent evenings reading to each other or discussing the daily happenings, and their nights in the perfect rhythm of their affection. It was during their lovemaking, just as the sun was setting that she knew she would be with child. There was no surprise when a few weeks later her bleeding did not come. She had felt the baby before it was inside her. Standing by the window she told Henry. His eyes lit up when he pulled her into him, before they clouded over, and a deep crease appeared between his brows. Her face was on his chest, yet she sensed the tiny change and looked up. When he noticed her raising her head, he smiled again and kissed her forehead before the look of worry again settled over his features.

They kept up their Sunday trips to church as she was not showing yet. She did not speak of her happiness to anyone, and only Margarita knew at first glance. The Cuban set an extra plate of collards in front of her and removed the coffee cup: "You had one already, another one will make the bebé restless. I made you your favorite cake with chocolate filling and dates."

"My taste for sweets has only gotten stronger."

"Is this even possible?" Margarite said with loving mockery. They were alone in the kitchen. "Your Monsieur has been in the Mother Superior's office for quite some time," she remarked, "Will he tell the Sisters?"

Zulimé shook her head.

"What are you worried about?" Margarita asked.

"That he is not as happy as he says. And I do worry, too. I am his property. Will my child grow up a slave when I did not? When I was not one until the night before he bought me?"

It was the one subject Zulimé had never broached to Henry de Roche.

"He does not treat you like one, he never has..." was all Margarita could reply, knowing that this alone would not get rid of Zulimé's doubt.

When de Roche emerged from the Mother Superior's sanctum his step was heavier than usual. He had accomplished what he had set out to do, but there was no trace of joy in him. He knew that what he had to tell his beloved would hurt her deeply. They sat silently in the carriage on the way back, silently they walked into the house, and silently they made love that night. It was not until after, when she lay in his arms as always and his free hand was stroking the small bulge of her belly that he turned his face and stared at her for a long time.

"Henry..." she whispered, "speak to me of whatever it is that pains you..."

He pulled her even closer: "I asked the Mother Superior for Mademoiselle Mariette's hand in marriage."

Zulimé body jolted upwards, but his embrace was too strong. She felt the desperation with which he held her.

"I do not want this, but I cannot marry you. A plaçage is one thing, but a metissage is another. I cannot protect you and our child unless I keep up appearances."

She struggled free from his embrace: "You could if you wanted to! But you never ever believed me! Or refused to because it is convenient this way! You get what you want, and I have no choice!"

Henry had never seen such an outburst from her. But before he could respond, she put on her clothes and left his room. She ran downstairs and grabbed the small satchel with her belongings. She slung it across her body and left. She only realized that she was running when she reached the edge of the de Roche plantation. There she jumped over the fence and kept on going. She had no plan, no direction, just pain and anger that propelled her forward. It was dark, and she looked at the glimmer of the moon to guide her through the bayou.

Henry half expected her to return after a time of cooling off. The other half of him could not shake a fear that she had run away for good.

Why did I fool myself into believing a spirit like hers would simply accept an arrangement like this without rebellion?

It was this rebellion after all, this strength of conviction that he loved about her. When Zulimé was not back by daylight, he was forced to make a decision; ride out to find her, send Touton after her or alert the authorities. The only other option was to let her go and this he could not bear any more so than letting police punish her for running away. He got on his horse and instructed Touton to search every corner of the plantation, no matter how hidden while he would look for her on the roads. They spent the whole day trying to find her to no avail.

∽

Zulimé had wandered aimlessly through the night, one thought playing over and over in her head:

Is his love for me enough if he cannot bring himself to defy the rules society imposes on men like him?

By midday Zulimé was exhausted from walking, from the sun burning down on her, the lack of water and her own inability to break the cycle of her thoughts. She sat under a tree, its shade comforting her. She drifted into sleep. In her dreams she saw hands reaching out to her with one painting a circle over and over again. When she woke up it was late afternoon, and she remembered the visions but could not tell how many hands she had seen and if they were those of females or males.

What am I to do? Did the Gods show me the hands of the nuns that would surely take me in if I begged them for shelter? Or was it Henry's hand reaching for me?

She wondered about the circle, too. She got up and felt a sharp pain in her womb.

What have I done, endangering my child by running through the night?

The sudden pain in her body did not compare to the pain in her soul, but it did serve as a reminder that her highest responsibility was to her baby. Her memory of what her mother once said after Monsieur Larrác had visited her came to mind: I know that I am loved. That I am cared for and that you and grandmère are protected. That is enough for me."

Would it be enough for her, too? Zulimé remembered her response, the response of a child who did not know better: "But Mamán, why can you not visit him in the big house? Why is he always coming to our little house?"

And her mother's sad face, the inability to explain it all to her small daughter.

Was it best to enter an arrangement like this or leave and fend for herself and her child? And if she stayed, could she carve out her own place and stature? One that was better than her mother's, who never questioned that she was dependent on Monsieur's whims, his rules and his timeline?

Will I be relegated to a shack and hidden away, too? How will I explain it to MY child?

It was then that Zulimé stared into the horizon and saw it—the big oak, her sacred tree. And suddenly, the pointed circle in her dream made sense; all night she had walked in a big circle on the outside of the plantation only to end up almost where she had started.

What are the Gods telling me? I must find an answer. And water...

She walked towards the oak knowing that the creek that flowed through the property was near. Its crystal water did more than quench her thirst. It cleared her weary mind. She embraced the tree, tired and strangely relieved to be back there. She half expected her tears to flow, but a sense of power and calmness came over her instead as she looked up through the canopy.

What we have is not an acceptable arrangement. It is not enough for me, even though I know he cares for me and our unborn soul. But this does not change how powerless I am...

An idea took form.

Dusk settled over the plantation. De Roche had returned, exhausted from a night and a day of worry and desperation over not finding Zulimé. He let himself fall into his favorite chair on the terrace, contemplating a life without her. It made his heart constrict. His own childhood came to mind, a life of privilege tainted by unease when he played with his friends, most of them the sons of French settlers. How they sometimes looked down on him, the subtle comments about his skin not being quite as white as theirs, about his mother, a quiet woman whose own color was a shade browner than his own. When he got older, he knew that he owed his privilege to money not pedigree:

"I have worked hard as did your grandfather. We built the plantation from nothing. We are true Creoles," his father had told him on his sixteenth birthday, "Your friends' fathers were born into riches, they brought their wealth with them from Europe. They do not know how to plow fields or grow crops. They have the means to have others do the work for them, and they consider this their birthright."

His father had sent him to work in the fields along with everyone else when he was only ten years of age. His appreciation of the hard labor that went into a successful harvest grew out of his own experience. So did his affinity for the laborers, the enslaved and the free people who worked for a few livrés, barely enough to get by. He often wondered why he enjoyed their company more than those of his own class, but it also led him to an appreciation of the laborers that most of his wealthy acquaintances lacked. And an inner conflict about the concept of slavery that reared its head every time he felt injustice was added to the mix, especially where it concerned women. Like the day many years ago when his French friends had begun boasting about how easy the slave girls were in comparison to proper white women:

"They won't ever fight back if you give them the whip first," one laughed.

"Oui, and you can get them to do things a wife would never agree to!" hollered another.

It had made the young de Roche sick to his stomach. He had swallowed a forceful response until the night after a rum-fueled get-together on his father's terrace when one of them had grabbed the daughter of the family's housemaid, bent her over his knee, lifted her skirts and touched her in front of them. De Roche had jumped out of his chair and slammed his fist into the young man's nose so hard he fell back, toppling his chair. The others had to pull him off after he had been pummeling his young acquaintance's face.

"Do not ever even look at one of my family's servants again!" young Henry had screamed and thrown them all out. His father had made him apologize to both, the barely thirteen-year-old girl and his supposed friend:

"He was wrong to do what he did, but he has only ever seen his elders do the same. You cannot afford a feud with your friend's family. He has every reason to challenge you to a duel."

"He is no longer my friend!"

"Be that as it may, and it is certainly up to you to choose who you want to spend your time with. But we have different classes and structures in life and like it or not, a slave is not worth risking your life over," his father had cautioned.

The question of why one's life was worth more than another's and the necessity to own slaves if one were to run a plantation had created a chasm that had only deepened when de Roche met Zulimé.

The very least I can do is treat my servants like humans.

If he had ever questioned how deep his feelings for her had become, her disappearance gave him every answer he needed. It crushed his heart to ponder the possibility of losing her.

Zulimé saw him from afar, still hidden by the trees. She stepped out of the shadows. He looked up when he heard her. His face showed nothing but relief. She took a deep breath before she spoke. It had taken her an hour to come up with what she knew she had to say and how much she needed to tell him: "I know that you cannot marry me even if I were a free woman. Even though I am a free woman..." She let the words linger.

He nodded: "Je suis un negresse libre... that is what you said over and over the day I bought you."

"Oui, je suis un negresse libre."

She told him the whole story. Of her fifteenth birthday. Of what had happened before he bought her off the auction block...

∼

Zulimé was skipping down the street as the sun was setting. She was always joyful but today was special. Her mother had given her a pair of gold hoop earrings that had been passed down from her great grandmother. It was a sign that Zulimé was now considered a woman. The celebration of her birthday was planned for tonight. She was fifteen.

The last rays from the sun bathed her skin in a warm, golden glow. She was much lighter than Mamán and Grandmère. She knew the reason even though this was something never to be spoken of. Her family had been brought over from Africa, from a land called Senegambia after the slave catchers had sold them, but she, Zulimé, had been born here on this beautiful island of Saint Domingue. Grandmère had told her that Monsieur Larrác had so fallen in love with her as soon as she was out of Mamán's womb that he had given them all their freedom but insisted that they stay in a little house on his plantation on the outskirts of town. Her mother crafted beautiful pieces of jewelry and walked to town every day to sell them. Mamán also had clients in the rich houses who required her advice and healing herbs as she put it. Zulimé knew that she assisted them mostly with vodou spells and gris gris. She loved the bustling city and tried to join as much as her mother would permit, which was not very often. All this would change now that Zulimé turned fifteen. She was almost dancing in anticipation of this glorious future. The sun had set, and it was getting dark.

I must hurry. Mamán does not like it when I am out late.

She was on the dirt road that led to the plantation, the sounds of the city behind her. Zulimé never saw them coming. They jumped her from behind some banana trees, stuffed a rag in her mouth and threw a dirty sack over her head. She tried to cry out, but the rag muffled her scream. She felt ropes binding her on the outside of the sack from her feet to her neck. She could not move as she was lifted and thrown over a man's shoulder. When she tried to raise her head, the ropes almost strangled her. There must be two of them for she had felt four hands on her.

"That one should fetch a lot more than the others. The merchants love the golden ones."

Oh, no! They think I am a slave!

Zulimé felt an icy grip around her heart despite the heat. When the slave catchers reached their destination, she heard wailing. They loosened her ropes and pushed her into what must be a barn. She stumbled and fell against something. The something moved.

Another woman!

One of the men took off the sack but immediately tied her hands behind her back. She could barely see anything except wooden sticks. The men slammed the door shut, pulled a thick chain around it and left. Her eyes slowly adjusted to the darkness. The wailing came from a little girl, no more than seven years of age, who cowered in a corner. Zulimé spit out the rag. "Where am I?"

"In a shack. A cage."

The voice came from the other corner. Another girl. She must be close to her age. Zulimé yelled: "I am not a slave! *Je suis un affranchitte*! Ma mère est un affranchitte! Ma grandmère est un affranchitte! We are free women of color!"

"Do you have your papers? Can you prove it? Then you can show them tomorrow on the market."

She could not. The papers were with her grandmother. They had never needed them.

"If you can't show your papers, you will be sold like the rest of us."

The girl next to her spoke out loud what Zulimé feared most. Her feet gave out, she sank to the floor. A sound came from deep inside her, some untapped well she never knew was there. It started as a low growl and at first, she looked around to see where it originated until the trembles that rippled through her insides became so overwhelmingly strong from her navel to her heart that she realized in horror it was her who had lost control. She tried to stop it, but the silent scream threatened to suffocate her. She frightened herself more than the others when she let go and a voice broke out of her, so foreign and inhuman, it may have come from hell. She knelt on the ground with her hands bound in the back, her head thrown forward and upward waiting for the sound to disappear. When the last breath had left her, she slowly curled up, gasping for air with tears streaming.

Zulimé did not know how much time had passed when the cage door was opened by the two men, only that it must be morning by the light that was flooding the barn. She had not slept, nor had she been awake, caught in a spirit world suspended from earth yet knowing she was very much on it.

"Ah, merde!" the bigger of the man cursed: "Look at this dirty bunch of females! Now we must clean you up!"

He pulled her to her feet, she did not resist or help, like a ragdoll in his grip even when she was dragged outside with the other girls and women. The smaller man disappeared while they were tied together in a line. When he returned, he carried a wet rag.

"Not this one."

He stopped his companion from tying the youngest girl to the rest, put the rag in her hands and ordered her to wipe the faces of the others. The scared child did as she was told. Zulimé felt and smelled the stinking wetness on her tear- and dirt-stained face. The long walk to the market led them through the backroads, the men taking the long way there to avoid the busy main streets. As Zulimé stumbled along some of her strength came back.

I will not go quietly! Je suis un negresse libre…

∼

"I believe you," Henry said, "I knew you were different from the moment I laid eyes on you. You did not fit in with the others. You never behaved like a slave. You take freedom for granted because this is how you were raised."

He paused, and she was about to tell him what she promised herself under the oak a short while earlier, but he was faster: "I will rectify this. Our child will not be born into slavery."

It was the moment that broke the well. It was what she had wanted to tell him as a condition for staying. And now he had met her not just halfway but with his full conviction and commitment. He took her wet face into his hands and kissed her cheeks, her eyes, her mouth. "Don't cry, ma petit chèrie, please don't cry."

She smiled at him and shook her head: "Henry…my tears have changed. They no longer emanate from my knotted stomach but from my radiating heart. I shall be free. An affranchitte again."

De Roche kept his word. A week later he gave her the papers. Zulimé felt reborn. A free woman of color. All he asked of her was that she not leave him. That she would bring up their children—for he wanted many more—right here on his plantation. It was an easy promise, she said, if he allowed her to make her own money just as her mother had. He did not ask how she would earn her wages assuming she would accept his salary for housework. She had other plans.

CHAPTER 21

The Lord has blessed us with good timing after the rough winds of the past concerning the Casket Girls. Marriages are beginning, things are falling into their rightful place...

Sister Stanislaus sat in the backrow of the chapel and could not help smiling as she put down her journal. Another woman was about to get married and not for a moment did the Sister doubt that it was pure love that had brought together the blessed couple.

Margarita smiled to herself as she was chucking beans for the day's meal. The previous night Señor José Castro had asked Señorita Margarita Cortez for her hand.

"I made him wait a whole year," she chuckled when she told Sister Stanislaus, "What a patient and consistent man."

Margarita was still smiling when hours later she was walking down Rue St. Pierre and bumped into Geneviève who was exiting her house: "*Bonjour*, Margarita, so nice to see you!" Margarita returned the greeting after which the two women stood awkwardly for a moment. "Would you like to see my house? I was on my way out but catching up with you takes precedence. Will you join me for a cup of tea?" Geneviève finally asked.

Margarita hesitated but curiosity got the better of her. After a tour of the home and a few sips of the tea— "I do not dare serve you coffee, no one makes that better than you", Geneviève had laughed—the two women settled into their old familiarity. Margarita shared her happy news, and after congratulating her Geneviève felt a tinge of sadness: "Sometimes I wish I was open to a new husband. But my heart tells me otherwise."

Of course, I have a bigger obstacle to overcome than the Cuban. She only hit her ex-husband.

"Where will you get married? I would love to host you." Geneviève said.

～

Margarita and José wed in a short ceremony in the chapel next to the church. Sister Stanislaus served as a witness at the registry where Margarita signed her name on the marriage certificate, and José made an X on the document.

This must change.

Margarita was determined to teach her husband how to read and write. José never had the chance to learn, but she considered herself lucky to be taught at the Ursuline school and had every intention to pass her education on to him. Some of the Ursulines along with her fellow Cuban cooks and a few of the Casket Girls attended a small reception where, following a Cuban tradition, the unmarried women pulled on colorful ribbons that had been baked into the wedding cake, one of them attached to a ring. Whoever pulled it was next to be married, so the superstition. To everyone's surprise, and not the least her own, it was Louise, the most reluctant participant, who got the ring. The look in her eyes spoke of embarrassment, disbelief and downright revulsion. It was not until Sister Stanislaus came back to the convent that night and told the Mother Superior about the reception that the Sister was informed of Henry de Roche's impending proposal to Louise Mariette.

"Mother St. Augustin, if you don't mind me saying so; Louise loathed being the one who pulled the ribbon with the ring. I do not believe she is ready to be married."

The Mother Superior waved her off: "Mademoiselle Mariette should consider herself lucky. Monsieur de Roche is a generous, noble soul who could do much better than to take a simple country girl for his wife."

Sister Stanislaus could agree with this sentiment. But another suspicion gnawed at her conscience; that the generous, noble merchant loved another.

Louise was the last one to know about her fate. Acadia had overheard Zulimé telling Margarita who in turn mentioned it to Geneviève who had already been made aware by Sister Stanislaus. The Mother Superior called Louise into her office and informed her of the decision, one that did not include Louise's consent. When the girl left the office, she looked like she was about to be led to the gallows instead of the altar.

No one cares about my wishes. No one ever did. My father sold me to the Ursulines, and now the nuns sold me to a man I barely know.

Louise had no tears left. She had cried too many after the soldier had violated her. And again, when Sister Stanislaus had rejected her wish to join their order. It was the Sister who recognized the dead look in her eyes and took her to the chapel: "We believed you would be joyful if not happy that your biggest fear of no man ever wanting you as a wife has been averted. This gentleman came to us with the proposal, we did not ask him. He must feel something for you."

The nun went on to praise de Roche's kindness, his generosity towards the convent and listed the many occasions he had come to their aid. Louise listened without response.

What could I possibly say? I do not have the strength to rebel like others would and did…

The Sister was still talking: "I am not supposed to put importance on his worldly possessions, but you will not be left wanting. Monsieur de Roche is a successful merchant with two plantations to his name. You saw the one in Saint Domingue, and I hear he plans to make this one here just as beautiful. You will be the lady of the house."

Louise perked up at these words.

The lady of the house… If I am to marry the man, at least I will not be like my poor mother who married for love but never had more than two dresses to wear and not enough money to pay for the doctors that could have saved her life.

In the coming days Louise's disposition changed. The future lady of the house had yet to talk to her betrothed, yet she was already planning a lavish wedding ceremony in her head. Unbeknownst to her de Roche was planning the opposite. He did not want to cause Zulimé more pain by flaunting his wedding, and he was trying to hold off the nuptials until their baby was born in the summer. When the merchant met with his fiancé shortly before Christmas, he courtly informed her that they would have their wedding in the chapel in a year's time. Her disappointment showed, and he reluctantly agreed to a compromise; they would have the ceremony on the plantation, but he could not move up the date. He cited long travels to the islands as the reason. In truth, he did not want to leave Zulimé's side more than necessary and planned to keep his journeys as short as possible.

Down at the port Florence met the brothers' ship when it returned from the islands. She always took inventory right there at the offloading of the goods the Bèrangers brought back from their voyages. She expected to see the usual barrels of rum and possibly a few casks of champagne and crates filled with jewelry or gold. Instead, a group of dark-skinned women were ushered down the gang plank by the pirates.

"Housemaids," Michél informed her as he walked them past her, "from the islands. They need work, and we can rent them out."

Florence grabbed his shirt: "Do you think I have gone blind while you were at sea?"

Jean stepped in: "Shouldn't you count the rum barrels?"

"What do you want with them?"

"The rum?"

"The women, your new commodity!"

"Like my brother said, we shall rent them out as housemaids and make a profit from their earnings."

"You will make a profit from their earnings, no doubt, but it won't come from housework!"

If Florence's anger surprised Jean, he did not show it. Her voice got louder: "Look at them! They barely know how to clean themselves much less a house!"

Jean had to admit the truth to his business partner. He had known all along that Florence would never believe the housemaid story Michél had come up with. "The girls were employees of a brothel in Port-au-Prince that recently burnt down and left them penniless on the streets and in the harbor. That is where Michél had found them."

His brother intercepted: "They were begging us to take them along in the hopes of a better life."

Florence almost laughed: "And you, smelling a new business opportunity, happily obliged. Did you even think of the fact that we do not have room to put them up?"

"They are sleeping on the ship for now, and yes, we do know that this is not a permanent solution."

Jean paused and shot his brother a look. Michél took over: "Which is why we want to rent the building in the back of Madame Cocotte's cabarét and put them to work."

Florence could not believe what she was hearing: "La Cocotte is the best brothel in the city, if you can say that about an etablissement like that. They are supplying their own women to their patrons, and those are much cleaner than the filth you dragged across the seas. So, why would Madame Cocotte agree to this arrangement?"

Now Michél looked at Jean who coughed: "Because we told her that you would run the women, and she trusts you."

Florence jumped up: "Are you mad? I will not run a brothel and pimp out a bunch of putains! Not now, not ever!"

∽

Florence had long since given up on her secret dream of merging the business and the personal when it came to Jean. The pirate never hid his dalliances with streetwalkers, but when he showed up at La Cocotte with Jeanette Crozat that night who sneered at Florence while she sat spread-eagled on Jean's lap, frocks up to her knees, and corsage barely covering her large bosoms, Florence as tightly wound as she was, lost her composure: "Sit on someone else's cock!" she raged while yanking her off him: "How dare you bring your putain to a business meeting! Of all the whores on Rue de Bourbon, it had to be the dirtiest one?" she screamed at Jean, "Are you not afraid of catching some disease?"

The pirate laughed: "Calm down, partner. Our business is over, time for pleasure."

Jeanette, empowered by his words sat back down on top of him. But Florence was not done. She grabbed Jeanette by the sloppy bun on the back of her neck and threw her to the ground.

"Mesdames et Messieurs, a fight!" yelled Michél.

The patrons gathered around the two women. Jeanette, struggling to get out from under, hissed: "Let me go, you thieving forçat!"

Putting her foot on the woman's chest, Florence's voice became icy: "At least I'm not selling myself to every limping sailor on the docks!" She bent down: "You better watch yourself. I will have you thrown out of the convent." She took off her foot, and Jeanette got up. The woman knew she was no match for Florence. She brushed herself off and left the cabarét under jeering from the crowd.

"Ah, women. Never a real fight. All they use is words," an older man commented with a nasty smirk.

"I don't hit women," Florence responded, "but I have no qualms about using my fists against men!"

Jean stepped in and grabbed her arm: "Take a breath." Florence watched the old man, eyes narrowing as Jean pulled her back to the table. "You owe me another," he said when she sat down.

"Another what?"

"Another woman. You disrupted my plans for the night."

"Find one yourself. And use better judgement. There are some who do not reek of sweat and cheapness."

He laughed again. She pointed at one of La Cocotte's house girls, a pretty, light skinned mulatto who smiled when she noticed she was being talked about. Jean turned to Florence and put his hand on hers: "You pay for her."

She brusquely shook him off but took out her *portemonnaie* and dropped a gold coin between the girl's breasts. The mulatto bowed slightly and sat down on Jean's knee. Florence downed her drink and got up: "I have had enough of your entertainment."

Jean's laughter rang in her ears until she was blocks away from the cabaret. His rebuke still stung, but she found satisfaction in having gotten rid of the putain from Biloxi, as she referred to Jeanette.

I must form another alliance. I cannot continue to count on the loyalty of the brothers.

The knowledge that she would need another man pained her. With these thoughts on her mind, she spotted Josephine at a tavern entrance. Their friendship had been strained since the Casket Girls' ball, but lacking another woman she could confide in, Florence asked: "Mind if I join you?"

Josephine nodded, and Florence shared her thoughts with the

Vicomtesse. And was met with a blank stare: "Why reject the protection of a man?" The aristocrat was incredulous: "Is that not what they are there for? To ensure our safety, our well-being?"

As soon as the words were out of her mouth, Josephine questioned their sincerity.

What good has it done me?

It suddenly occurred to her that she had never considered true independence. It was not how she was brought up. Men always made the decisions.

But was it not this very arrangement that cost me my way of life?

Florence interrupted Josephine's thoughts: "And do you believe that is really the best arrangement? Protection comes with a cost. Every time. In the end we all pay for it…"

That evening neither of the two women stayed late. On her way home Josephine pondered Florence's words. But when she looked at her grand mansion and thought of her loyal husband, she shook off the doubts. Despite her obsession with Michél and the complicated way they arranged their tete-à-tetes, she did not want to leave her husband or the life he provided for her. To keep Valdeterre in a happy state Josephine pretended that she was willing to try for a child. And was relieved at the first drop of blood every month. She had a suspicion as to why she could not get pregnant.

Something went wrong in France…

Josephine did not call what she felt for her husband love but contentment. She had a deep appreciation for his innate goodness. He was a better man than any other, including her father, uncle and brothers. He was the saintly knight who came to everyone's aid, the perfect gentleman who would get up when a lady left the table, adjust her chair, refill her glass and make sure her feet do not touch the mud when climbing into a carriage. The kind of man who anticipated her next move before she knew what it was. The lover who was as gentle in the bedroom as he was at the dinner table. And that was what made her think of the painting on the wall, slightly tilted toward the left, the curtains that needed mending and the tiny scratch on her dresser while he was inside her, instead of the spine-tingling ecstasy she felt with Michél. The pirate had remained a forceful lover who cared enough to make certain he pleased her. She liked that he was so sure of his skills, and his skills where many, sending waves of wanting through her even when he was far away, and she was only imagining his touch.

The only time her body erupted in the same way with her husband was when she closed her eyes, pushed the picture of her bedroom ceiling out of her mind and conjured up a vision of Michél instead. The Commander's shock at his wife openly showing her pleasure made her feel shame, and she never did it again. She reserved her most abandoned passion not for the man who loved her with tenderness but for the pirate. Whatever had repulsed Josephine about the man in Paris all these years ago, she now craved like an addiction.

Funny, how men can never hide their true nature while inside a woman. Or in the moments after their satisfaction ebbs.

CHAPTER 22

For Zulimé life on the plantation was almost blissful in this new year. She pushed Louise out of her mind, enjoying every moment of her pregnancy instead. Her beloved Henry was intent on making her happy, worrying about every little discomfort her condition caused. She laughed when she saw his concerned look, assuring him that she was fine, that the baby inside her was doing well and that she knew enough about pregnancy to take the right herbs for her morning sickness. She did not tell him of the other remedies, said nothing of her long walks to the creek, her moon ceremonies with the serpent that lived near the oak, a sign to her that the great Damballah was there to protect her. The breakthrough that had come with recognizing her own intuition, had grown into a heightened stage since she was with child. She saw the signs clearer, the colors brighter and heard the messages louder. She would have a boy, a son.

Zulimé sang to both her men, beautiful melodies of contentment and joy but also of strength. Henry's worries disappeared, now that he was invited to listen.

Papa Legba nan ounfò mwen	*Papa Legba is in my temple*
Atibon Legba nan ounfò mwen	*Atibon Legba is in my temple*
Alegba Papa nan ounfò mwen	*Alegba Papa is in my temple*
Ou menm ki pote drapo nan Ginen	*You bear the flag in Ginen*

> *Ou menm ki pote chapo nan Ginen* You wear the hat in Ginen
> *Se ou menm k a pare solèy pou lwa yo.* It's you who will shade the sun for the lwa.

When Henry had to leave for a few weeks, Zulimé felt safe with Touton in charge. In March, she felt her son moving inside her for the first time. That night de Roche returned from his journey. She flew into his arms and took him to the bedroom. She lifted her dress and put his hands on her belly. The baby's kick was so strong that they could see it on the outside of her stomach. The couple's apparent happiness was tainted only by the knowledge that their open show of it would end on the day of Henry's wedding to Louise. That these remaining months might be the best time of their lives and the freest.

When the heat turned stifling at the beginning of July, Zulimé felt that her time was coming. She asked Henry to fetch Bebé from the convent to help her after the birth. Her labor began a few days later. Henry insisted she give birth in the house, not in the hut the servants used for births. The labor lasted a day and a half as heat and humidity made it difficult to breathe. In a dark vision during the night, she saw a lion struck down by lightening, his dead eyes staring up to the sky. Her breathing became frantic for she had referred to her baby as a lion just the day before her labor began. At noon the following day, with Henry pacing the hallways, their son was born with a healthy scream. Zulimé was relieved that her baby was alive but could not shake her vision. They named him Stephane. His father was overjoyed and did not leave the house for four days carrying the baby around when she was not nursing him and tending to her every need. Then he sent for a priest. His son was a free man of color and would be baptized. De Roche also put Stephane's name on a deed of land adjacent to the plantation that he had secretly set aside for him.

Zulimé's entire being was filled with love for Stephane, this tiny yet strong creature. If she had one regret, it was that her mother and grandmother were not here to witness her new life and meet their grandson and great-grandson. The birth of a child had always been a cause for celebration and rituals that had one common goal: to protect a new soul against the earth's harsh forces. She pushed the fearsome vision out of her mind. Henry rode to the city to meet a ship and receive his cargo at the harbor. He was going to stay for a few days to carry out some business with the market vendors. One night, just before the first moon was over in the newborn's life, Zulimé carried their son to the creek at midnight and presented him to Damballah. She asked the spirits to protect him.

Zulimé danced and chanted the words to appeal to the spirits. She saw the serpent crawling out on the extended branch right over her head. She was comforted by its sight, reading it as a sign that the Gods had heard her and received the message. When she was in her last round of chanting the moon that had shone clear and bright was suddenly covered by a dark cloud. The serpent hissed and disappeared rapidly into a hole in the oak's thick stem. Loud thunder was followed by lightening. Little Stephane began to cry as heavy raindrops fell on him and his mother. Zulimé wrapped him in his cloth. Clutching the baby bundle to her chest she ran back to the house. Her face was wet, not from the rain but from her tears. For the next few days, she was inconsolable. Her milk dried up until Stephane screamed from hunger, and she was brought out of her despair by his needs. She made a soup to get her milk flowing again and a salve to soothe her sore breasts. When de Roche returned everything seemed normal save for her reluctance to let go of the baby when he tried to hug his son.

Henry misread her behavior: "Are you angry with me for being away these past days, mon amour?"

She shook her head and slowly handed him Stephane. She could not share her fears and dark foreboding with him.

He will never understand it. I am the only one who can protect Stephane.

∼

In the city, Florence had a dark foreboding of her own. The brothers kept bringing up the idea of the brothel:

"With your skills, you could turn it into a high-class etablissement, you have the best taste! You can run everyone out of business including Madame Cocotte.

"Flattery? Is this how you think you can change my mind?"

Her deadly stare made them change their tone: "We can throw you out and run our own business!"

Their threat was met with a hearty laugh: "Why don't you do that? I can't wait to see your bookkeeping and math skills. Talk to me when you have learned additions and the alphabet." Florence knew she had the upper hand. For now. She had another worry; with one girl after the other leaving the convent to get married or finding employment somewhere, the attic was getting emptier.

I cannot risk my casquette to be the only one left up there.

Florence had heard of Louise's impending nuptials to Monsieur de Roche. The Mariette girl's casket was the one stacked just above hers. She had considered this an insurance against anyone going through her belongings. Now her casket would be left exposed.

I must find a way to get it, but short of breaking into the convent...

A solution came when she engaged one of the cooks in conversation and found out the date of the wedding, the fifteenth day of December, a Saturday at the noon hour, because the merchant wanted to take his bride all the way up to his plantation right after. Everyone from the convent would be there.

And I shall be at the convent when everyone is in the chapel.

~

Louise Mariette of Trèves, France did not look like a happy bride about to be united with the man of her dreams, when she walked up to the altar to be given in marriage to Monsieur Henry de Roche of La Nouvelle

Orleàns, La Louisiane, but she carried herself with an unrecognizable confidence to those who knew her. Her wedding gown was simple but adorned with a veil of delicate lace that her betrothed had gifted her with. De Roche stood with dignity, his hands folded when she walked down the aisle, while his thoughts were with his true love and their son. He reminded himself that he was marrying Louise to protect them from gossip. And admitted that he was protecting himself from the same.

I am marrying a shy and kind woman who will treat Zulimé well and run my household with dignity and care.

He could not have been more wrong. The merchant and the country girl said their vows in front of the whole congregation.

Less than a stone's throw away from the chapel, Florence gained entrance to the convent by slipping the only Cuban cook who had not gone to the wedding a few coins to let her in. She climbed up to the attic.

There it is, the casquette with my initials.

It was too heavy for her to carry, with the many stolen treasures in it. Florence had anticipated this and removed a sack from underneath her skirts. She opened her casket and began moving jewelry, rolls of coins and other valuables. She carefully closed the casket after the only things left in it were a wedding gown, a pair of lace-up boots and a bible, none of which she had any use for. When she climbed down the ladder the sack slipped out of her hand. Her treasures hit the floor and made a sharp, clattering noise that brought one of the cooks running upstairs. It cost Florence another roll of coins to buy the woman's silence.

A few hours upriver, Zulimé tried to calm herself with tea and prayer. Her year of bliss was over. There were to be no more nights in Henry's bed, no more roaming freely across the plantation hiding neither her joy nor her love. From now on she would have to stay in her place, hoping for a visit from the father of her son when time and his new wife permitted. It did not help that she knew Louise as a woman who had always looked down on her, and Zulimé's intuition told her that Louise would not be pleased when she learned of their arrangement. De Roche had built a small house on the property close to the creek and the oak, her healing place. It was far enough from the big house as well as the slave quarters to afford her privacy. She decorated it with old furniture that she found in the barn. Henry built a crib for his son with his own hands and the largest bed Zulimé had ever seen for the two of them. The house was beautiful, but nothing could chase away her sadness, not even her happily gurgling Stephane, whose prominent nose was a copy of his Papá's and whose heart-shaped lips reminded her of her mother. Henry had forewarned her; he would return tonight with his bride.

～

De Roche took his new wife home in a carriage after the ceremony. They tried to talk about pleasant, unimportant things, but the conversation halted every few minutes. Only when he brought up his plans to make the plantation more like the one, Louise had visited in Saint Domingue did her eyes light up. She would do her best to make the mansion as splendid as the other one, she said.

"Don't be disappointed when you see my... our home here. It is not as grand."

Louise thought he was joking until the carriage pulled up to the house. For that is what it was, a house not a mansion. The disappointment was written all over her face. De Roche asked her to join him on the balcony outside of their bedroom for a cup of rum. He did not want them to spend time together on the porch that carried so many memories of delightful, romantic evenings with Zulimé.

I must push Zulimé out of my mind. At least for tonight.

Louise declined his offer of a drink. "I am very tired."

When de Roche left the balcony a little while later, Louise was asleep in her nightgown with the high collar and the sheets pulled up to her neck. The marriage was not consummated that night. Or the next. Or any day of the following week. Louise came up with a new excuse every day. Mostly it was that the preparation for their big celebration the following weekend kept her busy and exhausted. De Roche did not push or try to seduce her. Instead, he found a few moments with Zulimé and Stephane. Both mother and son had not left their little home and the surrounding area since the new Madame had arrived. Zulimé knew of the festivities planned for the next Sunday. She did not expect an invitation but had made it clear to Henry that she would not work as a servant that day. These were the occasions when she was put in her place; when being an affranchitte did not matter, when the lines were drawn between master and servant. It was in these moments when Zulimé summoned all her vodou goddesses to find strength.

At the behest of the new lady of the house, the entire delegation of nuns had been asked to attend the reception. De Roche saw to it that Valdeterre received an invitation over the objections of his bride: "I do not want Madame de Valdeterre at our festivities. Do you know we called her mighty Princess? She is a dreadfully entitled woman."

De Roche insisted: "My dear, the Commander is not just an important man, I also consider him a friend. And I cannot possibly ask him to attend without his wife, that would be disrespectful. You will have to welcome her. I do not expect you to spend the entire evening with her, you can avoid her after a few words. And considering how many people you already invited, that should not be too difficult." He could not resist the comment, having tried to keep the celebration small and low-key to no avail.

∼

On Sunday, de Roche got an idea of their future life together, and he did not appreciate it. Louise may have called Madame de Valdeterre mighty

Princess, but it was she who acted like one. Louise stood beaming on her husband's arm, welcoming the guests like a reigning royal greets her subjects. It seemed studied, as if she had read it in one of the female novels about forgotten dynasties. She looked like she expected her guests to bow to her. But she need not have worried about the Commander's wife. After a quick 'bon jour', Josephine rushed past her to catch one of the waiters with the tablet of champagne. She took a goblet and disappeared to the back gardens. There she took a deep breath. She had lied to Michél about her weekend plans after trying to get out of this obligation unsuccessfully; the Commander would have none of it when Josephine suggested that he should attend the wedding celebration by himself, any more than de Roche would allow Louise to invite the man without his wife. Josephine had hoped to spend the day with her lover not at this dreadfully boring féte. She had told Michél that her husband had to attend a military march outside of the city, and she needed to accompany him in fear of Michél causing yet another scene at someone's house. Josephine was not sure the pirate believed her but there was no way for him to find out. She ventured deeper into the gardens and out through a gate. She followed the path along a creek when she felt eyes on her.

The slave girl! Of course, she lives on her Master's plantation.

Zulimé, with Bebé at her side, stepped in front of Josephine who said: "You know, I always wanted to buy you."

"You are too late for that, Madame."

"Oh, I know, you are the merchant's property."

Zulimé knew she should not respond, but her pride would not allow her to keep quiet: "I am no one's property, Madame. Je suis un affranchitte."

Josephine laughed: "You always had such a high-minded attitude about you."

Zulimé shook her head: "Non, I always was a free woman. But now Monsieur de Roche signed my papers, so it is legal in this land, too."

Josephine was surprised. "Well, too bad. You would have made a good addition to my household." She glanced at Bebé. "Maybe you are available..."

Bebé with fear in her eyes snuggled up to Zulimé, her hand clenching her friend and mentor's.

Zulimé turned away: "Bon nuit, Madame." She left Josephine standing on the dark path with her half empty champagne goblet.

Back in the house, Louise's forced joyfulness took its toll on the guests. Conversations were strained. Sister Stanislaus watched the former country girl, a crease of worry between her brows as she went outside onto the porch. The torches on either side of the road illuminated the surroundings and the Sister walked on, drawn by curiosity about this plantation that Louise now lived on. She saw a little house ahead, much smaller than the main one yet much bigger than the huts the enslaved lived in. A light shone through the window, and the nun heard a baby crying. A rustling sound was coming from the overgrown trees on the side of the house, and she saw the glimmer of a pair of eyes.

"Is anyone out there?" she asked.

Bebé stepped out of the shadows. The girl's curiosity had gotten the better of her, and she had circled the house trying to catch a glimpse of the new Madame de Roche and her guests. She had seen Sister Stanislaus who had always been kind and fair to her leave the porch and had followed her down the path to Zulimé's home.

"Have you been well, Bebé?"

The girl nodded.

"Where is Zulimé?" the Sister continued and the eleven-year-old pointed to the door. Sister Stanislaus knocked. Zulimé opened with her six-month-old son strapped to her hip. The nun's eyes widened in surprise: "Whose baby is this?"

Zulimé tried to come up with a story, but it was too late, so she chose the truth: "Mine. My son. His name is Stephane. We live here."

The Sister, however curious, did not ask about the little boy's father. "Do you not have to work?"

"I do some housework, that's all."

"Your master does not have you work in the fields?"

Zulimé swallowed hard before she answered: "Sister, he is not my master. And I am not his slave. I am a free woman, as I have always been, from the day I was born. Now I have it in writing again. Monsieur signed the papers. If I so choose, I could go wherever I want. I could come back to the convent and work in the kitchen. For pay, of course. Right now, I choose to stay here and get paid for my housework."

Twice in one evening I told my story to two very different women.

A kind smile appeared on the Sister's face. She took Zulimé's hand in hers: "So, you always did tell the truth. I am glad he saw it and acted accordingly. If you ever plan on working in the city, please come to us first."

Zulimé nodded.

It gives me comfort to know that there is another open door for me to walk through if—for whatever reason—this one closes on me.

On her way back to the city with her fellow Sisters, Marie Madeleine Hachard was unusually quiet. She thought of Zulimé and her son and the little boy's color of skin, too light to belong to the offspring of an African.

∼

Zulimé had avoided her new mistress all through the Christmas holiday. On the first day of the new year 1732, Madame de Roche decided to have a small soirée with the neighboring plantation owners and their wives. She needed help preparing, so Cecile called on Zulimé. When the two former Ursuline charges came face to face Louise's surprise was written all over her tight features: "I did not know my husband gave you permission to work in the house."

Zulimé took a deep breath. She had prepared for the confrontation and was angry that Henry had neglected to inform his wife of her status. "Louise… Madame, your husband signed my papers. I am not a slave, and I get to pick my chores around the plantation for which I get paid for. I am glad to be of help in the house."

Louise had no response. She could not go against her husband's decision, but that did not mean she liked it. For now, the former slave was not what was on her mind first and foremost. After Christmas, she had run out of excuses to fulfill her marital duties. Sexual relations had happened but once, and she had endured them as she knew she was supposed to. It had not been as bad as she had feared. Her husband was a gentle man. But when he touched her, the memories from that dreadful evening in the tavern floated to the edge of her consciousness, and it took all her strength not to scream out loud.

I must get used to this if I want to have a family.

De Roche had not looked forward to consummating the marriage any more than his wife. He knew of the incident at the tavern and had no idea how it would affect her. They had decided on separate bedrooms after their wedding night. When Louise did invite him into her chambers on Christmas Eve, he did his duty on top of a woman who would not move once and lay there with her lips pressed together. He tried to embrace her afterwards, but she curtly informed him that she preferred to sleep alone.

The living arrangements between Monsieur and Madame de Roche were very much in Zulimé's favor. Henry spent most nights in her arms. He would walk down the path to her little house after Louise had retreated to her rooms which was always early. Zulimé and Henry read to each other after little Stephane fell asleep. Henry often brought leftovers and stayed until dawn. His wife preferred to eat breakfast in bed, a luxury that noble women indulged in, so she had heard. Henry used his early mornings to play with his son before returning to the big house. He felt much more married to Zulimé than to Louise. One day at dawn, Zulimé broached the subject that had been on her mind ever since the new lady of the house had moved in: "Does Louise know about our son? Considering that you left it up to me to tell her about my freedom?"

Henry had feared this question. He avoided looking at her when he answered: "I see no need to tell her."

"But I cannot keep Stephane hidden from her," Zulimé responded. "And once she sees him, she will recognize the resemblance. He has your nose, mon cher. Your chin and even your laugh. It could be very bad for me and Stephane if she does not hear this from you."

He could not deny her reasoning.

"Plaçages like ours are widely accepted, she will have to come to terms with it," he said.

"Once Louise has children of her own, she will hardly concern herself with you."

"How can she get with child if you are spending every night in my bed?"

Henry sighed: "I am trying, mon amour, I am trying."

De Roche had every intention to tell his wife about his lover and son but thought it better to wait until after Louise had given birth to her own child. He made every effort to gain entrance to her bedroom. She consented no more than once every other week. Zulimé suffered those nights, caught between her loneliness and the certainty of knowing that she, not Louise had his love. Still, she never took Stephane with her to the big house when she worked, leaving him in Bebé's care. On his first birthday in July, his father gave him a little wagon made of wood. The boy giggled and climbed in immediately, trying to move it by wiggling back and forth. That elicited chuckles from his parents, until Stephane realized he was not getting the thing to move and started crying. Henry laughed, grabbed the handle and pulled him in a big circle until he giggled again with spit dribbling down his chin.

None of them saw or heard Louise coming down the path. She had followed the laughter, curious as to who was enjoying themselves on the outskirts of the property. Louise had never been this far to the edge of the plantation. She was surprised when she caught sight of a house behind the cypress trees. And stopped short when she recognized her husband and Zulimé. She hid behind a thick trunk and watched the playful scene. She felt a bitter taste in her mouth when she took a look at the little boy. The discovery left her with conflicting emotions. She did not feel love for her husband and yet, when she saw the joy on his features jealousy rose up in her.

I have never seen him like this when he spends time with me. What kind of spell has this dark woman cast on him?

Henry picked up the little boy and threw him in the air. Stephane gurgled and let out a delighted scream when his father caught him in midair. Louise stepped on a twig, and it made a creaking sound when it snapped under her foot, but the three of them were too engaged to notice. Louise stood still, trying not to breathe.

I will have to do my duty and make him come to me more often. Once I have a son of my own, he will forget about them.

Every Sunday from then on Louise insisted that her husband sleep in her bed in the hopes of getting pregnant. Every month those hopes were dashed. She could not shake her resentment of the former slave girl who had ascended to be the number one woman in her husband's heart. And she let Zulimé feel it, coldly ordering her around, making her repeat simple tasks, complaining about the smallest things, like a place setting at the dinner table that was a finger width too far to one side or a candle that had too many wax drippings run off it. Nothing the servant did was ever right, and Zulimé gave up trying to please Louise.

Henry must have told her of us. And now she is even more unpleasant than before.

Zulimé felt protected by Henry's love for her and their boy. As a further assurance she had begun to hold vodou rituals on the nights that her beloved spent at his house. These gatherings near the creek were attended by many of the enslaved, some of them remembering similar events in their native Africa. When the wind blew from the right direction carrying the sounds away from the main house, a few of the males accompanied her chants with drumming. They used wood sticks, boards, metal scraps and furniture as their instruments. Whatever they could find and turn into a drum, cymbals, a banjo or a *cajón*. Zulimé provided the voice during parts of the ceremony. Her song was different from the ones she reserved for Henry. It was monotonous, in rhythm with the drums, repeating the same words over and over. A song of their past. A song of survival.

Si pa te gen Lwa, nou tout nou ta neye!	*If there weren't Lwa, as for us, we'd all drown!*
Si pa te gen Lwa, nou tout nou ta peri o	*If there weren't Lwa, as for us, oh, we'd all perish*
nan peyi letranje	*in foreign countries.*

Zulimé had found a snake that she kept in a cage. She would take it out and hold it high above her head at the culmination of each ceremony asking for safety and health for all the attendees and for continued protection for her son. These rituals were the only way to keep her dark visions at bay. Visions that had not disappeared over time.

CHAPTER 23

At the convent Acadia grew more and more restless. With Zulimé, Bebé and Margarita gone, she had no friends left and as much as she enjoyed caring for baby Ayita, she longed for grown-up conversations that extended beyond school hours. One late afternoon she was called in by the Mother Superior: "Today I received a visit from Monsieur Perault…"

Acadia was confused. Monsieur Perault was the blacksmith from Rue Royale who had been fixing door hinges and other broken metal things at the convent.

Why is Mother St. Augustin talking about him?

"Abondance, you know that he is a widower, don't you?"

It was not so much the question, but that the Abbess called her by her real name that made Acadia uncomfortable. Even the head of the convent had only used this name in very serious conversations or when she had chided her for some wrongdoing.

"He is looking for a new wife and a mother for his children."

Why is she telling me this?

Acadia still failed to understand. The Mother Superior cleared her throat: "Abondance, we would like you to consider his proposal…"

"Proposal? Me? He wants me to…"

The idea was so outrageous in Acadia's mind that she could find neither the right color nor the right words to describe it. When it finally sank in, everything became a deep crimson, her color of rage: "I will not marry an old man and play mother to a bunch of children I have never met!" Acadia took a deep breath and before the Abbess could respond, she ran out of her office.

"Abondance Gravois! Come back here this moment!"

The sharp tone stopped Acadia in her tracks. There was no running from this. She had to take a stand. Slowly she turned and walked back. Her demeanor was no longer obeisant. With a straight back and a raised head, she spoke: "Mother, I will not marry a man of your choosing. I will marry when I am ready. Then I will find a man on my own. I am not ready. My most important goal is to find mon père et mon frère, not marry. I did not come over on some ship from France. I am not a Casket Girl."

Acadia did not wait for a response she feared would be harsh. She had spoken her peace. When she left the room, she caught a glimpse of Sister Stanislaus. The nun had overheard the last part of the argument and knew what she had to do. When the Sister walked into the Abbess' office, she saw a most unusual expression on her superior's face—utter discomfiture.

"Did you hear what this young woman said in response to me proposing she marry? How... defiant... disrespectful..." The Abbess was at a loss for words, and Sister Stanislaus felt a tinge of pity. When she responded however, it was in the voice of Marie Madeleine: "Acadia is a rebel, Mother, but she is not wrong. She did not sail here on the Gironde. She did not come with a casquette. There is no dowry. She is no Casket Girl."

"She was thrown at our door by the members of her family!" The Mother Superior had found her voice again and it was strained. "She may not be a Casket Girl in the proper sense, but we have treated her like one. And the Vicomtesse de Chavin left her dowry which we gifted this young woman with. She has attended the Casket Girls' ball. In my mind all this makes her one."

"And yet we cannot force her into a marriage that she resents. Or any of them if their disinclination of such a union is this strong."

"Sister, I am aware of your feelings on this matter. You have been defiant of a practice we agreed to before our journey, though you have only quietly resisted. Until now."

Marie Madeleine knew she had to tread lightly: "Mother, you have my conviction that your efforts to find husbands for the women under our care is rooted in your desire to ensure a safe and better future for them, not your worry about our order's inability to take in more women in need because of lack of space. But can we in good faith force them into a life they reject? Are we going to threaten them with expulsion when they have not violated any of our rules and when all they have is the safety of our convent?"

Unlike some of the others, Acadia has been a helpful boarder and a decent pupil. I must appeal to the Mother Superior in this sense.

"Of course not. I am not about to throw Mademoiselle Gravois out on the street."

The Abbess would not admit that the crowded convent was indeed a reason for her proposal. The nuns could not know that the problem would solve itself soon...

One late evening when she was tossing and turning in her bed, Acadia thought once again of her father and brother. She had not given up on finding them. She got out of bed and went downstairs to the courtyard. Outside the convent walls she heard loud yelling. She remembered the hole in the wall that Florence and the mighty Princess had used to sneak in and out of, and that she and Zulimé had crawled through when they went searching for the snake that had gotten her friend into so much trouble. Acadia climbed halfway through the wall and carefully looked for the source of the yelling. Two sailors were fighting over a girl, a prostitute who kept a safe distance to the two men who pushed and shoved each other. Acadia recognized the woman as Jeanette who stood there watching and grinning.

Clearly, she does not care who wins this argument as long as they pay.

One man was taller than the other and used this to his advantage. He pinned the shorter one up against the wall and used him as a punching bag. When he turned around to look if Jeanette was still there, his victim used that moment to duck under his arm and run. The sailor laughed, put an arm around Jeanette, and they sauntered off. Acadia noticed a satchel on the sidewalk. The smaller man must have left it. She grabbed it and pulled it through the hole. When she opened it a sailor's uniform, pants, shirt and a cap spilled out of the tight bag. Acadia held them up and put the cap on top of her head. It fit perfectly. She stared at the clothes, then dragged the satchel to the back of the yard, behind the shack and took off her cotton dress. She rolled it up, put it in the bag and tried on the uniform. It was a bit loose on her, but the length fit since the sailor had not been much taller than she. She tied her unruly curls in the back of her neck with a ribbon from her dress, hid the satchel between some tools and snuck out of the convent.

Acadia had no plan and no clue as to where she was headed. She had heard Jeanette talking about the taverns along the river where sailors went for rum and girls, so she walked in that direction, practicing a man's stride which was easy for her; no one had ever considered her mannerisms particularly female or dainty. When she saw the lights of the taverns, she pulled the cap lower. Taking a deep breath she entered the darkest tavern. Some men were hollering at the bar. She moved closer. One of them took a look at her, slapped his companion on the shoulder and laughed:

"Look at that! Aren't you a little young to be drinking, my boy?"

The other one grinned and put a cup of rum in front of her: "Never too early to start. What ship are you on?"

She was caught off guard by the question and quickly pointed towards the port: "That one."

"The Augustias? Did you come over from Spain?"

She nodded.

"What's your name?"

"Amaro Gonzalez," she answered quickly, hoping the name sounded Spanish enough for their ears.

"Well, Amaro," the first one said, gripping her arm: "Have a drink with us. I am Francois and this is Nicolas," he said, pointing to his friend.

Acadia felt the effects of the rum immediately which caused more laughter from the sailors:

"Not used to this Cuban stuff, are you? The rum on your ship is watered down, I bet. Don't worry, one week in this city and you'll be gulping it."

They told her about their adventures on the high seas, and she made up some of her own. They spoke of a pirate attack they had fended off.

"Come to think of it, you look more like a pirate than a sailor, young friend. With your hair this long. On French ships we must get cuts all the time."

She swallowed: "No time for that. Our voyage was rough. I will have to get a cut in the morning."

On her way back to the convent she thought of what they had said about her hair.

I will never pass as a sailor in daylight... but I quite like being mistaken for a boy...

Acadia began to offer her services for market runs. She dressed up as a sailor twice more after that first night out and ran into the same problem every time; the men at the taverns were commenting on her long hair, so she began using the trips to the market to acquire different clothes. Having no money of her own, she stole them; a pair of black trousers, a white shirt, a few pieces of silk that she tied into a scarf.

With meager sewing-skills she managed to take in the pants and shirt, so they would fit her. She tied the scarf around her hair and left the convent at night whenever she could sneak away. She frequented different bars and kept her ears open to find out about places pirates, smugglers and *fliebustiers*, the freebooters and the buccaneers went to, always careful to avoid the taverns that Florence controlled or did business with, knowing she would almost certainly be recognized by the woman.

She felt safe at Flamand's. Florence had mocked the place on so many occasions in the convent's kitchen that Acadia was sure she would not run into her there. Flamand's had become a run-down mess of a bar that patrons only went to for the cheapest drinks in the city and for the show its owner, Jan Lamesse, provided. No one could remember the last time he was sober or the last time he did not spend the night ranting about some injustice done to him. And no one ever wanted to get too close to him; the man had not washed himself in a decade, he reeked of sweat, tobacco and rotten food. Acadia gagged the first time he came close. Over time she had gotten used to his stench and the dirty bar. The main reason she came back again and again was that on one rainy night, she had heard her brother's name mentioned: Pasquerette dit Gravois had become a smuggler who brought grains and other foods from up north to the city. She tried to find out more without attracting attention, but the only information she could get was that, when he was in town, he liked to have a drink at Flamand's. No word on her father's whereabouts, but she assumed that he was with his son.

When the summer heat thickened the air with humidity so heavy it dripped off the skin, Acadia's restlessness grew.

I must get out of this religious prison. I need to find my family and go about my life.

Acadia had perfected her impersonation of a pirate by now, including speech and gestures. She wiped her nose on her sleeve, sat with legs spread, hollered when she entered Flamand's and her burping after taking a sip was as crude as the rum in her cup. She had begun wrapping her small bosoms to make them look completely flat. She had had fine dark hair growing on her upper lip since she was twelve years of age and that came in handy now. Everyone called her the boy-pirate, some even referred to her as baby-pirate. On this night, she loudly announced to the whole tavern:

"Messieurs, I am looking for a ship. Time to bid goodbye to this town for a while."

Unbeknownst to her Jean Bèranger had watched her for weeks.

Interesting boy. I wonder if he can carry his weight.

Jean stood and waved her over. His eyes narrowed; he sized her up. He measured her strength in his mind, her ability to fight when necessary.

"I have a spot on my ship."

Acadia's eyes lit up. He put up his hand: "Not so fast. I first need to determine why I should give it to you. You don't look like you can lift a musket, much less roll a cannonball across deck."

Acadia put her hands on her hips: "I can assure you I know how to do that and more."

He laughed. "Oui, but have you ever killed a man in a fight?"

She told him of made-up sea-battles and swordfights on board of captured vessels.

He shook his head: "It all sounds wonderful but where is the proof?"

Acadia swallowed hard. It was time to reveal the gruesome secret she had kept for the past two years: "Captain, you remember the case of the soldier who violated one of the convent girls some time back?"

Jean furrowed his brow. Florence had told him about Louise, and he had overheard two drunken police officials bragging about the perpetrator's body floating in the river. The men had found him with his chest split open by a broken alligator tail. He had thought the story wildly exaggerated.

How would the soldier have ripped the tail of a gator after it had attacked him? And since when did gators kill people with their tails instead of their teeth?

Jean knew that the police had kept quiet about the cause of death for that very reason.

What is this boy talking about?

"The soldier was killed by an alligator. But not a live one. I had a dried gator tail in my hand when I attacked him and made him pay for what he had done to the girl. It sliced into his heart like a knife. I had a hard time dragging him to the river, he was of heavy built."

Jean could not hide his astonishment.

It makes sense; the tip of a dried tail used with enough force can easily cut into a man's flesh.

"Impressive..." was all he managed to say.

"Will you hire me then?"

Bèranger twirled his beard. "I shall take you on the next journey. For half the pay for you are only half as big as my other men."

Acadia nodded. This was better than being rejected.

"We leave the morning after next. Be at the port by dawn."

They shook hands.

Two days later, Acadia stole herself out of the convent before sunrise. All she had with her was the sailor's satchel. Bèranger's men hollered and laughed when she joined their crew. Most of them knew the baby-pirate from the tavern. They set sail at first light. Acadia had no idea what direction they were headed, nor did she care. She was bursting with excitement. Her world was now painted a bright, shining green.

At the convent, her disappearance was discovered when she did not show up for morning prayer, Baby Ayita was wailing—it had always been Acadia who had gotten her a bottle. It became obvious that she had left of her own free will when the nuns realized that she had taken all her belongings. While Sister Stanislaus was deeply concerned about the young woman, she was not surprised. Acadia would rather brave the dangers of a life in the city than be forced into a marriage she did not want. The Mother Superior's feelings were mixed; worry tinged with relief.

CHAPTER 24

On August 29 Zulimé woke with a jolt. The night's dream was a dark one, and her thin cotton sheath clung to her body. She was drenched in sweat, and it was not just because of her nightmare. The heat had become unbearable in the past few days. She had sent Bebé back to the convent to finish school. The house was quiet, Stephane still asleep. Zulimé got up and walked outside. It was early, and there was no breeze. The air was as thick as the gooey salve she had made for Stephane to ward off the insects, it felt as if she could hold the density in the balm of her hand. The sky was a greenish grey, and she could hear the mooing of Henry's livestock in the distance. It was unusual for them to be this loud this early in the morning. She had a sudden flash of fear. The sky's color had intensified into something that resembled glowing algae. She walked to the creek and sat under the oak. But this time her sacred place could not calm her.

In the main house, Louise was up early, too. She had not been able to find rest all night. Henry De Roche had left on a voyage two weeks ago. They had laid with each other the night before his departure, both hoping this time would result in a child. At first, she thought it was just sweat dripping down her legs when she got up. She only noticed the red stain on her bed sheets when she pulled back the covers.

Ah non! Not again. How many more times do I have to subject myself to this awful physical act until I can get what I want? I want a baby and respite from being touched by him for a while.

She cleaned herself up and took off the sheets. Normally she would have ordered Zulimé to do it, but she would be damned if she gave that woman the satisfaction of seeing her monthly blood.

∼

In the bedroom of their home on Rue de L'Arsenal, Margarita and José woke up sticking to each other. The hot weather never stopped them from falling asleep in each other's arms, so great was their love, but this morning was hellish even for them. They laughed when they disentangled themselves. José got up and fetched a wet towel for his wife. They discussed their day's plans over cold coffee. Margarita had perfected brewing the dark drink and storing it in a stone casket in the back of the house during the summers. José expected a shipment and needed to spend the day at the market. Margarita got ready to go to the convent to deliver a few bags of coffee and rice and visit with her Cuban friends and her favorite, Sister Stanislaus. When she kissed her husband goodbye, she suddenly had a foreboding of danger and held on to him longer than usual.

∼

At the Valdeterre mansion tensions ran high. Josephine hated the summers and made no qualms about it.

"Why can we not sail to Europe in May and return in October? Or at least travel up north to the coast? Anywhere but here, in this dreadful heat," she complained and not for the first time.

Valdeterre, patient at first, became frustrated: "You are well aware by now that my position does not permit such frivolity."

"Frivolity? You should be aware by now that I am a woman of noble descent and not accustomed to wiping sweat off my face a hundred times a day!"

"Does this mean that my noble wife will grace another lowly cabarét again just to spite me?" he asked mockingly. By now he knew about her penchant for the lower classes. He considered it a rebellion against her aristocratic upbringing, and against him whenever they had a fight, like this one. Today he was in no mood to put up with her yelling and left for his office early. Josephine paced the salon until even that made her too hot and decided to send her lover the agreed upon signal that she was available by parting the curtains in her boudoir. It occurred to her that today was risky for a rendezvous, yet her anger was stronger than her precautions.

I need Michél today. And the distraction only he can give me.

Margarita reached the convent at the same time as Geneviève. When they walked through the door the wind slammed it shut behind them before they could close it. Suddenly a loud crash followed by screams in one of the classrooms echoed through the halls. They ran searching for the cause. When they entered the classroom, all they could see was shattered glass and little girls crying. There were droplets of blood on the floor, on their clothes and all over their skin with shards sticking out of them. The big window above them had been blown out. Pierre rushed over and began removing glass. Geneviève looked proudly at her son while she helped clean the cuts.

This one may well become a docteur.

She looked around for her daughter. The little girl sat huddled in a corner, crying. Geneviève examined her, but Delphine was unharmed, just frightened. The Mother Superior ordered the teachers to fetch wood from the storage and board up the broken window and others who were exposed.

Michél had not gone to bed after his argument with Florence and was walking past the Valdeterre mansion when he saw the parted curtains. He entered through a backdoor and quietly walked up the winding staircase to her boudoir avoiding the hall and kitchen where the servants might notice him. Josephine was not pleased to see him in her chambers: "You are careless. What if someone sees or hears you?"

Michél pulled her to him: "Ah, we shall sneak out the way I came in and go to my house... after a welcoming kiss, that is."

Josephine's addiction to him was stronger than her worry, and she relented. They both left through the back entrance. The clouds above them were almost black and the gusty wind blew up her skirts. They hurried towards Rue de Bourbon and made it to his house just before the rain started to fall. He wasted no time and bent her over the table.

Josephine moaned and screamed and fought against him, but it was all a game. She could not get enough of him. He grabbed her hair. She arched her back, took his other hand and put it on her breast. One of the window shutters came lose and banged against the frame, drowning out their passion.

~

At the market, José could not find the merchant at the men's usual spot on the riverside closest to the port and went looking for him where the boats from Cuba were docking. José paid no attention to the wind or the grey clouds. Weather like this was a normal occurrence during the summer, and he was not afraid to get wet. He found who he was looking for on the last boat.

"I doubt, you will be able to carry the crates back to your house. Not in this weather."

José laughed: "A little summer rain will not stop me."

The man had an incredulous look in his eyes: "A little summer rain, you say? Señor Castro, this storm has been chasing us since we left Cuba. We avoided running into trouble when it changed course, but now it is back and is catching up fast. There is no more outrunning it now. I have seen these kinds of clouds before, and they are the nightmares my ancestors spoke of. We got lucky to have made it to shore. All I want now is to find shelter before it hits with full force."

José had heard stories of hellish storms before but had never experienced one himself. Worry took hold of his features while he hoisted two crates onto his cart.

∼

Under the awning of the nice woman who sold fish and beans, Sister Stanislaus sought refuge when the skies darkened, and heavy droplets began to fall. Like all the citizens of La Nouvelle Orleáns, she too was accustomed to the summer storms and knew they would not bring relief but worsen the humidity.

I must wait out the rain, I do not want to be drenched when I get back to the convent.

The Sister traded stories with the fish vendor, a little rumor about a smuggler who was in love with the woman's daughter but got rebuffed, a story of a drunken soldier who incurred the wrath of the Choctaw trader whose market stand he fell asleep under. They laughed until a sudden gust of wind ripped off the awning, and the water soaked them. Within minutes the wind kicked up so badly that other awnings were flying all over the place.

The Sister had seen the weather change but never this fast. She could barely catch her breath when she turned into the wind, and in the opposite direction her veil stuck to her face.

~

The wind had turned into a storm by the time Florence had decided to go to the port to await a smuggler's boat with the promised crates of champagne that he had stolen from a French ship. Madame Cocotte had asked for the luxurious drink to serve to her wealthier clients.

With Jean on a voyage and his brother his useless self, I'll have to bring them over to her by myself.

Florence was in a foul mood and barely made it a few blocks with her parasol overturned and the rain whipping against her. She held on to the walls of a building to catch her breath and gave up on the idea of fetching her goods. A block from her home she saw a familiar figure with his arm around a woman, running past on the opposite side of the street. She recognized Michél and Josephine.

The wind almost knocked her over, and she forgot all about them, fighting her way to her own place. As soon as she was back at her house, leaving a trail of water all over the floor from her wet frock, the heavy door came off its hinges and crashed to the floor.

Ah merde! Every time I need this useless coquin Michél to fix something he is with Josephine!

Florence ran to the back room and began rolling barrels towards the entrance. She was on her third one, sweat dripping down her face from the effort, when she saw two hands, gripping the frame from outside. Fighting against the storm, the figure of a woman slowly came into sight.

Not her!

Florence quickly weighed her enmity toward Jeanette against her need for help.

I will never be able to raise the door by myself.

Reluctantly, she pulled Jeanette inside not allowing the woman to catch her breath or wring out her wet clothes before ordering her to pick up the door. After a few tries they were able to move it to the frame, and while Jeanette pushed against it, Florence rolled the barrels up to hold it in place. Both women sat down on the floor from exhaustion while the storm raged on. They eyed each other suspiciously, not quite deciding on whether to start a conversation.

~

José rolled the cart up the dock when a sudden gust of wind stopped him. It felt like pushing against a wall. The river's tide seemed to recede, the air sucking out all the water. From the corner of his eye, he saw awnings ripping apart, the vendors' stools and even tables moving faster and faster. Sellers were trying to hold on to their goods, fighting against the forces of nature. He heard a scream and recognized the woman with her arms flailing.

The nice Ursuline nun from the convent!

Sister Stanislaus bent down to a body on the ground. José let go of the cart which rolled back down the dock. He ran towards the Sister who was hunched over the fish seller. The woman was not moving, blood pooling underneath her. Her head was covered by a table.

"It hit her when she picked up her goods. It just turned over..."

Sister Stanislaus was shouting the words into the howling wind. José helped lift the table off the woman's head when the beam that held the awning in place came flying towards them. He tried to push the nun out if its way, but it was too late. They were both hit by the pole and knocked over.

~

In the convent's kitchen Margarita cried out. Geneviève stared at her from across the kitchen table.

"Are you alright? It is just a storm."

Margarita's eyes were blank: "José… something happened to José…"

Geneviève calmingly touched her arm: "José will be fine. He is a strong man… come, let us prepare food for the children. They need us."

Margarita turned to the stove and as if in trance, and she began doing what she had done so many times before in the convent's kitchen; cook a meal. Her hands did the cutting and chopping, the mixing and stirring, but her mind was not on the food. Outside the storm raged on, shaking the shutters.

∼

At military headquarters, Valdeterre was hunched over his desk. He was trying to concentrate on the papers before him, but the roaring wind made reading impossible. He called for Major Dumont.

"Major, please send soldiers to fetch my wife. The command can withstand a storm and my house probably can, too, but I do not want to leave Madame Valdeterre frightened and alone at home."

When the Major left the office, Valdeterre got up and looked out the window. He could see the sails shaking in the distance and the water turning the streets into muddy rivers. The Commander had been a young man, newly stationed in New France ten years ago when he had lived through a similar storm. It had left the city devastated for years. Valdeterre was one of the very few who knew what to call this by its proper name.

This here is not a storm. It is another hurricane. God help us.

Officials had ordered levees to be built after the hurricane that ravaged the city in 1722, but those were considered more a protection from high water along the river resulting from the annual rains than as a safety against such a strong threat of nature. The Commander inadvertently made the sign of the cross while staring into the rain that now hit sideways.

∼

Outside of her little house, Zulimé wrapped a sheet around her waist in which she held Stephane.

This is just like the legend of the God who blew his breath across a chaotic water to destroy the earth that had expelled him.

As she was fighting her way towards the main building, a structure that would surely protect them better than her own place, she remembered the tales her grandmother had told her of the god Hurakan who raged against the people. It was a scary tale, one that had made her shiver as a child just like she was shivering now. Her dress got heavy from the water as every step became a struggle against the wind's force. She tried her best to shield Stephane, but he, too, was soaked and crying. When the de Roche home came into view, she breathed a sigh of relief. She climbed up the steps and opened the door. Cecile came out of the kitchen. The old cook raised her hand as if to warn her, but Zulimé was too concerned with her baby boy to pay attention. She wrung out his clothes and the wrap, leaving a puddle on the polished wood floors. When she bent down to wipe it up a pair of shoes and the hem of a dress came into view. She looked up.

Louise, hands on her hips towered over her: "What do you think you are doing?"

Zulimé looked at her in shock.

What am I doing?

"Getting my child dry. Seeking shelter…"

"Not here. You have your own house, so I am told. You and your… bastard are not welcome here."

Zulimé clutched Stephane to her chest. He would not stop wailing: "But Louise… Madame… It is not safe out there."

"Not my concern. Leave!"

Louise opened the door and pushed Zulimé out.

With Stephane in her arms, Zulimé tried to throw herself against the door, but heard the lock being turned from the inside. She screamed and begged in vain. When she heard Louise's footsteps disappearing, she sank to the floor on the porch, trying as best as she could to comfort Stephane.

Henry would never let her to this to us if he were here…

∼

On the soaking wet floor of Florence's house, Jeanette finally broke the unpleasant silence:

"Why do you despise me so much?"

Florence, a rag in one hand with the other firmly planted on her hip, pursed her lips and studied Jeanette's face: "You are everything I have fought against becoming my whole life. Women like you make it that much harder for women like me to be taken seriously by men, to maybe one day even be respected by them. I refuse to sell myself or be taken care of. I was not born into privilege and riches any more than I assume, you were. And yet I never sank to your level."

Jeanette got up. A strange blend of anger and pain appeared on her face: "What do you know about fighting? What do you know about survival? I was not born a whore!"

"No woman is born a whore. But some of us resist the urge to take the easy path."

All of Jeanette's bent up fury and hurt broke free. With tears streaming down her face and contorted mouth, she raised her voice: "Easy path? You think I took the easy path? I killed not one but two men!" Her words hung in the air.

"Oh, are you going to tell me some teary story now?" Florence derided her.

After a long and heavy pause, Jeanette continued in a quieter tone: "Just the truth…the first one was the man who took my virginity when I was no more than a girl. My body did not even look like a woman's. I stabbed him with my father's bayonet. My father should have done that, but he threw me out instead. I was on the street when I was barely eleven years young."

"What got you thrown into Salpetriére prison? The murder?"

"Not the murder. What gets all the working girls thrown into jail when a noble man refuses to pay, and we steal from him what is ours… and a little more for compensation." Jeanette looked down on the floor.

Slowly Florence asked: "And your second victim?" She tried to hide a hint of compassion under the guise of mockery.

"They were not victims. I was. The second one was the *souteneur*, the pimp who raped me. I drove a nail into his chest that I pulled out of the fence he had me up against."

Florence quickly added up these facts: "In Biloxi. You ran all the way to this city because of the murder you committed."

Jeanette shook her head: "Non, I ran from Biloxi because he beat me every day. All this led me to become a putain. When I ran from the pimp, he followed me."

Florence studied her for a moment. "Still, once you got to the convent you had every chance to save yourself. Instead, you did what putains do best; lie down first and get up last. Taking advantage of some dirty sailor when you could have gone to school, learned the alphabet. But you ended right back on the street. I bet the nuns will take you back if you show them remorse, or at least pretend to."

In front of the door of de Roche's home, Zulimé forced herself up. Stephane had exhausted himself crying, the only noises coming from him now were tired little wails. She picked him up and walked back out into the storm, pressing her son against her chest, staggering slowly from tree to tree and whatever she could hold on to just to catch her breath. It took an hour to make it halfway to her house, a distance that usually took only minutes. The thunder and lightning now happened as one with not a moment between. The sky had turned black. When the thick branch hit her, she fell backwards into the mud, consciousness draining from her.

∽

At Place d'Armes Major Dumont bolted into Valdeterre's office: "Commander, my men just returned. They were not able to find Madame Valdeterre."

Valdeterre's face darkened.

Where could she have gone? She did not mention any plans to shop or visits with a friend.

"Send out a search party. My wife must be found."

The Major hesitated: "But Commander…my two men almost did not make it back. The storm has taken off roofs and parts of homes… I am certain, Madame has found shelter at whatever friend of hers she was visiting with…"

He has a point.

"Alors, Major. We shall wait. For now."

∽

Zulimé looked up and saw a white opening in the sky with dark grey swirling around it. It seemed like a pirate's blown-out eye to her. She tried to move, but her leg was caught under something heavy. It was dark as night and her vision was blurry. She felt moss and mud.

Stephane!

She frantically tried to find her son, but without the ability to move and see anything but the eye of the storm, she was relegated to searching with her hands. Her body felt like fire despite the cold wetness and the water that was still falling.

I must free myself, I must find mon fils!

Zulimé ripped her leg from the trunk that trapped it, not caring about the searing pain or the blood. She screamed for her child hoping his cries would lead her to him. She crawled on the ground, feeling around her with both hands until she touched him. On her knees she picked him up, held him close with tears streaming down. She touched his little legs, his arms, his cheeks and round head. And then, as lightning struck, she saw the dead eyes of the lion. His soul had left, and she felt as if life was draining out of her in that moment, too, just as it had out of him. She fell back on the ground, still holding on to his little body.

Chapter 25

All through an excruciating night when the hurricane moved on, and the rain became lighter, but hearts became heavier, people all over the city and her outskirts worried about missing loved ones. No one dared to venture outside to search in the darkness. The streets and roads were deep, muddy rivers, and the water reached up past the piliers and kept many trapped in their homes, mopping up the overflow with whatever cloth, blankets and rags they could get their hands on.

At the convent Margarita had not closed her eyes during the night's ordeal. She paced the hallways, anxious to go and look for José. She glanced out the window and saw that the rain, although still falling, was lighter now and the winds had stopped. She opened the heavy door and felt a hand on her shoulder:

"Please, don't…" In Mother St. Augustin's voice was a quiet urgency and the look in her eyes, illuminated by one of the last candles in the convent was filled with a deep concern.

"I cannot stay here. I must find my husband." Margarita could barely get the words out, so constricted was her chest.

"I know," the Abbess simply replied. "But what good would it do him, if you got hurt?"

Margarita held on to the door handle, her hunched back suddenly heaving. The tears, so unusual for the otherwise composed woman, streamed down her face. The Mother Superior made the sign of blessing and put a calming hand on the cook's shoulder.

"When one finds love that is true there is no letting go or going back," Margarita said, slowly lifting her head. "I never thought this kind of love was possible for me, I cannot let it go…"

The Abbess took her hands in hers: "Give it a few hours until daylight. I shall send men with you, servants who are strong enough to move debris out of the way and can help you look for him and Sister Stanislaus, as well. She never returned… In the meantime, let us go to the chapel. Prayer will help calm us all."

She led Margarita through the muddy courtyard into the church.

On the plantation's wet grounds Zulimé came to, Stephane's body still clutched to her chest. The storm had passed, there was a sliver of sky and a deathly silence in the air. Zulimé had no breath, no command of her body or senses. When she got up, she saw her house through the trees, much closer than she had thought during the night. The roof was caved in, one wall tilted to the side, the shutters ripped off the windows, broken glass and wood splinters scattered everywhere. She sat down, staring at the wreckage around her and the wreckage in her heart, holding on to her son, rocking back and forth. This was how Touton found her. He picked her up and carried her to the slave quarters. There, he gently laid her down in the square between the huts in front of the fire they had built, and a few women came and wrapped her in a blanket. They pried the dead child from her arms, and she fought them. She let out a sound so scary that the women moved backwards as she threw herself over Stephane, gripping the dirt and beating the ground. They let her be until she calmed down. Touton wrapped her in the blanket, picked up the child and wrapped him, too.

"We will take care of him. We will send him to the heavens. Not to worry, little woman," he whispered in her ear, and she finally let go. The women cleaned the wounds on her leg with water and herbs as she herself had taught them, and Touton used two small logs wrapped in cloth as a brace for her broken bone.

∼

Valdeterre had been up all night, giving orders to secure the command as well as the prison. In between he had paced the halls, wondering where and if his wife had found refuge from the hurricane. At first light he hurried home, accompanied by Major Dumont. He found his mansion without the kind of damage he had seen on the other houses he had passed. Except for a few broken shutters, everything appeared to be fine. He paid no attention to the small puddles of water in the entry hall and called Josephine's name, but only the frightened maidservant came out of her room to tell him Madame had not returned.

∼

At Michél's house, a loud crash shook the walls towards the front of the street as Josephine was lacing up her dress: "I really must go. Otherwise, the Commander will send out a search party."

Michél grinned: "How will you explain your absence all night?"

"The storm should suffice as an explanation."

Josephine walked to the door and tried to open it. It did not move. She pulled and finally it gave way only to reveal heaps of stone and pieces of wood, too thick to move. Michél was behind her trying to help, but neither one of them could lift the mountain of debris. He closed the door, went to the only window and pushed against the shutter. It too, was stuck, the wood swollen from the water. Josephine's agitation increased as she saw his futile efforts. "Really, who does not have a back door to their house?"

Michél turned around: "Well, I do. When I bought the house, it was one of its selling points. It limits the chance for intruders to get in and steal my loot."

"And now it keeps me captive in here!"

She sat down on the bed. He managed to push the shutter open wide enough to see what was blocking it, but not leaving enough space for anyone to crawl through.

He craned his neck: "A large part of a roof from the opposite side of the street came down and must have fallen against my wall. We are, indeed, stuck here. Je suis desolé, it can't be helped. We must wait until the city officials have the debris cleared or some neighbor comes to our aid."

He moved toward her: "This might take a while. So why don't we continue to enjoy each other's company?" He took the two silk ribbons that held her dress together and pulled on them.

"You are insatiable," she said with a lot less anger than a minute ago.

"So are you, Josephine, so are you," he responded while she felt his breath on her neck.

~

On Rue du Maine Margarita was on a quest, hurrying down towards the river with Geneviève by her side. The two women walked close to the buildings and used fallen logs as make-shift bridges when they needed to cross the street. Margarita's shoes got stuck in the mud, and she dragged them out. They passed by unimaginable devastation; torn roofs, crying women and shocked children who could not comprehend what they were experiencing. Some men were trying to lift parts of their homes out of the mud. An old man was hunched over the body of a woman caressing her face.

Once they reached the market, Margarita called her husband's name and Geneviève shouted for Sister Stanislaus. They searched what had been a vibrant square only a day ago but now looked like a battlefield;

not one stand had survived the storm, vegetables, sacks of rice and beans and other wares were strewn around or had been washed away. In the distance they saw overturned boats. They stepped over dead bodies, their breathing coming in short gasps as the anguish over José and the Sister took hold of them. Geneviève tripped over a woman's leg and let out a scream when she recognized a nun's habit. The cloth was trapped underneath a wooden pillar and something that looked like a large bag was wedged in between, burying Sister Stanislaus.

Margarita touched the mud-soaked bag and froze: "José…" Her voice was barely a whisper as she tried to lift his head.

"Do not move him, we have to get the pillar out of the way first," Geneviève cautioned.

The two women tried to remove it with every ounce of strength they could muster, Margarita driven by pure desperation. When they could not lift it up, they carefully rolled it off them. Margarita cradled José's head, while Geneviève held the Sister's. The nun let out a muffled sound.

"She is alive!" Geneviève shouted.

José's head moved an inch, and Margarita cried out, too. The women looked around for anyone strong enough to come to their aid, but the market was deserted. They frantically built a stretcher from broken wood, ripped bags apart to tie to the rods and carefully rolled José's body onto it. He moaned. As soon as his weight was off her, Sister Stanislaus moved and sat up. She touched her arms and legs and found them not broken.

"Can you walk?" Geneviève asked as she was helping her up.

"I think so…"

Geneviève reached under the Sister's arm to hold her up and tried to help Margarita drag the stretcher. When they reached the convent the Mother Superior sent one of the servants out to look for a doctor. José was unconscious still. Sister Stanislaus was not injured save for some scratches and a sprained ankle. She told them that José was the only reason she had survived. Margarita's tears streamed down her face as she buried it in his chest and listened to the nun. It was not easy to find a doctor—too many citizens were in desperate need—but the Ursulines carried enough importance to be tended to first, and the servant returned with Docteur Lagarde who confirmed what Margarita had feared: José had a broken back where the beam had hit him. The doctor tied a wooden cast around José's back and chest and implored the women to keep him stable. They hoped he would come back as soon as time and the hundreds of other patients permitted. Sister Stanislaus' eyes met the Mother Superior's, both silently admitting for the first time that having a military hospital would serve a lot more people.

So many will perish because two Catholic orders cannot agree on this matter…

The Sister had not felt this much regret in a long time and could see on the Abbess' face that the head of the convent shared her contrition.

∼

On Place d'Armes Valdeterre had Major Dumont organize the rescue team. Their task: clear the streets and take citizens to the barracks whose homes were too damaged to be safe.

"And find my wife. I shall accompany you." The Commander and a group of soldiers began looking specifically for those houses that seemed like they had occupants trapped inside. They searched on Rue de Chartres and Rue Royale, the area where the well-to-do citizens lived. No one had seen Josephine.

Did she go to one of the seedy cabarèts again? Why does she enjoy spending time in questionable company?

Valdeterre began to knock on every door. One of those was Florence Bourget's.

Her friend, the woman Josephine always calls one of the poor souls who, unlike her, was forced to travel to the colony…

Florence opened on the third knock, clearly expecting someone else.

"I told you to go to the convent…" Surprised, she stopped talking when she laid eyes on the Commander, not Jeanette.

"Commander…What do I owe this pleasure?"

The hint of sarcasm did not go unnoticed by Valdeterre. "I am looking for my wife."

Florence laughed: "You lost Josephine."

"I gather, you are friends. Have you seen her?"

"I would not go as far as calling her a friend, more of an… acquaintance."

Florence was not about to explain their complicated friendship, or that they were on the outs, currently. She saw the anguish in his eyes.

Damn fool, he really loves her.

"Commander, let me tell you about your wife…" She had the decency to pull him inside before continuing.

No need, to humiliate the poor cuckold in front of his men.

"You are a good man, Commander. Too good for a woman like her. You do not deserve to be deceived for another year or more."

His eyes widened.

What is she talking about?

"I did see your wife just before the storm got bad. She was in the company of her lover."

A thousand cannons went off in Valdeterre's head. As his world came crashing down, the realization that his wildest suspicions proved to be true hit him all at once.

"Where does the man reside?" was all he could say.

"Two blocks up. And I would not call it reside. It is more like shacking up. He is not a nobleman."

Stone-faced, Valdeterre walked out without another word. During the short walk up the street, a flurry of thoughts flew through his brain. It all made sense now, her many late nights, her stories of where she had been and most of all her feigning exhaustion, headaches and any excuse to avoid making love to him. And even when she relented, she seemed to be somewhere else. A part of him hoped that she would be one of the many victims of the storm they had encountered in the past few hours.

Better to bury her than to deal with a scandal.

When they reached the house Florence had described, he surmised the scene; whoever was in there was trapped by the neighbor's roof that had come down and was blocking the exit. Valdeterre's men removed it and broke into the house on his orders. Josephine sat upright. The noise had woken her. She was naked, the legs of a man entangled with hers. Michél had slept through the wreckage and only opened his eyes when she pushed him. She pulled the sheet over herself, staring at her husband. No story she could make up would be believable now.

"I shall have your belongings sent over. To your new home."

His voice was lifeless and betrayed the rage, the sorrow, the humiliation inside him. He turned on his heel and walked out.

"Clearly, he is not serious. You moving in? Here?" Michél was dumbfounded: "If another man had seduced my wife as I have done with you, I would have killed him."

Josephine slowly came out of her shock: "You would prefer that he killed you?"

"I would have understood if he had tried. But this? What kind of man just walks out?"

Her humiliation turned to anger: "The kind of man who knows that not everything can be solved with a sword or a gun! The kind of man who can provide properly for a woman of my standing!"

Michél's laugh and nasty tone belied his hurt over her words: "A woman of your standing who carries on a liaison with a scoundrel like me."

Josephine got out of bed, gathered her clothes and hastily got dressed. Michél watched her, the mixed feelings still stirring inside him. When she walked to the door, she turned to him and said in a voice tinged with regret and despair: "And the kind of man I am going to get back…"

He shook his head: "Good luck with that…"

The man did not kill me. Maybe he will forgive her…

Michél was not certain he liked this idea. It was clear to him that he would not mind her living with him and having her all to himself. Out in the open…

~

When Josephine arrived at their house, she found Valdeterre sitting in an armchair in the salon, brooding. She walked up to him, but his raised hand stopped her. He would not look at her when she fell on her knees: "Je suis desolé, mon amour, je suis desolé…"

When he finally spoke, it was with a bitter quietness: "Mon amour? This is not love. This is betrayal. And if it really has been going on for years…"

How does he know? Did he have me followed? How can he possibly know that I have been seeing Michél for years?

Valdeterre got up. "I shall get a divorce."

Josephine jumped up and hurried after him: "Non! You cannot! We married in church!"

He looked at her with sadness: "Which has not stopped you from breaking your vows. I can never trust you again." And with that he walked out.

No amount of begging and pleading could change the Commander's mind. He slept on a cot in his office and had the divorce papers drawn up within a week with the help of the court. It was during this process that Valdeterre decided to make the kind of inquiries that he knew he should have made before he proposed. This was how he found out that his high and mighty wife was herself a Casket Girl.

In a fit of anger, he confronted her: "You have been lying to me from the beginning!"

She cried and told him about the man in Paris. Told him that he was her brother-in-law, her older sister's husband. That he had seduced her, the then barely fifteen-year-old Josephine. And confessed that she had become infatuated with him in the way only a fifteen-year-old would. That he had cast her aside and made sure she was shipped off to this colony after she had shamed her family with this scandal of which he was the instigator. That there was a child she left behind. A child raised by strangers, she assumed, given away minutes after the birth.

Valdeterre did not believe her.

"You are making this up. Especially the part of having a child. Nice touch to get me to feel compassionate towards you. You would say anything to not lose your status."

After he left, she broke down. Of all the lies she had told over the years this was not one of them.

The Governor's wife, Madame de Bienville, suggested to the Commander to buy his soon-to-be ex-wife a small house on Rue de Bourbon— "where she belongs"—to get her out of his life for good. Josephine had no choice but to sign the papers. Two soldiers moved her belongings into a decrepit building, barely fixed after the storm and not too far from Michél and Florence. Valdeterre had given her a small sum of money to make the utmost necessary purchases, but other than that, she was left with nothing but her old name: Josephine de Chavin. In the beginning she only ventured out when she absolutely had to. Every walk was one of shame; she could see the looks of scorn that former acquaintances and the noble wives gave her when she got too close to their mansions along the river, and the snickering from the les petite gens on her own street. She was a pariah, an outcast again, only visited by Michél who could not be kinder to her, but who she blamed for her fall from grace. Her loneliness was the only reason to permit him his visits.

CHAPTER 26

In his office at military headquarters Valdeterre buried himself in work, and there was plenty. A tense conversation took place two months after the disaster. He had cautioned about opening all storage facilities and, with the Governor's consent, only distributed food to the neediest and most desperate citizens. But Lieutenant de Roy Louboey, a member of La Nouvelle Orleàns' Conseil Superiéur was of a different opinion and lamented the major setback caused to the colony's development by the shortage of food: "We are victims of events we cannot ever foresee. The hurricane of August 29 ravaged the whole harvest, overthrew the houses and destroyed three quarters of the foodstuffs, tobacco, sugar and other crops that would put the settlers in the saddest situation of the world! Three quarters of our population will perish from famine if we do not open the city's warehouses that hold the stored rice."

The Commander made his case: "Lieutenant, were you present ten years ago, when another hurricane caused this much damage? Because I was, and I have learned from the mistakes of its aftermath. The warehouses were opened then, and the victims were given access to all rice, sugar and beans that were stored there. The result was a disaster that by far outweighed that of the storm when a terrible drought a short time later caused real famine, one that could have been avoided by rationing. I refuse to subject the citizens to a similar situation. I have and will continue to inspect every demand on a case-by-case basis and distribute necessities accordingly."

Excluded from the distribution of food were the plantations upriver. Most of them had fields with crops, not all of them destroyed by the storm. This included the de Roche property whose owner returned a few weeks after the hurricane to a "holy mess" as he called it. As Henry rode up to his house, he was relieved to see that aside from some minor damage—a porch railing that had cracked, a few shingles that needed replacing and a broken window—his house had withstood the onslaught of nature. But everything else was in disarray. Louise, incapable of running the plantation, had not made sure that the fields were tended to, the ruined crops removed, and the mud cleared. Touton had taken over but without outside help that only Madame de Roche could have hired, he and the handful of slaves who were strong enough were fighting a losing battle against the rotting tobacco. The rice was lost, drowned in the runoff water. After surveying his fields, Henry was anxious to see Zulimé and his son. When he got to their house, he found it in shambles and abandoned. Alarmed, he ran back to ask Louise.

She shrugged her shoulders: "How would I know. That woman is no concern of mine. And neither is her bastard child," she added in a cutting tone. The only reason Henry contained himself was that his fear for Zulimé and Stephane by far exceeded his anger at his wife's comment. He called for Touton.

"Where are Zulimé and the boy?"

The big man's voice cracked when he answered. "Zulimé is safe, Master… she is staying with us. Had to after what happened to her house…"

Henry saw a tear in Touton's eye. A suspicion gripped him.

"Master… we lost Stephane… The storm's demons took his soul…"

De Roche had to hold on to the back of a chair, his breath knocked out of him by a greater force than even the hurricane.

"Master should come see after Zulimé…" Touton said.

Without a word Henry followed the big man out, every step closer to his beloved heavier than the one before. He found Zulimé in the same paralyzed state she had been in ever since her night of loss. Her dead eyes looked past him, no sound escaped her lips and when he took her into his arms she hung there like a ragdoll. No emotion flickered across her features. He took her head in his hands and looked deeply into her faraway eyes: "Mon amour, I will take you back to my house and have Cecile make up your old room."

"Non!" She pounded his chest. "Not your house! I cannot, I shall not live near her!"

She cried out with a mixture of unmeasurable grief and uncontained anger, the first time since the storm that she had any feelings at all. He tried to calm her, but she would not let him and tore herself away. Helplessly he turned to Touton: "Take care of Zulimé. And make sure that her home is rebuilt as quickly as possible. I will get you help from neighboring plantations."

The plan to hire out workers from friends like Louis Blanchard proved more difficult than de Roche had anticipated. Their properties had sustained damage, too. Labor was the most difficult commodity to come by and the most expensive. Eager to get Zulimé back into her own home, he found himself doing the repairs, a task performed in stoic monotony and one designed to take his mind off his own grief. He was still mystified by her violent reaction upon his suggestion to move her into his house and her comment about Louise.

After a few weeks of long days and nights with barely any sleep Zulimé's home was restored, and she moved back in. Henry had removed the broken crib and any toys that he had found during the cleanup. When he wanted to be with her on her first night back, she rebuffed him and only allowed him to take her to bed and sit with her for a while but sent him away when he tried to kiss her. He left, sad and empty and above all lost.

My grief is not any lesser that hers, why won't she share it with me and allow us both to find some solace in each other?

Henry de Roche, a gentle man but still a man could not understand her emotions. And yet, he did have a suspicion that there was more behind her reactions. That he was missing an explanation and owed one.

After he had left Zulimé got up. Her heart was cold, but she knew that this was not a state of being she could allow to go on. She would lose her gift if she was not open to the flow of life. And so, she walked to the creek and sat underneath the oak. She prayed to Papa Legba first, the God who holds the key and guards the doorway and the roads between the worlds. She imagined him showing little Stephane the way into the afterworld where the little boy would be protected from evil. She thanked the deity for taking care of her son. Her worship of this Sun God gave her a peace she had not felt since the tragedy. She knew she had work to do, and until it was completed, she would not let Henry stay with her.

At the convent, just after classes had finished, Sister Stanislaus found herself in the strange position of having to plead with the Mother Superior over the return of a woman both had been all too happy to see leave only a few weeks earlier. To make matters even more confusing, it was another Casket Girl who was asking for mercy and consideration for someone she herself had fought and despised when both were still living with the nuns.

Jeanette's life story had moved Florence more than she had let on, so when the woman came knocking at her door in a desperate state, she did not turn her away: "You look like you've been sleeping in a doorway."

Jeanette's downcast eyes told her that she was not far off in her assumption. "Not even Madame Cocotte would take me. She said I was too cheap and too dirty."

"I have no room for you here, my house is not big enough. You know what you must do. If I were you, I would throw myself at the mercy of the Ursulines. They have taken in many victims of the storm."

"Will you come with me? S'il vous plait?"

"Fine. If it means that you won't have to degrade yourself for a while…"

Sister Stanislaus was in no mood to make it easy for the pair when Florence made her case: "Sister, I realize Jeanette did not leave under the best of circumstances…"

The nun interrupted her: "Neither did you if I recall."

"I am a businesswoman and saw no reason to take advantage of your generosity any longer when I was quite capable of supporting myself. This poor soul, however, has no place to go. Would it not be the Catholic thing to do to give her shelter?"

Sister Stanislaus inhaled sharply: "Do not lecture me about Catholicism, Mademoiselle Bourget!" She turned to Jeanette: "Do you promise to go to class and attend church services? To not disrupt or corrupt the other boarders and their children?"

Jeanette gave a slight nod.

"Then let me try and convince the Mother Superior."

The Sister waved Jeanette to follow her. Florence lingered for a moment.

Maybe this time the convent and its strict rules will bring a sense of balance…

~

The moon shadow rose above the waters when Zulimé armed with a cup, logs, stones, a snake she had found and caged and above all a fierce determination, set out from the slave quarters to the utmost edge of the plantation where the creek ran into the swamp.

It is time.

Zulimé had practiced for weeks, for tonight's new moon would seal all her efforts with a ceremony so powerful, its magic and its repercussions would be felt strongly by the two women who were her targets: herself and Louise. If she succeeded, they would be felt for a lifetime. All her qualms about using her powers only for the good were clouded by her grief and need for revenge.

The French woman will pay for what she has done to me.

Zulimé chose a clearing surrounded by cypress trees with moss hanging off them. She built a fire from the logs that she had drenched in oil earlier and put the cup in front of it. It contained rum and gunpowder, a *hommage* to the spirit of Kalfu who lords over bad luck, destruction, and all manners of injustice. She purposely cast out all Ghede, the deities of death and excluded Ayida, the fertility goddess. The former because she did not dare cast death upon her enemy and the latter because she would have thwarted the whole point of the ceremony. Ayida was to be called on later for an entirely different purpose. The snake represented as always, Legba whose blessing she asked for first and whom she begged to accept her dark spell to right a wrong.

As she fanned the flames and inhaled the smoke from the perfumed oil, Zulimé began to feel lifted from earth. She chanted to invoke Kalfu, asking him for his dark powers to punish Louise for the pain she had brought. Zulimé danced around the fire, saying the same words over and over: "Kalfu, hear me! May she be void of joy; may she be forever barren…"

She danced faster and faster, her arms flailing, her body shaking until the fire died, and she collapsed in front of the cup. After a few breaths, she pulled a doll out of her pocket. It depicted a thin woman with long limbs but no breasts or belly. She put it on the ground and stomped on it, then lifted the cup over her head and poured its content into the embers with a loud cry. She jumped up as the gunpowder ignited the flames once again and made them rise as high as the cypress before burning off the last log and dying out. Her body drained and her senses clouded by the smoke she had inhaled, she passed out.

When she woke it was almost morning, and the new moon had faded. On her way back to her house, she gathered some herbs. The ceremony was one thing, a poisoned tea quite another. But for it to work, she had to return to de Roche's house. The urgency to put her plan in motion overcame her dread of dealing with Louise in person.

Zulimé was spared running into Louise, when—a few days later—she learned from one of the servants that the mistress had left for the weekend to attend church services in town. Under the pretense of visiting Cecile, Zulimé walked into the mansion and was greeted so friendly by the old woman that she was almost taken aback. Cecile felt badly for having witnessed Louise's refusal to shelter to the young woman and her son and not having been able to help. Zulimé hesitated to confide in her, though, fearing that she might not be as complicit in administering a concoction to her mistress that would keep Louise from ever conceiving a child. While chatting with the cook Zulimé learned that Madame closed out every meal by drinking a cup of chamomile tea while Monsieur preferred a rum liqueur.

Zulimé asked Cecile for some cotton rags she knew the old woman stored in the back room. When Cecile shuffled off, she removed the pouch with the herbs she had collected and mixed them into the jar with the chamomile. They did not change the pungent smell or change the color.

Besides, Cecile is half blind.

When Henry returned home and came looking for her, Zulimé greeted him with a small smile for the first time since the hurricane. He was relieved but regretful. Geneviève LaCour had told him of the tragedy that had befallen José and Margarita and had asked him, if he could send Zulimé to help the poor man.

"It is, of course your decision. I do not want to let you go but understand if you would like to come to your friend's aid. Margarita seems convinced that you and only you can heal him."

Zulimé contemplated her choices.

I could use a change right now. Everything here reminds me too much of Stephane. And maybe, doing something good for José will calm the Gods…

For truth be told, she feared the wrath of the spirits for what she had done to Louise. Her grandmother's words 'only use the gift for doing good onto others unless they are so evil, they need to be punished', were echoing loudly in her head. She justified her actions with the second part— 'unless they are so evil…' Louise had done the worst deed a woman could do: cause the death of another's child.

"I shall go to La Nouvelle Orleàns if Margarita needs my help."

Henry pulled her close and buried his face in her hair: "I shall miss you terribly, mon amour. And I promise to visit every Sunday, so we can attend church."

He kissed her gently and for the first time in weeks she felt her body responding to his.

Walking along Rue St. Philippe, Geneviève observed how life in the city had returned to a normal state, when one discarded the food shortage and the rationed portions that Valdeterre had imposed on the citizens. While the workmen's families suffered, the wealthy people thrived. Belonging to the latter group, she took advantage of the low price for properties and was buying up houses, lots and even field property along the city's Eastern border. On this late October Sunday when the hot summer rains had finally given way to cool breezes and clear sunshine, she was on her way to one such building right behind the Cortez' home. She knocked on Margarita's door to invite her on a stroll. Their now regular Sunday walks gave Margarita a few hours away from the strain of caring for José. Her husband had gotten better and there was even hope he would walk again, but for now they had the carpenter make a wheelchair and José was mostly housebound. Geneviève took Margarita to see the new acquisition, and the cook was impressed by the large courtyard that was separated by a wall from her own, and the vast kitchen that took up one whole side of the house: "I did not know that there was a restaurant right behind my house."

Geneviève smiled: "It had not opened yet when the hurricane came. As you can see the place is not livable now, and the owners abandoned it. It needs a lot of repairs."

"But it would make a fine restaurant!"

"Yes, it would. Especially if it was run by you."

The Cuban's eyes widened as her friend continued: "Margarita, I would be delighted if you were to open your own place. I was so bold as to have the deed drawn up in both our names with me sharing in a small part of the profits. But it will be your restaurant for you to do with as you please."

Margarita had tears in her eyes when she took Geneviève's hands in her hers: "Gracias! A thousand times gracias! I will make this the best place in town."

"I have no doubt. And it will lift your husband's spirits when he has something to do again, a place to go."

José was overjoyed when he heard about the restaurant. A few days later Zulimé arrived, and she came prepared. She brought salves and ointments that she rubbed on his neck and spine and taught Margarita how to do it, too. In a vision, Zulimé had seen José floating in a large tub of water, happily moving his legs while she spread salt and herbs in all four corners of the room and chanted healing words for him. She described her vision of it to the women, and Geneviève ordered the workmen to build such a tub in the Cortez' courtyard. Together they lowered José into the water and made him move his limbs. Whether it was Zulimé's chants or the simple movements, José improved steadily over the next few weeks and by month's end he was able to walk with a cane within the confines of his home. The doctor was astonished and called it a miracle, having been spared the more unusual details of Zulimé's cure.

Zulimé's disposition improved the better José healed and the longer she was away from the plantation. Henry came to visit every week as promised and even though they could not sit together in church, they always found time and a quiet spot afterwards. He never spoke of Louise until, one day, Zulimé asked if his wife was with child:

"Non, she is not," he responded solemnly. "And our relations are not improving because of it."

Zulimé took his hands in hers. They were standing on the river's edge on the upper corner of the market that had still not resumed business completely. There was no one else in sight as the sun began to set.

"What if I told you that I am…"

His eyes burnt into hers with a mixture of shock and elation. "That you are…"

"With child. It happened the night before I left for the city."

His embrace was at once joyful and desperate. "I want you to come back with me," he said after a long pause.

She pushed him away: "Non!"

Again, Henry was taken aback by her strong reaction. Zulimé took another step away from him, her eyes burning with anger. "She killed my son! I will not let her kill another one! I will never go back to the plantation!"

Bewildered he reached out for her, but she retreated even more:

"S'il vous plait…" His hand touched hers. "Please… I do not understand… what did she do?"

Her anger and sorrow came flooding back when she told him what had led to Stephane's death, her voice breaking: "Why do they call bad things black magic when it is the white woman who commits such evil deeds?"

Fury replaced desperation as he listened. His fists clenched, knuckles white, he did not say a word when he accompanied her to Geneviève's house and kissed her on the forehead before he mounted his horse.

All the way back during his ride he contemplated how to handle Louise.

Kindness is not a commodity she trades in. I made a mistake when I chose her.

By the time de Roche reached his home, his mind was made up. He marched in and called for his wife. When Louise walked into the salon, he roughly grabbed her wrist and forced her to sit on the chaiselongue. She was too surprised to protest. De Roche was towering over her.

"When I married you, I imagined a quiet life with a kind woman, a woman of faith and compassion. You are neither. You caused the death of an innocent boy and almost killed his mother, too. From now on, I shall spend as much time away from here as I can. You are to run the household to the best of your ability when I am gone. You are not permitted to travel to the city."

He thundered out of what would never again be his real home and left her, stunned.

Back in La Nouvelle Orleàns de Roche met with his neighbor Louis Blanchard at the newly opened coffee stand in front of Margarita and José's yet unfinished restaurant. Margarita had come up with the idea to turn her coveted brew into a business opportunity. While the two merchants sipped the invigorating hot drink on this cool autumn morning, de Roche came right to the point: "Louis, I know you have been acquiring properties here in the city since the hurricane, like so many other people with means. I failed to do the same but am now on a search for a house. I am somewhat pressed for time but hope you will be able to help me out for a reasonable price."

Blanchard scratched his chin: "I do not currently own anything large enough to fit your needs, unfortunately."

"It is not for myself that I am searching. Although I plan to spend a lot of time here. What I need is a modest but comfortable home, preferably one you have already restored, for there is no time to rebuild for months on end."

It was not difficult for Blanchard to add up what his friend was really saying. He was aware of de Roche's fondness for the beautiful former slave, enjoying a similar arrangement with one of his own: "Come with me. I just might have what you are looking for."

Blanchard took de Roche to a house on Rue St. Anne close to the corner of Rue Royale. It was situated between a carpenter's home and a glass blower's shop. Its piliers had been recently replaced and the roof looked new, too. Blanchard opened the door to a comfortably sized living room adjacent to a kitchen that led out into a small backyard. The one-story house had two bedrooms, one large, one slightly smaller, and another next to the kitchen just big enough to make space for a narrow bed and a nightstand. It was intended for a servant or cook.

"I shall make you a fair price if you want it. The same amount I paid for it plus reimbursement for the restoration."

They shook hands on the deal. The rest of the week was spent buying additional necessities for the house, such as a chandelier, dishes and two beds, one for each room. De Roche ordered a crib from one of the artisans on Rue Royale, then went to the convent to fetch Bebé who was all too happy at the prospect of being reunited with Zulimé who knew nothing yet of all these arrangements. The Mother Superior asked de Roche's permission for Bebé to continue attending school which he reluctantly granted: "Her first priority has to be Zulimé's well-being, but oui, she may keep studying."

Once the new home was finished, he picked up Zulimé and hurried her along towards Rue Royale. She was wondering what was causing such excitement. In front of a lovely house, he pulled out a large brass key and handed it to her: "Go ahead, open it."

She slowly turned the key and walked in. Bebé had been waiting and came running from the back, skipping steps until she reached Zulimé and threw her arms around her.

Henry smiled broadly: "This is your house. I shall not force you to go back to the plantation. You shall live here with our child. Bebé is here to help with the daily chores, and I shall come visit as much as I can."

Zulimé was too stunned to speak, but for the first time in many months her silence originated from joy instead of pain. She looked up at him with gratitude and relief.

I own a house. In the city and close to my friends. My child is safe now.

Bebé retreated to the back as the couple shared a long and intense embrace. It was not until hours later, when he had left, that Zulimé noticed the tiny crib next to the bed in her room. The tears took her by surprise. She cried over the memory of her Stephane, out of love for the man who had done so much to make her life better, for his generosity of heart and from a sense of a new beginning.

Chapter 27

The market was still not as lively as it had been before the hurricane, Florence observed when she went to meet Jean whom she had avoided for weeks even though he had returned from his months-long journey shortly after the storm. No matter how apprehensive she felt about it, she could no longer evade a conversation.

"You did not waste any time joining the carpetbaggers who now take advantage of people's misery," she said without so much as a greeting.

He grinned: "I take it you got word from my brother about the new building we acquired."

"Acquired? You just took advantage of the owners' misfortune when they left after the disaster because they could not afford the repairs. And you wasted no time to move in your whores."

"They abandoned it, so it was mine for the taking. And don't you like how close it is to your house? You don't even have to walk two blocks to work."

Florence pushed down the bile of anger rising in her throat. Jean made it very clear that he expected her to run the new brothel.

"I told you; it is either that building that will house all the women—with you in charge, of course—or I will use your house which is in my name for the same purpose. Without giving you any control."

If I say no to his blackmail, every business arrangement between us is at risk. I'd have to fight for my home and reveal the forgery on the deed.

The house was legally hers, but the brothers would seek revenge for her betrayal, she was certain. And so, Florence became a Madam against her will.

∼

After Florence left, Jean walked down to the port to the gang plank that led to his ship.

"I know you're in here," he shouted towards the cabins below. "My ship is not an accommodation for stranded sailors…"

A lone figure climbed up the stairs to the deck. Acadia's hair was loose, her wild locks falling all around a face darkened from the sun. She wore no hat. He grabbed her elbow.

"You need to pay me. Without money I cannot find a place to stay," she said quietly, avoiding his eyes.

"I will consider your wish over the holidays, but there is no way you will get as big a part of the loot as the other men… as the men…" he corrected himself.

Acadia freed herself from his grip: "You saw I can hold my own. You saw how I proved myself. I deserve my fair share."

Jean grinned. As with Florence before her, he admired strong personalities, unhindered by fear and lack of confidence. The discovery that the baby pirate was a girl had come as a shock, but Acadia had proved herself with determination as an integral member of his crew. Still, he was not about to give in easily: "I am not even certain I will keep you on. You are a distraction to my men. That does not make for successful voyages." Before she could protest, he held up his hand: "You may stay at my etablissement until you find a more permanent solution."

She looked at him incredulously: "Your etablissement? You mean, your brothel?"

He laughed: "I did not suggest that you work there. Just find a bed to sleep in and food for nourishment. If you truly want to stay on you better not get skinny and weak."

Acadia reluctantly agreed but found herself stupefied when she discovered who was running her new accommodations.

~

In the salon of the building on upper Rue de Bourbon Florence, hands on her hips and having been forewarned by Bèranger, gave Acadia a cool yet not unfriendly welcome:

"Oui, it is me. And since I am giving up a bed for you that is normally used for business you ought to pay me respect."

Acadia shrugged her shoulders. "I would have never taken you for a madam."

Florence let out a wry laugh: "And I would have never taken you for a pirate. So, there you have it. I suppose we are both not what we seem to be. You can wash up in the back, and you can get one meal per day after the girls have eaten. And you will pay me fifty livrés every week. I heard you made off with quite the loot, therefore money should not be a concern." She walked away but turned around as an afterthought entered her mind. "Oh, and you owe me the whole story. Jean only hinted at it."

A few nights later over a cup of rum or two in the brothel's bar, Acadia satisfied her curiosity when Florence asked: "How did they find out you are a woman? You fooled them for months, Jean said."

"We got into a battle with a Spanish crew after we had captured their vessel. We were throwing up ladders, and I climbed up first, as I always did because I am the fastest. I was barely onboard when a shot rang out and I was hit in the stomach. I fell over and into the sea. I don't remember much more and know only what the Captain told me when I came to in his cabin." Florence laughed: "You were unconscious in Jean's cabin? Well, bless the Lord that he is such a gentleman!"

Acadia responded angrily: "What would he have done with me, all bandaged up and in pain? Two of my shipmates threw a net into the sea and pulled me out. I lost consciousness and was told that a big dark stain was visible on my clothes. Jean must have instructed the men to rip open my jacket and shirt to look at the wound."

Acadia thought back to the day of her discovery…

∽

The looks on the men's faces would have made her laugh under different circumstances. They jumped back as if they had been bitten by a snake. One of them yelled: "Bloody hell, baby pirate is a woman!"

They hollered and pulled her pants down to check if they were indeed correct. That was when Bèranger stepped in and hit the one nearest to her so hard, he flew halfway towards the port beam. "Get off her! And you and you—he pointed at two others— "carry her to my cabin. And bring me salt, rum and cotton."

Jean cleaned her wounds and removed the shrapnel with his knife. She recovered, none of the metal had hit an organ, and as soon as she had regained consciousness, he asked her for an explanation.

Acadia told him her story and begged him to keep her on after he had threatened to leave her on some island along the way. She had heard tales of Anne Dieu-le-Veut and Jaquotte Delahaye, the two famed female pirates who had ruled the seas in the past century.

"Why can I not be one of them?" she had asked him.

∽

"But Jean did not make a decision whether he would keep me on," she continued, looking at Florence. "He never even spoke to me much all the way back to La Nouvelle Orleàns…"

"If you are as good as he said, he will keep you on," Florence declared.

"He said I was good? Because that is the truth."

Florence grinned: "He also said, you do not know how to shoot straight. You can wield a knife like the best of them, move faster and fit into the tiniest hole—no surprise here—but that you need to learn how to handle a gun."

Acadia was aware of her shortcomings, but Bèranger's words, as recounted to her by Florence, filled her with hope. Because aside from enjoying her adventures tremendously, she had yet to accomplish her goal of finding her family.

Drifting from one seedy tavern to the next, Josephine de Chavin had no goals. She rarely dared to cross Rue Royale, drank day and night and ended up hunched over a table at La Cocotte's until the Madame woke her roughly and threw her out in the early morning hours. When Michél was in town he called on her a few times a week and she obliged him.

One afternoon, as the day drew to a close, Josephine found herself on the corner of Rue Royale and Rue Toulouse. The old familiar streets were no longer welcoming. Well-off residents who would have given their last heirlooms to be invited to one of her soirées, deemed her unworthy of so much as a disdain-filled glance. Josephine was loath to venture nearer to the river, nearer to the mansion she had called home, but her feet seemed to follow their own call and one step after another she got closer to her all-too-recent past. She lingered on the corner and stared up to the window of her former boudoir, a room she had spent so much time in, getting her hair done, reading French romance novels and fantasizing about Michél. Now that their liaison was no longer a secret, the fantasy had become lifeless, a constant reminder of what had prompted the demise of her whole existence in the upper echelons of society. The crimson curtain was gone from the window, it looked bare without it. She imagined how Valdeterre had erased any sign of the feminine in the house, how he had thrown out the soft linens and replaced them with coarse cotton sheets, the kind he was used to as a soldier who had spent considerable time in the field. How he had workmen carry out her slanted settee, the one he had not sent over with all her other belongings. And how he had gotten rid of the delicate porcelain he had ordered from France upon her request right after their wedding.

He probably gifted it all to the Ursulines… as if the nuns and slaves and les petite gens would know how to appreciate such beautiful luxuries…

Josephine had lost her status but not her superior way of thinking. The skies were cloudy, and it rained every few hours. She crossed and found herself in front of the steps that led to the entrance. She had never paid attention to the fine detail of the artfully carved door or the intricate curving of the cast iron hinges. She put her hand up and touched the wood as if by magic, it would open into her old world. She felt herself sliding down, a sunken bundle of despair on the front steps of a home that was no longer hers nor would it ever be again. She pulled herself up when she saw a man hurrying past. The rain had started and the water dripping down her face hid her tears as she ran back towards Rue de Bourbon. Soaking wet she found herself where she always ended up, at La Cocotte's. The doorman would not let her pass at first until Madame saw her and waved her inside. Instead of sending her to the bar, Madame steered her upstairs to her fleet of rooms where she kept her desk and all the ledgers that contained notes about her business.

"Sit down. Do not touch anything. I will fetch some towels to dry you off."

Madame Cocotte went to the back while Josephine tried to wring out her dress without making a puddle.

"What are you going to do when your money runs out?"

It was a question Josephine had been asking herself, never coming up with an answer other than the hope that Michél would somehow take care of her. "Are you proposing that I work for you?" Not long ago, Josephine would have been offended at the suggestion of becoming a prostitute, but now she had no fight left.

Madame Cocotte patted her hand: "I doubt you are cut out for that, but how would you like running things?"

Josephine's interest was piqued. "Running the cabarét? The brothel? For you?"

The Madame smirked: "Ah non, we never call it a brothel, my dear. A cabarét, yes. And not for me, really. Rather instead of me. I am thinking of retiring. You are an educated woman; you can read and write and most of all you can count. I would still get most of the profits, of course, but over time, if you prove yourself, this place could be yours."

Before Josephine could object to the profit sharing, Madame raised her hand: "Do not get high and mighty on me now. You have neither a lot of choices nor another offer. But you have enough class to attract wealthy customers. Once you clean yourself up," she said, pointing at Josephine's torn sleeve. "Think about it." Madame Cocotte walked away.

Josephine took the last swig from her cup and, for the first time in months, went home before midnight. When she mentioned the proposal to Michél, he urged her to accept. The fact that she would be in competition with the Bèranger's own brothel escaped him.

"Imagine, how much money you could make! You will never again be accepted by society, but as the Madam of the finest establishment in the city, the men will have to respect you. You will know everything about them, everything they want to keep secret from their wives and each other. This is what power is."

For a woman who had rejected independence her entire life believing she could count on a man of her own stature to provide for her, a woman who had encouraged her friend to go into business while never taking the same approach herself, Josephine began warming up to the idea in her moment of need.

∽

Henry de Roche became a savior of sorts when he drained his plantation in Port-au-Prince and shipped all available bags of rice and beans and sugar to the city. Food was running out in La Nouvelle Orleàns brought on by a horrendous drought in April and May that turned the earth brittle in such a way that it was hard to work the soil. The relentless summer rains that followed added to the despair of the colony's people and affected the plantations greatly. Valdeterre was forced to open the last storage facilities and release rice to the starving citizens, while everyone eagerly awaited supplies from France. It was everything Valdeterre had feared.

In agreement with the Commander, de Roche distributed the food for free to the poor and made up for it by charging the wealthy more. When an argument broke out among the rich over the inflated prices, Valdeterre called in Father de Beaubois as an intermediary. The priest went up on the pulpit one Sunday and spent the entire sermon preaching about the grace of charity. And to make his intentions very clear, he ended with a warning: "Those who let the poor suffer while their coffers are full, shall not call themselves Christians and shall be banned from receiving holy communion."

There was no more argument after that mass, proving how much power the Catholic church held, even over the wealthiest patrons.

∽

The small house on Rue St. Anne made Zulimé feel settled and truly independent for the first time in her life. It was during Henry's travels that she gave birth to her second child. Bebé was by her side and this time her labor was short, but the child was in the wrong position and ripped her almost apart. Zulimé's screams could be heard from blocks away. She had known this before, had seen the baby's backside coming out of her first in a vision a few weeks prior to the birth.

Bebé held Zulimé's hands through her pain. Getting the baby out took longer than the labor. Zulimé lost the will to push a few times, so exhausted was she. When it finally came, she was not surprised that the child was a girl. Her elation that the baby was healthy when Bebé placed her in her arms was overshadowed by the tears for the one she had lost. Her recovery was hard. She had no milk, and Bebé went to find a nursemaid, but this caused Zulimé so much anguish that she spent an entire night praying for guidance to make a tea, a salve or an ointment that would help her milk flow. She was relieved when she came up with one, but her exhaustion made it difficult to take care of her daughter. Bebé went to Margarita for help. It was the Cuban who suggested that Zulimé begin selling her teas, salves and ointments.

After she recovered, she got up and knocked on her neighbor's door: "Monsieur, would you consider making small bottles and jars for me?" she asked the glassblower. "I have no money to pay you upfront, but as soon as my items sell, I shall give you what I owe and hopefully order more."

To her relief the man agreed after she offered him a healing salve for a cut on his hand that immediately took away his pain. Her next visit was to a shopkeeper around the corner who sold hair potions and face creams: would she consider selling her ointments for a portion of the profit? They too, agreed on a fair share.

By the time Henry returned, Zulimé's endeavor had taken off, and she could barely keep up with the production so great was the demand. Despite the hardships that had befallen the city, her potions were second on the list of the poor as well as the rich, right after food. Soon, word spread that her teas could ease pains, aid in sleep disorders and cure stomach illness. Her ointments were coveted by ladies and workers alike for their potential to speed up wound healing.

Zulimé had come up with the idea of creating paper labels whenever paper was available, and she wrote the names of the potions on them in her beautiful handwriting. Bebé added little drawings of the ingredients for those customers who did not know the alphabet. Zulimé had found joy again when she looked at her daughter and purpose when she stood in her kitchen creating her salves and herbal mixes. Henry, too, was overjoyed when she placed the new baby in his arms upon his return.

If he had hoped for a boy, he hid it well: "She is as beautiful as you, ma chèrie," he said while rocking her to sleep.

"I named her Marie Catherine…" she whispered.

He was delighted: "After your mother."

She smiled. Marie Catherine Larrác would live on in her granddaughter.

"We shall have her baptized as soon as possible," he declared.

"I will ask Margarita and Bebé to be godmothers."

"Certainly," he agreed.

After the baby fell asleep and Henry had put her in her crib, Zulimé told him about her newfound business. As expected, he was proud but insisted that he pay off the glassblower. She objected: "Allow me to do this on my own… and there is another thing I need to speak with you about…" She took a deep breath before continuing. What she was going to ask may or may not be received in kind. "I want to buy Bebé's freedom."

His eyes widened in surprise, then narrowed in contemplation. "I doubt you have the money for that."

She looked at her hands folded in her lap: "Not yet, I know…"

He put his fingers under her chin and made her look him in the eye: "Then it will have to be one or the other." She did not understand. "You can either pay off your debt with the glassblower or buy Bebé's freedom and allow me to pay the man."

She threw her arms around his neck. He picked her up and carried her to the bedroom. That night they slept in each other's arms after Zulimé had told him about the painful birth and her need to heal before she could become his lover again.

It took Bebé a long time to realize that she was free, an affranchitte, after Zulimé informed her. The girl stood in the kitchen unable to move, her mouth open which made Zulimé laugh. When the news finally sank in, she began crying uncontrollably, giggles interspersed with her tears. Bebé had been born enslaved and never known freedom. After a few minutes of laughing and crying, she asked: "But may I still stay here and live with you?"

Zulimé's relief was palpable when she answered: "I had hoped you would want to, but from now on I shall pay you for your work."

~

Geneviève was coming back from a construction site, hurrying along the river and turning the corner on Rue Orleàns when she bumped into a man, dressed too elegantly and warmly to be a citizen. It was dusk and in the fading light, she did not see his face. But his smell.

Oh, his smell.

How could she ever forget that nauseating blend of tobacco, perfume powder and something that reminded her of gun smoke from a recently fired pistol? The memory was so strong, she jumped back and hit the wall of a house. The impact left her without breath, but all her senses told her to run. And run she did, the narrowing eyes of the man the last thing she saw before turning another corner onto Rue de Chartres. She did not stop until she reached her home, making sure at every turn that he had not followed her. She threw the door shut behind her and went up to her bedroom two steps at a time. She did not want her children to see her in this state. She splashed water on her face and forced herself to calm down.

Did he recognize me? What is his business in La Nouvelle Orleàns? What is this vile man going to do to me? Will I ever be safe?

Geneviève's thoughts were jumbled, piercing her brain and constricting her chest.

This city is not big enough to escape someone, and what about everything I have built for me and the children?

She spent the following days in fear of discovery, spied around every corner, turned to see if she was followed, and every sighting of a man in an overcoat made her heart race. She was certain she had spotted him at least twice lingering near the better homes along the river, clearly searching for something. Or someone. One evening a week later, after accepting a supper invitation at the Castro home, Geneviève sat down in the courtyard with Margarita when her ever-observant friend quietly asked what was wrong. She confided the whole sordid story and her paralyzing fear of being found by that man. Margarita's hand flew to her mouth. The Cuban knew that Geneviève had every reason to be frightened. And short of selling everything and running up north, there was no solution other than the hope that the man would give up and go back to Paris.

"Can you ask the Commander for help? You are on friendly terms with him, are you not?"

"What would I tell him? If he hears the truth, he will have no other recourse than to put me behind bars. If I lie and make up a story that this man is following me and scaring the children, he may have him questioned and the truth will come out regardless. I have no way out." Geneviève's voice was quivering, she was near tears.

Margarita put a hand on her arm: "It was self-defense."

"I cannot prove that. There are no witnesses other than my Pierre who was a tiny toddler then."

A few days later Geneviève woke up to loud knocking. She ran downstairs in her nightgown and opened. Commander Valdeterre stood next to one of his deputies, a regretful look on his face. Behind them was her nemesis.

"Madame, you will have to accompany us to command. There have been serious allegations made by the Baron…" Her knees gave out and Valdeterre stepped forward to prevent her from falling. "Madame, if you would get dressed, s'il vous plait."

Geneviève dragged herself upstairs, slipped into a dress, her hands shaking and unable to tie the laces. She threw a shawl around her shoulders, shivering despite the warm morning. She woke a boarder, a woman her age and asked her to take care of Pierre and Delphine. The children looked on helplessly, as the Commander and his deputy led their mother away followed closely by a tall man with a grim mouth and cold eyes.

"Why is she not tied?" the Baron asked in a harsh tone.

"Madame LaCour is not a prisoner, Baron. She is merely being questioned."

"She should be hanged; she is a murderess!"

"These are your allegations, I am aware. They must be proven, and Baronesse LaCour has a right to defend herself."

"She is not worthy of this name or title!"

"Regardless, she will be questioned, and your presence is not permitted. We already have your statement, now we need hers. I could not prevent you from accompanying us now, but I can keep you from being part of the police inquest."

In Geneviève's ears their conversation played through a tunnel far away yet echoing in her mind. She felt as if she were outside of her own body, one thought circling in her head:

What is to become of my children?

CHAPTER 28

On upper Rue de Bourbon Florence ran the new house with a tight hand. Her girls were clean, and their mornings were spent learning the alphabet and some additions. Florence who had resisted school when she had first come to La Nouvelle Orleàns, was now determined to pass on to the girls the same education she had received from the nuns. She came to enjoy those morning lessons as much as she dreaded the night's business.

There was light on the horizon for her, and it came when Alexandre Pascal entered the etablissement one night. Pascal was a smuggler who Florence had met when he sought the services of one of her girls. From the moment they laid eyes on each other, it was obvious that he would have preferred to bed her instead of the prostitute he paid for. After that night he came back regularly, never again to seek the pleasures of the flesh. Instead, he asked for a cup of rum and the pleasure of her company when she joined him at the bar. They talked all evening, and Florence learned a lot about him.

Alexandre Pascal is a much better businessman than the Bèrangers. He never gets himself in trouble like they do.

Alexandre Pascal bought up goods from overstocked manufacturers in Cuba, Saint Domingue and the Grande Antilles islands and found routes through the waterways of the Delta to avoid paying taxes to the Compagnie of the West Indies. When he was in the city, he paid Florence nightly visits and always came bearing gifts. Most times it was a necessity like corn or rice that enabled her to feed the girls better than most people who had to survive on the rationed portions. One day he brought her a personal present. When she opened the small box, she gasped: rubies and emeralds sparkled under the light of the chandelier. He took the necklace and put it around her neck.

"Befitting a queen." His gaze lingered on her neck before he kissed her slowly. "I am going down to the Delta in the morning to meet a St. Dominguan vessel. I shall be back in a week's time. I hope we can continue this…"

Alexandre raised Florence's hand to his mouth and bowed. Her eyes followed him out the door.

∽

Sitting in the big salon at La Cocotte's, now behind the bar not in front of it, Josephine contemplated her new life. A few months ago, it would have been inconceivable to imagine herself running a cabarét. The *grande dame* of the Commanders mansion could not have reconciled in her heart and mind a move from a posh riverside home to a tavern on seedy Rue de Bourbon. Yet here she was. Running a cabarét—she could not bring herself to call it what it was, a brothel—was a step up from barely getting by as a disgraced Casket Girl.

I better get very rich here for society will never permit me a place among them.

One day in late summer when the heat was particularly unbearable and the thickness of the humid air lay on the skin like a heavy blanket, Josephine left Madame standing at the counter to fetch them some cold water from the back. They had been going over the books, fanning themselves and counting the earnings from rum and girls. When Josephine returned, Madame Cocotte lay motionless on the floor, her fan covering her face. Josephine dropped the water, knelt down and felt for a pulse. There was none.

Madame Cocotte's funeral was a colorful parade made up of all her girls, who had painted their faces even more than usual, followed by a reception at her etablissement where musicians played sad tunes and many of the gentlemen that had made her rich, drank the last of her champagne. Josephine was immediately treated as the deceased's heir apparent by prostitutes and gentlemen callers alike. Upon further examination of Madame's desk, dresser and nightstand, there was no last will or testament found, and after Michél threatened the notary, Josephine's name miraculously appeared on the deed. It would cost her twenty percent of her earnings, for now a small price to pay for the pirate's protection.

I shall find a way to get rid of him when the time comes, and I tire of him.

Being a madam came much more easily to Josephine than she thought. Ordering the prostitutes around was second nature to her, and charming men to get what she wanted was a skill practiced since childhood. Except now she did it for profit not for marriage or status. She was always on the lookout for new girls, building on the 'stable of variety' as Madame Cocotte had called it. The old lady had been famous for women of all colors, builds and special skills, serving a clientele as colorful as the city's social structure itself.

La Cocotte's was also a place for regular women who came to enjoy a drink. Artisans who could not afford the high prices for sexual favors, simply got to enjoy watching wealthier patrons make their choices over a cup of rum while listening to music from a mandolin player or a singer in the back of the salon. Josephine intended to keep it that way. The rich paid for the pleasures of the flesh but often refused to spend more money on cheap rum, when the champagne ran out. For the fancy libation one still depended on shipments from France while there was rum aplenty from the islands, and the poor paid their hard-earned livrés as they drank themselves into a forgetful stupor.

Either way I make a profit.

∾

A few blocks up the street Florence smashed four plates and two jugs when she heard who had taken over La Cocotte's.

"So now the city has a high and mighty madam? I thought she only whored herself out, not others! I knew there would be trouble when the Bèranger brothers involved themselves in two similar businesses…"

"…that are now run by two fiercely competitive women with a complicated history?" Alexandre Pascal finished her sentence. He took a long look at her before her yelling ceased, and he finally spoke: "Why are you still doing this?" He reached out and took her hand between his in a gentle gesture. "You never seemed comfortable running a brothel. Your skills can be put to better use elsewhere."

Florence lowered her head to avoid his intense eyes. Alexandre had just put into words what she had been feeling for a long time. "What choice do I have? I am bound to a devil called Bèranger…"

"You are bound, you are not sold. Those ties can be undone." She looked up, as he continued: "There are those who are pirates, and there are those who are smugglers. There are those who are madams, and there are those who are businesswomen. You and I are not the former but the latter. Bèranger is a fool. He still believes he can get rich off the ships he attacks while the governors of every colony, every island keep coming after the pirates. He believes this fallacy can sustain him to the end of his days when the end of his days may not be too far in the future. Making money is now about trade and business. One can bend the laws but not break them, or one ends up at the gallows. Give it up, Florence. Find a girl to take over and deal with Bèranger. Untie yourself from him. You could own this town, invest in homes, in bars, in shops."

"I already own a home. The one I live in. My name is on the deed. But Jean does not know this. He will come after me, and I cannot fight him on my own."

"You are not on your own anymore." Alexandre got on one knee. "Florence Bourget, marry me. Say oui."

With widened eyes and her free hand at her mouth, she hesitated but for a moment before she breathed her 'yes'. He got up and pulled her with him. Their kiss seemed unending.

In a sea of happiness, the forçat from Paris had never thought possible, Florence kept putting off the confrontation with Bèranger. Her fiancé, Alexandre Pascal, had left for Barataria Bay, and she wanted to wait for his return, for the first time in her life relying on a man and being comfortable with it. Her plans to wait with the news was thwarted when Jean Bèranger burst into the house one evening, red-faced and angry: "Mon frère, le *bastarde*!"

Florence was surprised. Jean had never called his brother a bastard, never spoken a bad word about him no matter how often Michél had endangered one of their enterprises with his short temper and impulsive actions.

"Michél? What has he done now?"

"He plays protector to the mighty Princess! Or I should say 'mighty madam'! He convinced two of the best girls we brought back from our last journey to work at La Cocotte's instead of our etablissement!"

Florence sighed: "About that… How would you like to have our etablissement turn into yours and yours alone?"

"What are you talking about? You are running it, and I pay you a good price, do I not?"

"What I am saying is, how would you like to save your money? I have other business to attend to and no time to keep playing Madam."

Jean came up to her until there was barely an inch between them. Florence did not budge. His voice was icy: "I will not allow that."

"You do not own me. I am not one of your prostitutes."

"I need you to continue running my business, not yours."

His big hand went to her neck, cutting off her air. She reached around the side of his belt and pulled the pistol out of the holster. He let go of her when he felt the muzzle of his own weapon digging into his stomach. She took a step back, not lowering the gun.

"I shall go about my own business. You and I are finished. As a show of good faith, I will help you find a replacement who can take over my duties. D'accord?"

Jean narrowed his eyes: "What replacement?"

"I was thinking of Jeanette. She can read, write and do the additions. She knows the business better than I ever did, never having been a prostitute myself. You know her. She can do this. She is not afraid of anything." Florence waved the pistol: "Now get out."

After the door closed on him, she locked it and sank into an armchair.

I cannot trust him to leave me be, but maybe he will think about it and recognize the generosity of my offer.

∽

Acadia was sitting on the dock at the port when she spotted a fuming Jean Bèranger coming towards her, his boots loudly clattering from his heavy steps. The man oozed anger.

Maybe not the best time to bring this up, but I will not let my world turn dark again.

"Jean, I would really like to get back to sea…"

"I have a lot more pressing troubles to handle than your wishes to sail off!" he thundered, "and besides, I have not decided whether to keep you on yet!"

"What troubles?"

"That wretched woman decided to quit working for me!"

He slammed his fist into a pole. Acadia knew instantly who he was talking about: "But if Florence is not running the brothel anymore, where do I sleep? We must get back out."

"You think, I don't want to set sail?! I do, but this unresolved situation here has kind of disrupted my plans."

Acadia decided it was best to not press the issue for now, leaving him on the dock staring out at the water.

I have become too dependent on that woman. I should have never let her have this much control over my business.

Secretly he admitted that Florence's suggestion to replace her with Jeanette was a good one. Jeanette would be the only madam in La Nouvelle Orleans who had started out as a prostitute, which certainly gave her more insight than Florence ever had, and that aristocrat could ever gain.

Josephine de Chanvin may whore herself out to my brother, but that is a far cry from Jeanette's years of experience. As a prostitute Jeanette has the desperate skill of a woman who had to come up with a repertoire of tricks to survive. She could teach the girls a whole lot. But of course, no one is better at the business end than Florence…

Jean's thoughts meandered back to Acadia. Despite not having told her yet, his mind had been made up weeks ago. She did not just fight like a man; she was better than most of his pirates. Instead of simply using force, she had the ability to calculate any situation. This was apparent in the narrowing of her eyes before she raised her sword, knife or gun, the way she changed from a wide stance to a quick step when she attacked, and above all her fast way to duck and slip in between the enemy when she assessed that there was no way to win. Unlike his men who all too often got beaten to a bloody pulp, she hardly ever injured herself by charging into a fight when she was outnumbered. And there was something else about her. After she had been discovered for who she really was, he had one day laughingly commented that she had cleaned herself up at long last. Acadia had responded with indignation:

"It is not like everything coming out of the Acadian territories has a bark, gills or claws. I may not be a pretty girl that smiles all the time and curtsies in a powdered wig, but I am not an animal."

Jean had begun looking at her differently from then on. She was certainly anything but conventionally pretty, and yet her lithe body which he had seen plenty of when she was wounded, and her sharp determination impressed him. She possessed a haunting beauty he had not seen in any woman before her. He sighed.

Why is it that I am always so drawn to women of such raw toughness? I should know that they are all a world of trouble.

~

Florence had taken it upon herself to go to the convent and tell Jeanette of her plans. The irony of her offer in the city's center of Catholicism did not escape her, particularly when the only quiet place to talk was the chapel.

"You want me to take over your brothel? I thought you dropped me here to get away from selling myself," Jeanette asked incredulously.

Florence rolled her eyes: "You will not have to sell yourself any longer. You will oversee selling the others."

"So, you want me to be the Madam?"

Sometimes this woman has the brains of a swamp frog.

"Oui, pending Bèranger's approval. And this is why I am here. I need you to come tonight, when I am going to convince him to let you take over. You must prove yourself and make him understand that you can do this. That you can now read and write and most of all count. He must see you can fetch the best price from the customers. Jean loves money. You need to show him that you can keep his place running at a profit."

One could have cut the air in the room into slices with a bayonet when the pirate entered the brothel after sunset. Florence, standing next to Jeanette at the bar, noticed him the minute he walked in. Their eyes met, and every girl and customer moved out of the firing line. Florence and Jean were shooting invisible daggers at each other. If it was a show of strength, neither was winning, so they stared each other down until Florence moved her head in a welcoming gesture and put her hand out as a sign of conciliation. Bèranger slowly crossed the room.

"Bon soir, Jean. So nice of you to join us. I believe you have made the acquaintance of Mademoiselle Jeanette Crozat…"

"… who you are proposing moves up, from Mademoiselle to Madam?"

"Getting right to point, are you? Alors. Let us save time. Oui, Jeanette is wholly capable of taking over…"

Jeanette interrupted: "I can count, I can read and write, and I am very good at negotiating."

Bèranger sized her up: "Oui, I seem to remember the last part… I am willing to let you try. If profits are not up, or at the very least the same in three months from now, you are lucky if I even let you stay on in your other profession."

Florence smiled: "I am confident about the profits. Do we have an agreement?"

Jean nodded and they shook hands. Florence poured them all drinks. Pretending as if it were an afterthought while she handed him his cup, she added: "Now, there is the matter of my house."

"Your house? You do not have a house. You have a place to sleep as long as you keep handling my other businesses."

A voice coming from the back was deep and had a sharp edge to it: "Which Florence Bourget, soon to be Madame Pascal shall not be doing any longer."

Alexandre Pascal stepped from the shadows right up to Bèranger who was slightly shorter than him and not as muscular in build. The pirate had a hard time hiding his surprise.

So, this is why she wants out.

Jean had heard of Pascal, the fliebustier who controlled the waterways to the south and east.

She found herself a smuggler.

"Good, then you will not need my house."

Florence was in his face, ready to scratch it faster than Alexandre could pull her back. "It is my house, you coquin, and I will not give it up! I would rather burn it down!"

Bèranger's hand was at Florence's throat, but before he could tighten his grip, he felt a searing pain shoot across his face and found himself on his knees dripping blood. "My nose, *cochon!*" He screamed as he got up and drew his knife. Alexandre Pascal grabbed his wrist before he could strike and stepped on his foot rendering the pirate defenseless. Holding him at arm's length, he said in a deathly quiet tone:

"If you ever touch my fiancé again, I will break much more than your nose."

Pascal pushed him back, and Beranger holding his bloody face, staggered out. The silence of those present in the salon, slowly turned into hushed whispers.

Alexandre put an arm around Florence: "I believe I have made an enemy out of Monsieur Bèranger."

"I am not giving up my house. I have a deed."

"Ma belle, you do not need the house. Let him have it and be done with him. His greatest punishment is the loss of your business skills. You shall own this town. Not just one house."

Florence knew he was right.

I will take over the city…

∼

On her wedding day Florence got reckless when she put on the prettiest and most expensive dress she had ever worn. It occurred to her that a certain pair of earrings would complement her appearance.

The wedding is a small affair, no one will notice their value. And their original owner is not invited.

The rift between her and Josephine had grown so deep thanks to competing brothels and Michél's meddling, it could not be bridged. The wedding was indeed small, only a handful of people, most of them the groom's acquaintances. Jeanette and Acadia were present in the chapel next to the church. Florence, however, did not count on her groom, a man of many surprises who put together a parade through the city, hired musicians who played their drums and had horses adorned with colorful ribbons. The bride was serenaded, and their celebration attracted many onlookers who either stood clapping on the sidewalks or joined the parade.

The sound of the drums brought out artisans, merchants and tavern owners. Inside La Cocotte's Josephine heard the noise and curiosity drove her outside. She spotted the parade's main attraction in its midst and was about to walk back inside, dismissive of the former forçat, when Florence's elaborate hairdo caught her eye as the groom was twirling his bride in a dance move. Another dance at another wedding, with a female guest she had not been able to unmask, struck her memory like lightning.

Josephine threw herself into the crowd, her hands closing in on Florence's ears: "Thief!" she yelled, "I should have known it was you! I saw you at the Mardi Gras ball, forçat!"

Florence grabbed her wrists and shook her off: "I do not know what you are screaming about, Madam Josephine. Get out of my parade!"

Alexandre Pascal's friends took hold of Josephine's arm and removed her from the street, while she raged on: "The earrings are in the design of my family's crest! You stole them from me! I shall have the police hunt you down and pay for your thievery!"

It was not until the following morning that Alexandre inquired about the jewelry. He lay with his arms around his wife when a rueful smile crossed his lips:

"She is not wrong, is she? Madam Josephine?"

Florence looked at him unapologetically:

"Non. I took them. She is rich, and I needed to insure my future."

He laughed: "She is not rich anymore if the stories are to be believed, and you, ma belle, do not have to insure your future. You have one with me. So why not give back her jewelry?"

"Because she does not deserve mercy. And she cannot have me arrested, either, given that her ex-husband is the head of police. That man would rather throw her in prison for disgracing him so publicly than helping her in any way."

He nudged her: "Then at least wear them only at home. You do not need to show off in public, you are beautiful without these adornments."

Florence gave him a reluctant nod.

Over at the military command, Valdeterre felt badly for his most prominent prisoner and worse for her children. He was forced to jail the Baronesse when she refused to speak or answer any questions. He implored her to defend herself against the Baron's allegations, begged her to explain to avoid a trial, even petitioned the Governor to keep her under house arrest instead of throwing her into a damp cell, but none of his efforts were met with success. Geneviève LaCour would not say a word, every inquest was met with blank stares, and the Governor refused to allow an exception being made for a suspect who was accused of murder. It would set a bad precedent, he declared.

But no one said I could not make her as comfortable as I can.

Valdeterre ordered a room at command to be cleared and stationed two men outside. He had proper food delivered and allowed the boarder woman who took care of the children to bring a change of dress once a week. He also permitted Sister Stanislaus to visit for an hour each day and implored her to persuade the Baronesse to cooperate with the Councilor. The one who did all the talking was the Baron. Not a day passed without him marching into the Commander's office, pounding his silver cane on the floor and demanding a trial. After weeks of silence on Geneviève's part, Valdeterre knew that he could no longer avoid it. When the Sister heard that a date had been set, she rushed to see him:

"Commander, I beg you to give her more time!"

"I have no more excuse. And I fear that the trial will end in favor of that man, if she continues to stay silent."

"I have tried to make her state her case, but to no avail. The Baronesse only asks questions about the children, not even her homes. Permit me one more try. I would like to bring in Señora Margarita Castro. The two have a very close bond."

He twirled his moustache. "Permission granted."

Valdeterre convinced the Councilor to close the trial to the public and call on witnesses to attest to the accused's character. The Baron objected loudly and violently, trashing a lamp on the desk which prompted the Commander to have him thrown out.

On the first morning of the trial, Sister Stanislaus and Margarita walked into the courtroom together. The Councilor opened the proceedings by reading the allegations and calling Baron LaCour to the stand.

"What happened on Christmas Eve in the year 1726?"

The Baron puffed up his chest: "That woman, my daughter-in-law who I have disowned, shot and killed my son in cold blood. She shall hang for this!"

"That is not for you to determine. You say, in cold blood. Are you implying she planned his murder?"

"This is precisely what I am saying."

"Were you present when this occurred?"

"I was standing right there and witnessed the murder, oui."

"Baron, what was Baronesse LaCour's reason for killing her husband?"

"You shall not call her by that name or that title!"

"Answer the question, s'il vous plait."

"She is a greedy woman; she wanted his fortune. She would have killed me, too, given a chance."

"Are you alleging that she threatened your life?"

"She was the one with the pistol, was she not?"

"How did she get the pistol?"

The Baron stood quiet for a moment. He knew that whatever he said now would determine the trial: "She must have stolen it from my son."

Geneviéve who had sat still with her head down until then, looked up and for the first time in weeks appeared to be present.

"So, she came into the room with his pistol? When did this occur? Before the meal or after?"

The Baron began to stutter: "Oui, she must have. It was after Christmas supper was served... The servants had cleared the dishes and only I, my son and she were at the table."

"Liar!" Geneviève's shout rang out suddenly and unexpectedly. Sister Stanislaus exchanged glances with Margarita.

"Madame, be quiet! You shall get your turn!" the Councilor warned before continuing: "Baron, if, as you claim, the murder was planned, why would she wait until after supper and then commit the crime in front of you?"

"She is a ruthless woman!" Waving his finger, the Baron pointed at Geneviève. The clerk called for a break after excusing the witness. Margarita and the Sister huddled around Geneviève for the half hour until the trial commenced with the Councilor calling the two women to the stand. Sister Stanislaus was first. The nun described the defendant as a calm and measured woman who was neither prone to violence nor to sudden outbursts. The Sister spoke to Geneviève's virtues as a mother and her deep faith.

Margarita was next, confirming what had been stated before. The Councilor was about to excuse her from the stand, when she looked straight at the Baron while she addressed the court: "Would you agree that the Catholic faith prohibits a man from beating his wife?"

The Councilor was thrown off by her question. Valdeterre raised his eyebrows. There was no sound until the Councilor regained his composure: "Señora Castro, what are you implying?"

"I am not implying; I am simply asking. Does the Catholic faith permit beatings by the husband?"

"Non, of course not…"

"Then I would humbly suggest that you ask the Baronesse the true reasons for what she did. Only then will you understand why she had to defend herself."

On the other side of the courtroom the Baron erupted: "It was not self-defense, it was murder! Do you really believe the word of that brown woman over mine? I am the eyewitness!"

"Order!" yelled the clerk. "One more outburst and I shall have you removed!"

After another break Geneviève took the stand. She seemed a changed woman.

"Whatever you said to her, Sister, must have worked," whispered Margarita.

"I simply reminded her of her duty as a mother. It was you who convinced her not to give up but stand strong against the lies."

With a straight back and a strong voice, her head held high for the first time since her arrest, Geneviève took a deep breath when asked to recount her version of events.

"Councilor, I do not deny shooting my husband, but this part is the only truth out of everything being told so far." She looked at Margarita: "My husband had a violent temper just like his father."

The Baron jumped up and was held down by two clerks before he could interrupt again.

"He would hit me during disagreements," she continued, "throw me against the bedpost when I refused his advances after he had beaten me and lock me in my boudoir for the slightest infractions of whatever rules he came up with. No zinc, no powder could cover my bruises. When I begged my father-in-law for help and asked him to talk some sense into his son, he laughed and said that I must be a bad wife. That someone like me had to be put in her place. That I deserved the punishments just like his own wife had until she learned proper behavior and how to satisfy his every need."

"How long did this go on?"

"It began shortly after the wedding when I came back late from the dressmaker one day. It ceased for a while after Pierre was born, and he was proud to have a son. But my daughter was not conceived of love but of brutality. And the beatings became worse. That Delphine did not die in my womb from his kicks to my belly, that she came into this world a healthy child is a miracle. And this man, my former father-in-law was an eyewitness to that, too. He stood laughing while I was in pain."

The Councilor crinkled his forehead: "Is there any proof of all this? A witness perhaps who is in the city?"

"The only witness is that man over there," Geneviève pointed at the Baron, "and he is lying."

"So, there is no one else who can confirm your story?"

She hesitated: "My children... but they were too young..."

"So, we have no evidence."

"Non, we do. The evidence is me. My body."

Geneviève slowly raised her hand, craned her neck towards him and brushed back her hair, thus exposing an ugly scar that reached from her ear all the way to her shoulder.

"He took his bayonet to my throat and sliced me open. There was so much blood that I lost consciousness..."

There was a pause and a hush in the courtroom.

"What happened on the night of the killing?"

"I was used to the beatings, the threats to my life. But on that night Pierre, barely five years of age, was playing with his cake. This enraged my husband who tore the fork out of my son's hand and stuck it into his arm." Her voice broke: "Pierre ran screaming and bleeding from the room. I jumped up. My husband raised the fork and grabbed my wrist. I heard my father-in-law laughing behind me while I tried to wriggle out of my husband's grip. All I wanted was to run after my boy, but I could not get free, and he hit me across the mouth. I turned my face away and saw the pistol in my father-in-law's holster. I pulled it out with my free hand and shot my husband in the stomach."

Silence lay heavily on the courtroom. Sister Stanislaus made the sign of the cross. Margarita stared at the ceiling, incapable of preventing tears. Valdeterre had a look of worry and compassion on his face.

Then the Baron jumped up and began yelling: "This is the proof! She murdered him!"

Valdeterre had heard enough and had enough of the man. He got up and motioned the soldiers who stood at the door to remove the Baron. The Councilor asked Geneviève how she got away. Her brother, she said. She recounted how she ran upstairs, took Delphine out of her crib, found Pierre crying under the bed, carried them both out the door and ran to her brother's house who sheltered them until he secured passage on the Gironde.

"I came here to make a new life for my children. A life without beatings, without violence. My own inheritance and my brother's help made this possible…"

Geneviève's voice trailed off; her shoulders sagged. She appeared to be shrinking. Every wall she had built so carefully around her heart had fallen. She saw clearly in this moment: this tale that she had herself so convinced of, that she had to do everything for the protection of the children and her own, was a myth. Erecting the walls had not come out of strength but necessity and desperation. But right here on this stand, she felt strong when she told her truth at long last. Never had she shown more courage, no matter the outcome.

The court retreated to deliberate the verdict.

PART FOUR

OF SECRETS AND SCARS

"Do nothing secretly; for time sees and hears all things and discloses all."

— *Sophocles*

CHAPTER 29

It is the year 1745, and we have moved into the new convent at long last. We need all the room we can get, educating more girls than ever. The city continues to grow at a most rapid rate. It is almost inconceivable that this is the same place we found when we set foot on this soil so many years ago...

In a quiet corner of the Saint Louis Basilica, Sister Stanislaus put down the pen and fanned the paper for the ink to dry. Her father had been faithfully publishing her letters for the past eighteen years. She felt a pang of guilt for omitting some things. She reported on the successes of the school and the discussions and arguments with Jesuits and Capuchins, described the growing city in detail, but left some of her more ambivalent feelings for her journal. And she mentioned the Casked Girls only in passing. Through the years, she had become even more critical of the practice to send women across the seas, and lately she had gotten distraught by the new Mother Superior's decision to turn away the undesirable kind and refuse them not only education but shelter. On this day, a ship carrying another sixteen girls was to come into port.

I wonder who will be the lucky ones that are permitted to stay...

The Sister's thoughts went back to the day twelve years ago, when she had entered the Abbess' office only to find Mother St. Augustin slumped over her desk. The head of the convent had passed from yellow fever, a disease she had hidden from all with the exception of her most trusted nun. Mother St. Augustin had sequestered herself so as to not infect the others, but had refused to seek the help of a doctor.

I should have at least called on Zulimé to help her…

This regret weighed deeper on the Sister since Mother St. Augustin never got to see the milestone for the Ursulines that she had worked so hard for: the move to the new convent a few months after her passing. The newly installed Superior Jeanne Melotte, called Mother St. André, had turned the day into an unnecessary spectacle. As Sister Stanislaus described it to her father:

On July 17, 1734, the convent bells rang a merry peal, and the citizens led a procession through the city to our new building. The children of the orphanage, the pupils of our school and the respectable ladies all bore lighted tapers while singing pious hymns. Behind them were twenty young girls dressed in white, and little ones dressed as angels. This was not the only reason for some of our discontent. It was the figure of a young woman impersonating Saint Ursula who wore a costly robe with a mantle and a glittering crown of diamonds and pearls from which a veil descended to the ground that made us feel as if this were a Mardi Gras march. A heart pierced with an arrow in her hand, this young woman was surrounded by companions, dressed in white like her, carrying branches of palm in some sort of victory pose. We had to march behind them with the rest of the clergy, accompanied by loud military music. Only the singing of praise and gratefulness once we reached our new abode was befitting such a ceremony.

The Ursulines' new home at the corner of Rue de Chartres and Rue d'Arsenal finally housed the hospital that the Jesuits had insisted on per their contract. A wing, separate from the convent, the school and the orphanage had been built solely for this purpose. As relieved as the nuns had been to escape the inadequate living quarters on Rue de Bienville, their elation over the new building soon disappeared. The new convent was made of *colombage* which usually called for a protective covering of the exterior, but the timbered walls had been left exposed, and after a few years, the humidity had begun to erode the house. The Jesuits, fearing it would become a fire hazard had agreed to build a new structure next door, the Mother Superior informed the nuns on this morning. For now, the Sister worried less about a new building that, judging by the wait for the current one, would take years to be finished and focused instead on the task at hand—the arrival of a new group of Casket Girls.

Mother St. André received them one by one in her office. Sister Stanislaus took one look at a couple of them and knew with certainty that they would not pass. Not since a robbery of the sacristy two years ago, had forçats been allowed to live at the convent. The Sister saw the list of the new arrivals and the fleur de lis branding on their shoulders that all women of questionable pedigree were asked to expose. As expected, the Mother Superior denied them room and board. Most of the remaining girls were not from Paris or another big city in France, but from villages in the countryside. The Sister did not anticipate any of them being turned away from what she had seen on paper. Country girls were usually the easiest to control and the best behaved, and most of them ended up in decent marriages. Suddenly her glance fell on a young woman with blonde locks, and she stopped dead in her tracks. Some of the girl's features were different, and the look in her eyes was demure, but there was no mistaking the resemblance to another Casket Girl from long ago. Curiosity got the better of Sister Stanislaus, and she followed the girl into the Mother Superior's office.

"Mademoiselle Cheniér, I have been told very troubling things about your upbringing and more disturbingly about your behavior on the sea voyage these past few months..."

The Abbess closed the black ledger on her desk and folded her hands on top of it. Isabelle Cheniér, her back hunched, stared at the floor.

"What do you have to say for yourself?"

"Mother... I shall work hard. Whatever chores you assign me..."

"The work that you seem to be good at is not tolerated in the holy house of our order. I cannot and shall not in good conscience permit the likes of you to stay here and influence good, decent girls. Je suis desolé, Mademoiselle. You will have to find another place to live."

Sister Stanislaus was not going to be deterred from speaking her mind, but as soon as she opened her mouth the Mother Superior held up her hand: "It is of no use, Sister. There are rules. Rules that have not been followed by my predecessor with terrible consequences that I can neither condone nor have any inclination to repeat. You are dismissed. Please return to your lessons."

Sister Stanislaus knew that it was in no one's best interest to argue. The mood and tone had changed in the past few years. Like her predecessor the new head of the convent stood up to the Jesuits and Capuchins, but unlike Mother St. Augustin, she did not listen to anyone's advice and was quick in judging others. Sister Stanislaus had happily settled into her role as the headmistress of the school and found that she was no longer torn between her religious beliefs and her secular common sense. Yet seeing a young girl condemned without even looking into the reasons for her alleged behavior brought back Marie Madeleine Hachard with full force.

She hurried outside hoping she would be able to catch up with Mademoiselle Chenier. It was not just worry for what would become of the young woman but curiosity. She searched the corners closest to the city but could not spot her. In her defiant mood Marie Madeleine turned the corner on Rue St. Anne and walked into Zulimé's small shop to buy a few healing potions. The Sister had been doing this for years with the full knowledge of Mother St. Augustin, and later secretly, knowing full well that the new head of the convent would never condone purchasing from a vodou priestess. The Abbess believed that the potions and salves came from a pharmacy, and Sister Stanislaus never corrected this assumption. She left the shop with a feeling of dread about returning to the convent and decided she would indulge today.

I shall take a walk down to Castro's and enjoy some of the gumbo Margarita is famous for.

~

Isabelle Cheniér dragged her casket towards the harbor. The nuns had handed it back to her when they refused her at the convent. It was heavy, and Isabelle was tired. Tired of the struggle, tired of surviving. She had nowhere to go and no other option but to find the ship that had brought her here and the only person who would possibly help her now. It was a last resort, one that she had tried to avoid in the hopes of finding a new home with the Ursulines. Isabelle thought back to that day when she had boarded the ship. Heartbroken, lonely, ashamed and despaired, she had found solace in the First Mate, because he had a few kind words for her. The sailor had felt sorry for her but liked what he saw and seduced her one night in his cabin. He had given her a few coins in the morning and invited her back the next night. And the next. She had obliged him not for his lovemaking but for a handful of livrés here and there and a few scraps of better food than what was served to the other girls. He had taken what he wanted and sometimes allowed her to spend the night in his cabin. Other times he had told her to leave, and she had crawled back to her cot, trying not to be discovered by the others while knowing that everyone was aware of her dalliance. The shame had never left her until she had walked through the convent's door this morning. Until the glimmer of hope for a better life was extinguished by the Mother Superior's harsh words. Some of the other Casket Girls must have told the Ursuline nuns that she was a prostitute.

Isabelle saw the First Mate as he was about to walk down the plank, having safely secured the vessel. He stopped and grinned: "Forgot something? Or do you miss me already?"

She dropped the casket. "I have no place to stay… I would do anything for you if you would let me be with you…"

"Anything? An offer I cannot refuse. But I am only renting a room until we ship out again. Whenever that is."

He took her with him and made her wash his clothes, clean his room and service him in other ways. And when, a month later, her lover set sail to return to France, he left her with a few hundred livrés that would pay for the room for a week's time. In seven days, Isabelle would be without a roof over her head. That was when she heard about La Cocotte's cabarét.

∼

At Castro's Restaurant Geneviève listlessly picked at an étouffée, usually her favorite of all of Margarita's famous dishes. Geneviève had been acquitted of killing her husband when the Councilor had ruled it self-defense. On Commander Valdeterre's recommendation, he had threatened Baron LaCour with prosecution for aiding the abuse of his daughter-in-law and endangering the lives of her children unless the Baron returned to France and never set foot in La Nouvelle Orleàns again.

It had taken Geneviève a long time to recover from the months of incarceration and separation from Pierre and Delphine. She had become withdrawn and dispirited and left the daily routine entirely in the hands of others. Margarita and Sister Stanislaus had stepped in and taken care of the children as much as their time permitted. It was the Sister Pierre came to when he got into a fight with another boy. And when Delphine had her first monthly bleeding she asked for Margarita to teach her what to do.

Geneviève was even more consumed by her desire for security after the trial. She bought more properties along the first two blocks from the river and had plans to develop plantations outside of the city. Her already vast fortune grew with each new acquisition, and she became La Nouvelle Orleàns' richest woman, but Margarita sensed the emptiness in her heart:

"On death's bed what will you look back at? A new grand mansion? Buckets of gold? Or the love of your children? And possibly a good man?"

Margarita's words echoed in Gneviève's soul, and she could not banish them as she had for years or distract herself with more purchases. For too long she had turned inward out of fear and necessity, her friendship with Margarita being an exception and only coming about because of their similar experiences and shared pain. In a strange way that had always belied their different culture and social status, Geneviève looked up to the Cuban woman.

After lunch Geneviève walked to the church. The nave was empty, and she found the priest ready to hear her confession.

"Father, I fear that I have neglected my children and my own life in pursuit of wealth to secure the future of my family…"

The priest listened to her regrets. "My child, have you raised your children in the Lord's faith, true to his word?"

"Certainly, Father."

"A mother's highest quest is her children's well-being. A woman's place is in the home. She shall not seek earthly treasures. It is the husband's responsibility to feed the family."

It took all of Geneviève's restraint to not storm out of the confessional. "I am a widow, Father. There is no choice for me."

"You must find a husband then."

The priest absolved her of her sins, urged her to pray and ask God for modesty and guidance. Geneviève had hoped a confession would calm her. Instead, a seething anger began boiling inside her.

Men have caused me nothing but pain. But how could a priest know and understand…

She briefly thought of marching back into the church and reminding the good Father of all the money she had given to the Jesuits, the Capuchins and the Ursulines over the years.

MY earthly treasures were certainly never refused by them!

Geneviève's mood did not improve on a long walk along the river.

Unlike Margarita's gentle suggestions on the same topic, the priest's judgement on her life did nothing to open her heart. It merely brought on anger and hurt.

Men are cruel creatures. Even so-called men of God…

She stopped at the French market and sat down on a bench near one of the stands when she saw a man coming towards her whom she had never considered more than a distant acquaintance, albeit one that had always shown great respect tinged with a gentleness uncommon in other men she had known. Commander de Valdeterre doffed his hat and greeted her with a smile.

"Madame LaCour, a pleasure."

"Commander."

Despite their many conversations and interactions over the years and after her trial, their formality was a remnant of his former marriage to Josephine. He joined her for lunch, asked about her children and her work, and she felt her anger abating, at the world in general and men in particular. Valdeterre had always made her feel comfortable, and it was comfort she mostly craved these days. When he invited her to accompany him to a soirée at the Governor's home the following week, she readily accepted.

On a beautiful night with the stillness of the sky above, they rode up to the magnificent mansion. Geneviève had not felt this kind of serenity for a long time, if ever, and sensed that her companion was right there with her, ready to simply exist in this space of kindness and tranquility.

As if reading her mind, he said: "We have both been through so much, how nice to enjoy each other's company."

That evening marked the beginning of a friendship. Neither of them felt that it should become more. Too much had happened in both of their lives to make them want a deeper connection than they already had. For two people whose trust in marriage had been destroyed, the wounds were too deep to overcome. Valdeterre became her companion on social occasions, the gentleman who joined her at balls and soirées, and if there were rumors, they both laughed them off. He was there for her children when they needed advice, never offering any without being asked or overstepping into the role of a father figure. He loved spending time at Margarita's and José's restaurant and savoring their delicious food whenever Geneviève invited him to come with her.

Margarita, of whom it was said that "her coffee is like the benediction that follows after prayer", had become a legend not only amongst the *le vendeuses*, the women who sold the invigorating drink from their stands along the quay, but for her dishes that were the finest in the city. With José's help she had turned their restaurant into the best that La Nouvelle Orleàns had to offer. Aristocrats and simple people alike flocked to it. Margarita had hired four more Cuban cooks to help her while José was directing the wait staff—all of them free men of color—like a conductor with his orchestra. He hobbled around the place with his cane faster than most healthy men. The Castros had long since paid off their debt to Geneviève which was helped by the simple fact that theirs was one of the few restaurants that never had to pay the Bèrangers any protection money. Florence had made sure of it.

"Call it a favor to me as I am calling it a favor to the cook who kept all of us women fed very well when the Ursulines had no money to spend on good food," she had told Jean and that was that.

～

On the high seas, Acadia was sitting at the stern of the ship, knowing that sailing back to Saint Domingue was a bad idea. The island's Governor had taken a page out of the anti-piracy lawbook enforced in more and more regions of the Caribbean. The governments of all island nations were showing no mercy to the ones that got caught. Pirates were hanged or shot or rotted in prison until they died from disease or hunger.

"We have to start looking for a better way to make money," she kept repeating to Jean, who brushed aside the danger.

If only he could take this one journey without attacking a ship…

The two had a very good reason to go to Port-au-Prince, and she wished they would do it under the guise of buying sugar for rum making, still the only legitimate trade the Bèrangers were registered under. Yet the second a sailing vessel appeared on the horizon, the devil in Jean took over. The capering of a ship had become routine for Acadia, and the one they were about to attack was no different from all the others they had overtaken through the years. Or so she thought when they fired the last cannon shot before taking off towards the island. It was not until later, after they had been anchoring in Caille St. Louis for six days, that she spotted the passenger vessel she was convinced they had sunk, coming into the port. Acadia's beautiful day with all the colors of the rainbow suddenly turned dark.

She ran to the house that Jean and she were staying in: "We must go! The ship… it just came into the harbor…" She was out of breath.

Jean jumped up, the little girl he was holding still on his arm. "Did they recognize our ship?"

"Of course! And they will tell the authorities."

"Let them. I can deny anything. I sold most of the loot and hid the rest."

Acadia had a bad feeling but knew it was pointless to argue with him. The little girl, no more than three years old, started crying. Acadia took her from Jean's arm, barely holding back tears herself.

Jean stroked the child's cheek. "I will spend the night on the ship and tell the crew. Are you coming?"

Acadia nodded, pressed the girl to her chest and walked outside to hand her to a local woman. She held on to the child that was wailing for a while longer, then tore herself away and ran, wiping tears off her face.

The night was restless, and Acadia woke when she heard loud voices outside. The police were on the docks.

"Jean Bèranger, we are here to seize twenty-eight barrels of rum, sugar cane and indigo that you have not paid tax for!"

Ah non, Jean did not pay?

Everyone agreed that the inflated tax was a crime of itself, but of all the times Jean refused to pay up, this was the worst, she thought. It was obvious that the police had come to the docks to find a different cargo, one they could jail him for. The officers boarded the ship and went through everything for two hours but found nothing—Jean had only kept a pouch with jewelry hidden away inside a sugar barrel. The officers again asked for tax on the goods. Jean pulled his weapon. His men followed suit. After a heated argument with the police, Jean forced them off the ship at gunpoint and ordered his pirates to set sail. The winds were slow during the night hours, but everyone was convinced that the police boat would not follow them into the darkness.

They were wrong. The authorities must have taken off after them as soon as the winds kicked up at early light. Jean was sure that his ship was at a safe distance from Port-au-Prince by then, but suddenly everyone on board heard them, the unmistakable horns of the Saint Dominguan authorities.

"Let's turn east, a little more into the wind," cautioned one of the sailors, "this is our only way to outrun them and make a faster getaway."

Acadia agreed, but Jean would hear none of it: "I am done running. I have had enough of the island police." Bèranger felt bile rising in his throat.

Acadia ignored him and shouted: "Let's turn the sails into the wind! We must get away!"

Jean stomped towards her and grabbed her arm: "We are doing no such thing! I am going to show them who rules these waters once and for all!" He yelled at the men to turn the ship around. Acadia put her hand on his shoulder: "Non, s'il vous plait… we cannot win this. Their boat may be smaller, but they have more weapons. Better to leave and not risk our lives…"

He shook her off.

"Jean, think of…"

"She is all I am thinking of!" he thundered and ordered the men to get the cannons ready.

Is he going to fire at the police? This is crazy.

Acadia had never seen him like this. The decision he was making now was nothing short of irate.

One police officer was yelling at them to throw anchor. "We are here to collect what you owe us! We shall board your vessel to do so and expect full compliance!"

Acadia could only make out a few words against the wind: …anchor… board… compliance…

"Do not fire the cannons, Jean! Their revenge will be fierce, and we will never be able to get close to the island again!"

Her plea had an urgency only he would understand. He turned to her for a second, and it seemed she had managed to convince him.

"You are right. Why waste cannonballs on these bastards. They are close enough. Fire your muskets!" he instructed the crew.

Whoever was closest to the bow shot at the police boat. Their action was met with a rain of bullets and a shot from the police cannon. It hit the hull of the ship. In the commotion, Acadia did not see the officers who threw up ropes and climbed aboard. What ensued was sheer madness. One of the pirates stabbed a policeman and was shot in the stomach. Another had an officer in a headlock, and they both went overboard. A second cannonball ripped into the starboard beam and when it came down, it crushed two pirates. Blood splattered everywhere. Acadia saw the back of Jean's head amid the fight and a musket pointed at his back. She threw herself at the man holding the gun, but it was too late. A shot rang out and brought Jean to his knees. She grabbed on to his shoulders and dragged him behind the wheel. The blood stained his white shirt and grew bigger with every second.

Jean's eyes glazed over as she held him in her arms: "Save the ship, my love… and save her…"

Acadia screamed, shook him and took his face in her hands,

imploring him to open his eyes. She drowned out all the noise, the shots, the cries of pain until one of her crew mates pulled her off. Jean's last words rang in her ears: 'save the ship'… and she did. Acadia and the men killed every last one of the officers. The ones who retreated drowned in the waves. Their boat was shot to bits until it sank. Acadia had no memory of what happened after. She was living in a cloud of blackness. They gave Jean a sea burial, and Acadia assumed command of the ship. The only reason they survived was due to good weather. They boarded up the hole in the hull but were left with only one sail. They threw half their cargo overboard to make it to Barataria Bay alive.

At their house on Rue St. Anne, Henry de Roche watched Zulimé adjusting the pillows on the chaiselongue, straightening the curtains and placing little pouches of herbs on shelves. He had gotten used to her rituals and never asked too many questions. He had his suspicions about the caged snake in the garden shack, and he knew that she did not keep chickens solely for their eggs. He noticed how admired she was for her medicines and cures and was proud of her for it.

The rest of it, I do not want to know. As long as she does whatever she does when I am not here.

Zulimé's eyes met Henry's for a moment, a smile appeared and vanished quickly as she continued with her chores. She did not look a day older than when he brought her to La Nouvelle Orleàns, only her gaze held the wisdom of age and the melancholy of a pain that had long since turned into a scar. She had become a fertility specialist of sorts. It was her way of atoning for the one big sin of her life; the wrong Zulimé had done to Louise by cursing her womb. The spirits had punished her for it. Two more children, a boy and a girl had died of malaria barely old enough to walk. Henry had become withdrawn after their deaths, refusing to speak for months, staring off into the distance as if his soul were searching for theirs. He had neglected his business and rarely touched her. She had her own grief to overcome and went to church every morning. When the loneliness of her pain threatened to swallow her, she turned to her vodou again and feverishly appealed to the spirits. It was then that she started regular rituals and held ceremonies in the fields that bordered the city. Those were attended by an ever-growing group of free people of color and enslaved women and men who on their one free day of the week could do as they pleased as long as they did not leave the city limits.

Henry found out about these gatherings by chance; he was on his way home one early evening when he saw Zulimé sitting on top of the small carriage he had given her a while ago. She never used a coachman, preferring to hold the reins. He shouted out to her, but she either could not hear or decided to ignore him. He spotted the big cage next to her, covered with a cotton cloth, and he was certain of what it contained.

What is she doing with the snake?

He had a sick feeling in his stomach.

It is one thing that she keeps a snake in the garden shed. It is quite another that she takes it on rides through the city.

Henry followed her while the sun set and watched her entering a pathway canopied by trees and barely wide enough for the carriage. They were close to Bayou Saint-Jean.

Why is she not taking Grande Route. St. Jean, the portage trail much better suited for carriages? What is she hiding?

Zulimé disappeared into the overgrown pathway, and he almost galloped into the carriage in the dark before stopping his horse. She was gone and so was the cage. He heard strange sounds and followed them. The trees opened to a field bordering the bayou, and what he saw made him recoil: at least a hundred people, both male and female were dancing to the drums. Zulimé was on top of a wooden block looking up into the sky, rocking her hips with her arms raised above her head, holding the snake. Henry had caught glimpses of vodou ceremonies before on his St. Domingue plantation, but they had seemed peaceful compared to the feverish chanting, dancing and drumming before him. The males barely wore any clothes, the females were grinding their bodies into the men with abandon, drenched in sweat. Nothing shocked him more than Zulimé's eyes—her dead look staring up into the night sky. He came close to expelling his dinner when two of the females jumped up on the block next to her, raised a chicken over their heads and cut its throat, letting the blood drip all over them. This made him turn around and run back to his horse.

Henry waited up for her that night, sitting in his armchair, drawing from his pipe. He had no plan as to what to say to her when she returned an hour after him. She had completely changed, with a peaceful look in her eyes and smiling when she walked in and gave him a kiss on the cheek. Only the faint smell of sweat betrayed her calm demeanor.

"Where have you been?" he asked.

"Just some business," she replied.

"Business? I saw you! Is that what you call business? Leading vodou dances or whatever you call this on the bayou at night?"

Her eyes narrowed slightly, and she shrugged: "What did you see that so upset you?"

"A ceremony so pagan and distasteful and so unworthy of you that I am having a hard time describing it! Chicken blood? Men and women barely clothed?"

"Did you stay until the end?"

Her calmness astonished him. "What end? When the women sliced the chicken open and bathed in its blood?"

"No. The end of the offering. When the music stopped, and we sent a prayer to the heavens. Had you stayed until then, you might understand what it is all about."

Henry got up and paced the room. The more composed her responses the more upset he became. "This behavior is unbefitting a woman like you."

It was in that moment that Zulimé lost her composure. "A woman like me? A woman like what—a colored girl stolen from her home, sold off as a slave? A woman who must be grateful to the man who bought her and then luckily came to love her and gave her back her freedom? A freedom that should have never been taken from her in the first place! Or a woman who carries on the tradition of her ancestors? Who brings solace to her people and to herself with ceremonies that are as old as time? That woman?!"

It all broke out of her; the years of resentment that had been there despite her love for him and her joy over being loved back.

"I am not like you and neither will our daughter ever be. If you had not fallen in love with me, I would have been working in your fields this past decade. I would be invisible to you. You would not have cared if the serrated leaves of the sugar cane had cut into my body. You would not have paid any attention to my infected wounds, to the blood, the sweat or even my death brought on by work no human should ever have to do. Because I would not have been human to you. Just another piece of property for your gain, your riches."

Henry's voice was filled with pain when he responded: "I have always prided myself on treating my slaves better than most plantation owners… and I did fall in love with you, mon amour…"

He had not called her that in a long time, and she softened a little: "But you could not marry me…"

They sat down on the chaiselongue before she spoke again. "The loss of our bebés has torn my heart out. It has caused me as much pain as I know you must feel. I faithfully went to church every morning yet did not find relief. I lost my song because of it. It has never returned in the same way again. The Lord's prayer may be enough for you, but I must pray to my other deities. It helps me in ways a Catholic mass cannot. I am asking you to let me grieve and heal in my own way. I am asking you not as a woman beneath your standing, but as the mother of your daughter. If you cannot honor and respect my culture, I ask you to accept it in the same way I accept yours."

Henry sighed. He had known for a long time that accepting her traditions, as strange as they may seem to him, was his only way of not losing her. She had become a successful seller of potions and creams, coveted by artisans and nobility alike. She could afford her own house even though it might have to be in a less affluent part of the city. She had the strength to live without him, something he doubted about himself; he loved her deeply and could not let go of her. They made a truce that night: he would accept her vodou work, and she agreed to hold the gatherings only when he was travelling. Zulimé never told him that she was not appealing to the spirits for her own peace of mind but on his behalf as well, that his pain was very much on her mind. She firmly believed that it was those ceremonies that worked their magic. She even began to sing again in her old voice. Henry had gotten better, too, and they both had found joy in their only daughter.

Marie Catherine was a bright twelve-year-old with glowing almond skin and a joyful disposition. She went to the convent school where her favorite teacher was Sister Stanislaus.

"She was the first white woman who never believed that I was a slave," her mother told her. "The kind Sister has the gift of not seeing everyone through the colors of her habit… black and white," she mused, prompting her daughter to ask a naive question of such simple logic that it surprised even Zulimé who was as used to her daughter's wisdom as she was proud of her girl's dedication to her studies.

"But is she not a woman of God, supposed to treat us well in all the many colors we come in?"

Zulimé sighed: "If it were only this simple. They are not all like this, the nuns. Not every Catholic reads the bible for what it really means."

"Is that why you never go to church anymore?"

Marie Catherine had touched on a sore subject, and one of the few reasons her parents argued. Henry wanted his beloved to attend mass with him on Sunday. She objected to the segregation:

"I have never gone WITH you. While you sit up front on one side

I have to sit in the back rows on the other. It is not the opposite sides I am bothered by—all women sit there—but the front and back part of it. If we are all equal in the eyes of the Lord, can we then not sit on the aisles of the same row?"

Henry never had an answer, of course—there was none that would have satisfied either of them—and the argument always ended with him throwing his arms up and burying his head in a book or furiously stuffing his pipe.

∼

It was on a night like this when they needed their space from each other and retreated to opposite ends of the house, that Zulimé saw a shadow in front of her bedroom window. The glowing pair of eyes was instantly familiar to her, and she motioned towards the back entrance.

"Acadia, is that you?" she whispered into the darkness.

The pirate took a step toward her old friend: "I need your help…"

Zulimé pulled her inside: "Henry is in the salon, do not make a noise and follow me."

She carefully pulled the kitchen door shut behind them and held up a candle to illuminate Acadia's face. Her friend's features were gaunt, the dark eyes had the hollowed look of someone who had seen too much for her soul to bear. Her clothes hung loose on her wiry frame, held together by a leather belt. The two women had not seen each other in more than five years. Through the city's rumor mill Zulimé had heard of her friend's rise within the ranks of Jean Bèrangers crew. Acadia had attained an almost mythical status as the only woman pirate in the Caribbean Sea. In her heart Zulimé had felt Acadia's loneliness whenever she thought of her.

"When did you last eat?"

Acadia waved off the question: "We ran out of food halfway back to

La Nouvelle Orleàns. There was no time to anchor on the shores to stock up on supplies with all the damage the ship had sustained."

Zulimé ladled some cold bean stew into a bowl. Acadia hesitated for a moment before devouring the meal. She wiped her mouth on her sleeve and stopped when she noticed Zulimé watching her:

"Excusé moi, one does not learn good table manners at sea."

Zulimé put her hand on Acadia's arm: "I don't care about your table manners. I care about the dark brown cloud that surrounds you. When was the last time you had a brightly colored day? What happened on this last journey?"

Acadia avoided looking at her friend. Her eyes darted across the room, up to the ceiling and down to the floor without fixating on anything or anyone.

"What are they saying?" she asked.

"I don't know what they are saying. There were rumors a few months ago. I do not listen to rumors. I want to hear the truth from your mouth."

Acadia found a strange comfort in sharing the horrors and the loss with her old friend even when her voice, raspy and deep from years at sea, smoking tobacco and drinking crude rum, broke at times. She was reliving the nightmare as she was telling it for the first time.

"Jean and I… we became lovers a few years ago. He gave me more responsibilities on the ship, sometimes even sending me out on my own. It was hard at first because some of the men did not like following my orders, and when Jean was not around, they ignored me or worse. I learned to fight with my words and my fist. Jean helped. He made it clear to the whole crew that I was to be respected. I know that most people do not hold him in high regard in this town, but he is… was… a considerate man, a fair captain and a gentle lover. That morning, I begged him to make a getaway. But his anger at the island police was stronger than his smart mind…"

Acadia did not tell Zulimé of that last night of love making and the desperation of it, as if they had both known that it was their last moment together. Her eyes fixated on the empty bowl in front of her while she continued the story of that fateful day. Zulimé listened intently, never interrupted and only touched Acadia's hand when the pirate stumbled at a particularly painful part. When she was finished, Zulimé caressed her cheek, dry and rough from the salty air and the sun.

"Can you find a place to sleep for the next few days? I will put you up once Henry leaves for a trip. He cannot know about it, though. You are too famous now, and he will never permit me to host a pirate in our home."

Acadia nodded: "Do not worry about me. I can always sleep on the ship."

Zulimé was loath to let her friend go: "If you don't mind the snake, and I know you don't, I can make up a cot in the shed, at least for tonight. Henry never goes back there. And... I know she has never been our favorite, but I can talk to Florence. She has a bigger home on Rue du Maine, and she rents rooms to boarders, travelers and merchants, and no longer to prostitutes. She gave that up long ago. She is much kinder now."

There was a glimmer of hope in Acadia's eyes as she listened to her friend's proposal. "I would be so grateful if she took me in, and I can pay her."

The next few days brought a renewal of their friendship. Acadia saw her dark cloud transform into lighter colors and felt like she could breathe again after the harrowing months. One morning as she looked over to Zulimé talking to her daughter, she smiled, imagining herself a few years down the road. Zulimé, too had a trace of a smile on her lips while she watched Marie Catherine mix up a potion for a client, a woman desperate to get the attention of a young man. Chanting to Erzulie, the vodou goddess of love, Marie Catherine was thoroughly caught up in her work and did not notice her mother. Zulimé had long ago decided that she would not try to stifle the girl's interest in what she called the family business the way her own mother had done.

I cannot keep my daughter from the deitys' call if she is destined to serve them.

Zulimé had known that Marie Catherine would enter the vodou tunnels of mystery when she had caught her with the snake years ago. There was the then four-year old girl singing to the serpent to calm it after one of Zulimé's ceremonies. At eight, Marie Catherine had prepared her first gris gris-pouch, and at eleven she knew how to create healing potions that were more potent than Zulimé's own.

Marie Catherine shall become the most powerful priestess of La Nouvelle Orleàns.

CHAPTER 30

On Rue de Toulouse, Michél Bèranger walked up to the entrance of La Cocotte's only to be rejected by the doorman, a portly African who Josephine de Chavin had hired to keep the undesirables out.

"We are not open yet," the doorman curtly informed him.

"I am not your regular customer. Get out of the way!"

The man towered over Michél: "The lady of the house is not receiving visitors."

The old pirate hurled insults at the doorman but did not dare get into a squabble that he knew he would lose. He retreated, cursing and spitting: "Lady of the house, merde!"

The years had not been kind to the younger Bèranger. His face was blotchy, he was nearly blind in one eye, walked with a limp and suffered from a permanent cough from years of smoking. He had become useless to Jean when he had lost his strength; too slow to work on the ship, too weak to participate in the takeover of vessels and too dangerous when he was angered. Jean had not permitted him to travel to the islands where Michél was still a wanted man, but rather tasked him with overseeing Jeanette's girls. Michél had only agreed because his brother had asked him right after he had just returned from an argument with Josephine. Michél still cared for her and hated when she treated him badly. In a moment of resentment, he had gotten some satisfaction out of accepting the offer, making him a direct competitor to Josephine in his mind, if not hers. The Madam considered La Cocotte's so above any other etablissement that she shrugged off any attempt on Michél's part to lure the good clientele to Jeanette's.

Jeanette Crozat, the former prostitute had turned into a skillful madam, if skillful meant teaching the girls how to get into their customers' pants to grab their wallets while doing their business. Jeanette had originally perfected this during her escape from Biloxi. It required a girl to make sure that she was the one undressing her prey and lay his trousers on the bed next to him. Sitting on the man made the thievery easy, other positions demanded quicker fingers. After the customers had finished, Madame Jeanette made sure the poor bastards got served so much cheap rum that they could barely remember their name much less where they may have lost their coins.

Jeanette did not like Michél, but she faithfully reported her earnings to him, paid him the Bèrangers' share and put up with his drunken rantings. Florence had taught her well, and she had developed a talent for creative arithmetic. The side-income never made it into the books. So far, Jeanette had resisted Michél's urging to move the brothel out of the old house on Rue de Bourbon and into the building that housed Flamand's Tavern, which he had taken over after the original owner's demise.

Flamand, the unsavory little weasel had died the same sad way he had lived—after being bitten by rats in his own bar. With an infected wound he never treated, his body was too weak to withstand the yellow fever. Michél declared himself the new owner before Flamand's body was cold. He found no resistance. In truth, no one cared enough about the run-down tavern as long as the price of rum did not go up.

Michél learned of his brother's death when one of the crewmen showed up at Flamand's. The younger Bèranger was devastated. Jean, his protector, his mentor, his savior was gone. Without Jean he would have languished in jail or worse. If Michél was overcome with grief at first, his second thought was one of greed.

I am the heir to his fortune.

In his mind, it was a fortune amassed through years of ruling the seas. From the beginning Michél had considered Florence a threat to the Bèranger assets. With her out of their business after she married the smuggler Pascal, he had breathed a sigh of relief. It was short-lived when Acadia made a name for herself as an invaluable member of the crew. Jean's infatuation with the woman had driven a wedge between the brothers. The elder's refusal to take him on voyages to Port-au-Prince had angered Michél greatly. He still dismissed the argument that it was for his own protection and saw it as a ploy by the couple to keep all the treasures to themselves.

Jean and his women… He couldn't have settled with one who obeyed and indulged him? He had to be with a knife-wielding devil who controlled his mind?

Michél walked up to the brothel, certain that he would run into his old shipmates at Jeanette's. He was disappointed to find the place empty save for some sailors who were too poor to pay Madam Josephine's prices and had to settle for Jeanette's girls.

"You need to make this etablissement more desirable for wealthy customers!" he yelled at the Madam, who shrugged her shoulders:

"I am making you almost as much money as that old harridan Josephine makes at Cocotte's. I have more girls and more turnover to fill your pockets, and if you don't like it here, go be with your mighty shrew."

Jeanette dodged the flying cup he threw at her. She had hit a nerve. Michél's relationship with Josephine had soured over the years. In the beginning of her reign at La Cocotte's, she had hired him for protection, and they had continued to see each other. As soon as she was established, she got tired of him and when he came to her with a proposal to merge their businesses, she laughed in his face. Not for a moment did Josephine consider making the worn-out pirate a partner.

"You run your whorehouse, I run my cabarét," she told him.

La Cocotte's was Madame Josephine's empire, and she ruled over it like a queen with an elevated fauteuil at the far end of the salon as her throne and a leather whip as her scepter. Her stable of girls was well chosen. As varied as they were in color and provenance, they all had the traits in common that set La Cocotte's apart from the common brothels. Josephine saw to it that they all got an education by sending them to the convent school on Sundays, when even the strict Abbess did not turn away women of dubious character. Madame Josephine insisted on cleanliness and required of them a talent besides the one in the bedroom. Most of them were dancers, some had a decent singing voice, and one even knew how to play the harpsichord. Their combined skills made for a pleasant atmosphere every night, and the wealthier patrons appreciated La Cocotte's for it.

A man like Michél Bèranger did not belong in such an environment, nor did his crude manners fit into Josephine's salon. His old charm long gone, resentment had replaced charisma, and if she could have banned him from her cabarét she would have. Yet she depended on his barrels of rum, crates of wine and champagne and other items that no one else would sell her. Her former husband had made sure of that. So, Josephine let Michél sit at the bar and made excuses to her patrons, describing him as a strange mascot— 'just another colorful character'—she often was overheard saying. She allowed him to share her bed occasionally, out of boredom, her obsession for his touch long gone. Her only goal was to be rich and wield influence, both of which she had achieved after the first few years. She knew everyone's dirtiest secret and never shied away from using blackmail if it was to her advantage.

Josephine encouraged unions between her employees and her patrons, should they present itself, only asking that the girl stay on until she had found a replacement. Over the years, many had married artisans, traders and in some cases even noblemen. The Madam was known for taking in stranded Casket Girls that kept arriving even though a new generation of women was growing up in La Nouvelle Orleàns. From her own experience Josephine knew that not all the Casket Girls were forçats and Parisian street walkers or damaged goods like Jeanette.

While the Ursulines had been tasked with finding suitable husbands for their charges, it was Madame Josephine who had more girls marry well. Just last month one of the mulattos had become engaged to a free negro who owned a small farm outside the city. A week later, her fairest Parisian girl informed her of her pending nuptials to an army lieutenant. The dark-skinned girl was easy to replace, the city was full of them, but the French one posed a problem. She had been La Cocotte's highest priced and best earner.

Into this predicament walked Isabelle Chenier, eighteen years young with her golden locks and violet eyes. The doorman looked like he had seen a ghost when he let her in. It was late morning, and the Madam was still indisposed. Josephine never rose before early afternoon when an enslaved woman served her corn cake with fruit preserves and a cup of hot chocolate. This delicacy was all the rage in Paris, she had heard, and since cocoa was a commodity easily available in La Nouvelle Orleàns, she had instructed her servants to always have a supply on hand. Sometimes at night, she spiked it with rum to put her in a slumber.

The shy young girl waited patiently for hours, perched on the edge of a chair in the hallway, not noticing the peculiar looks from anyone walking past. With her eyes downcast and her hands hidden in the folds of her dress, she seemed out of place, looking more like a lamb about to be led to slaughter than a young woman seeking employ in an establishment like La Cocotte's. Isabelle heard the rustling of a heavy gown before she saw the woman wearing it.

"What is your want?"

Josephine towered over her. Isabelle winced and quickly jumped out of the chair, curtsying before the Madam. When she raised her head, Josephine took a step back.

This girl's nose! I have only ever seen a nose shaped like this once before...

Staring at the young woman she tried to banish the memories she had hidden in the dark tunnels of her consciousness for decades. She shook off a feeling of *déjà vu*.

"What is it you were saying?"

Josephine had missed the first part of Isabelle's introduction.

"My name is Isabelle Cheniér. I arrived here a month ago from a small village in France. I have no means to support myself other than… to dance…"

"You are a Casket Girl."

"Oui, Madame." Isabelle took a deep breath: "I was supposed to stay at the convent of the Ursuline Sisters but…."

"They threw you out." Josephine narrowed her eyes. She knew all about the new Mother Superior who did not take kindly to young women of disreputable status and abhorred the shiploads of Casket Girls that were dumped on the convent each year.

"Do you have experience as a… dancer?"

Isabelle lowered her head again. Almost inaudibly she said: "Oui, Madame. A little."

Josephine walked around her in a circle taking in every detail.

Lean figure, small bosoms but nicely rounded, wide set eyes in a pleasant face… Save for that long, pointed nose! But a narrow waist that emphasizes her breasts…

"Smile."

It was Josephine's way of making sure a girl had good teeth. Isabelle passed the test. Josephine was not looking forward to training Isabelle, but the loss of her best French employee had left a void, and young blonde women were not that easy to lay hold of in this city where skin color got muddied by plaçages and metissages. Josephine was still a snob, but it was this trait that made her a good businesswoman who understood that certain noble clients preferred to bed women who reminded them of their own.

This one will have to do.

"Gabrielle! Octavie!" she called out to a brown-haired German and a slender *negresse*: "Take Isabelle upstairs, she can have the vacated bed next to Claudine. And give her a dress from the wardrobe chest."

Josephine sat down at her *secrétaire*, pulled out a piece of paper engraved with the La Cocotte crest, something the original owner had drawn up, and began writing a note with her feathered pen:

'Mon préféré Monsieur de Richaud, I am pleased to inform you of a new arrival that, I am certain, shall meet your special tastes, a fair young woman of noble pedigree with a pleasing disposition. She can be of service to you any time you so desire. In the hope that you shall grace my house with your visit very soon, I remain yours, Madame J'

∾

Isabelle Chénier had a hard time adjusting to her new profession and cried herself to sleep at night. Again and again, she had to endure the gross, sweaty body of Monsieur de Richaud on top of her, his flabby belly slapping against her stomach and breasts. He was not just fat but tall as well, and she was always afraid to suffocate under him.

"Be happy that it was the *cochon grasse*, the fat pig who broke you in," Gabrielle had said after her first encounter, "at least he only knows one position and does not have much stamina. Or a sizeable *zob*. *Le phallus* more like it."

"What are you going on about?" Octavie interrupted, "at least a nice, big cock would add some pleasure to Isabelle's hard work."

Pleasure? I only once experienced a sliver of pleasure…

The memories of her former life in Soisson, the village a day's journey away from Paris, came flooding back…

∾

In the small garden of the caretaker's house, Isabelle hid from her siblings. She did not enjoy playing with that rowdy gang of five. The father was easy to anger and took off his belt to give the boys a good beating at least twice a week. The two girls got screamed at and punished by the mother who made them do labor that they were too young and weak for, until their hands were raw, and their backs ached. Isabelle was spared all that. The parents were distant, treated her as if she were a piece of furniture, like she did not exist at all. That way she escaped the scolding and the beatings, but it turned her into an outcast, and the children let her know it. The older brother found her behind the hedge, and there it was again, the taunting:

"Porcelain doll, you think you're better than us? You won't play? This will cost you; we promise."

Just this morning the younger sister had stolen Isabelle's meager meal, and she knew what the brother's promise meant: there may be worms put into her shoes or a dead frog in her bed. It was nothing new. She shrugged and retreated further into the hedge until they got tired of her and continued playing on their own, rough and loud until the parents returned from their work tending the grand mansion and vast gardens of the wealthy nobleman who employed them. Isabelle could not complain about the children's mockery to this couple that never laughed, never touched and never uttered a tender word to each other.

Porcelain doll...

The description fit. She not only felt different, she looked it, too. The other five were robust little things with reddish-brown hair like their mother and a stocky build. Isabelle was thin like the man she believed was her father, but unlike him she had a much fairer complexion. Her interests were different, too. She adored school and read the one book in the house, a mystery tale that the wealthy employer's wife had given them, over and over. While the others amused themselves by throwing rocks at the ducks, she loved to sneak into the rose garden near the pond behind the big mansion. That was her haven, her sanctuary, a place she could hide in and read her book in peace.

It was there that the *Comte*'s younger son found her one day. Startled, she clutched the book to her chest, thought of an apology, but he smiled at her with his kind eyes and said:

"Keep reading or whatever it is you do. No one ever comes here. My father and brother are too busy, and Maman suffers from pains in her knees that make it hard for her to walk on the grounds."

Like Isabelle, the young man loved mysteries and brought her more books from the library in the house. They were the same age and found that they had common interests. His favorite tutor was his history teacher, and he told her all about the Celtics, Huns, Romans and Greeks. She had a vivid imagination and made-up fantastical tales of knights with heads like wild beasts and the fair maidens they courted and fought over. When the weather got too cold for them to be outside, he snuck her into the pantry through the side door where they ate delectable sweets and fresh bread that the cook had stored there. Isabelle spoke more during their meetings in the rose garden than she had spoken in the little caretaker's house her whole life.

When he kissed her one afternoon she did not resist—it seemed so beautifully natural to her. He took her virginity one warm spring day on a soft blanket on the grass, and she felt a happiness she had only imagined for the characters in her stories but never dared dream of for herself. He brought her gifts. A silk ribbon that she tied to her undergarments, afraid her sisters would steal it, and a small pendant that she hid underneath her cotton blouse. One day he gave her a ring with his family crest on it. It had belonged to an old aunt who had passed away and no one would miss it he said, his mother owned much more valuable jewelry. To Isabelle the ring was a magical treasure regardless, and she kept it in a pouch that she hid under the mattress with her books.

Her dream came to a crushing end when one day they were discovered by his father, the Comte. "Cover yourself!"

The Comte screamed at her as he yanked his son by the arm and threw the blanket at Isabelle. He ordered her parents to come to his study. When they returned her father took off his belt and beat her for the first time while her mother yelled at her and tore at her hair.

"You are a disgrace! A whore like your mother! Is there a bastard in your belly, too? A bastard like you?"

The words were out and with it the truth, the explanation for everything she had sensed but never quite understood before.

I am not their daughter…

Isabelle felt elated and scared at the same time.

Who am I? What will happen to me now?

The answers came faster than she expected. By the next morning, her friend, her lover was sent away. No one would tell her where to. The caretaker, who she now knew was not her father, searched her belongings out of fear that she might have stolen from the Comte who would punish them and send them all away. When the caretaker lifted the mattress, he found the books and burned them. Isabelle begged him to let her keep the ring. He took a long look at it, and she feared he would throw it out or make her return it to the nobleman. To her surprise, the handed it back to her.

"Keep it. It shall forever remind you of your disgraced mother."

The shock hit her all at once.

The ring was my mother's… What then, is my relation to the boy I love, if his family crest is mine, too?

The conclusion was too much for her to face. The Comte called her into his study and informed her that he would no longer pay the caretaker and his wife a monthly stipend to raise her, and that therefore she was to board a ship to a place called Louisiana to marry a colonist.

"Or whatever it is you shall do to survive," he added.

If this is what the Comte meant by that, I might as well have drowned at sea.

Isabelle had gotten ill after her first encounter with Monsieur de Richaud. It was nothing like the tender lovemaking with the boy who was her first, and did not compare with the roughness of the First Mate whose hard body she was nonetheless drawn to. She had thought herself prepared for this profession, but when de Richaud undressed, she wanted to gag, the smell of his sweat mixing with that of his powdered hair. The others she had to service were not much better. It was mostly the older noblemen that fancied her, and some of them asked her to do the most ridiculous things to them. There was the one who made her take him in her mouth while he yelled out his wife's name adding curse words, and another who wanted her to ride naked on his hairy back while he crawled around the bed on all fours. It was almost a relief when she had to take one of Octavie's regulars one evening, a Cuban plantation owner who tied her hands to the bedposts. At least he was not fat and old, and their encounter did not feel like the silly games of an obsessed child.

After a few months, she began to understand how Madame Josephine ran her etablissement. Every girl was different and satisfied different needs. Gabrielle was the best earner, because she did not shy away from the most special requests. Octavie was the most exotic and the best dancer, charming a wide variety of customers but being the favorite among the better-off free men of color. There was the girl from the tribe of the Choctaw who was called the lion tamer for her skills involving whips, and the twins who played the harp, dressed only in silken corsets and always servicing their clients together.

Isabelle knew what her part was, Gabrielle had explained it to her on her first day: she was the replacement for a recent departure, a fair girl with blonde hair just like hers. She was to play the aristocratic role, never curse or act in a lewd manner. That is until she closed the door to her room. When with a customer, she had to be willing to do whatever he wanted. Those were the rules laid out by the Madame, and they also included strict regulations on cleanliness and attending Sunday school.

"No patron of La Cocotte's shall ever find you boring," Josephine was famous for saying:

"The talent of a pleasant conversation based on knowledge will make you more valuable to educated clients who come here for more than just the pleasure of your bodies. None of them shall ever leave thinking that you are dirty and uneducated. If they want that, they can go to Madame

Jeanette's. None of her girls have special talents. Here, we are selling a fantasy."

Isabelle often wondered what her special talent was. She could not dance like Octavie or play an instrument like the twins. Her singing voice was not as strong as Gabrielle's, and she did not speak Spanish like the other French girl, a petit, black-haired waif with bright red lips. It almost made her laugh that she, who had grown up in a tiny house as the caretaker's daughter, sharing a bed with five other children and wearing old hand-me-down cotton dresses, was now considered the princess of Madame's stable of girls. It struck her as strange that the role came so effortlessly. So many questions remained.

Who are my parents? Are they alive?

Isabelle pondered all possible scenarios and knew that she would never feel complete without the answers. As a reminder to never stop searching for them, she kept the ring in a pouch and often wore it hidden in her corset, in the crease between her breasts when she was not working.

It was during the Easter parade, a festive event that drew the citizens to the streets, that Isabelle got lost in the crowd on Rue Royale and found herself standing behind a tall woman with her hair in an up-do. Everyone was cheering the musicians and dancers, when the woman turned her head slightly. There, in front of Isabelle's eyes, dangled a golden earring in the same design as her ring. With halted breath Isabelle moved with the crowd, not wanting to lose sight of the woman.

Florence had not given much thought to the earrings since marrying Alexandre Pascal. She had not gone out often or attended soirées, focusing on building her business instead. The Easter parade was an exception and an excuse to wear jewelry that her husband gifted her with as well as the earrings. When the parade came to a halt near the church and the crowd dissipated, she was surprised by a young girl's hand on her shoulder and an anxious voice.

"Madame..." Isabelle said, "are you my mother?"

Florence almost laughed: "Non, Mademoiselle, I think I would remember that!"

Struggling for words Isabelle pulled out the pouch containing her ring. Florence took one look at it and all the little pieces of information Josephine had alluded to in their early years together fell into place.

She looks just like her! Except for the nose.

The girl was still holding on to her, a look of such despair on her face that Florence knew she had to tell her the truth without admitting that she had stolen the earrings.

"Mademoiselle, I am not your mother. But I know who is. She... gave me these earrings a long time ago. Her name is Josephine de Chavin. She owns a... cabarét, La Cocotte's..."

Florence caught Isabelle before the girl fell. All color had left Isabelle's cheeks, her eyes were hollow, her breath came in gasps: "And she owns me..."

Isabelle's voice was barely audible. She pulled herself up and walked away, every step heavier than the one before. Florence was shaken. Despite her past disagreements with Josephine, she felt nothing but sympathy upon realizing the tragic truth.

∽

Isabelle was still in a trance when she got back to La Cocotte's, plagued by more questions.

"What is eating you? Are you ill? You look like you have seen a ghost," Octavie crinkled her forehead. She was used to seeing Isabelle shy and withdrawn at times, but this was different. "You should lie down."

"Where is my... Madame?"

"At her *secretaire*. Tell her you feel too weak to see customers."

Octavie yelled after her, but Isabelle had already disappeared. She found Josephine sitting behind her desk, writing on her ledger.

"What is it?"

Josephine did not look up. When the ring fell in front of her, she dropped the pen and spilled the ink. She pushed her chair back and stared at the girl: "Where did you get this?"

"It is my mother's…"

"Who gave it to you?"

"The nobleman my supposed parents worked for in Soisson."

Soisson…

Josephine looked at Isabelle and for the first time saw the resemblance, her features, her hair, her figure. And the nose which was her former lover's. All at once it hit her. The past she had buried, the memories she had banished, the shame she had concealed.

Isabelle's voice had the anguished urgency of knowing the answer to her next question but having to ask it regardless: "How did you come here? How did I end up with that family? Talk to me… say it. Who are we to each other?"

Josephine raised her head, her eyes fixating on the curtain rods instead of the young girl before her. "I can't," she whispered, "please leave."

Isabelle stared at her, unable to move.

"Go!"

It was more a cry of a most crushing despair than an angered scream. Isabelle ran out of the room. When the door slammed shut behind her, Josephine began to shake uncontrollably. Her legs gave out, she sunk to the floor.

I have turned my own daughter into a prostitute…

～

Back home, ensconced in her bright and airy living room, Florence was trying to recover from her encounter with Josephine's daughter. The former forçat had softened after marrying Alexandre Pascal, and she had found it easier to forgive. She felt sad for the young girl, but it was Isabelle's mother and her pain when she found out in what cruel way her past had caught up to her, that brought out Florence's empathy. She had hurried home after the parade, finding Alexandre bent over big sea maps spread out on the dining table, drawing out the route for his upcoming journey. Alexandre hated being interrupted in this planning stage, so she quietly closed the door, leaned against the wall and waited. When he looked up, he sensed something was wrong. His eye caught the shimmer of her earrings. He furrowed his brow, about to berate her.

"I know, I know. Do not scold me. From this day forward I shall never, ever wear them again," she said.

Florence told her husband about Isabelle and Josephine and the tragic fate that tied them together. "If I had gotten rid of these damned baubles just like you asked me to, the poor girl would have never found out," she lamented as she ripped them out of her ears.

"And what would that have solved?" Alexandre gently took the jewels out of her clenched fist.

"She is selling herself in her own mother's etablissement."

He lifted her chin: "Look at me. If she had not found out, she would continue doing that. Now there is hope that she can find a way out."

"What about Josephine? I cannot imagine the pain this kind of revelation causes."

"It is always better to know than not to know. For them both."

Wife and husband hugged. It was moments like this that filled her with gratitude for this man, this life and this contentment that she could not have dreamed of before she met him. Not that Alexandre was a simple and even-tempered man to be with. Their marriage had its up and downs. Never one to give in easily, Florence had found her match in the strong-willed smuggler. Their fights could be heard all the way down the block, yet they always made up and believed that their volatile disagreements kept their passion alive.

A few hours later, the Pascals were sitting in the small salon of their raised Louisiana cottage on Alexandre's old lot, with front and rear galleries, a double-pitched roof over Norman trusses, windows of sixteen lights, and two fireplaces. Florence had always wanted a courtyard, so they had added one in the shape of an L, as well as a separate kitchen building. Never the most skilled at domesticity before, she had begun collecting the most beautiful porcelain serving dishes, the finest wine and furniture such as a mahogany bed with silk mosquito netting and two card tables, indulging her husband who had a weakness for *Vingt-et-Un*, a popular game among the men.

The couple had an argument.

"I will take our boy with me and teach him the trade!"

"No, you won't! He will have an education and decide in a few years if he wants to join you!"

She slammed her hand on the table and made the mugs jump. Arguments with Florence always involved broken dishes, and Alexandre found the humor in it when she asked him to replace them, but this time he did not feel like laughing. His only child brought him nothing but joy, and he took pride in telling the boy about the trips. Now his son was old enough to accompany him. Florence would have none of it: "I will find the money to pay for a tutor."

Having experienced the advantages of education by the Ursulines, she had become a big believer in schooling. *If only there was a school for boys already.* The Capuchins and Jesuits had given up on it after the Company of the Indies that had a contract stipulating that they were responsible for everything pertaining to religion, failed to make a payment for a new building that had been purchased to house said school.

"I heard about apprenticeships for boys and will inquire about a good teacher I can afford," Florence continued a bit more calmly. A crease appeared between her brows.

My wife, the thinker. She is always three steps ahead.

Alexandre was secretly proud but not willing to give in to her so easily. He was preparing to embark on his next trip along the Gulf trading routes between La Nouvelle Orleàns, Havaña, Veracruz and Cartagena, Colombia. Even though he made a large part of his income from smuggling, he cleverly incorporated his illegal dealings within his legitimate trading company.

"I give you a few weeks to find a tutor. If you cannot, I will take our son with me when I leave."

Florence loved a challenge, and within two weeks she engaged a noted teacher, Sieur Duparé who taught writing, reading and arithmetic as well as the practical skill of building and architecture. She was paying him from her income renting out the building next door. When Alexandre sailed, he always gave Florence power of attorney to manage their business interests. She signed their documents and applied the skills she had developed for almost twenty years. It was she who came up with the idea of turning the property into an inn for ship captains and traveling merchants. With the proceeds, she invested in real estate. The ever-growing city was expanding to the east, beyond what was originally the divider behind Rue de L'Arsenal, and the lots on the new street were not as expensive as the ones closer to the Place d'Armes.

∽

It was the inn on Rue du Maine that Acadia moved to. Florence had followed Acadia's rise as a pirate and secretly admired her courage. Florence was aware of the rumors of a long liaison between Acadia and Bèranger. Such a relationship did not surprise her; Jean had always chosen what was most convenient and after all the easy women he had dallied with over the years, his hidden admiration of strong women had won out after all. Florence did not regret that it was not her he had chosen and admitted that Acadia was a much better fit for a man like him. When Acadia told her of his violent death, she felt a tinge of sadness but hardly any surprise. Alexandre Pascal had predicted long ago that Bèranger would die at the hand of one of the many authorities that had been fighting piracy so vehemently for the past few decades.

"This is what happens when a man is lost in the past and does not keep up with the sign of the times," she could not help saying to Acadia: "Do not make the same mistake. Piracy is a relic from an era when lawlessness ruled the seas. There is too much risk involved now. You want to make money? Smuggling is a much safer way to financial freedom. My husband knew this years ago and turned to trading."

"How can I become a smuggler? Or a trader? All I have left is a broken ship..." Acadia replied. The answer to her question arrived one evening when Alexandre Pascal brought an acquaintance to dinner. Acadia entered the dining room and gasped. Pascal's friend and she stared at each other.

"Abondance?" the man finally uttered.

"Papá?"

"Non, *ma petit sœur*, it is me, Pasquerette."

The long-lost brother she had searched for reached out his hands and slowly pulled her into an embrace. Pasquerette was the spitting image of their father. When he told her of the older Gravois' death—their papá had passed of an infected wound after being bitten by an alligator on one of their journeys to the swamps—Acadia cried for the first time in a decade. Her tears were for much more than the loss of a father that had abandoned her at the door of the convent. Brother and sister retreated to the parterre garden after supper. Pasquerette told her of his regret over leaving her with the Ursulines, his hopes that she would be taken care of and the long absences from the city while he and their father established smuggling routes to and from the Northern territories. It was not that they had forgotten her, but the hardships they had faced for years had prevented them from taking her back.

"We had nothing to offer you. No home, no shelter. We lived off scraps. I did not make enough until after Papá died. He had always resisted partnering with other traders. The old man was stubborn like that."

Acadia remembered. Once her father had made up his mind there was no one who could persuade him otherwise.

"I searched for you for over a decade," she said, "I joined a ship because I had heard you became a pirate…"

The crease between his eyes became deeper. "I hired with a captain after a disagreement with Papá, but piracy was not my calling."

"It was mine…"

He raised his head: "What did you say?" All the stories he had heard over the years, of a woman pirate from La Nouvelle Orleàns came to mind. He had never connected his sister Abondance with the legendary Acadia.

"Oui. The Sisters and the other girls at the convent kept calling me Acadia and having never liked my given name, I was grateful for a new one. I disguised myself as a boy at first but could not keep it up for long. By then Jean and the crew respected me enough to keep me on."

"Jean? Jean Bèranger?"

"The one."

"Is it true that he got killed on the last voyage?"

Her nod was almost invisible. She so desperately wanted to tell Pasquerette that he was an uncle, but her throat closed, and she could not get the words out. No one knew about the child, not even Zulimé who she considered her only true friend, and she and Jean had sworn the men on the crew to secrecy. Acadia was afraid her brother would not look kindly on a child born out of wedlock to a couple of pirates and left on a far-away island, so instead she asked: "How did you end up here tonight?"

"Monsieur Pascal and I are working together. I carry the goods up north that he cannot sell here. Abondance…" He corrected himself: "Acadia, the authorities are chasing pirates all over the Caribbean Sea.

They know no mercy. It is too dangerous for you to continue this line of work."

He is the second person to urge me to end the only way of life I know…

"What would you have me do? Marry? No man would have a wife that beats him in a sword fight, shoots better and knows how to use her fist harder than most soldiers. I will not join the convent. Not that they would have me. And I would never sell myself to Madame Josephine or Madame Jeanette."

He interrupted her agitated speech: "Work with me and Monsieur Pascal. He is looking for another ship to double the load."

"I have a ship. It needs repairing, and he would have to send me on voyages to Saint Domingue."

Pasquerette leaned forward: "We have no dealings there, but it is an interesting idea to expand our routes…" He stared at her for a moment: "Why would you want to return to that island? Isn't it the one where Bèranger got killed?"

Acadia folded her arms: "I have my reasons," was all she replied, and Pasquerette once again recognized his indomitable sister whose stubbornness had been a constant cause for quarrel when they were young. No prodding on his part would get him an answer.

"I shall have a talk with Monsieur Pascal. Get your ship repaired."

Chapter 31

Josephine had not left her quarters at La Cocotte's since the revelation. It was assumed by all that an illness had befallen her.

"She must be contagious," whispered Octavie.

"Why else would she lock herself into her rooms?"

Josephine had spent the last weeks in the twilight of her past. All the memories, concealed for so long and masked by her outer station in life emerged like ghosts, dancing around her through sleepless nights and empty days. The most persistent ghost was Josephine's own mother…

Little Josephine was playing her favorite game, hide and seek, between the thick brocade curtains. Only, on this day no one was around to engage with the six-year-old. Her older sister was no longer interested in the game, the servants were busy, and her maid had been called to help out in her mother's rooms. Josephine was bored, but just when she was about to step out, the door to the salon opened and her parents, the Comte de Chavin and the Marquess de Moutonne rushed in, or rather, her father was dragging her mother into the room:

"You shall not behave in this manner in front of guests from Paris that have come to discuss important topics with me! These *dîners* are not for pleasure, and even if they were, you cannot drink yourself into this despicable state and then disparage the wives of these important officials!"

"Their wives are endlessly boring, what else would you have me do?" her mother screamed back.

"Show manners suitable to your status!"

"A status that is above yours!"

"As you never tire to point out! Too bad your family lost all their riches, and you had to marry someone like me!"

The Comte yanked his wife's arm and ripped her sleeve as he did so. Her mother was indeed ranked higher in the nobility of France, a source of quarrel between her parents whenever she brought it up.

"I could have married a Duc or at least a Marquis!"

"Sadly, you were never beautiful enough for them to consider you."

Her father's face took on a sadistic smile. He knew he had hit a nerve, the most aching one for his wife, for the Marquess was plain looking with thin lips and small eyes.

"At least our daughters inherited my eugenics, especially Josephine," he added cruelly.

This brought a smile to the six-year-old behind the curtain.

I am beautiful, even more beautiful than my sister. Mon Papá said so.

Her mother began to cry and clawed at her father: "Bastarde! I shall not subject myself to playing host to your oh-so important acquaintances and their dull wives again!"

Anger took hold of the Comte's features, and he hit her mother so hard that she staggered across the room before falling to the floor. He pulled her up, his hand under her chin and put his face close to hers. In a tone so icy it made Josephine shiver, he said: "You shall do as I say. Today, tomorrow and forever."

With that he left the salon and her mother a whimpering mess curled up on the floor. Josephine had not flinched when he had used his hand against her mother. She had seen it before, unbeknownst to her parents. She stepped out from behind the curtain and slowly went over to the crying woman. Her mother did not hear her steps and flinched when the little girl touched her. The Marquess recoiled, got up, straightened her skirts and fastened her hair that had come lose. She noticed the torn sleeve: "See what you have done!"

"But Mamán, it was not me…" Josephine meekly responded.

"Do not contradict me!"

Her mother's hand came down on her cheek and left a red mark. Josephine's tears flowed, but the Marquess was unimpressed. Her face turned almost as cruel as her husband's when she scolded her daughter: "You are not to eavesdrop on conversations between grownups. Or approach me without asking."

"But Mamán, you were crying…"

"I was not. A lady does not cry. A lady does not show her true feelings in front of anyone. Never forget that."

∼

And Josephine never had. Sadness was not something one ever admitted to, her mother had said.

Downstairs, the rumor mill kept churning after the cooks told everyone that Madame was leaving plates outside her rooms, with barely touched food. Octavie suspected an ailment of the stomach, Gabrielle suspected poison. The only one who could have dispelled all the gossip kept to herself. Isabelle refused to see customers.

"It is my time of the month," she said.

"You've been using this excuse for almost two weeks now. A damned long time of the month… Someone needs to talk to Madam J… Octavie," Gabrielle commandeered,

"Go upstairs and see about Madame!"

"I? What if she gives it to me? Whatever disease she has got."

"Have you seen a doctor come over? Don't you think she would have called one, if she were really ill?"

Octavie reluctantly walked upstairs. She hesitated briefly before knocking on Josephine's door. No sound came from inside. She knocked louder, then slowly moved the doorknob. She did not see Josephine at first, so still was the room. Only a sliver of evening light fell through the drawn curtains. The parlor seemed empty. Octavie was about to move to the bedroom when she drew a sharp breath. There between the desk and the window was a shadow. Josephine, with one hand holding on to the frame stared off into nothingness, a ghost removed from life but stuck on earth.

"Madame… are you alright?"

"Isabelle… go fetch my… Isabelle…"

Josephine's tone of voice was soft, barely audible, tinged with an emotion Octavie could neither understand nor explain.

"Oui, Madame, right away," she said, happy to escape the stale space. She bolted downstairs. "Isabelle, Madame wants to see you."

"She probably wants to know why you have not worked for two weeks," Gabrielle remarked snidely.

"I don't think, Madame knows…" Octavie replied, "I don't think she knows at all what goes on in the world…"

Isabelle did not follow the order immediately. Instead, she went for a walk as she had done almost every day since the encounter with the lady with the earrings. She was searching for this woman hoping to find more answers after not having gotten a response from her mother. But she neither knew the woman's name nor where she lived, so Isabelle wandered the affluent part of the city, asking about her in shops, described her to the workers in front of the wealthy homes, all the while assuming that Florence was a noble woman by the way she had been dressed that day and stating that Josephine had gifted her with the jewels.

When the sun set and again, Isabelle had not found the woman, she returned to La Cocotte's and went straight up the stairs. She entered Josephine's boudoir without knocking.

"I am here," Isabelle simply said.

Josephine turned around: "I am your…"

"I know who you are," Isabelle interrupted her, "that part is clear to me. What I want to know is why you abandoned me."

Josephine took a breath: "I grew up in Paris. My family owned land in Soisson. It is where I gave birth to my child before she… you… were taken from me, and I was shipped off to this city. I hoped my uncle and his son, my cousin would raise you…"

"They said you disgraced the family."

"I made the mistake of falling in love and trusting a man. I never made that mistake again."

"What mistake? Me? I am the mistake then."

"I was fifteen and in love with my brother-in-law. I could not resist him, and he took advantage of that. When I got with child, he disavowed me."

Josephine's lover's words still rang in her ears…

∼

"She bewitched me, Comte! She has uncontrollable desires. No man could resist that. She threw herself at me!"

"You are a liar! How can you claim that when it was you who seduced me?" Josephine heard herself shout; her voice so high-pitched it sounded like another's.

Her father raised his hand: "You are to be quiet and let the man speak!"

"Merci, Comte. Do not tell my wife, your daughter, s'il vous plait. As I said, it is not my fault that I was tempted."

"You were clearly more than tempted, son, but it is also clear to me that Josephine acted like a putain. We shall not tell your wife. We shall not tell anyone. You are dismissed."

He calls me a putain. My own father calls me a putain.

Josephine looked over to her mother, desperate for support. The

Marquess stared at the table as if it contained the world's wisdoms and would not meet her daughter's gaze. After her lover left the room, Josephine could no longer hold in her anguish:

"Mamán, Papá, please do not abandon me! And my baby..."

The Marquess still refused to look at Josephine and addressed her husband instead: "She has brought shame to this family. She is no longer my daughter. Do with her as you please."

Her last words echoed in Josephine's head thousandfold. She tried to respond, say something, anything. Beg her mother for mercy, for forgiveness. But no sound passed her lips.

∽

Josephine drew in her breath and looked at Isabelle:

"My father threatened me with the Hotél Dieu at first, the place in Paris where women of the lower classes give birth after unwanted pregnancies. Instead, he took me to Soisson and instructed his younger brother, my uncle, to "take care of it" as he said. I almost died giving birth to you. They let me suffer, too. They would not call the docteur, and the midwife cursed me during my labor. They hoped I would perish in childbirth and you with me. It would have solved all their troubles."

Josephine paused before she continued: "I was in love with that man... your father..." she repeated.

"And I had relations with my own cousin without knowing it!" Isabelle shouted.

The abandonment, the lies, the betrayal— they all became a searing torch in Isabelle's soul. Josephine reached over, but Isabelle rejected the outstretched hand. She left her mother's quarters.

"If Monsieur de Richaud shows up, please tell him I will see him," she told the girls downstairs.

∽

The day after, Josephine left her rooms for the first time in weeks but did not resume her business. Her duties fell mostly to Gabrielle who kept the ledgers. Josephine sat in her fauteuil in the back of the salon as she had done before, but she now seemed more a frozen statue than the lively grande dame she had been. Customers who had enjoyed witty banter with the Madam had to resign themselves to one-word answers. Josephine barely mastered a 'bon jour' and 'bon nuit'. Any attempts on her part to reach out to her daughter were rejected with a dismissive wave of the hand. Any tries to keep Isabelle from seeing clients met with defiance; Josephine's daughter went about her work as if it was an act of rebellion. Shy before, she now spoke only to the men who came to see her.

One afternoon, the doorman let in an unusual guest. Florence had been dreading her visit to Josephine's etablissement. Yet it was as if Florence's feet had a mind of their own ever since her run in with Isabelle. On several occasions in the weeks past, she had circled the building on Rue de Toulouse that housed La Cocotte's. On this day she found the courage to walk in. The salon was quiet. Most of the girls were resting or preparing for the night ahead, only Gabrielle sat at the bar going over the books. She looked up when Florence entered.

"Can I help you?"

"I came to see Madame de Chavin."

"I am not sure she is receiving anyone."

Gabrielle shrugged but something in Florence's demeanor made her get up and look for Josephine. When she found the Madam in the back of the hall near the kitchen, she whispered: "There is a woman here to see you, and I don't think she will leave."

Josephine did not show her surprise when she recognized her former friend, enemy, co-conspirator and whatever else the two women had been to each other since the day they met on the Gironde. A moment of awkward silence passed between them. Florence took the first step:

"I had to come. You have been on my mind. I am so deeply sorry for your pain. And so distraught over being the one who told your daughter…"

Josephine fixed her eyes on Florence. It was the first time in weeks that she had looked directly at someone: "It was inevitable. How did I ever think I could bury it all…" she said in the voice of a woman way beyond her years.

Florence opened her *poche the bourse*, her small purse and pulled out a pouch. Out of the silky wrapping peaked the earrings. "I should have returned these to you years ago. Again, I am so very sorry."

"They belong to my daughter now. You can leave them with the doorman. Maybe Isabelle will accept them from him. She refuses to speak to me."

Florence wanted to reach out her hands and comfort Josephine but thought better of it. There was an impenetrable wall around the woman they once called 'the mighty Princess'. Yet unlike before, when it was built of arrogance and superiority, this one was of unspeakable despair and abandoned hope. There was so much Florence wanted to say. Instead, she turned, handed the pouch to the doorman to give to Isabelle and left.

∽

As fate would have it, the repair of Jean Bèranger's ship took a lot longer than Acadia had anticipated, and she was forced to stay behind when her brother and Alexandre Pascal left. Acadia did not trust Bèranger's crew quite yet, knowing that Michél would try anything to make them change their minds and their allegiance. So, she spent her days in the harbor and her nights keeping Florence company. She shared more stories from her pirate days with the former forçat, yet never revealed her big secret of the child left behind.

Michél, meanwhile, went to the harbor to inspect what he thought was his ship now. He noticed port workers removing rotten planks that

Acadia and the men had put up to cover the big hole in the hull, the result of the cannon shot. The ship tilted slightly to one side, weighed down by seawater that had seeped in.

"Who told you to begin the repairs? And more importantly: who is paying you?" Michel asked.

"The Captain."

"Which captain?"

Michél knew the answer before the man could respond.

I will destroy her.

Michél limped back as fast as he could and put word out to the crew to meet him at Flamand's. Not all the men showed up. The First Mate informed him in no uncertain terms that the crew had voted to make Acadia captain.

"She has proven herself over and over. She is a true leader. You, on the other hand have not been on a voyage in years. You are too old to fight," the First Mate said. He neglected to tell Michél of the proposition Acadia had presented them with; of becoming legitimate traders and sometime smugglers, giving the old gang of bandits a chance to live out their years outside of a prison wall.

"I will destroy all of you! I will cut your guts out and feed them to the alligators!"

No one took the old pirate seriously. One by one they left, shaking their heads, laughing wryly.

∼

Both, Florence and Acadia expected their men, husband and brother, to return in two months' time, and both knew immediately that there was something very wrong when Pasquerette came back only a few weeks after they had left. At first, they did not know who the lone figure was who walked down the dark hallway until Acadia recognized him by his gait despite his limping. Pasquerette's face was black from soot and grease, his back hunched and smelling of a mixture of sweat, smoke and sea. He held on to the doorframe and avoided looking at either of them.

"Where is my husband?" Florence asked quietly.

"We had a fire on the ship… we didn't know where it started… but that it erupted very quickly… too quickly to put it out… we tried… but Monsieur Pascal was too close when it reached the mast… the sails were so dry from the hot winds and caught fire immediately. He was consumed by the flames…"

"Papá!"

The anguished cry came out of nowhere. There, behind Pasquerette stood little Alexandre, his mouth turned downward, his eyes wet. Florence rushed to him and took him in her arms where he began sobbing loudly. Florence stared off into a bleak void, unable to shed a tear, holding her son tightly. Acadia took her brother's hand and led him to an armchair. She brought him a cup of water, and slowly the whole story emerged. The men had been just off the coast of Veracruz, and the weather had been so hot and dry that the fire grew faster than the crew could pull up seawater. After Alexandre Pascal succumbed to the flames and the vessel began to break apart, many jumped into the ocean only to be hit by falling debris or drowning. Pasquerette was the only survivor, because he was the only one who could swim. He fought his way back to a beach from where he saw a cloud of ash and glimmering pieces of what Monsieur Pascal's ship had been. For days after, Pasquerette dragged himself to the city and begged the captain of a ship that was about to set sail to La Nouvelle Orleàns to grant him passage.

Florence did not leave her parlor for days after the news, clutching her son and having food brought up for him. She did not eat more than a few scraps of bread and could not fathom going downstairs, instead holding on to the only person left to love.

Acadia was concerned about Pasquerette. She knew her brother well. Sitting around a house that was not theirs with nothing to do, would only put him into the darkest mood, a deep black she did not want to imagine. He blamed himself for his inability to save Alexandre Pascal and rescue the crewmen. Being confronted by a grieving widow and a bereft son every day would not get him over his guilt.

Florence did not speak to anyone but her son, even after she left her bedroom. She was barely able to tolerate the comings and goings of the boarders, much less the siblings. Acadia knew that she had to make plans, and not only to get Pasquerette away from this house of mourning. Her ship was almost repaired, and she had told her loyal band of pirates who all called themselves fliebustiers, freebooters now, to prepare for departure. Acadia had burned the old pirate flag, given the ship a new paint job and a new name. There was to be no more evidence of the vessel's former purpose. With Pasquerette by her side they set off one morning. She chose Port-au-Prince as her destination.

Florence began attending church more regularly, seeking solace in a God she had not worshipped since she was a child. She raised her son in the Catholic faith as best as she could and arranged her days around him; little Alexandre, so like his father in looks and mannerisms, was a considerate and affectionate child with a keen interest in anything that had to do with building. One day she called out for him, thinking he was in the kitchen. No one had seen the boy leave. Florence anxiously ran out of the house and searched the surrounding buildings. Finally, she spotted him sitting on a big slab of marble on a construction site on Rue St. Philippe. He was watching the workmen put the roof together shingle by shingle with such utter concentration that he did not hear his mother calling his name at first. After a relieved hug, she scolded him:

"You cannot run out without asking me. I was worried sick."

"But Mamán, I must learn how to build houses. I am the man of the family now. I must take care of you, and I like observing the workers. I can learn so much from them. Someday soon I will build you the finest house in the city," he said with confidence.

Florence could not hold back tears as she pulled him into her arms:

"Ah, *mon courageux petite homme*, my brave little man…"

On their walk home, his small hand in hers, she thought of how she had neglected her businesses for months, how she could no longer afford to pay the tutor and had to let Sieur Duparé go. Alexandre missed his teacher and the lessons. No wonder he had wandered off in his longing to learn.

On Sunday after mass, Sister Stanislaus took the widow aside and enquired about her little boy. Florence confided in the nun her worries over his education and asked if the Ursulines were willing to make an exception for him like they had done for Geneviéve's son Pierre.

"This, I am afraid is no longer possible," Sister Stanislaus sighed and spoke of the strict and rigid rules the new Abbess had implemented. "The Mother Superior would declare this idea abhorrent, but can I offer a solution? I could use my spare hours to teach the boy during the week…"

Florence's face brightened, and with gratitude she vowed to be a good Catholic henceforth. During the dark and sleepless nights when she felt cold in her large bed, longing for her love who would never again be next to her, she forced her thoughts onto her son who would have much better chances in life thanks to the good Sister.

It was at the market a few weeks later that Florence noticed a familiar figure standing on the levee, peering out over the river. Florence walked over and put a hand on Josephine's shoulder, startling her.

"Let us walk over to the food vendors, get some lunch," Florence said softly.

They sat down at one of the rough-hewn tables in between the workers who spent a few coins on simple dishes during their short breaks.

"I am not sure if you heard… I lost my husband…"

It was the first time that Florence detected a shimmer of emotion in Josephine. For a moment Josephine's gaze fixed on her old friend, her eyes registering surprise and sorrow: "I had not heard," she said.

"We have both lost a lot in this life, and we have both overcome even more," Florence said, expecting a response but none came. Their connection was lost with Josephine staring off again, her mind drifting to a place no one could follow. Florence took her hands which Josephine allowed, but without reciprocating when her old friend squeezed them: "We have our children to live for," Florence said with conviction.

Barely visible, Josephine shook her head.

On her way home, Florence was overcome with sadness. As much as Alexandre was the light that illuminated the darkness of her soul, Isabelle was for Josephine a reminder of her life's biggest failure. Florence pondered loss and redemption, past pain and future hope. A smile appeared on her face when she walked into her house and found Alexandre reciting a poem Sister Stanislaus had taught him. Watching her son blossoming into a young boy who took pride in learning helped her recover and find some sort of peace.

EPILOGUE

The morning light was still faint when Josephine left La Cocotte's. What was at first an aimless wandering became destined certainty when she reached the Mississippi. The wind caressed its surface as she stared at it for a long time. It was a cold day and none of the market vendors were rushing to set up their stalls this early. Josephine had but one thought in her mind:

I have turned my own daughter into a prostitute.

The river's currents swirled faster and more turbulently as the wind kicked up. She lifted her skirts and took a step closer to the edge. Instead of wading in, she let herself fall. The water slowly seeped through the thick fabric of her dress. She was wrapped in coldness.

A life wasted. A love lost.

Josephine never struggled as she drifted further out, and the sound of her thoughts became frozen. For the river had its own voice. And before her spirit left her body, she imagined it was God's.

Sister Stanislaus slowly rose from the pew. She had stayed after holy mass, praying. It was not really a mass but a memorial service that had taken place in honor of Madame Josephine de Chavin. She had disappeared a few weeks ago, and when a fisherman found a monogrammed handkerchief swept on to the river's edge, the Commander had her declared dead. Josephine could not have survived the Mississippi with its unforgiving currents. Valdeterre ruled her death an accident to insure a Catholic burial. Content with his life now, he had long since forgiven his former wife for her indiscretions and did not want for her disgrace to continue beyond her passing.

Rumors of Josephine's relation to one of her prostitutes had caught Sister Stanislaus' ear, and she had gone to talk to the girl. The Sister was not surprised to find that it was Isabelle Cheniér. The resemblance between mother and daughter had struck her the day the Casket Girl had arrived at the convent only to be turned away. When Isabelle came to the door—despite Marie Madeleine Hachard's worldly approach to life outside the convent, she was wearing the habit of a holy order and could not very well enter an etablissement like this one—Isabelle was in deep mourning. The Sister asked her to walk with her. She tried her best to bring solace to the young woman who grieved not the loss of a mother she had not known, but the loss of time to do just that, to get to know her. Sister Stanislaus recognized the deep layers of this grief, the missed chances and the guilt over having confronted and rejected her mother, all piled on top of each other. As much as the nun tried to console the girl, she knew that her words echoed in the airless chamber of sadness and that, with God's grace, only time might bring healing. Of the troubles, the hardships and the sorrows that the Casket Girls had gone through, Josephine's and Isabelle's story was the most tragic.

At least the daughter could have been saved if we had just taken her in…

Sister Stanislaus, standing in the house of the Lord, could not help the anger rising in her. Even after the loss of her mother, the Abbess had refused to give Isabelle room and board and a purpose beyond selling her body.

"She was a sinful girl when she first arrived. Now she is a prostitute! What makes you think I will ever permit her to poison the holy halls of our convent with her godless ways?"

"The halls of this convent are not so holy, Mother Superior. The halls of this convent have shown neither mercy nor forgiveness to too many! We are conspirators in trading women, making decisions about their lives, with no regard as to what this may do to them!"

Marie Madeleine Hachard had not realized how loudly she had screamed until the door to the Superioress' study crashed into the frame, thrown shut by her own hand, and a congregation of fellow Sisters, alerted by the yelling, stared at her in the hallway. Mother St. André had punished her for her outburst and insubordination by taking away her favorite classes for a month and ordering her to see the priest about a confession. She had refused, having her own conversation with God instead of admitting to a guilt she could not feel. She wrote in her journal:

"Lord, forgive me for what I am about to do. It is not righteousness that leads me to action, it is an 18-year journey that so often left me in doubt about the chasm between your true teachings, and how the church has chosen to interpret them. So much of what I have seen, the decisions made that have caused pain to the children of God, I cannot condone any longer without doing my utmost to change the earthly rules upon which they are based. Arguing for what I believe is right, in the discussions I have with my superiors, is no longer enough."

Sister Stanislaus looked at the mourners. It surprised her how many had come to pay their respects. There was Madame LaCour next to Margarita Castro. Zulimé, now a successful artisan, kneeled next to them holding hands with her daughter Marie Catherine. A few of the wealthy noblemen, patrons of Josephine's etablissement, stood off to the side, and in the darkest back corner huddled the sunken figure of Michél Bèranger. Florence Pascal neé Bourget had come, honoring her unique friendship with the deceased in her own way. Florence had confided in Sister Stanislaus her regret of not being able to save Josephine.

A few days later and without the Mother Superior's knowledge,

Marie Madeleine Hachard set in motion what she had confided to God in her writings. She had a long conversation with the Commander who, agreeing with her, relayed her concern to the new head of state. Governor Vaudreil-Cavagnial wrote an important letter to Paris with an urgent suggestion which was accepted by the French government. And so it was that Isabelle Cheniér neé Chavin became the last Casket Girl to ever set foot on the shores of the Mississippi.

THE END

Thank you...

To my parents, Helene and Anton Sereda who made me love, learn and breathe history as soon as I could talk.

∼

This novel is dedicated to Al Jarreau who told this twenty-one-year-old new arrival to America that she had a special gift and to keep on writing.

∼

To everyone who encouraged me to finally write a novel, especially Eva LaRue, my very first reader who sent me the funniest text message after she devoured the first draft in one long sleepless night.

Thomas Castaneda for being my first and very diligent lector and all-around supporter.

Nicelle & TG Herrington who allowed me to be a squatter in their beautiful New Orleans home where most of the book was written. A special shout-out to Nicelle's unmatched PR- and marketing skills, and to TG for the author photo.

Alexa Pulitzer for championing my work, connecting me to writers and other artists, and above all, contributing the extraordinary cover art.

Laura Bilgeri for lending her beautiful–tri-lingual and accent-less–voice to the audiobook version.

Peter Vieweger for the studio time and feeding us brilliantly through heatwaves and rainstorms.

Helen Eisenbach for the best developmental edit I could have wished for.

Shani Silver for telling me to "keep your money" and self-publish.

Leigh Abraham for the best writing advice this author could have hoped for.

Tina Lifford for her wisdom and teachings.

George Clooney for pushing me to go for the challenge and staying the course.

And Octavia Spencer for believing I could.

∼

Those of you who supported the self-publishing endeavor: Dr. Alfred Gusenbauer, my dear cousin Harald Pfaffeneder, Ruth Ann Jones, Linda Deleo, Milli Adler, Victoria Bousis, Theano Apostolou, Kristin Shannon, Maryam & Josh Lieberman, Monica Lepretre & George Hutchinson, New Orleans Songbird Robin Barnes, Mamta Melwani, Sara Costello, Rainer Hosch, and Christa Baum, who always had words of encouragement, from way back when we were both teenagers, writing poetry.

∼

To the Faulkner House Bookstore where I found the first mention of the Casket Girls, and The New Orleans Historic Society where I spent countless hours doing research, and for allowing me to use the map of the old city.

∼

And deep gratitude to my family of friends in Vienna and all of you in New Orleans who opened their homes and their hearts and so generously connected me to everyone, from historians to bookstore owners and beyond: if friends are defined by lifting each other up, y'all have won the master king cake! Or as we say: Go'head, baebeey!